The Taste of Light

"A girl with dawn in her eyes didn't belong in Pedro's shadows, but now that she floated into his life, he will battle whoever dares take her from him."

Giovanna Siniscalchi

Praise for The Taste of Light

"Rich historical detail, vibrant prose, and engaging relationships... A plot that never lets up, weaving a delicate tale of a man who believes he is undeserving of love and a woman who expects love to be everything it is not." ***Booklife - Editor's Pick***

"Mind, body, and soul of characters like Jamie and Claire Fraser of Outlander. This romance charges like a bull from page one, and you are swept into an arena of haunting past secrets, political intrigue, and the fierce intensity of love." ***The Historical Fiction Company***

"The tension and pacing throughout the book are impeccable and sprinkled with incredibly human-like reactions. The evolution of both Pedro and Anne makes for an exciting, adventurous, and satisfying read." ***Reader's Choice Reviews***

Acknowledgments

I dedicate this novel to my daughter, Olivia, and both Marcellos in my life. The light of your love and support shines over my writing path. Every time I sit to write, I remember my grandfather's intrepid recitations of Camões and the action-filled stories he told starring my grandmother. I strive to replicate the excitement he created in my young mind. I'm also indebted to my kind editor, Ceara Nobles.

Prologue

Mozambique, 1861

"Corruptio optima pessima. The corruption of the best is the worst." Ancient Latin saying

Pedro adjusted the rifle over his shoulder. River fog, insidious and thick, crept over the tents. The north wind bowed the campfires, spreading the scent of burned straw and humid wood. When the breeze hushed, the teardrop flame stilled. Exhaling, he pressed the trigger. A yelp and a string of colorful curses rose above the cicada's call. Gabriel's candle burst, plunging his cousin's bivouac into darkness.

Fernando, the Duke of Braganza, whistled, a grin splitting his chubby cheeks. "Officer Gabriel will not like that you snuffed another of his candles, sir."

Pedro's lips quirked. "It will teach him to go to sleep instead of drawing the entire night."

They needed to march at first light to lead the tribe under their protection to safety, and at the rate Gabriel consumed paper, Pedro would have to write his letters on brick. How would the Marshal receive such a weighty dispatch? At least his cousin obeyed curfew. If only his brother had the same discipline. Cris had missed drills this morning. Again.

"Can I conclude the bulletin, sir?" Fernando grimaced at his ink-stained hand and glared at the leaking pen.

Pedro cocked the rifle's action and recharged the cartridge. "Without our demands for provision? Tell the Marshal I cannot wage war here unless he sends horses, aguardente, uniforms, flour, and gunpowder."

A soldier survived three days without water, seventy without rations, but only five seconds without powder.

Fernando's smile wavered, and his gaze strayed to their meager wine supply. The Portuguese queen had sent the boy to Mozambique's cantonments to conclude his military education. Since he had become Pedro's aide-de-camp, the reality of the African colonies had claimed several of the youths' pounds, and Pedro wondered how long it would take to claim his wide-eyed idealism.

"Include three caskets of port and whatever books the Marshal can fit in the frigate."

"Thank you." Fernando grinned and wrote eagerly.

"Greetings, Almoster." The Viscount of Beira poked his powdered head inside the tent. "I would knock, except there is no door."

How had his father's secretary found their position? He was supposed to stay in Mozambique's capital, where he could not report Pedro's doings to the hawkish Prime Minister's eyes. Pedro hid his surprise under a blank facade and lifted his chin, the only cordiality he could force himself to show the old sycophant.

Beira tiptoed inside Pedro's quarters as if afraid to taint his ancient hussar uniform. The last time his bearskin had seen action had probably been in the civil war, and even then, from above the fence, ready to jump at whatever side was winning.

"Never say Father sent you just to celebrate my birthday." If the Duke of Titano thought to keep maneuvering Pedro from his lofty seat as Prime Minister in Lisbon, he would soon know the error of his ways. Pedro's twenty-first birthday had freed his mother's inheritance, severing his father's last hold over him.

"Yes, yes, how could he not?" Beira tapped the box he carried as if only then noticing it. He placed it atop Pedro's makeshift table and opened the lid. "A magnificent chess set. The Prime Minister bought it in St. Petersburg."

Pedro inspected the contents. Besides the chess set, veiled by tissue paper, was his father's whip. Pedro stared at the ivory handle and twisted thong, and bile rose to his mouth. He shut the lid, telling himself he had risen above his father's lessons. "It is hard to play the game in bivouacs. Not enough light."

"I'm sure your majesty provides adequate funds to deploy his troops comfortably. In fact, if you protected Portuguese interests in the capital, instead of escorting some negroes down the river—"

Pedro gritted his teeth. "When I arrived, the East African colonies were a disgrace to his majesty's coffers. If he so wishes, the Duke of Titano can take the credit for my improvements. Unless the Prime Minister is against progress here..."

Beira sucked in an affronted breath. "Progress? You court-martialed Mozambique's governor."

"He acted under the influence of slave traders."

"You expelled the priest."

"I arrested him for a public commotion." Pedro lifted his brows. "Inside the brothel."

Beira sighed, dropping his shoulders. "Look, your father applauds your enlightened endeavors. As always, your fervor and nobility... amuses him. Creating a primary school, a hospital, even a civil code? But this is Africa, not Europe. Your mission was to curb rebellions against the crown and safeguard the gold miners' interests."

If it depended on the Duke of Titano, Pedro would employ all resources to patrol the ivory and gold routes instead of curbing lawless slave traders from terrorizing villages.

A gunshot report drowned the secretary's long-winded arguments. Pulse speeding, Pedro flung away the tent's canvas screen. A line of torches lit the black mountains behind the Zambezi River, and Swahili war cries pierced the night.

"The Chikunda," Fernando mumbled, waving the dispatch like a peace flag.

The bands of enslaved warriors oppressed villages from Mozambique to Luanda, raiding the tribes for slaves to feed their masters' ships. Pedro cursed under his breath. How had they found their location?

Grabbing his rifle, Pedro strode outside, followed by Fernando and Beira.

The mist-shrouded night had turned into a battlefield. A shell exploded the camp's oven, showering debris over Fernando.

Ears ringing, Pedro pulled his aide-de-camp to his feet. "Are you hurt?"

"I'm all right, sir." His fair skin had brown smudges, and his eyes were wider than a cannonball. He shook the letter, cleaning the paper. "Now I won't need to blot the ink with sand."

One had to admire his grit.

Beira's face was whiter than the powder he used over his receding hair. "You should stay out of the Chikunda's way. You know what they want."

Of course, Pedro did. They wanted slaves.

Ignoring Beira's outburst, Pedro flung the bugle at his aide-de-camp. "Assemble the men."

Fernando blew on the instrument, his cheeks hollowing out. Most of the soldiers had already left their tents and, under the battle call, deployed into a single column parallel to the encampment.

"Almoster, think before you act," Beira whispered grimly, a hint of desperation making his voice sound like a brass flute. "Your recklessness is legion, but you have a royal duke serving under your command. All officers in your regiment are sons of peers of the realm."

Nice of Beira to remember their band of aristocratic misfits. Each had been sent here to learn a lesson. Henrique's father thought his son lacked patriotism, and the cure would be to fight for the country's colonies. According to Gabriel's father, the service would force him to forget architecture and make him a brilliant soldier. Fernando, fourth in line to the throne of Portugal, would benefit from a shock of reality, while Santiago needed to curb his wildness.

Pedro clasped Fernando's shoulder. "Are you afraid of the Chikunda?"

The boy lowered the horn and grinned. "They file their teeth into sharp points and kill elephants bare-handed, but to bullets, all men are equal."

Pedro chuckled and turned to Beira. "See, you worry for naught. Now, if you excuse us, we have a more binding commitment." Pedro grabbed his Dreyze rifle and attached the bayonet.

Gunshots got louder, and women's screams rose above the explosions. The bastards had reached the villagers under Pedro's protection. Locking his jaw, Pedro advanced toward his soldiers. If they could concentrate the fire over the enemy's left flank, cutting their retreat line, the Chikunda would be scared into surrender.

"Stop!" Beira laid a manicured hand over Pedro's uniform. "Your father is ready to negotiate your return to Lisbon."

What for? The woman Pedro loved had married. Julia was lost to him forever.

Pedro yanked his arm from Beira's touch. "You better seek shelter."

"The offer includes a commission in the North Army. You can leave this malaria-ridden hellhole. You will be a brigade general in the corps supporting our allies in France. Can you imagine it? Fighting against honorable soldiers instead of these savages?"

Pedro shut his eyes, his hand twisting the bayonet until there would be no hope of removing it. Damn his father and his cruel manipulations. Why flaunt Pedro's dream, his life goal, after cruelly denying it last year? Since when was he blind to the Duke of Titano's lessons? Father's offer was a carrot to tempt Pedro from his obligations and crush what he called Pedro's useless morals.

The gunfire stopped, the lull eerily like the silence before a storm. Fernando lowered the trumpet. Their gazes met. They had talked about dreams. Fernando wanted to experience the infinite passion of his heroes, Dom Pedro and Inês de Castro, Portugal's most haunting love story. The villagers under Pedro's protection had dreams, too. Whatever those were, Pedro could bet his warhorse none included a one-way trip in a rat-infested hull.

Understanding flicked in Fernando's eyes—their dreams would have to wait.

Nodding at the aide-de-camp, Pedro shouted orders to the rank and file.

"What should I say to your father?" Beira shrieked.

"Tell him the Count of Almoster places this malaria-ridden hellhole's interests above the duke's."

Chapter 1

Anne welcomed the sunrays filtering through her umbrella pine tree. It was one of those days in Portugal when the brilliance of the sky led you to believe it would be quite hot, but the shade still carried a cold bite. Her unwilling pupil had made no progress, even after changing his setting from the nursery to the garden. Lying on his tummy, Tony made faces at his notebook, some exasperated, some downright murderous.

"Greek isn't all that bad," Anne said, accommodating her pug in a cradle formed by the pine's root. Sunlight poured there, and James loved the warmth. The dog had come with her to Portugal, her only comfort on the shivering nights aboard the clipper, and had been her faithful companion ever since. The old boy had more than earned his rest.

Tony rolled his eyes and dropped his head on the notebook, hiding the white pages under his chestnut mane.

"I promised your mother you would finish your verbs today." Helping with the eight-year-old boy's education was the least she could do to repay her sister-in-law's hospitality. After her brother married Julia and left Oporto to reside in the country, Anne's mother closed their townhouse to stay with friends in London. Anne had moved to the vineyards, and Quinta do Vesuvio's picturesque scenery had become home. Sure, this should be the year she made her debut in polite society, but who needed a schedule filled with exciting balls, glittering court receptions, and carriage jaunts at Parque da Estrela?

Anne exhaled and caught her locket, pressing the heart-shaped jewelry between her thumb and forefinger. The necklace was a replica of the one Prince Albert had given to Queen Victoria when he proposed. It helped Anne remember no matter where she was, her dream suitor, who would love her selflessly, was already there, somewhere in the world. As long as she kept her heart open, a higher force, not unlike the mysterious pull of magnets, would bring him to her.

Tony grumbled and pushed away the notebook. "Why do I need to learn this? I bet Vasco da Gama would beat these Greeks senseless if he had the chance."

Anne didn't gush about the classic works of Aristotle and Plato's dialogues or Greek playwrights like Aristophanes. It would only make the boy groan. "An explorer can only profit from learning languages. Why, if you find yourself stranded on some remote island—"

"Your brother is teaching me English. Is it not enough? Why is your Portuguese different than his? You don't sound as if there is a frog in your throat."

Anne chuckled at the slandering of her brother's pronunciation and the boy's blatant change of subject.

"When Griffin came to live here, he was an adult, but I was not yet your age. Plus, my best friend is Portuguese."

"I think *mamã* is his first Portuguese friend."

"I guess you are right."

Before Griffin fell in love with Julia, he was the most stalwart peer of the British community in Oporto. Made of port wine traders and their families, they inhabited a separate society in the city, with different schools, clubs, churches, and even bathing spots at the beach. Anne disliked the transparent walls between the British and the Portuguese. But thankfully, Griffin now embraced this country as if it was his own.

"Soon, I will go to the Indies, like Vasco da Gama. I will have my fleet and go exploring new worlds. If you drop the Greek, you can come," he said, his voice solemn.

Anne placed a hand over her heart. "I will be delighted to accompany you, Mr. Ferreira, after you finish your verbs."

He rolled his eyes, scribbling furiously. "Aninha?"

"Hmm?"

"What will you be when you grow up?"

How to explain she was a grown-up woman? Girls her age were married or with children —she was eighteen, after all—and her dreams were more fluid than his aspiration to explore the world and its frontiers.

She had a great idea of who she was... not. She was not a prudish English lady, nor a meek one waiting for a convenient marriage, not a bluestocking and not a coquette. She wasn't a winemaker like her brother and new sister, nor religious like her Portuguese friends, and God forbid, she wasn't ambitious like the Crofts.

Anne exhaled and toyed with a fallen pine leaf, making round circles over the grass. "Since I cannot make you memorize the verbs, I must rule out teaching."

"I would finish the lesson much quicker if you picked me some pine nuts," Tony said, caressing his tummy and gazing at the wooden buds poking from the pines' branches.

Anne loved the waxy nuts and eyed them with longing. "A lady does not climb trees."

Back in Oporto, she used to scale her tree all the time. It gave her the perfect spot to peek at their neighbors' garden swing. While Mr. Nogueira sent his eight children frolicking to the sky, she would close her eyes, pretending the breeze kissing her cheeks was from her turn at the swing.

Tony sniffed and turned away. "My father used to pick me pines. He was the best tree climber in all the Douro, but since he died, no one bothers."

Anne's chest tightened, and she patted Tony's back. Being an orphan, she was no stranger to the ache of growing up without a father. Her brother had adopted Tony, teaching him all kinds of manly stuff. Still, he couldn't replace Julia's first husband in the boy's heart. "Oh, don't cry. Please, if you stop, I promise to get you some pines."

After a quick glance at the house to assert they had no audience, Anne removed her slippers. Her feet fit on the bark's grooves, and she used her arms to propel her weight up until she reached a horizontal branch. The umbrella pine's crown was alive with drones and chirps and tweets. Midway to the top, pine's flower pollen stuck to her nose, and she sneezed, startling a swallow into frightened flight.

Tony observed her, shielding his eyes. She could not see his expression but could bet her quick progress had amazed him. A little winded, Anne twisted a bulky pine from its branch and threw it in the boy's direction. The wooden flower landed on a tuft of daisies. "You better rush, Tony, or you will miss them."

Tony shoved his hands in the pockets of his short trousers and shrugged. "Never mind. Pines taste like sawdust."

Anne sucked in a breath. "What?"

He blew a raspberry and whirled to leave, laughing like the little devil he was. "I'll be at the stables... not studying."

He had fooled her! Brushing hair away from her face, she watched as the boy swaggered out of the tree's shade. His trick would work with his disgruntled nanny, but not her. Anne stretched over a sturdy branch and hugged it with her legs, crossing her ankles below her. Ha! She would give him a scare he would not soon forget. Spurred by giddy mischief, Anne dropped to the side and let go of her hands. With a swoosh, she went upside down, hung by her crossed ankles.

"Argh! Help. Somebody help!" Anne swung to add to the effect, and her bonnet fell. Her blonde hair swept the daisies below.

Tony halted mid-run. Anne clamped her mouth shut to keep from laughing as shock, fear, and a heavy dose of guilt played on his boyish face.

"Does the lady require assistance?" A deep, manly voice came from behind her.

Anne gasped, and her ankles gave way. Like a potato sack, she dropped, her back hitting the pine cone. Anne swallowed the pain and sealed her eyes shut. In a heartbeat, she had lost her hold on the tree and her dignity. A wave of heat climbed to her face, no doubt leaving her fair skin a patchwork of carmine blotches. If only the daisies' stems were long enough to cover her mortification.

"What have I done?" Tony said, his clammy palms cradling Anne's face.

Anne opened a slit in her left eye. After spotting a red coat and golden epaulets adorning very tall, very male shoulders, she closed her eyes again. Who had misplaced a handsome stranger in Vesuvio's garden? What would she do? Ladies didn't hang from trees, not even to teach Greek to truant boys.

She should say something. But while she could be quite eloquent inside her head, when she spoke to strangers, especially of the dashing variety, the words would bore a nun. Perhaps... perhaps she would just open her eyes and greet him with a sheepish smile.

"Is she dead?" Tony's concern doused her musings.

"I think she fainted," the stranger said in a cultured, slightly amused voice. "If you sprinkle water on her face, she will revive."

That was her cue. The instant a few drops fell on her person, she would flutter her eyelashes and pretend confusion. Holding her breath, she heard a lid being unscrewed and counted her heartbeats.

A gelid torrent splashed her face and chest. Where did the stranger collect this water? The alps? Anne sputtered and scrambled to a seated position.

Dropping the canteen he had used to drown her, Tony attached himself to her neck. "Aninha, I'm so sorry. Are you hurt? Please don't tell my mother."

Anne sifted her fingers through his silky curls and comforted him. When Tony calmed, Anne stood. Avoiding the stranger's curious gaze, she shook her day dress into a semblance of order.

The officer cleared his throat. "Antonio, it is the gentleman's duty to climb the tree while the beautiful lady observes from the ground."

Anne's cheeks flushed at the compliment, but with her tongue pasted inside her mouth, she had a better chance of turning into a grapevine than coming up with a witty phrase.

"Tony, won't you introduce me?" He was leaner than her brother and a tad younger too, high twenties at most. A beard shaded his square face, adding a touch of roughness that suited him.

"Aninha, this is Mr. Gabriel Fontes. I met him yesterday in the village. He is staying at Quinta da Esperança. Mr. Gabriel, this is my new aunt, Miss Anne Maxwell."

"A pleasure to make your acquaintance." Anne curtsied and admired the medals lining his chest.

"You are famous, Miss Aninha Maxwell."

Startled at her nickname's casual use, Anne tilted her head. "How so?"

"Mrs. Maxwell sang all your praises. She just told me how you decided against a season to help her. Your effort is commendable." Taking her hand in his, he smiled, his brown eyes exuding warmth and admiration.

At once, she felt a kindred connection, as if they had traced similar steps in life. "It's no sacrifice. My sister-in-law was gracious to receive me, and I cannot be thankful enough for how happy she makes my brother."

It seemed like a long time had passed. Had he been looking at her all this time? Tony tugged at Mr. Gabriel Fontes's sword, breaking the spell. "Have you been to the Indies?"

Mr. Fontes ruffled Tony's hair. "Only to Africa. Does it count?"

Tony made rapid-fire questions about the army and the duties of a soldier. Mr. Gabriel Fontes answered them all with patience.

"I'm here on an important mission. As the head of the king's guard, I must prepare for his majesty's visit to the Douro."

Her family talked of nothing else, as the king had promised to include Vesuvio in the tour. Phylloxera killed all the grapevines last year, and without Julia and Griffin's cure, the wine industry would have been devastated. Their effort had granted them a baronetcy.

Tony bounced with excitement. "Will you fight criminals, then? Spies?"

"Always." After a wink that could melt the alps — perhaps it explained where he got the water — he checked his timepiece and frowned. "I must go. May I visit you, Antonio?" Mr. Fontes's eyes shifted to Anne for a second and then back to Tony.

"That will be grand. Griffin is teaching me fencing. You can join our practice, too. He has some brilliant moves, for an Englishman, of course."

After tipping his hat, Mr. Gabriel mounted his dignified chestnut horse and cantered away, his posture straight. Anne's gaze followed him until he crossed the courtyard's iron gate.

"Aninha?" Tony yanked her hand.

"Hum?" Anne shaded her eyes, waiting to catch the last glimpse of Mr. Fontes's coat when he took the road to the village.

Tony placed his hand over his chest. "I've changed my mind. I want to be a soldier."

An enormous sigh escaped her chest, and she smiled dreamily. Anne would rather marry one...

Tony eyed her askance. "Are you really all right?"

"Really, really," she said, kissing her crossed fingertips.

"If that is the case, then... *Tchau tchau*!" He spun, racing so fast his heels touched his bottom.

Laughing, Anne picked up her skirts and gave chase. "Come back here, you rascal!"

Chapter 2

Cavalry Academy, Mafra Palace

Pedro tugged the right rein and pressed his left heel to Erebus's flank, and the stallion leaped from a contained walk to a brisk gallop. Pedro allowed the horse freedom of the arena. When it no longer felt as if Erebus was trying to demolish the ground with his hooves, Pedro turned him into a wide circle, reducing its diameter until Erebus cantered.

After the stallion spent his explosive energy, Pedro led him through his dressage training. No Lusitano in Lisbon, or even Portugal, could passage, pirouette, and piaffe like Erebus, and the horse well knew it. When they finished the side canter, Pedro halted and tapped the horse's neck, praising the effort.

Cris opened the gate and stepped inside the arena, a stripped coat flung over his shoulder, the high points of his starched shirt stark white against his tanned neck. They shared the duke's blood, but few believed them to be brothers. Pedro had his mother's fair skin and blond hair. Cris's coloring was dark, with black hair and olive complexion, like their father's. His clear green eyes contrasted with Pedro's cynical brown ones, and, in battle, Cris counted on brawn while Pedro preferred cunning.

By his dishevelment and day-old stubble, Cris had spent another night indulging Lisbon's demimonde. "You drew quite a crowd today. You should consider the poor troopers' sleep and exercise Erebus later. Must you rise in this ungodly hour?"

Pedro glanced at the raised dais erected for watchers. Cavalry recruits filled the benches and crowded the hill behind the arena. "If they wish to learn, they will adapt to my schedule." Pedro jerked his chin at a brown parcel Cris carried under his arm. "What's that?"

"Package for the Count of Almoster. The Duke of Braganza's valet delivered it last night."

Like a circus performer, Cris balanced the volume on his finger and took a careless step closer. Bullet quick, Erebus flattened his ear and bit Cris's shoulder.

Cris jumped, cursing like a conscripted sailor. "Jesus! Shoot this savage before he commits murder."

Pedro's hand went protectively to the old wound on Erebus's neck, below his mane. The shrapnel, shot point-blank by the Austrian artillery, would have pierced Pedro's chest if Erebus had not reared mid-charge, taking it in his stead. "If I shoot every grumbler in Lisbon, the queues would be longer than the guillotine's during the French Revolution."

Keeping a safe distance from Erebus this time, Cris threw the package. Arm lifted, Pedro caught it before it could sail over his head.

Pedro unraveled the twine and oiled paper, revealing Fernando's worn book. *The Infinite Love of Dom Pedro and Inês.* Fernando never outgrew his obsession with Portugal's most famous love story. Why send this now?

Memories from Mozambique resurfaced, but Pedro pushed them back to the hole they belonged, concentrating instead on Fernando's hasty scrawling.

'Take my Inês to the Douro with you. I've made a discovery that will shock even a cynic like yourself. Ever yours, Braganza.'

Pedro frowned at the cryptic words, hoping Fernando didn't mean to pull him into his missions at the colonies again. While the officers who returned from East Africa strove to forget, Fernando kept attaching himself to Mozambique's problems.

"What does he want?" Cris asked.

"Nothing." Pedro stored the book inside his coat. "Have you brought your luggage to the yacht? We'll leave at first tide."

Cris clucked his tongue. "Why don't we enjoy the summer elsewhere? I've heard French modistes brewed a bathing suit that reveals juicy tidbits of ladies' arms and legs. Think about it—a few weeks in Dieppe and then Paris. We'll attend the *Bouffes-Parisiens*, the *ball publiques*... Just like when you were the ambassador to France. That was living! What's in the Douro? A year since we set foot in the north, and well—"

"The king will be there."

Cris pawed his hair out of his forehead. "I saw Carmen yesterday. Imagine my surprise when, after some pretty tears, she told me she would not sail with us to the Douro."

"She spoke the truth." Except for the tears. She left their arrangement a rich woman. Unlike the wide-eyed court ladies who cloaked themselves in laces and frigid dispositions, Carmen enjoyed his unique demands with abandon. Still, Pedro's plans had no place for a kept mistress.

Cris whistled and nodded several times. "Gone were the days when I received such news from my older brother. Now I have to scramble for gossip like the rest of the rabble."

Pedro had no patience for his brother's information digging. He must have heard the rumors. Soon Lisbon's court would talk of nothing else. "Why the sudden interest in my mistress? Ask what you wish to know."

"You sent her away because you are courting the princess? The one who lives in England?"

At this point, Pedro had not set eyes on Isabel, but that would happen in the fall. "If by courting you mean to pay for her brother's debts and not require a dowry, then yes."

"But... why?" Cris frowned, his brows meeting above his aquiline nose. Political life baffled him. Even more than the intricacies of war strategy.

Pedro exhaled and spoke in measured tones. "The princess is a cousin to Queen Victoria and Frederick of Prussia. She has blood connections to all the royal houses of Europe."

Connections that would ensure no one ever ousted him from power as they did to his father last year.

"There was a time when you wanted to marry for love."

Pedro's shoulders tensed, and he fisted his hands. Erebus sensed the change in his mood and pranced. "There was a time when you didn't question my tactics."

Cris's naivete kept him from seeing people's true nature. In their world, Pedro either advanced or he would perish, and with him, Cris, the Almoster legacy, and all he possessed. No one would steal from him again. His marriage to the princess would be the concrete to reinforce the foundations of his future.

Pedro pointed to the brick tower flanking the Mafra palace. "She will be my Torres Vedras."

The fortified construction could hold twelve eight-pounders and three infantry brigades. A line of a hundred and fifty-three similar forts defended Lisbon—the Torres Vedras. During the first Empire, only two obstacles halted Napoleon's advance: the Russian winter in the north and Torres Vedras in the south.

While the army relied on earthworks, high grounds, and bridgeheads for defense, Pedro would construct a fortification carved on influence and power.

"I don't like it. These people are treacherous. I fear for you. With the duke gone, you are vulnerable."

Pedro closed his eyes, remembering his father's defeated face. A misplaced son's obligation had urged him to act and help the Duke of Titano flee to England before his imprisonment. He forced a smile. "Fretting like an old lady doesn't become you."

"I don't understand you, really. Since Mozambique, you have faced some challenges, but after last summer, you changed. I—"

"Don't say it."

Cris prodded on, a mulish expression on his face. "I much preferred when you fought for Julia, for the woman you loved."

What good had love done to him? Ten years waiting to make Julia his, only to have her stolen by the Englishman. "Love. A mockery of a word poets invented to justify lust, jealousy, hate, the need to possess. Unreliable emotions we are better off without."

Cris's mouth dropped open. "You cannot mean that. You sound like our father."

The comparison pierced him as Cris knew it would, which proved the closer people got, the higher their power to strike. Pedro gritted his teeth. "More reason for you to heed my words. Were you not the one who licked Father's boots when he was the prime minister?"

Cris's face blanched, and his eyes took on a haunted look. No one could say Pedro was selfish with pain. Cris had a bourgeois need for their father's affection. Their father, on the other hand, had never recognized his bastard son. To the Duke of Titano, Cris had been a by-blow of his baser needs and a rotten influence on Pedro's life.

"Have a nice training, brother." Cris dragged his feet to the exit, leaving tracks over the arena's sand.

Pedro had gone too far. He despised the duke's disdain for Cris, and had even fought with his father to keep his brother close. Pedro was striving to push an apology out of his throat when Cris stopped at the gate.

"Julia is pregnant, and she goes by Mrs. Maxwell now."

Chapter 3

T he last of the Saint John's party fireworks had exploded over the night sky when Maxwell's carriage rolled to a stop at Vesuvio's courtyard. Pedro gulped port straight from the bottle and moved past the orchard to catch a better view. Last year, he had arrived here, the guest of honor, confident in his ability to marry Julia and reclaim the fate his father had taken from him. Now he lurked in the shadows, exiled from his own destiny. Vesuvio's scent, old wood and wine, invaded his being, carrying memories of the long-ago summer when Julia had healed more than his wounds. The sense of peace it had brought then, before Maxwell had sailed into their lives, now reeked like an empty cellar.

What the hell was he doing here? What was it to him if she expected the poacher's child? For once, his brother had been right. He shouldn't have come back to the Douro. He should've summered in Paris and resumed his campaign to win the princess's hand in September. Still, his legs would not carry him away.

Maxwell alighted first and helped Julia descend the steps to the paved walkway. Pedro stared at them together, and the port singed his empty stomach. It should have been Pedro helping Julia out of the carriage on St. John's eve. It should have been him shedding his coat to shield his wife from the cold. It should have been him ushering her into the safety of the house. It should have been him sleeping through the night by her side, free from nightmares.

Pedro's chest tightened, and he gripped the port with enough force to shatter the bottle. A single torch burned on the wall, and Pedro could not see their faces, but Julia's shape was unmistakable.

Cris had been right. She was pregnant.

Pedro took a swig from his bottle and stepped out of his hiding place, making no pretense of being silent. The full moon swept over his black clothes, casting shadows over the schist soil.

A wolf howled in the distance. Twigs snapped to his left. Pedro's lips tugged up in a feral grin. He didn't have to wait long. The Englishman strode into the clearing, blocking the view of the house. Pedro didn't bother reaching for his pistol.

"Stop hovering outside Vesuvio like a damn robber." Maxwell crossed his arms above his chest. By the low tone of his voice, he didn't want to alert the others of Pedro's presence.

Pedro sneered. "Robber? How ironic. Did you forget who did the theft?"

"Instead of haunting my property, why don't you take better care of yours? Your vineyards are the largest in the region after Vesuvio. You keep the grapevines killed by phylloxera. If you don't plan on rebuilding them, sell Salgueiro to me."

The vines would have to rot twice over in hell before Pedro allowed the Englishman to own anything else fated to be his.

"You lost no time filling her with your brat, did you?" Pedro said, his words dripping with disgust.

Maxwell caught Pedro's lapel, his metallic eyes flashing with hatred. Pedro tensed, his hands craving the feel of the Englishman's windpipe. He wouldn't boast if he could no longer speak.

Laughter chimed in the breeze. It wasn't Julia's throaty laughter, but sugary and heavenly. Startled at first, as if she had been tickled out of it, then rolling out in nuances and waves. Her melody lifted the hairs in Pedro's arms and vibrated a chord in his chest.

Pedro shoved the Englishman out of his way and cocked his head to the side, tracking the women as they climbed the steps to the front door. Julia entered the house first. The other paused with her hand on the doorknob. The torchlight crowned her with an aura of light but hid her silhouette. Her willowy shadow played over the whitewashed facade. Pedro strained his eyes to no use. Her face was veiled from him, but he imagined he wasn't invisible to her, even surrounded by darkness.

"A house party? And you didn't invite your neighbor? Who is she?"

"Stay away from my family," the Englishman said between gritted teeth. Maxwell couldn't hide his reaction. His fear was tangible—the fear of a man with too much to lose.

Pedro chuckled, savoring the upper hand. "You think you can avoid an introduction? I might impose on your household the *droit du seigneur*—"

"Bastard! Remove your aristocratic ass from Vesuvio, or I will—"

"Do what?" Pedro invaded his personal space, staring him down.

The women had long since entered the house. It was just Pedro and the Englishman under the shadows of Vesuvio's palm trees. Pedro realized why he had come. Last summer, he had punched Maxwell's eye when he should've crumbled his entire face. There was always time to right a wrong. Pedro dumped the bottle and fisted his hand.

Before Pedro could connect the punch, Cris flung an arm around him, holding him back. "You two organized an impromptu dance here, and no one thought to invite me? Shame on both of you."

Pedro tensed to push his meddling brother from his fight when the front door opened.

"Griffin, is something the matter?" Julia exited the house. She carried a candelabra, and the light flicked over her worried features.

Pedro sobered. The port and the will to fight cleared from his head, leaving numbness in its wake. He shouldn't have come to the Douro. He shouldn't have come to Vesuvio.

Pedro jerked away from Cris's hold and vanished back into the shadows.

"There you are. After your performance at Vesuvio, I was prepared to look for you in the gutter. Care to explain?"

Pedro blinked awake. The ballroom wavered once and came into focus. With the curtains drawn, the sun attacked his eyelids. The duke's life-sized portrait creaked open, and Cris emerged from the hidden passage.

Pedro shut his eyes. "Are we under attack?"

"Of course not."

"Then use the damn door."

Cris shrugged and closed the painting. "I'm all for a dramatic entrance."

His boots thumped on the marble, resonating in Pedro's skull.

Pedro applied pressure over his temple, willing the headache to recede. "I'm not in the mood today."

"The steward asked me when you will allow him to rebuild Salgueiro's vineyards. He said it should start soon, or phylloxera will compromise the vintage. He pleaded for the workers who depend on the wine—"

"Salgueiro's vineyards will remain as they are. A field of dead grapevines." Pedro managed a sitting position on the chaise.

"Even the *Arinto* grapes? You love the white wine from that hill. As the only producer in the region, if you don't rebuild, *Vinho Luz* will cease to exist."

Pedro exhaled and dropped his weight back on the chaise. *Vinho Luz*. Delicate, it grew on the highest hill, closer to the sun but far from the heat, delicious to drink, a blend of acacias and passion fruit, perfect for sharing. Nowadays, the wine stunk of ashes and crushed desires. "My taste has evolved."

Cris sniffed one of the port bottles scattered over the side table and grimaced. "I doubt it. If you want to get drunk properly, let's go to the madam. At least we'll have better company."

"Better by what standards?" The thought of having a jaded whore brought a sourness to his mouth. Pedro felt with his hand for the decanter on the floor and took a hearty swig.

Cris sighed and ran his hand through his hair. "Until when are you going to brood? It is becoming predictable, and isn't predictability dangerous? You taught me so yourself."

Pedro threw away the empty bottle. It rolled over the Persian rug and vanished below the lacquered piano.

Cris grinned. "You are getting soft. I bet if we fight now, I will win."

"Not while I draw breath, little brother."

Cris pulled his cavalry saber from the scabbard and tested its balance with practiced movements.

Pedro stood. The floor swayed underfoot. With brittle legs, he went to the sword display and chose his favorite, the saber he'd used in the Battle of König Gratz in Bohemia. Lifting the Prussian steel high, he faced Cris at the center of the ballroom. Once a scenery for extravaganzas, it became their arena, the high ceiling and vast space allowing the swords to swing unperturbed.

Light flickered over the blade, glinting off the family motto—*non ducor duco.* Never the conquest, always the conqueror. Fingers around the grip, hand engulfed by the cross guard, Pedro was in his element. War. In a muddy plain, in a ravine, in a dispatch room, be it fought with a sword, a rifle, or a pen, this was what he was made for.

Pedro circled his brother, bare feet silent. In battle, Cris's height and brawn scared the breath from his enemies. But in their private matches, he never won a single bout. Too decent, he couldn't strike with blood in the eyes.

Pedro slashed forward, testing the sword's weight on his wrist and shoulder. Cris feinted to dodge the attack and parried, his arms flying madly. Pushing and drawing, Pedro cornered his brother between the Grecian column and the window. Using his distraction, Pedro grappled, locking Cris's blade between their bodies. Cris widened his eyes, a trail of sweat raining down his forehead.

"Keep your left arm close to your body. When will you learn proper technique?"

"I don't mind using energy. I have enough to spare." Cris forced Pedro's sword back with sheer brute force, and Pedro had to withdraw several steps.

"If only you had used it in Mozambique." The words escaped Pedro's mouth before he could check them.

A flush blotched Cris's neck, and he pushed Pedro away with his fists and raised his weapon, slashing out with right and left cuts. Pedro stepped back, heaving his breaths.

"I knew coming to the Douro would be a terrible idea. Julia moved on. When will you?" Cris panted and withdrew, splaying his hands on his knees.

"You don't know what you ask." Pedro flung away the sword. The saber clanked twice and stilled near his mother's harp—a twisted pair on the pristine marble.

"Tell me, then. Make me understand."

He'd hoped marrying Julia would bring him peace, would cleanse his soul. Pedro pointed at his chest. God, how he hated his brother's concern. Exhaling, Pedro paced away. The statue drew him as a load-stone, a pull impossible to deny. Hands folded on her lap, hair flowing over her breasts, nude spine flaring to rounded hips, she gazed at him, a gaze too vivid to be true. She was beautiful, and Pedro recognized beauty in all forms—but this artist's skill went beyond coaxing emotion from stone.

It was in her eyes.

Her gaze was at once playful and alluring, girl and all woman, mother and lover, sister and friend. Pain erupted in his chest, and he extended his arm, his black-gloved hand hovering near her cheek. Years of waiting, and still the statue mocked him with all he couldn't have. His hand closed in a fist, and he whirled lest he shove the slender sculpture, shatter-ing its untouchable passion.

Julia had looked at him with tenderness, with pity for his father's beatings, but never like the statue, never that way.

"Why don't you forget the past? Forget Julia, forget—" Cris would no doubt say Mozambique, but stopped and exhaled forcefully. "The future is all that matters."

Pedro laughed, the sound like rocks grating on iron, and covered his face. By Saint George, he could not bear a woman's touch. His skin, the nerves and muscles underneath, must have been wired differently than everybody else. For ten long years, all his adulthood, he had hoped Julia would heal him. But after last summer, he understood his wishes to be delusional. Touch was repulsive to him. How did one forget that?

"My future is set." When the king arrived in the Douro, he would sign the betrothal. "But you should, Cris."

His brother sheathed the saber. "A political marriage with a prudish princess is a mistake. We should get away from court, give it time to... For you to collect yourself."

"The maxim that time helps is a fallacy made by hopeful fools. You should go. Choose any of my properties. Marry, proliferate, be gone."

Cris shook his head and whirled, a frown creasing his brow. "Just like that."

"Call it a gift. A prize for your long-time loyalty."

Cris flinched as if struck. "So now my loyalty has a price?"

"Call it what you may."

Cris nodded several times, then he ambled to the exit. He opened the French doors and leaned on the threshold. Through the blue glass, the light fluctuated as if his brother were underwater. The house would be quiet without his boisterous laughs and lewd jokes. The heavy silence fell on Pedro's shoulders, and the days ahead loomed with no sounds other than the ones inside his head.

Pedro ignored the ache in his chest. His brother would be better off without him. "I am glad you understood."

Cris turned, and their eyes locked. A mischievous grin lit his face. "I am due for the madam's house. The girls are missing me. But fear not, I will be back before dawn. Perhaps I'll send you some entertainment."

Pedro groaned. "Don't."

Chapter 4

Through her bedroom window, Anne could almost taste the river. But today, instead of gazing at the placid green depths of the Douro, her eyes kept straying to the courtyard. If she craned her neck just so, she would see any visitor before he knocked at the front door.

"Interesting book?"

Anne jumped from the chair and dropped the leather volume on the sheepskin rug. "Flor, you startled me."

The maid laughed, the sound lazy and warm, and sashayed inside. She was the typical Portuguese woman with luminous olive skin and abundant brown hair. Whistling a soft tune, she placed a tea tray on the vanity. "You can sweeten it. Wentworth ordered beat sugar after your sermon."

"How thoughtful of him." Brazil kept exploiting slaves in their plantations. The least Anne could do was avoid their goods.

Anne rolled the sugar cube in her fingers, her gaze straying to the front gate.

"Your officer won't come today. This is a small village. He must know your brother left for Regua city."

Anne hid behind the book, a smile stealing to her lips. "Who?"

"Child, when you take the corn to the mill, I am already coming back with the cake. Here, the post boy delivered this to you."

Anne opened the perfumed paper and admired the precise handwriting. Mr. Gabriel invited her to meet him in the square tomorrow. Anne perked up, but then deflated. "Do you think my brother would approve a courtship?"

After her father took his own... after he went away when she was six, Griffin had assumed his place with the determination of a thoroughbred. She was grateful for it...most of the time.

"Is this officer rich?"

"How can you say these things?"

"Oh, I forget wealthy people consider it rude to speak about money. Come, let's do this hair of yours."

Anne held her skirts and plopped on the chair behind the vanity.

"Mr. Maxwell means well." Flor took a brush from her apron and combed Anne's flowing blond strands.

"If he scares all the suitors, how can I find my soul mate?"

Flor stopped brushing. Through the mirror, Anne saw her brown eyes dimming.

"What is it?"

Flor sniffed and shook her head. "Love isn't the stuff of fairy tales, where people are perfect and do all the right things. Love is messy, primal, and flawed. It wants to control and be controlled. It takes effort and maturity, Aninha."

Poor Flor. Anne learned from a rushed conversation the maid had suffered a terrible disillusion. But Anne wouldn't follow the same path.

"You fret for naught. Here." Anne removed the clasp from her neck. After carefully opening the locket, she withdrew the thumb-size paper. "It is a list. A guide to finding my dream suitor. He should have a kind heart and love animals as I do. A pleasant sense of humor would be nice but not required, and of course, he needs to get along with my brother. This would be the most challenging. Above all, he must be noble." She wouldn't fall for someone who couldn't put others' interests above his own.

Flor's eyes widened. "Child, this is—"

"Ingenious, right?"

"You know what? Let your brother choose for you. He has excellent taste in spouses."

Anne shrugged and stored the paper safely inside her locket. Her gentleman would fall in love with her as Griffin had fallen for Julia, and he wouldn't leave at the first challenge.

Images of her mother's loneliness after her father died flashed through her mind, and Anne flinched. No. Selfishness would not be in her suitor's vocabulary.

Perhaps she had already found him...

Anne traced Mr. Gabriel Fontes's signature.

Julia waddled inside the bedchamber, her tummy preceding her by a foot. "Anne, there you are. You are so talented with a needle. Would you help me?" She held a piece of butter-colored cloth by the seams. It was either a dog dress or a troll's nightcap, but Anne would not discourage Julia by asking.

"Mrs. Maxwell doing embroidery?" Flor cocked her hip. "Are you feverish?"

Julia gave the maid a mock scowl. "If I am to be the mother of a lady, I need to learn."

In Anne's dreams, Julia's child appeared as a black-haired, blue-eyed, rosy-cheeked girl. So, they took to calling the new baby a girl, to Griffin's and Tony's consternation.

Anne picked up her sewing basket. Julia had two left hands for needlework, but what she lacked in stitching, she more than made up for in winemaking.

On the way to the morning room, Julia halted, holding the back of a chair, her face frozen in pain.

Anne linked arms with her sister-in-law and guided her to the couch. After a quick recovery, Julia dismissed Anne's concern, but her smile stretched her skin as if plastered on her face.

"When will Griffin be back?" Picking up James in her lap, Anne settled by Julia's side.

Julia turned to the painting on the wall. By the play of emotion on her face, it looked as if she was searching for Griffin on the painted landscape. "Three days. I'm having these contractions. I am sorry, I should not be speaking thus."

The baby was due in October. Wasn't it too soon for her to feel so? Anne's stomach knotted. "Did you talk with the midwife?"

"I sent for her. I shouldn't burden you with my problems. You are too young."

"I want to help." She forced a grin and a lightness she was far from feeling. "Bear with me for a moment, will you? Maybe, just maybe, you could stay inside for a few relaxing days. I have a new novel. It's about an English family living in Oporto, and guess what—"

"I promised to visit the neighbors tomorrow and teach them the grafting process. Many have not reconstructed after phylloxera." Julia leaned back on the couch, and her tummy bulged.

Julia and Griffin worked so hard, and their efforts to save the vines from the plague were inspiring. But she couldn't risk the pregnancy by overworking.

Anne threw her palms and subtlety into the air. "You can't go away from the house. Not in your state."

Julia shook her head. "The king will visit the properties. We must show him we are making progress with phylloxera."

Anne had no experience with births, but if Julia kept bouncing on that buggy, her niece would come out too soon. But if she went in Julia's place, she could not meet Mr. Gabriel Fontes...

She crushed his message over her chest. If he were her dream suitor, he would understand. "What if I go?"

Chapter 5

Who said Anne couldn't drive the buggy? Shaggy, such a lovely horse, responded to her inexperienced nudges. The morning air was crisp, the sun was shining, and she had a purpose, a meaningful one. Anne clicked her tongue, and Shaggy managed an easy trot, crossing the vineyards. Emerald grapes dangled from the branches like jewelry on a princess, infusing the breeze with their sweet scent.

When they bridged the Douro, the scenery changed. All the way to the horizon, the hills had sprouted thorns. The staked lines, where once the grapevines must have leaned for support, now were empty, standing atop the granite terraces like crosses. Anne yanked on the reins, and the wheels screeched, lifting plumes of chalk. James popped out from his carrying basket, and Anne scooped him back atop his pillow.

Shaggy raised his head, his ears flicking to the right. Plunged in shadows, a side path winded from the main road. The way to this forsaken property? Sunlight brushed the leaves of twin willow trees. Flimsy and wispy, the foliage flowed as if calling her inside.

Julia had trusted her to accomplish this mission. To visit dead vineyards in Villa Nova and explain the cure for phylloxera. Anne couldn't shy away.

Yes, she would bring light back to this property.

Clicking her tongue, Anne guided the carriage down the side road. They crossed a gate designed with twisting ropes of iron. Over the top, a plaque read, 'Quinta do Salgueiro.' A mansion presided over a formal garden, its two neoclassical wings hugging the hill. It would be beautiful if it weren't for the dead vines flanking it. Why allow an enchanted home to turn into a graveyard of vines? Perhaps the owner did not live here or had not heard Griff and Julia's advances in beating phylloxera. The rebuilding was a slow process. Even in France, many vineyards were still barren hills.

No footman came to greet them, and she continued on the circular drive until it ended in a baroque stable with gaping double doors. She halted the buggy and secured it on a hitching hook. James snored, his head drooping. He deserved a rest. She closed the door to his basket and placed it securely on the carriage floor. This was just a polite call, and he would be better here.

Anne strolled to the front entrance and fluffed her new dress. Made of ivory satin, the bodice hugged her torso, and the overskirt opened to show layers of white tulle. The tiny grapes, a compliment to her embroidering skills, added just the touch to the ensemble.

Satisfied she appeared both feminine and businesslike, Anne reached for the brass knocker and made it resound two times. Several heartbeats passed. No birds chirped on the cypresses, and no insects droned over the manicured flowerbeds. Even the breeze had hushed. She gazed longingly at the stables and lifted her hand to knock again when the door swung outwards, missing her by an inch. In the doorway stood a gray-liveried butler, his pockmarked face scrunched in a frown. He eyed her as if she was a bandit bent on invading his master's home.

She forced a smile. "Hello, I'm Miss Anne—"

The servant grabbed her arm and pulled her inside the unlit vestibule.

"Wait, what—"

Barking Portuguese words she didn't understand, he steered her along a palatial foyer and a hallway decorated with impressive military paintings. She had to take quick steps to avoid tripping on her skirts. When they arrived at a set of French doors adorned with blue panels, he halted.

"Sir, if you will—"

Without knocking, he shoved it open and signaled impatiently for her to go inside. Anne entered gingerly, heart beating in her throat.

"*Espere aqui.*" The butler banged the door shut and left.

What was wrong with him? Anne stared at the stained glass, catching her breath. The poor man must have confused her words. Either her Portuguese was not as good as she believed, or he spoke a dialect. Soon she would laugh at this over a steamy cup of tea.

Anne spun in a slow circle, her slippers reflecting over the travertine floor. Light peeked from slits on the velvet drapery, hardly enough to satisfy her curiosity. Shadows played over the Venetian mirrors and on the gilded leaves and roses festooning the ceiling. Opposite a grand piano loomed an assortment of guns and wicked swords. Anne touched the tip of a curved saber, and pinpricks rose along her skin.

A chaise longue stood at the other corner, pillows scattered over its damask upholstery. A coffee table had liquor bottles as adornments. She brought one to her nose and grimaced at the alcohol fumes. What a shame to ill use such a superb room.

Anne touched the piano keys, the notes echoing through the high ceiling, conjuring a dazzling ball—windows open to the moonlight, candles sparkling on the crystal chandelier, ladies and their pastel gowns twirling to a full orchestra. Vila Nova's residents would enjoy coming here to dance. How selfish to keep it hidden.

On top of an oak desk lay an ancient tome. Anne trailed her fingers over the red and gold title—*The Infinite Love of Dom Pedro and Inês de Castro*. Her gaze flitted to the door, and seeing it still closed, she opened the book.

Albuquerque castle, June 1312.

Inês searched the Castilian sky. Arcturus, the queen of stars and star of queens—her star—shone mightily. It must be a sign. Had the witch not said her fate awaited in Portugal? Out in the courtyard, the mules brayed, jingling their harness, impatient to take her there. Just a moment more. With agile fingers, Inês braided the flowers into a fragrant bouquet. Odd numbers for luck—daffodils for truth, bluebells for luck, roses for love, and the hyacinth for joy.

She couldn't begin this journey without happiness.

Before the tale swept her away, Anne stopped reading. The romance was another oddity. This quinta must be the richest in the region and by far the most desolate. Who lived here? The question gnawed at her insides, spurring her to explore further.

She paused before a life-sized painting of an officer wearing the Marshal's uniform. His face was vaguely familiar, with a severe mustache and white hair. What if war had left him deformed? That's why he would not socialize and allowed his vineyards to die. Anne could help. Why not bring him into Vesuvio's society? A breath of light would soften the heart of a weary soul.

A draft lifted the hairs on Anne's neck, and the top of her ears pricked. The butler must have upset her nerves. Brushing the exposed skin on her arms, Anne turned.

On the darkest side of the room, hunkering in a throne-like chair, features concealed by shadows, was a man. Had he been there all this time? Anne thanked her bonnet for concealing the fierce heat that coursed through her face. How would she convince him to re-build his vineyards after he caught her snooping?

He rose, unfolding his lean, tall frame graciously.

Anne waited for him to speak, to introduce himself, her heart battering against her ribs. He crossed the ballroom with purpose and force, the gait of one who commanded all with a wave of his gloved hands. Anne's gaze was drawn to his unfashionably long hair, the bur-nished gold strands reaching his shoulders. He wore it tied at the neck in the style of a noble from France's first empire.

He stood before her. His expression could be carved from marble, so little feeling it showed. Was he dis-pleased?

Anne inhaled to speak, but his eyes scrambled her apology—the irises nuanced from tawny to yellow, like a kaleidoscope made of shattered topaz. He tilted his head, and the aloofness vanished, replaced by a sardonic smile that caused her cheeks to burn. Anne hid her gaze behind her eyelids, and if there were a hole in the floor, she would hide her head too.

He wasn't an old general, and he most certainly wasn't deformed.

Chapter 6

"I can explain," the girl said, wringing her little hands.

Pedro blinked several times, but he had not invoked the image—an apparition in a cloudy dress stood in the middle of his hangover. Mayhap the port had made him delirious. Light from the stained glass danced on her gauzy skirts. A wide-brimmed bonnet covered her hair and face. Still, her swanlike neck, dainty shoulders, and trim back offered tantalizing glimpses of her curves. Nothing like the jaded whores the madam had sent last time. This must be his brother's doing. Still, Pedro hadn't had a woman since Carmen, and his body decided it was done with celibacy.

Pedro circled her. "You've smelled my liquor. You tested my blades. You've read my book. Care to try the couch? See if it's soft?"

He might be wrong, with the veil covering her face, but he could bet her cheeks had turned a pretty shade of pink. Her lace-covered fingers traced the grapes embroidered in her bodice furiously. Was she nervous? But he had barely begun. Was that her game? To pretend innocence?

Intrigued, Pedro took a step closer.

With a sharp intake of breath, she stilled. "I shouldn't have touched your things. I... I came here to— "

"I know why you came," Pedro whispered in her ear.

Her fragrance was layered like a delicate white wine. What did she look like beneath the tulle veil? Would the illusion of innocence keep after he removed the bonnet? With a swift gesture, he unlaced the bow under her chin and flicked the hat away. Her hair cascaded down her back and flirted with her hips, the unusual champagne strands curling enticingly.

"Please, this is improper." She crossed her arms over her chest as if he had bared her clothes, a flush rising on her pearly skin.

Her face. Blue, innocent eyes, and rose lips. Only a beauty mark above the left corner of her lip added a mischievous note to her celestial countenance. Loveliness such as hers belonged in a Raphael painting, peeking at humanity from a lofty pastel cloud.

What the devil should he do with an angel? "She shouldn't have sent you here. Didn't she tell you what I do with breakable girls?"

She laughed nervously and reached for her discarded bonnet, her hand shaking. "Why, I'm not made of porcelain or crystal. I'm quite strong. Indeed, I—"

"Then why do you tremble?" Pedro caressed her cheek, feeling the downy hairs rise to meet his fingertips.

She replaced the hat, her fingers fumbling with the ribbons. "I assure you, sir, I came here for a business reason, and I'm perfectly indifferent—"

Pedro caught the offending object and flung it away. Business indeed. She thought this was a transaction, did she? It was the only sensible notion the girl had spouted since she'd stepped into his life. While she watched him with widened eyes, Pedro brushed his thumb over the naked skin above her glove. She stopped speaking, and the tip of her tongue came out to lick her bottom lip. She wasn't indifferent to him. Why the knowledge mattered when he was paying, he could not say, only that it did.

A vision flashed of her touching him, trailing her delicate fingers over his arms, and he released her hand. "Are you new to this?"

"Why, yes, I've just started—"

"Say no more." Pedro silenced her with a fingertip over her mouth.

He would not touch an angelic whore new to the trade. He would not trace her frowning brows and would not relieve her of the tight corset. He would not tie her hands and bend her over the piano. He would not release her champagne hair and see it reflected over the lacquered surface while he pounded his lust on her until she screamed. Who was he fooling? The screaming would start before he brought her to release. Most likely when he showed her the ropes.

"Look at me." Pedro lifted her chin.

She obeyed, and her eyelashes unveiled the bluest irises he'd ever navigated. The depths swirled with emotion, and he got lost in the ocean of her eyes.

To hell with good intentions. Pedro cradled her face, his leather-gloved palms engulfing her cheeks. The girl clamped her eyelids shut. He came closer, their breaths mingling.

Kissing whores wasn't part of his transactions, but her impossibly soft lips lured him. He paused for a second and then tipped her head and joined their lips. Warmth flooded his body, the sounds and sights of his sins receding, leaving only roses and tea, silky strands of hair against his skin, and the pounding of his heart.

Pedro broke the kiss. Her pull was dangerous. It took him several seconds to still his breathing and push her away from him. "Run, little angel. Fly back to whatever cloud you came from and don't come back. Be thankful I'm not in the mood to give chase."

She raised her fist as if to slap him.

Pedro caught it before the strike and stared into stormy eyes. "You cannot hurt me with blows."

She tugged her hand from his grasp. "You... you abuser of unsuspecting women. Unhand me now."

A gunshot blasted outside, followed by a scream. Pedro straightened, gut hardening. The girl gasped, eyes darting to the door.

Pedro raced to the window. Light bounced on the white gravel of the courtyard. Three men paced, rifles leaning on their shoulders, hulking over Salgueiro's entrance. They dressed in militia uniforms, but he could not make out any crests. One of Pedro's guards, shot through the chest, lay in the flowerbed.

"*Merda*." Pedro closed the draperies. With the back of the chair, he blocked the doors. If they had three outside, they should have at least four inside the property. The mansion had several rooms, but they would come here. Outnumbered and encumbered by an inexperienced whore, he had one alternative—retreat.

Pedro grabbed a sheaf of money and Braganza's book and shoved them inside his pocket. The angel was next. She stared at the door, face pale, ready to bolt.

"Come."

He gripped her wrist and pulled the shocked girl through the door concealed behind his father's portrait. Meager light clung to the bare stones. A dripping sound echoed over the corridor. Empty. If luck was on their side, the attackers' intelligence had not discovered the duke's voyeurism and his habit of building secret passages in all his residences.

When the walls narrowed, she balked. "Where are you taking me?"

"I will lead you to safety, but you must stay calm. They can't harm us here."

"Who... who are they?"

"I don't know. Yet." But whoever they were, invading his property had slashed their life expectancies.

A point of light flickered ahead. A peephole to the parlor. Pedro's father had used it to spy on visitors and discover their intentions before accosting them in his private study. He brought his eye close to the opening, the smell of moldy wood and dust invading his nostrils. The room came into focus—an overturned settee, books and paintings scattered on the floor. Flavio, his trusted servant, lay on the oriental rug. The killing of an unarmed, elderly man had much to say about his attackers' intentions.

Faint breathing. Someone was inside. Curse this opening; it was too narrow. They needed out of the quinta. Pedro was pushing away from the wall when the parlor's door opened. A newcomer, dressed in the same militia uniform, entered the parlor.

With more pimples than a beard on his face, the youth took a shaky breath. "The count is missing."

A couch groaned, and then footsteps.

"Is this a joke?" The voice cut like a gelid blade on exposed skin.

João Ulrich. Pedro could recognize that voice anywhere. Cold sweat dampened his temples, his hand curling on the hilt of his sword. The slave trader from Mozambique came into view. Instead of the gold chains around his neck and the Chikunda bodyguards he used to have at his side, he wore a well-tailored short coat and a cravat. But the sleek black hair and thin mustache painted on his angular face were still the same.

"We cleared all the rooms."

"And the blonde pet?"

Pedro gritted his teeth at the lecherous glint in Ulrich's eyes.

The minion stared at his feet. "The woman is nowhere to be found, sir."

Flicking a knife, a cruel cigarette on his lips, Ulrich strutted around the newcomer as if presenting himself at a bullfighting arena. "My, my... So many mistakes. Gather the men. Burn this place down, if need be, but find the girl and the count."

"I won't kill a girl, sir."

"No one lives to tell of Almoster's innocence." Ulrich drew the knife along the minion's throat, below his jaw. A thin line of blood spurted from the olive skin. The distance separating them could not conceal the sick shine in Ulrich's gaze. "She will die, but who said I would give you the pleasure? Bring her to me."

The girl cried out, and Pedro covered her mouth. Her eyes looked enormous on her pale face. Her fear was justified, as he had seen firsthand what kind of depravity the slave trader had in his arsenal.

Ulrich swiped the knife on the minion's coat, cleaning the blood. "Anything else?"

"No, sir." The soldier bowed and left.

Alone, Ulrich booted the settee back in place and sat with his feet crossed on top of Flavio's torso. Pedro wanted to punch his way into the room and rip the bullfighter's eyes out. Ten years looking for the criminal, and now he was in Pedro's grasp. If he retraced his steps to the ballroom, he could surprise Ulrich in the parlor before he gurgled for help.

Pedro uncovered the girl's mouth. "You will stay here."

"But where will you go?" She posed a shy hand on his forearm, her eyes darting like a trapped bird. "Don't leave me alone."

He pulled away from her touch. He could end this, kill Ulrich and silence the voices in his head.

"Please." Her voice broke, her gaze shimmering with tears.

She would shed many more if he was caught and left her unprotected. Damn it. Why should he care? If he lost Ulrich now, how would he track him later? He had hideouts in every port of Europe.

A vision of her white tulle dress splattered with blood flashed through his mind. Against his better judgment, Pedro took her slight wrist, his hand engulfing the trembling limb, and guided her through the dank corridor.

"Who is he?" she panted, racing to keep up with his longer strides.

"No one you should concern yourself with."

"They are going to kill us, are they not?"

"Not if I can prevent it."

He opened the hidden portal leading to the stables' mezzanine. The place was quiet above the soft rustling and nickering of horses. They circled around sacks of Indian corn and bales of hay, the milky light from the skylight making dust motes float over the oak boards.

"I need you to be silent."

She nodded, her face bleached of color. From the vantage point on the second floor, Pedro spotted Erebus. The warhorse pricked his ears, alert. Other than an unfamiliar carriage, the space was empty.

Pedro descended the stairs, the angel close behind, and approached Erebus's stall. With no time for a saddle, he took a bridle and a cloth and, in seconds, had the horse ready.

"Don't make unnecessary gestures." Erebus usually accepted a second rider, but it was better not to test the horse's temper. Pedro placed his hands on her waist, spanning it with ease.

He had raised her level with his chest when she twisted with surprising strength, breaking free. Hair flailing, she climbed atop the cart he had glimpsed from the mezzanine.

He caught up with her. "What do you think you're doing?"

"I am going home!"

"The quinta is surrounded. How far do you think you can go in this rickety cart?" he whispered furiously and pulled her from the carriage.

She kept gazing above her shoulder as he dragged her away. "But—"

"You will obey me." This was madness. Justifying his actions to a slip of a girl.

"I can't leave James behind."

Pedro halted. "Who?"

"My dog, James, is over there." She joined her hands in front of her body, gaze rushing to the open exit and back to the cart. "Please!"

Pedro tugged her hand, but she dug her feet again, pulling against his hold."I won't abandon him. I won't!"

"Do it."

She climbed up and returned carrying a brown valise. Steps made Pedro turn. A shadow appeared at the stable's entrance. Pedro covered her mouth again, and she lifted her brows, the black of her eyes eclipsing the blue.

"Crawl back to my horse's stall."

Pedro hid inside the tackle room. The man entered the stable with a musket in hand, scanning the place. Pedro waited. When a greasy face came parallel to the iron-studded door, Pedro jumped, clasped the beam above his head, and used both feet to shove it open. It hit the assailant with a crack, and he crumpled. Pedro straddled the invader. Thrashing his beefy arms, the man struggled to unseat him, but Pedro punched his nose until he lost conscience.

A scream, her scream, pierced the silence.

A filthy attacker had snatched her hair, pulling her up with savagery. A blade flashed as he unsheathed a dagger. She flailed her arms and kicked, but the man overpowered her, pushing her head back to expose the whiteness of her neck.

Heart hammering in his chest, Pedro took off running, short sword prepared in his right hand. He vaulted over the first bale and climbed the second one, battle rage boosting his strength. When Pedro neared, the coward's eyes flared, and he shoved the girl aside. Her head slammed on the brick wall with a sickening thud, and she collapsed.

Pedro did not give the attacker a chance to defend himself, finishing him quickly. Throat dry, he fell to his knees by her side. She lay on the floor, white-blonde hair spread like a nimbus over the hay. The skin above her right brow was bruised and already swelling. Anger swept through him in red currents, and he forced it under control. Keeping his eyes on the portal, Pedro took his gloves off.

His hands loomed monstrous, so close to her pearly skin, but he brushed the hair out of her forehead and cradled her cheek. "Angel?"

She turned her face toward his voice, opening her eyes. Light and pure, the color reminded him of the Atlantic near Algarve. "Who's pounding in my head? Make it stop, please."

"I will get you out of here."

"Promise?" Her eyes focused on his face for a fleeting moment, then fluttered shut again.

Careful not to jostle her, he passed his hands under her legs and supported her shoulders. She curled into his chest, cheek pressed against his shoulder, hand looped around his neck.

Pedro kicked the door to Erebus's stall. His horse nickered, stomping the hay.

"*Parado*," Pedro commanded.

The horse stood still, neck high. After taking his raincoat from the peg, Pedro helped her up. Even fighting dizziness, she held tight to the mane. After showing more bravery than he expected, she now wavered, and he took the reins, preparing to mount. A pitiful whine brought his eyes to the floor—the dog. He shouldn't bother with the nuisance.

With a heavy sigh, he bent and grabbed the basket's handle with his left hand. Dog collected, he mounted behind her.

A few more feet and they would be out in the open. He could use speed and the element of surprise to avoid pursuit. If Ulrich had a decent rifleman... They needed to race to the hill and gain the cover of pine trees, out of range.

Pedro touched his heels to the horse's flanks. Erebus had reached the patch of sunlight at the exit when a flash of black rushed from outside. The stallion reared. Pedro increased the pressure on his knees and inclined his torso forward, holding tight to both girl and dog to keep their balance. Erebus knocked the attacker's chest with the front hooves and crunched him below steel horseshoes.

With a lurch, Erebus galloped free.

The gravel pathway leading to the back of the property was empty. Pedro lowered his torso to the horse's neck. Shouting and bullets followed them on the elm-lined path, but soon faded. Atop the hill, Pedro glanced one last time at his property, his chest burning with the need for revenge.

Chapter 7

Gabriel pinned the medals onto his officer's coat and combed his hair. The king's carriage would arrive this afternoon, and he still had to review the guard escorting the procession tomorrow. Dom Luis had high standards for the hussar's uniform, and Gabriel needed to ensure the officer's fastidiousness. It was tedious work, to be sure, and if it weren't for meeting Miss Anne Maxwell, his stay in the north would have proved utterly uneventful.

What a lovely girl. With her looks and prospects, she could have a successful season in Lisbon or Oporto, but she had relinquished her chances at a brilliant marriage to help her family. Gabriel sighed, his hand coming up to cover his medals. He knew the price of sacrifices intimately, and the choices that led him here were not so selfless as hers...

Gabriel forced his mind away from the past. Perhaps Anne Maxwell would be there. Of course, she would be. The whole gentry from Vila Nova to Regua would receive the monarch.

Where was his sword? A quick inspection of his belongings confirmed his suspicion. His sister had stolen it again.

Gabriel traveled the corridors of their rented residence, careful not to clank his spurs. Father had one of his sleepless nights wandering the garden, his hands clasped behind his back, an unlit pipe dangling from his lips. The cocks had started their cacophony when he retired. Would Father's sorrow of losing contact with Pedro, his precious godson, ever fade?

Gabriel hastened through the parlor door and emerged in the courtyard. The sun punched him in the face, and he blinked to adjust. Manuela hacked at a dummy with abandon, a few blows away from dislodging the damn thing from its post. Gabriel groaned. His saber's blade would be as dull as one of Santiago's sermons after Manu's abuse.

She riposted, hair flying in disarray, face sunburned and sweaty, her boy's clothes indecent. Madame Margot, the French governess, scrunched her snout as if she had smelled rotten eggs. No doubt he would receive her notice later. What was it? The third this year?

Gabriel placed himself in front of Manuela's target. "Enough."

The girl blew hair from her face. "Go away, Gabriel."

With a sigh, he avoided a blow to the head and disarmed his wayward sister. "Sword fight? I preferred the actress phase. Your Viola was quite spirited."

"Leave off, saint." She whirled and was dashing off when he grabbed her arm.

"Don't call me that."

"Why? It's the truth." Her nostrils flared, her fair complexion turning an unbecoming shade of red.

Gabriel exhaled and cleaned a smudge from her cheek. "Why can't you behave like the other ladies your age?"

She glared and shrugged away from his touch. "So you can marry me off and be rid of me?"

"Of course not. I want your happiness. Father wants—"

"Father doesn't even know I exist."

Gabriel stared at her moist eyes. "You know he loves you. He is just—"

"Preoccupied with matters of estate. I wonder how he gets the time for you." She tapped her chin, the strong, square chin that gave her face too much personality, and then her lips contorted into a sneer. "Of course. You are the perfect son. And I... I'm just the unwanted daughter that took Mother away."

"Manu, please."

She shoved him away and raced inside the house.

If only she knew who really mattered to their father. She had been blessedly too young when Pedro was around. Before Mozambique, Fontes had eyes and ears only for the golden boy, his precious godson. Gabriel exhaled long and hard. If he could not make their father care, he must be the one to care for her.

Hooves clattered outside his gate. Lieutenant Lopes, his second in command, limped inside the courtyard. What was he doing here so early? He was supposed to be escorting the king. Had he deserted their monarch? Gabriel opened his mouth to reprimand him when he noticed the state of his uniform. Blood stains marred his white trousers, and his coat had gunpowder burns.

Gabriel's heart ricocheted inside his chest. "What happened?"

"We've been ambushed."

Chapter 8

Erebus galloped at full speed, his hooves battering the macadamized pavement. A pained moan escaped the girl's lips. Pedro tugged the reins to the left, guiding the horse away from the road and over the hayfield. When the horse's gait turned smoother, her body went lax in his arms. How many times had he seen head injuries in soldiers? The consciousness loss, headache, and somnolence faded after two days. But they were men, stronger, used to battle.

What if she didn't wake?

She must lie in a proper bed, to be cared for away from the unprotected road. Any moment in the open left them vulnerable to further attacks. Without delay, Pedro needed to collect his brother at the brothel and retreat to the coudelaria. His horse breeding property near the border with Spain was impregnable. Once there, he could plan their next steps.

He pulled the edges of his black cape, protecting her from the wind and curious eyes. If there was someone's life more in danger than his, it was this girl. A nameless, angel-like whore with the devil's own luck.

That voice. The dagger slashing through skin. João Ulrich.

Flashes from Mozambique bombarded his skull—whimpers echoing in the bone-dry ravine, a whittled bird trampled on the trail, hungry flames licking the huts.

Pedro squeezed the reins, his palm moist. He kept his gaze ahead, counting the cork oaks on the field. Still, the memories came, threatening his sanity. Pedro gulped air and tensed the arm that held the girl, bringing her closer. Her warmth seeped inside him, and the past receded enough for him to concentrate on the road.

After they crossed the bridge over the Douro, Vila Nova's whitewashed lodges appeared in his line of vision. Pedro took the path hidden among a grove of pines. The madam's cottage stood away from the village's hypocritical sight but within walking distance.

Pedro reined in, lifting dust from the shabby entrance. A stable lad came running.

"Bring my brother. And the madam."

"Yes, Your Excellency." He bowed and scurried away.

The two-storied house had yellowed walls cracked as if shaken by an earthquake. Near the front porch, magnolias, roses, and daisies, their stems bent, wilted petals lolling, split the parched earth of terra-cotta vases.

He opened the cape. Without the flush of his kiss, the girl's skin was pale. Pedro traced her golden brows, the feathery lashes, but he refrained from touching her lips with his blood-splattered glove. How could she belong in this house? She'd said she was new to this, no doubt turned to this life by a desperate father or a debt-ridden widow.

A frown marred her forehead, and she groaned, her eyes shifting behind closed eyelids. Fighting the attackers in her dreams? Ulrich was a perverted, shrewd blackguard. If he wanted her dead, he would scourge the countryside until he found her.

The brothel slumbered this time of day, but the madam would appear any moment, and he would have to relinquish the angel's weight. Another man would press against her, tainting her with his lust, abusing her until her innocence would harden into greed.

If Ulrich didn't get to her first.

Pedro's shoulders tensed, and he brought her closer to his chest. Not in his lifetime.

Cris exited the porch, coat disheveled, shirt open. Pedro covered the angel with his coat, so not even her glorious hair showed to the outside world.

His brother stretched his arms, a grin flashing his teeth. "You joined me after all."

"Salgueiro was attacked. Take your horse. We need to regroup. Now."

Cris halted, his smile fading. "Attacked? Are you all right? And the servants?"

Pedro shook his head.

The madam sauntered down the stairs, her gaudy corset showing below a flimsy wrapper, her bleached hair framing a heavily painted face. "*Bonjour*. A pleasure to receive you, Your Excellency."

Pedro uncovered the side of the cape, revealing his precious bundle. "How much?"

"Who is she?" Fake French accent forgotten, the madam squinted her eyes at the girl.

Her practiced moves did not fool him. She would name her price now, as he wanted out of this place.

Every moment in the open placed himself and the angel at risk.

He goaded Erebus forward, and she jerked out of the way, her complexion turning gray beneath the layers of face powder.

Pedro lowered his voice. "Don't play games with me. I won't ask a second time."

Cris posted himself at the madam's front, raising his palms. "She is telling the truth, brother. I've never seen this girl before, and I know them all."

Pedro hid his surprise under a blank facade and clutched the girl closer.

Angel, who are you?

Chapter 9

Gabriel stood in Vesuvio's courtyard under the shade of leafy palm trees, a frilly concoction of a bonnet in his hand. Why was a flower of a girl, the sweetest he ever beheld, in the carnage that had become of Quinta do Salgueiro? He cleaned his feet on the rug and entered the parlor in the wake of an old British butler. It was Gabriel's duty to find out, wasn't it?

"If you follow me, sir, the baron will receive you in the study."

Gabriel inclined his head and followed the formal servant. Signs of restoration brightened the old mansion's public areas. New oriental rugs and silks gave vivid color to the vestibule and parlor, enhancing the sober oak parquet and tapestries.

With a quick rap, the butler opened the door and signaled for him to enter. Bright light washed the study from stunning floor-to-ceiling windows.

The moment he stepped inside, Griffin Maxwell vaulted from his seat. "You found her?"

The Englishman had dark circles under his eyes, and his hair stuck at odd angles. What a difference from the model of British restraint Gabriel had met at the village last week.

Gabriel cramped the bonnet, his palms moistening the cloth. "I'm not sure how to say this—"

The door opened without a knock, and Mrs. Maxwell waddled inside. "Wentworth said you bring news of Anne. Is it true?"

Maxwell exhaled and shook his head. "Why must Portuguese women be so stubborn? Didn't the doctor advise you to stay abed, Julia?"

She reached for the bonnet, her eyes brimming with tears. "Where is our Anne?"

Gabriel sighed. "I found the hat and her carriage in Quinta do Salgueiro, but unfortunately, your sister is missing."

Mrs. Maxwell gasped. "At Pedro's property?"

Mr. Maxwell's face turned red and then purple. "I'm going to kill that corrupt aristocrat."

"I don't understand. Anne has never met the Count of Almoster."

"Hasn't she?" Gabriel's heart lurched, and he lowered his gaze. She could have taken a fancy to him. It was hard to believe a sweet and innocent girl to be so disposed, but Pedro was nothing if not persuasive.

The baron narrowed his eyes to slits. "My sister is respectable, and anyone who even tries to disparage her name will—"

Mrs. Maxwell touched her husband's arm. "There must be an explanation. She left to meet winemakers. To teach how to graft grapevines."

"Then she was at the wrong place at the wrong time." Gabriel's throat felt dry, but he needed to say it. The family had a right to know. "There's been an attempt on the king's life. Dom Luis escaped unharmed, but Pedro Daun is the prime suspect."

Mr. Maxwell opened and closed his mouth. "That murderous bastard has my sister."

Mrs. Maxwell sagged on the couch and pressed her temples. "I met Pedro as a child. Despite his many... shortcomings, he is an honorable man. There must be some mistake. If he has Anne, he is protecting her. I am more tranquil now that I know she is with him."

Maxwell stared at his wife incredulously. "Pedro Daun hates me. He would delight in exacting his revenge." The baron whirled, a fierce scowl on his face. "I'm going after him."

Gabriel had an inkling where Pedro had taken refuge, but he would keep his silence. The last thing he needed was civilians interfering with the investigation. "Why? Why does he hate you so?"

The couple shared a tense look, and Mrs. Maxwell raised her brows.

Mr. Maxwell lifted his palm as if to stop her words. "The count is manipulative and a scoundrel, and he has meddled enough in our lives. Last summer, he attempted to marry Julia by force."

Gabriel startled. Julia had been the woman Pedro was obsessed with when they went to Mozambique? The one he fought so hard to forget? Could this be why Pedro had taken the girl? To settle a vendetta with the baron?

"I vow to you I will bring her back."

Chapter 10

Images flickered behind Anne's eyelids. Her mother knitting close to the fire, smiling at her antics, only to cry when she thought Anne wasn't looking. Griffin listening to her play the piano, his face hidden behind the Times. Then it all blurred, and she shivered alone in the cabin, the ship gray and chilly, tilting, rocking.

Anne fought to open her eyes, but a dark force shut her eyelids. The storm roared outside, threatening to swallow the boat. The shadows changed and now surrounded her, jerking her from the floor and snatching her hair.

Anne opened her eyes with a gasp. The nightmare released her, but her heartbeats raged as if she still wrestled with its grip. Blinking, she took her bearings. Dark velvet enclosed her in shadows. The strange bed had pearly sheets. A bright spot of light came from between the heavy curtains, piercing her vision. When she lifted her head, she woke a beast living inside her brain.

"Finally."

That voice. The smoky sound pulled a thread from Anne's memory, but trying to unravel it increased the pain. A brilliant glass-stained window. The walls, distant but clothed in burgundy silk. A massive painting. She squinted her eyes—two horses. One was ebony, the other white as light.

She turned to the left as black breeches came near. Panting, she raised her head and winced at the pain. "What happened?"

"You have been sleeping for several hours. Twenty-one, to be precise." The mattress dipped. "Here."

James padded closer, licking her face, and she cradled his small body, the relief of his presence making her dizzy.

The man came into focus, blond hair tied at the nape, golden skin, smooth. No imperfections chipped his face, no curves, all straight lines.

The memory of his kiss colored her cheeks, and Anne pulled the covers to her chin. "You stayed here?"

He lifted his palms. "I mean you no harm. I'm a bachelor, and females only visit my household to... entertain me."

Did he think her a woman of loose morals? Oh, the shame. Anne shut her eyes. "I'm not... that. I'm sorry if I gave—"

"I'm Pedro Daun, Count of Almoster." He bowed briefly. "I will send the housekeeper with food and allow you to rest." He turned to the door.

He would leave her here, alone?

"I must explain. I had a reason to visit. A perfectly innocent one. Why, my name is Anne—"

He halted and tilted his head to the side. His stare was unsettling.

Anne's skin tingled uncomfortably, and the explanation at the tip of her tongue eluded her. When he was leaving, she wanted him to stay. Now that she had his full attention, she wanted him to leave.

"It suits you. Ana."

Ana. The two long A's in his husky voice rolled on forever. Her name was far from unique, but on his aristocrat's lips, it bloomed, grand and secretive, the name of a medieval queen.

He waved his hand imperiously. "I don't doubt your innocence. And I expect to hear a full account of why a respectable lady landed in my ballroom—after I return."

The Count had said twenty-one hours, almost a full day.

Julia must be frantic. Please let Griffin be home.

Anne gazed at the door. "I'm well enough. I prefer to go back to my family."

"You will remain here while I hunt our attackers. It's not safe for you anywhere else."

"Not safe? Will those villains come here too?" Pain assaulted the left side of her temple. Anne moaned and pulled at the sheets, but the bed held her like quicksand.

He moved closer and sat in the bedside chair. Anne inhaled sharply, his scent of cedar bringing memories of unrequited, port-tasting kisses and, strangely, safety.

With a leather-clad finger, he pointed at the glass panes. "That is the Misarella Bridge. The only access to this property. I have it guarded day and night." A wry smile came to his lips. "Those villains, as you put it, won't bother us here."

Anne pushed to a seated position and brought her face close to the window, misting the glass. A gruesome bridge loomed above a sheer drop. Water foamed below, scraping now and then to show pointed stones.

"The granite construction dates to the Middle Ages. Common folk believes it was made by the devil."

Anne placed her fingertips on the glass. "Do you believe it so?"

"If it was built by the devil, he is on my side. The bridge makes the coudelaria impregnable." A note of pride colored the velvet tone of his voice.

Anne smiled wistfully. "My brother would admonish you for entertaining folk tales."

"Allow folk their tales. They have little else." His expression softened, and he lifted his hand, his finger reaching for her smile as if it were a delicacy. "You seem to like this paragon of rationality."

"I love him dearly. Griffin is an overbearing oaf sometimes, but he means well."

His hand paused in the space between them, and a pleat appeared on his fair brow. "Griffin?"

"Griffin Maxwell, of Quinta do Vesuvio."

One second, he was relaxed, the picture of a charming aristocrat. The other he advanced, holding her chin to the sunlight. Anne's breath caught, and she held still under his scrutiny, her heart accelerating. The Count of Almoster was as predictable as a feline on high alert, hind legs coiled, pupils narrowed, tail twitching—one never knew if he would purr or pounce.

"You don't look like him."

He released her as abruptly as he had caught her and stood. With his back turned to her, he stared outside, his unyielding shoulders haloed by sunlight. Even marble-still, he gave off energy, a hum she felt in the pit of her stomach.

Anne found her locket in the folds of the loaned camisole and held it tight. "Do you know my brother?"

"One could say we are old friends."

Anne exhaled, her chest light for the first time since she opened her eyes in this strange room. If the count were Griffin's friend, everything would turn all right.

"You will rest now," he said dismissively, already starting for the door.

She caught his hand, her naked fingers intertwining with his. "Please, can you send for him?"

His body went rigid, and he pulled away from her touch. "I believe we have already finished this conversation."

His face held the same comfort as his bridge. How could such beauty cut so deep? The safety she felt with him faded, opening a chasm between them. Anne lowered her weight back to the bed. She touched her forehead and winced at the lump there.

"I've agitated you. I will send the housekeeper with tea." He strode to the door, his hand opening and closing by the side of his body as if she had singed him.

She watched him until he shut the door, leaving her alone.

The windows creaked on a sudden gust of wind. The room's shadows taunted her with hidden depths. Safe? She shuttered her eyes with such force that her eyelids hurt. The attacker's blotched face flared inside her mind, pulling her hair, his fingers digging into her arms.

Anne blinked, her breaths coming in short bursts. She must get out.

With trembling hands, she pushed the sheets to the side and, shifting to the edge of the bed, stood with a shove. Her legs crumbled beneath her, and she fell to the plush carpet. The dizziness returned, and from atop the bed she heard James barking, the sound coming from far away. Her head throbbed, and she whimpered. Only a man's polished shoes, discarded under the bed, listened.

Chapter 11

The air felt toxic inside Pedro's lungs. He shut the bedroom door. The shadows of the empty corridor swayed, shifting into menacing shapes.

Maxwell's sister.

Panting, Pedro splayed his hands over the window's priceless stained glass. It hid all the light, all the air. He needed air. With one swift move, he wrenched a candelabra off a nearby table and hurled it. The glass shattered, raining down colorful shards over the bridge, and light attacked the hall. Pedro took great gulps of air, the wind lashing out at his face.

Though the panel was no more, the Misarella remained. Pedro stared at the diabolic rocks. Instead of security, it brought restriction. Fate had turned again, chaining Pedro in a play not of his making.

Maxwell's sister.

A laugh drained out of his chest, and he pressed his temples. His father would plan the most delectable revenge. Having his enemy's sibling under his roof. Pedro could still hear her laughter—a chiming of heavenly bells. The Englishman's fear had unfolded, had it not? How would Maxwell enjoy losing a loved one?

What was he thinking? That girl, that... that wingless angel sleeping on his bed, was Maxwell's sister. It could not be true.

Pedro rubbed his breastbone, the denial playing over and over inside his head. Why must the poacher have anything to do with her? Was it not enough to steal Julia and his promise of peace, and now this... a claim on an angel Pedro had discovered for himself?

Pedro forced his breathing under control and pushed away from the broken window. No. His upset had nothing to do with the girl. The surprise had tainted his judgment. If he was angry, it had to do with Ulrich. Yes. Maxwell had robbed him of his revenge. If it weren't for her, he would have ended Ulrich.

No matter. Pedro would do it now. He had lost enough time playing the girl's nursemaid. If Ulrich had left any trail, Pedro would find him and finish what the bullfighter had started ten years ago in Mozambique.

A thump sounded inside his bedroom, followed by barking. What had she done?

Pedro opened the door. The bed was empty. His pulse sped up, and he strode inside the room. She lay on the floor, her hair tangled around her face and arms.

Pedro exhaled and picked up her limp body. "You chose thc wrong place to fall, little angel."

She opened her eyelids, her gaze clouded, disturbed, but when she saw him, she relaxed as if reassured by his heartbeats. How could Maxwell leave her to roam the countryside? Pedro would never allow his woman to be hurt.

Carefully, he brushed the hair from her face, exposing the swell on her forehead. Rage coursed through his veins. Her slight weight, her fair coloring, the transparency of her skin... she was as delicate as light.

Pedro lowered her to his bed. She protested, but he covered her with the counterpane. "I will eliminate those who meant you harm," he vowed.

She turned to her side, her hands folded near her chest, and her eyes fluttered shut. "Then you will take me to my family. I know you will." The last words came out as a sleepy murmur.

Pedro watched her breathing turn even. The bed curtains rippled, and light danced on her cheek, a shine and diamond above her beauty mark, and another near her lips, guarding her against shadows. Sleep had claimed her when he tucked a strand of hair under her perfect ear.

"I wouldn't be so sure."

Pedro sharpened his blade, the strop's up and down swipes filling the study with rhythmic sounds. A knock on the door brought in Jair, his clothes dusted from the road to Salgueiro.

Pedro stood and sheathed the saber. "What did you uncover?"

The retired soldier cleaned perspiration from his brow. "The royal guard surrounds the quinta."

A neighbor must have heard the shooting and contacted the authorities. "Saddle Erebus. I will leave to meet them."

As if Gabriel's regiment could arrest Ulrich. More likely, they would bungle the tracks. No matter. Pedro would find the slave trader even if he had to climb the Picos de Europa. He collected cartridges for his rifle and moved to the door.

"On my way back, I bought this." Jair cut Pedro's exit and extended his arm, exposing a crumpled newspaper.

"That will be all," Pedro said and scanned the headlines of Journal do Comércio.

Attempt on the king's life. The Count of Almoster is the prime suspect.

Pedro sat behind his desk and stared at the sheet until the black typography bled together in the corners, but his mind couldn't absorb the meaning of the words.

The door opened and closed. Pedro didn't acknowledge the newcomer.

"You look like hell. What is it?" Cris grabbed the newspaper and gasped.

Pedro dropped his head on the chair's back and shut his eyes. "Read it."

Cris took a shaky breath. "'The attempted regicide happened on the fourth day of His Majesty's visit to the north of the country. He traveled on an open Landau, accompanied by the queen and the Duke of Braganza. They arrived at Vila Nova around four in the afternoon. The city's proud people carried flowers and rosemary boughs, crowding the village square in front of the cathedral. When the driver stopped for the queen to distribute coins, the first shot exploded. Chaos ensued. The shooter discharged two more times before he was taken down. But the attempt had not ended. According to the king's guard, a second offender awaited on the cathedral's belfry. With uncanny aim, he shot, missing the king by an inch. A witness affirms a blond man hastened away from the tower after the second shooting. The Count of Almoster was seen by one of the king's guards. The count has extensive military training. One of his former commanders, Antonio Fontes, affirmed he doubted any other officer could have taken that rifle shot.'"

Pedro gripped the armrests, trying to keep afloat. Fontes had accused him? For all his godfather's morality, he knew how to pierce a man in the back.

Cris shook his head and ran a hand over his disheveled hair. "Why are these journalists speaking such calumnies?"

Pedro pressed the sides of his temples. "Can't you see? This is not a writer's work. Ulrich's speech made no sense back in Salgueiro, but now I understand the plan. To incriminate me of regicide. What has he accomplished by eliminating our servants? He killed my alibi."

Pedro's blood flow returned, and with it, vertigo. He had survived this far by protecting his flanks, by never allowing the enemy to break his front, by attacking first. And yet, Ulrich had burst through his defenses and cut his retreat.

Cris gasped and lowered the paper slowly. "There is more. Here it says... the king's brother was killed in the shooting."

Cold seeped into Pedro's chest. Fernando could not be dead. He fisted his hands and shut his eyes. Why would providence spare Braganza? Only because his former aide-de-camp was the best man Pedro ever knew, the last who deserved to die young? Pedro knew too well no benevolent fate ruled the world.

Cris placed a hand over his shoulder. "I know he was your friend. It is all right to grieve."

Pedro shook away his touch, hardening his gut. "Read the rest."

"'The Royal Guard is searching for the count. The population is incensed by the attack. The king returned to Oporto, where the Duke of Braganza will be buried—'"

Jair crashed inside the studio, his face ashen. "Sir, there are soldiers on the bridge."

Cris lowered the paper, desperation twisting his expression. "Pedro, what will we do?"

Do? Pedro had a perverse curiosity to let this farce play to its bitter end. "What would the Duke of Titano say if his heir died a traitor?"

"When will you stop giving a damn about what the duke says? Will you play into Ulrich's hand and go to prison just to ruin Father's legacy?" Cris's voice cracked.

Pedro stared at his brother's wide eyes. If he was arrested, Cris could be implicated as well. And the girl. Ulrich's worlds rang inside his head like a death knoll.

The slave trader would not rest until he eliminated any potential witnesses.

Pedro stood and strode to the door. "How many, Jair?"

"At least twenty, sir."

Cris pulled his hair, panting. "If they block the bridge, we are locked here."

"We will use it as an advantage. Jair, tell the leader I'll parlay in the gatehouse."

Jair nodded and left to do his bidding.

Cris grabbed Pedro's arm. "Are you sure it's wise?"

"The guard must see me. They'll believe I'm barricading myself here."

Cris's eyes widened, and he wrung his hands. "But they will siege the coudelaria. Wait us out. The food can only last so long. Then they will arrest you and—"

"We won't stay here. I'll lead us out through the scarps." Pedro alone knew the mountain passes through the forest. If they reached the Douro River and Barca D'Alva, they could board the yacht and evade pursuit.

"It's madness. We'll break our necks."

Now wasn't the time for Cris to question his authority. "Enough."

Pedro moved past him and reached the narrow portico of the gatehouse.

Jair guarded the door, his face set in granite, and reached for the doorknob. "The leader refused to enter alone. Brought another red jacket."

Pedro crossed the threshold. Cris followed him inside and closed the door. The square room was spartan, a table in the center, one door leading to the bridge, the other to the coudelaria's inner courtyard. A single window gave scant light, and time and mildew had blackened the walls. Smelling of dampness and stale sweat, it was the opposite of the opulent interior grounds. The officer who had come to arrest him shifted his weight from side to side.

Gabriel. Why was he not surprised?

"The hour for uninvited callers is long past." Pedro narrowed his eyes and squared his shoulders. "You are remiss in your etiquette, cousin."

Gabriel exchanged a glance with the other soldier, a stocky middle-aged man, no doubt his second in command, and removed a missive from his red coat. His royal uniform was pressed, and he had shaved and combed recently, not the appearance of a man riding non-stop to find him this far north. Gabriel had been close, with time to partner with Ulrich and later place the blame on him. But was he capable of it? Not the cousin Pedro had grown up with. A shy youth afraid of battles, preferring paintbrushes to a bayonet, a disappointment to his military father. But Gabriel had changed, and a man could do any wrong for the right price.

Gabriel cleared his throat. "This is your arrest order, Pedro. If you accompany me without resisting, I can guarantee—"

"The only guarantee if you take me is a promotion for you. Don't be a hypocrite. This is me, not some half-wit from Lisbon."

The moment they had him, his life would be forfeited. The plebe would go wild, cheering whoever eliminated a king slayer.

"Still, I have my orders."

"And I'm impressed. First, Fontes accused me point blank, my own uncle, and now you arrive here to arrest me. Our family sure knows how to throw a welcome," Pedro said, unable to hide his bitterness.

"Father didn't mean to. The reporter distorted his words—"

"Spare me his excuses." Pedro gritted his teeth. At the worst moment of his life, when Pedro had needed his uncle's guidance, he had received contempt. If Fontes had failed to be at Pedro's side after Mozambique, why expect any faith from him now?

Pedro forced a leash around his temper. No point in reviving family grievances.

"Since you mentioned my accusation, who did you say was the prime witness?"

Gabriel inflated his chest. "The guard's lieutenant who accompanied His Majesty north."

Ulrich had a long payroll then, including this Dom Luis's bodyguard. "Does he still have access to the king?"

"I don't know why this changes anything—"

"Does he?"

"No. He asked for medical leave and returned to his home in Aveiro."

How convenient for him. He would retire with a heavy purse after selling Pedro out. Pedro stilled. If he caught hold of this crooked guard, he could find Ulrich and put an end to this treachery. Heart speeding, Pedro advanced another step. "His name?"

"I'm done answering your questions, Pedro." Gabriel's gaze strayed to the window. "I want to return before nightfall. We've lost too much time already."

"If I were you, I would increase Dom Luis's guard." Pedro cleaned an imaginary speck from his velvet coat. "Now, if you will excuse me, I have a tower to defend."

"Must you do this the hard way? Father would be disappointed in you."

Pedro tensed, fisting his hands. "Do you think I care?"

Gabriel exhaled and sought Pedro's gaze. "He changed after Mozambique..."

A weight descended over Pedro's shoulder. Nothing had been the same after Mozambique. "Ulrich is in Portugal."

Gabriel flinched, his eyes widening in shock. "Why is he here?"

Pedro pointed his chin at the stranger Gabriel had brought. "*Tu lui fais confiance?*"

"I trust him with my life."

Pedro nodded. "I will retell the events. Just this once. The day the king was shot, I was at Salgueiro. Ulrich invaded the quinta, and killed the servants. I never had dealings with that scum. At least this you can vouch for me."

A glint of sweat appeared on Gabriel's upper lip, and he adjusted his coat, his movements jerky. "I don't know, Pedro. Your story seems too convenient, and there are witnesses—"

"It's getting late." Pedro pointed at the exit. "I don't want you stumbling on a wolf on your return trip."

"Wait." Gabriel lifted his palms. "What about the girl?"

Pedro schooled his expression. "Who?"

"Enough with your games. We recovered her carriage from your property. Her family is frantic. If you act with chivalry and release her to my care, I will take your explanation to the king."

Pedro fisted his hands by his side. The girl could prove his innocence, and for that, Ulrich would not let her live. Pedro had vowed to protect her, and he kept his vows. "Since when does the king care for a commoner?"

"The girl may not descend from royalty like your exalted ancestry, but the king granted her brother a title. Griffin Maxwell is Baron of Boa Vista now."

Cris coughed to stifle his obvious shock and gave Pedro a charged look. He could well imagine what went on in his brother's head, wondering if Pedro meant to take his revenge on Maxwell's sister.

Gabriel awaited an answer, a hint of desperation furrowing his brow. "Christ, Pedro, she is an honest, sweet girl and—"

Pedro stilled, his muscles tensing. "Have you met her?"

Gabriel's face flushed, and he averted his gaze. Silence stretched. Gabriel splayed his hands on the scarred table, forehead damp with sweat, no doubt cursing himself for his outburst.

Gabriel would not be so overwrought if she were a mere acquaintance. What kind of relationship existed between them? Pedro would send the straight arrow to find pebbles in the riverbed. Keep to the plan, dammit. He should let Gabriel take her. What was it to him if her life was at risk? If Maxwell had proved totally inept at protecting her? Except for the hatred he felt for her brother, he had no claim to the angel sleeping on his bed. "When Ulrich invaded, she was there with me."

Gabriel advanced on him, his eyes wild. "You would use her as an alibi, Pedro? I should expect no less. You proved how little you value others in Mozambique."

Vision hazy, Pedro pinned him to the wall. Gabriel gulped, his face blanching.

"You pissed yourself after Ulrich ordered the Chikunda to point their carbines at us." Pedro slammed Gabriel's shoulders into the wall. "When I lowered my rifle, you were the first to sigh in relief. I bet you cried yourself to sleep that night."

Light flashed to the right. The stocky soldier had unsheathed a dagger.

To avoid bloodshed, Pedro lowered the straight arrow. As soon as his feet touched the ground, Gabriel pushed Pedro away to pacify his subordinate.

"You've overextended your welcome. If you cross the Misarella, I will pierce your shiny coat with lead."

He flicked his hand to Cris, and his brother escorted both men outside.

Pedro didn't wait for his brother to return and dashed over the spiraling steps leading to the watchtower. If he was to mount their defense, he needed to act fast.

Cris's panting breaths sounded behind him. "She is Maxwell's sister?"

Pedro didn't stop for his brother's inquisition. "Not now."

"This is madness. You cannot use the girl as an alibi. If you expose her... being found in your house, alone, she will be ruined."

Pedro flinched. He expected Gabriel to think the worst of him, but his own brother? "You heard Gabriel. The king's bodyguard, the one who accused me, is in Aveiro. If we get to him, we can get to Ulrich. We leave within the hour to the yacht. Prepare to sail. We can reach Barca D'Alva tomorrow and Aveiro in three days."

Cris grabbed his arm. "And the girl?"

Pedro stared at his brother's arm until he dropped it. "She does not concern you."

"I'll do what you say. For now." Cris saluted him mockingly and descended to the courtyard.

Pedro ignored his brother's outburst and climbed the rest of the steps. The tower's roof had been prepared for a long defense, ammunition and food safely stored, crenelation free of anything that could hamper the view. Below, framed by the tower's dented battlements, Gabriel had reached the river's opposite side, his head turning to gaze at the tower's windows.

"They are preparing to cross, sir." Jair handed him a binocular.

Pedro pointed the lenses at the Geira Mountains. Beyond the raging river, the soldiers armed themselves, their red uniforms like smears of blood on the wild countryside.

Gabriel stationed the men at the crest, where a patch of grass gave way to the canyon, only four hundred feet from Pedro's tower. Gabriel must have calculated a safe distance with the Dreyze's rifle range in mind, the standard issue of the Portuguese army.

Pedro approached the crenelation, and Jair handed him his Chassepot rifle. Handling the familiar weight, Pedro cocked the action and opened the bolt. The firing pin was shining clean, and he inserted the paper cartridge. Even though the new rifle could fire at least twenty times without cleaning the barrel, Jair had assembled the tools for cleanup, and they kept several rolled cartridges at hand.

Pedro settled the gun over his shoulder. The French weapon was a vast improvement over the Dreyze, and what his cousin didn't know was that the range reached a thousand feet. He closed his left eye and followed Gabriel, fingers caressing the trigger. A gentle squeeze and Gabriel wouldn't arrest him or pursue his angel. After the three seconds needed to recharge, Pedro could shoot the second in command. The rest would scatter like hens.

Pedro tensed his finger, the rifle's stock biting into his shoulder.

With a curse, he lowered the gun. The Duke of Titano would sneer at his useless morality, but Pedro would not attack unprovoked.

The sun reached the mountain's crest, coloring the river and the devil's bridge in the ember colors of hell. Gabriel raised his arm above his head. An infantryman raced to the Misarella, two more behind.

"Leave it to me." Pedro aimed at the soldier's bearskin and fired.

With the shot's impact, the hat flew and sailed to the riverbed below. His second discharge landed on the bridge's stone railing, an inch from the officer's torso.

Pedro watched as Gabriel shaded his eyes and gazed at the tower. "Go ahead; step over the bridge."

Clouds blocked the sun, plunging the ravine into shadows. Pedro held his breath, daring Gabriel to move.

When Gabriel signaled a recall, the three infantrymen abandoned their advance, and the regiment moved to their saddlebags, withdrawing supplies and faded bivouacs. It worked.

They mounted a siege.

Pedro released a pent-up breath and lowered the Chassepot. "Shoot in the air every hour, Jair. Light the torches and keep them awake all night. Tomorrow afternoon, I want you to send an informant, alerting them I escaped to Spain."

It would give them enough time to board the yacht.

"Yes, sir."

Pedro glanced at the Lusitano mares grazing, the lake reflecting the century-old cork oaks, and his fields of corn and rye. "Jair."

"Yes?"

"Keep the bridge, no matter the circumstances."

Chapter 12

Anne halted, her legs frozen. The mountain crest ended ten feet beyond her, giving way to a dome of blue. A group of horses awaited by the coudelaria's stone wall, their harness jingling. They couldn't leave through here. It must be a mistake.

Mr. Cristiano Queiroz took hold of her elbow. "I know it seems... er, daunting, but my brother is in control—"

Anne pulled away from him and plastered herself on the stones of the coudelaria, her safe place in the past day's turmoil. Cold seeped into her spine, her skin tingling. "The horses can't fly. No matter what your brother says. Please. There must be another way."

"Ana."

She startled. That voice. The Count of Almoster loomed on her front.

Pedro Daun. Half prince, half ruthless fighter.

"We spoke about this. Those men will not let you live. You are only safe with me. Now come."

She lifted her eyes to him, her chin trembling. His stern facade offered no comfort, no warmth.

Cristiano cleared his throat. "Pedro, I think she needs—"

"Ride ahead and scout the embankment."

The cheerful brother huffed, but then his shoulders drooped, and he collected the basket with James and mounted his horse, leaving her alone with the count.

Anne exhaled and forced her gaze to meet his. "I've been thinking. If they blame you for trying to end the king's life—"

"It's called murder."

"Yes. That. Won't the king still be in danger? Shouldn't we try to save him?"

His lips lifted in the semblance of a smile. "Shouldn't you concern yourself with your beautiful neck before worrying about others?"

Anne covered the mentioned part with shaky hands. Must he be so blunt? Though what he said sounded right, it was wrong to put their lives above the royal family. "What if—"

"After the sun sets, we won't be able to descend the scarp. We have no time."

A shot echoed over the stone walls, and the horses lifted their heads. Anne's heart bolted, and she stifled a scream. "Take me back, please."

"Do you wish those villains to bring violence to Vesuvio?" Despite his harsh words, his tone was soothing. "I want your trust. Do you trust me, Ana?"

He said her name that way again, the vowels reverberating inside her. Why did he have to say it so? She opened her eyes. He was too close and asked too much.

He tugged the reins of a white mare, the one from the painting in his room. "This is Hemera."

"Hemera?" Anne touched its nose in greeting.

"The Greek Goddess of Light. She scatters the night's shadows at dawn, bathing the earth in the ether's light. Her steps are sure. You have nothing to fear."

"She is beautiful."

He gazed at her intensely and placed Anne's hand on the mare's frizzy mane. "She is yours."

Anne gasped. "You are most generous, but I... I cannot accept."

"You'll need a horse for this trip." His expression turned aloof, and he spoke matter-of-factly as if he had offered her a glass of water or a parasol, not a prized Lusitano steed.

"I couldn't. It wouldn't be proper to receive a gift from you, and it's too valuable—"

The count placed a finger on her lips. "She will be yours as long as you stay with me. Is that more acceptable?"

Anne nodded but held her breath, unused to being touched like this.

He helped her mount. Astride the horse, she could not avoid looking at the void beyond the ridge. Anne failed to control her breaths, the bursts too loud in the hushed ravine.

"Ana?"

"Hmm?"

"Look at me."

She did. The setting sun mellowed the lines streaked on his irises, and though his expression was controlled, his eyes exuded a compelling force, a magnetism too hard to resist. Anne lowered her gaze.

"There is a path hidden on the rocks. I know it. The horses know it. I ordered their iron shoes removed so that they won't slip. If navigated carefully, it is secure.

Keep your eyes on me, not the canyon, your knees tight, the reins firm, and when we go down, bend your torso backward. Hemera will do the rest. Let her follow my horse."

He took a carrot from his pocket and spoke to Hemera in husky Portuguese. Hemera neighed and nuzzled his narrow waist until he fed her the treat. His black-gloved hand contrasted with the white mare as he tangled his fingers in her mane, so close to Anne's knees that pinpricks rose below her riding breeches.

The Count of Almoster was kinder to animals than to people. If Hemera trusted him...

Anne made her decision. She would trust this man for now and help him in any capacity available for her. "I will follow you."

He lifted his gaze, and a barely audible gasp escaped his lips. Then he bowed and left, his strides taking him towards his stallion. With a gracious move, he mounted his massive Lusitano and stepped forward—into nothingness.

After a parting glance at the fortress, she followed the count into the precipice.

When they reached the valley, Anne glanced up, her pulse steady for a change. The coudelaria had shrunk, now a speck atop the cliff. They were alive, and she had navigated a treacherous mountain by herself. But the ordeal wasn't done. The count guided them over a dense forest. During the long hours astride, the cheerful brother had kept a steady stream of conversation, and before the sun had vanished completely, he had convinced her to call him Cris.

They traveled until night had plunged the path into darkness, and her legs alternated between blessed numbness and unpleasant tingles and cramps. When they stopped for the night, Anne was drained. Cris came to help her alight. The count had his back turned, already rubbing down Erebus, his movements brisk and efficient. Cris took Hemera and his horse away, no doubt to receive the same treatment. Her legs could do with a thorough rubbing too...

She limped to where Cris had left James's basket and bent to pick him up, relishing the warmth of his body. "You are a brave boy."

Careful not to stray too far from the men, she took him to relieve himself, and when she returned, they were setting up a canvas tent. "Can I help?"

"You've done well," the count said. "Sit by the fire. Tomorrow you will rest in your own cabin."

Thanking his thoughtfulness, she plopped down with James on her lap. A comfortable position proved elusive, her buttocks and thighs protesting the hard ground. The brothers worked with quiet efficiency, the sort of expertize that hinted at previous practice. How many nights had they passed like this, surrounded by trees, out in the elements? And why would a wealthy, sophisticated aristocrat need to spend the night outdoors?

Anne leaned against the cork oak, caressing James's ears. Her pug snuggled closer to her tummy, snoring. A breeze ruffled through the tall foliage, mixing the rising smoke of the campfire with the fresh scent of pines. The summer night was balmy, but she welcomed the fire crackling close to her feet, the heat easing the soreness of her legs. At least she was too tired to think of how she had ended up sharing the fire's warmth with two strangers. But unlike the count, his brother befriended anything around him—the trees, James, even the hard schist soil—and he made her feel at ease.

Cris passed her a chunk of bread and ham. "You lived all your life in Portugal, and you've never been to the capital?"

Anne's smile wobbled, and she shrugged. "I was going to spend the season in Lisbon, but then, well, plans change... After reading many tourist guides and history books, I feel I'm a connoisseur."

Cris clasped his arms above his head. "It's not the same. You must cross the arches of the Praça do Comércio and eat sardines on Alfama's open grills."

Anne admired the flames sending sparkles into the quiet night. "I long to see the dawn from Saint George's Castle." She read that when the sun emerged from the Tagus River, it colored Lisbon's houses in all shades from white to deep red.

"Too tame. I'll take you to the Fado taverns. The best in the country."

Would she visit Lisbon at last? The count said as soon as he garnered evidence of his innocence, he would take it to Portugal's capital, straight to the king. Perhaps something good would come from this adventure.

Right now, she would settle for a bath and a soft mattress.

While Cris gushed about Fado singers, her gaze kept straying to the count. He had yet to speak, peeling an orange with precise cuts of his knife. Though he sat to the left of them, removed from the campfire's circle, long shadows emanated from his shoulders, touching her hip. Why did he isolate himself? Was it because of his social status? Or was he affected by the accusation? If she were more outspoken, she would ask. But even Cris left him to his musings.

The glow loved him, though, and had no qualms about touching him. While rolling a schist pebble between her fingertips, she imagined his skin to be firm and thick beside his straight nose but bristly over his chin. Covered in black leather, his hands were a mystery yet to be revealed, but she could bet his palms would be abrasive from wielding the sword. She couldn't guess the texture of his hair. Would it be fine and cool, like hers, or dry and thick like Tony's? She was staring at the golden strands when he turned to her. His eyes, luminous and alert, made her drop the pebble.

Cris rose and stretched his back. "I'll take first watch."

She peeked at the ominous trees surrounding them. "Cris?"

"Yes, sweet?"

"Please be careful."

He took his mean-looking gun and winked. "Always." With a last parting smile for her and a nod to the count, he swaggered away.

Anne followed his broad back until he disappeared into the shadows. She returned a sleeping James to his basket and hugged herself. Without the talkative brother, the camp became too silent.

"You spent the season hiding in the Douro?"

Anne lifted her shoulders. "I wouldn't say hiding, but my mother went to stay with friends in Bath, and Griffin moved to Vesuvio, and I didn't want to impose—"

"You sacrificed a year of husband-hunting so you would not bother anyone? How convenient. For them."

"My family wants the best for me," she said defensively and instantly regretted the tone of her voice. Why did she feel the need to justify their actions?

"That's not how the world works. If you don't pursue your desires, others will take them from you, or in your case, simply trample your wishes in favor of their own."

If everyone thought like him, where would the world be? Anne raised her brows. "Isn't this notion quite selfish?"

"Human nature is selfish. From our ancestors' fight for food to our industrialist society... it compels us to compete, get ahead of others."

Anne smiled mischievously. "Some may wish to *get along* with others, Your Excellency."

He lifted his eyes from the orange, and it may have been the light playing tricks on her, but his lips twitched. "Heaven hath no wit as an angel rebuked. She has a tongue, it seems. Call me Pedro."

"Oh, I couldn't."

His expression closed, and he cut the naked fruit in two. "You called my brother by his nickname."

"I'm sorry. It's just that he is..." She closed her mouth, stopping the words before she blurted out that Cris was far more friendly. That wouldn't be thoughtful, would it? Apart from when they met, the count had been courteous, but to call him by his first name... It was too intimate.

He offered her the fruit. "He is a natural son."

Anne refused, her hand finding and holding her locket. "Why are you saying this?"

He leaned away, his chin jutting out. "It's the truth. Or will you try to convince me an English lady doesn't mind? Would you marry a bastard?"

The crude word, spoken so callously, made her flinch. "I would not care if my dream suitor was born out of wedlock."

He chuckled. "Dream suitor? You would marry this paragon without considering his background? Would your brother approve?"

"I can't speak for Griffin, but a person's character is more important to me, Your Excellency." She drawled the honorific and then cringed at how petty she sounded. She shouldn't let him goad her so.

He crossed his arms, lifting his blond brow in challenge. "It explains the suitors you've been leading on."

She gasped. "What are you implying?"

"You tell me." He threw the orange, and it hit a trunk, leaving a wet mark. "Sweet."

Anne hated how the endearment sounded on his lips. "You are in a bitter disposition, and I don't want to form a poor opinion of you because of some sour words." She stood and paced away from the fire.

"Where are you going?"

"I need air."

She weaved between firs and oaks, her steps muffled by the carpet of pine leaves. Shadows soaked the forest, making it hard to see a clear path. When she could no longer hear his breathing, she halted. With a heavy sigh, she leaned against a birch tree. The bark scratched her cotton-clad back, but she was beyond caring. A heaviness spread through her shoulders and neck, and she slid to the ground, shutting her eyes, and resting her chin over her bent knees.

The calling of crickets and cicadas failed to ease the thumps of her heart. She never gave reason for people to treat her ill. One moment, he soothed her. The other, he taunted her. What did he know of her life to accuse her of leading men? Her reputation had been irreproachable, at least before now.

Anne tugged her locket, twisting it in her hands. If there ever lived a man more different from her dream suitor, it must be the Count of Almoster.

Twigs broke to the left, and then the air shifted by her side. It was him. His breathing ruffled her hair, but she ignored him, keeping her eyes closed.

"Do you hate me yet?" He sounded hoarse.

"No." She sighed. "Do you want me to?"

A forceful exhale. "No."

He was silent, but his presence made the air thick. Anne scrunched her eyes, burying her face in her arms, willing him to go away.

"Come to sleep."

"I'm not tired."

"Do you relish disobeying my orders?"

She didn't.

"Ana," he said in his low, impossibly low voice, and shifted closer, rustling the leaves. "You are exhausted." His tone turned gentle and warm.

Her skin stirred. Soft, whispery soft. Had he brushed a strand of hair from her cheek? She opened her eyes. He crouched by her side, his face mere inches away. She could be mistaken, but his angry energy seemed to have faded. Why such mercurial moods?

"Perhaps I'll sleep here."

A howl, long and eerie, pierced the night.

Heart in her throat, she shuffled to the side, a breath from touching his bent legs, and scanned the black trees for furry visitors. "What was that?"

"Cross your arms in front of you and stay still."

"Sir?" she whispered.

Before she could blink, he passed an arm below her knees, the other between her shoulder blades, and lifted her, pressing her against his chest.

She sucked in a breath. "What are you doing?"

"Shh. The Iberian wolf has excellent hearing."

Carrying her as though she weighed less than a child's conscience, he walked back to the fire. He was solid and lean, wired steel underneath warm skin, and goosebumps surged where her body touched his. So high from the ground, she resisted the urge to settle closer. He had carried her before, but she had been dizzy. Now that she was lucid, she felt about to faint.

The wolf howled again, and she whimpered. "He can hear us here?"

"This must be the alpha."

"Alpha?"

"The most powerful male. He hunts through the night. When he is hungry, nothing can keep him from his favorite prey."

Stomach quivering, she kept her eyes on the shadows, her heart thudding so loud the alpha would hear. Was he there now? Lurking in the stalks, brown fur bristling, sharp teeth waiting for a bite?

"What," she gulped, "is his favorite prey?"

He gazed beyond their camp, his neck tense, and then he narrowed his eyes. "Disobedient girls."

She gasped. "You goad me, Your Excellency."

Smiling smugly, he raised a brow. "Call me Pedro."

"After what you did? Never."

He grinned, and his eyes twinkled devilishly. "Do as I say, or I will drop you."

"You wouldn't." A nervous laugh escaped from her chest.

Just like that, his arms went lax, and she slipped.

"Pedro!"

He grunted and adjusted his arm below her legs, bringing her up again. Panting, she latched her hands around his neck, his silky hair teasing her wrists, and buried her face in his velvet coat, breathing in his woodsy scent.

After a sharp intake of breath against her forehead, the muscles of his chest and arms turned rigid. Playfulness gone, he kneeled on the ground and settled her atop the blanket, pulling the quilt to her chin. Anne stared at him, gripping the sheets. Had she hurt him somehow?

Without uttering another word, he grabbed his rifle and turned his back on her, hunkering on the ground, his shadow falling over her midriff.

She pushed her weight to her elbows. "Pedro?"

"Sleep. The wolves won't bother you."

Chapter 13

Dawn had not relieved the night's darkness when Pedro awoke. His brother snored by the last embers of the fire. The girl still slept, her hair shielding her face from him. Curled on her side, her hands folded near her chest, she was serenity embodied. A wave of warmth unfurled in his chest, and a need to lie by her side and share her peace took him by surprise. Pedro shook his head and moved to awaken her. Before he could touch her shoulder, he stilled, unable to disturb her.

Pedro strode to where Erebus had spent the night apart from the other horses and, after brushing his flanks, braided his mane. The girl was a danger to herself, and luckily, when her rosy beliefs led her astray, she would be far from him. She hadn't been far last night, though, and when she'd placed her hands around his neck...

Pedro cursed under his breath. The horse noticed his turmoil and banged his head.

"Good morning." She yawned prettily and eyed him warily, seeming unsure if he was a gentleman or an Iberian wolf.

His heartbeats sped like a besotted fool, and Pedro grunted, fumbling with Erebus's mane, the braids resembling knots.

A shaft of sun found her, painting her hair a shade darker than champagne but lighter than chardonnay. The night before, her scent had been layered, flowery, with a hint of citrus, of ripe neroli. A chaste kiss had tasted like roses and tea. What flavors did she hide under her lips? Perhaps she was indeed sweet. The endearment used by Gabriel and Cris grated on his nerves, and Pedro gritted his teeth.

She leaned her torso over a trunk, and her nimble fingers touched the cork bark as if measuring its length for a dress. Pedro had no patience for fidgeting, but in her, it was endearing. How she felt the texture of carpets, and petals, and pebbles. If no trinket was at hand, she touched her bottom lip, twirled a hair lock, the beauty mark on her cheek.

"Is he a Lusitano?"

"What do you know of Lusitanos?"

"Nothing, actually. But I love horses, and this one is the most magnificent I've ever seen. Does he have a name?"

At least she had a good eye for horseflesh. "Erebus."

She tilted her head. "I have to guess... the God of Darkness?"

He had to admit her deduction was not faulty either. His lips tugged up. "He created the night, filling earth's hollows with dark mist."

"It fits him." Her gaze rested on his hands. "I don't think you are an accomplished hair stylist. Why the braids?"

"To keep the reins from tangling in the mane."

"Why don't you cut it? Thoroughbreds have their manes cut all the time. It's the practical thing to do."

Pedro halted, the strands slipping from his fingers. "I wouldn't sacrifice aesthetics for the sake of practicality."

She clucked her tongue, an infuriating grin on her face. "I did not know."

He crossed his arms. "Whatever do you mean?"

Her smile turned impish. "You are a romantic."

Pedro laughed. The girl who wanted to save the realm, judging his beliefs? "And you are what, a dull realist?"

"Be at ease. Your secret is safe with me. I've seen the mares and foals outside the coudelaria. Have you been breeding them for a long time?"

He shrugged. "Eight years. When I returned from Africa, the army would sell the horses from my regiment to the slaughterhouse. I bought the lot."

"I'm glad you saved the poor animals," she said, the words tinged with admiration.

Pedro glanced away. "Don't mistake it for charity. The Marshal reduced the cavalry numbers, and the horse breeders turned to cows and corn. I did not want the Lusitano race to disappear."

He had grabbed the saddle when twigs creaked behind him. Pedro released the tack and whirled. She had floated into Erebus's space, delicate arms outstretched, inches from his nose. The stallion, his eyes rolling, ears flattened, was a second away from nipping her hand.

Pedro sucked in a breath, his heart shoving against his ribcage. He bolted behind her and circled his arm around her waist, bringing her against his chest. While Erebus neighed and reared, wrestling with his halter, Pedro retreated until his back touched a trunk.

"What—"

"Silence," Pedro panted.

She, too, breathed heavily, no doubt realizing her error. Pedro wanted to bury his face against her nape, feel her satiny skin, scent her fragrance. Instead, he dropped his head on the bark behind him, trying to slow his breathing.

Erebus settled, nickering and blowing from his nose.

The danger had passed, but his arms wouldn't push her away. Her lithe frame fit against him, the top of her head reaching his chin, her spine flush against his chest, her derriere cradled on his hips. If he lowered his mouth to her neck where her pulse throbbed, would she taste too sweet or fresh and elegant?

He could have her in this position.

The notion flooded him with heat. If he held both her hands folded on her front, she would be unable to touch him, and then tying her would not be necessary. No explanations required, no rules.

She tilted her head back, her eyes closed, lips parted, a flush rising on her cheeks. Desire.

If he whispered her name in her ear, if he clasped her waist, if he caressed a path down her collarbone—

Pedro locked his jaw and set her away. "No one taught you stallions are dangerous? This is a warhorse." He forced himself to release her arms. "He could have trampled you before you had the chance to scream."

"I'm sorry to have given you such a fright. I promise I won't forget. This will be my first lesson."

"Lesson?"

She lifted a dainty shoulder. "My first lesson on Lusitanos, of course."

"Stay away from him." Pedro steered her away from the stallion. He shouldn't allow her this close. She was

Maxwell's sister, a good Samaritan, and a distraction that could kill them all. "We've dallied enough here."

Chapter 14

Anne rolled the blanket and stored it in Hemera's saddlebag. Cris checked the mare's cinch while humming a soft tune. The count had yet to look at her since Erebus had rejected her friendship. She tested his name on her lips—Pedro. Peter, but he wouldn't like to be called that. Most Portuguese treated the British with deference, but not him. She couldn't picture him deferring to anyone. He watched the horizon with a binocular, an Olympian God inspecting his domain. She shouldn't be so fanciful, and if she had any prudence, she would avoid their puzzling interactions.

"Cris, are we far from Barca D'Alva?"

The safe brother stopped his work and grunted. "If we don't stop, we should arrive before noon."

Anne stretched her arms, her gaze finding Pedro again. Admiring him was much easier when he wasn't glaring or being outrageous, like picking her up, threatening to drop her, or—she touched her lips—kissing her. Cris's handsomeness was as inviting as a green field or a placid lake. Pedro Daun's beauty was of an altogether different sort. The kind felt in the pit of the stomach while atop a cliff, watching glassy waves crashing against the rocks, or when facing a tiger with its tawny head on his paws, eyes unflinching and magnetic.

Cris bumped her shoulder. "The brooding will stop when we reach safety."

"Is he always like this?"

"Not always." Cris frowned, lips twitching. "Sometimes he's worse."

"Sir! You should not speak ill of your own brother."

Dropping his head back, Cris laughed, the sound startling a pair of doves.

The count pierced them with his stare. "If you have time for jests, it means we have tarried too long." He mounted Erebus. The war horse was gentler than a kitten with him.

"Pedro's bark is worse than his bite," Cris whispered, helping her mount, and took James's basket with him to his steed.

They crossed hills, some arid, with the occasional oak or olive tree on a carpet of dry undergrowth, others lush with rye and corn. The sun was high when a meadow opened before them, tall grass rifling in the breeze. A silver ribbon glittered on the horizon—the Douro River. Barca D'Alva must be near.

"You are not smiling today." The count aligned his horse to Hemera's side. Atop Erebus, his knee loomed at least a palm higher than hers. "I did not know English girls were evil-tempered."

Anne perked up, looking at him askance. "Evil? I don't have a thimble of evil inside me."

"No?" He smiled a devilish smile, the dash and elan of all things outrageous. "I bet you have."

She raised her chin. "How could evil be inside humankind if God made us in His own image?"

He stared at her for a long moment. "Aren't you naïve? You have evil inside you, and so have I. Perhaps I'll prove it to you."

She scoffed. "How?"

"We have time."

Despite listening to his absurdities, or perhaps because of them, her stomach fluttered, and her hands soaked her gloves. Being near him compared to eating candied fruit while balancing on a tightrope.

Pedro said something in Portuguese, and the stallion danced sideways, right hoof crossing in front of the left, its neck arched, black mane flowing with the breeze.

"How do you do that?"

"It's called dressage." Pedro adjusted his reins and did a subtle movement with his knees. Erebus, the beast who had nearly killed her, waltzed like a ballet dancer. Pedro's smug smile made her breath catch.

She hid her reaction behind a cough. "I didn't know you were vain."

"I don't hide my sins. Now, if you wish for a lesson, you'd better be a better rider than you are a philosopher." He smiled, lifting a golden brow.

He would teach her about Lusitanos, despite his mulish denial. Anne smiled and corrected her posture, sitting high in her saddle. While she had been taught English horsemanship, she could learn the techniques the Portuguese used with their precious Lusitanos just as well.

Pedro pointed at her legs. "Keep a firm grip on your reins, and press Hemera's flank—" He halted, and the smugness washed from his face. Frowning, he stared at the ridge behind them. "We've been followed."

The earth vibrated in the wake of Pedro's ominous words as hooves pondered the turf. To their right, voices. A war cry. Anne's heart lunged to a frantic rhythm. Not again.

Cris galloped to their side. Hemera pranced, advancing over Erebus. Anne couldn't control the mare. The animal probably sensed danger. She searched the glade, but the pasture offered no hiding places. Just an ocean of grass. God, they were vulnerable like partridges.

"Soldiers. They must have discovered our ruse. Proceed to the yacht." Pedro yanked his reins, and Erebus stomped the ground, neighing.

Cris shook his head, reaching for his gun. "You can't face them alone—"

"If I don't arrive in two hours, sail without me."

"Brother, please, I couldn't—"

Pedro's gaze lingered on her face. "Take care of her."

A scream locked in her throat. He would risk his own safety for her?

Cris, eyes wild, face flushed, froze in place, but then with a roar, he grabbed her reins, and before Anne could ask Pedro to be careful, they were lurching down the slope. Anne looked over her shoulder but couldn't discern Pedro's expression. They were too far. Erebus reared, hooves punching the air, and horse and rider took off in the opposite direction. She kept her eyes on him until Hemera stumbled, and Anne bounced in the saddle, jarring her teeth.

She faced forward as the countryside blurred by their side. Her thighs were screaming when they reached a silent path lined by cypress trees. Cris released her reins and allowed the horses to catch their breaths. Panting,

Anne scented the humid, ripe air. She chanced a look back, but while the threat had not followed them, so hadn't Pedro. Had they gotten him?

Please let him be all right.

Towering sails peeked from the umbrella pines. A white mist blanketed the Douro as they passed rows of boats moored along a planked walkway. Cris guided them to an inlet in the river, revealing a secluded grove.

"The berth is here." Cris reined in and helped her dismount.

High above the stream floated the largest boat on the harbor, the size of a mansion. The hull gleamed in natural oak and navy blue, and the three masts poked the clouds.

Anne caressed Hemera's nuzzle before giving her to a liveried servant. Brushing her arms, she squinted her eyes at the ship. The sun glinted off the silvery letters of the yacht's name. *Dawn Chaser.* What did it mean to Pedro? An ache spread inside her chest, and she clutched her locket. She might never find out.

Tired to her bones, she dragged her feet closer to Cris. He spoke to a white-haired man that appeared to be the captain. The stocky man bowed and left. Cris's gaze had yet to leave the harbor's entrance.

She patted his shoulder. "He will prevail against this threat. He rescued me from a quinta filled with assassins."

Cris's eyes were brimming with emotion, and he kicked a pebble into the river. "He is not the easiest person to be around, I'll tell you, but—"

"Don't despair. Then I will cry, and if I do, James will, and then where will we all be?" Her chin trembled, her voice breaking.

"He is my only family."

"And your mother?"

"Never met her."

A flock of shallows flew over their heads, searching for the safety of the willows on the other riverbank. Anne shouldn't pry, as the subject of his birth must be painful, but sometimes speaking about the pain helped. Before Griffin had met Julia, he'd bottled his feelings so tight inside himself that it had left him with a perpetual frown.

"You grew up with your father, then?"

He scoffed. "The duke? He didn't acknowledge me. God knows I've groveled enough. The first time, I was ten. The Franciscan monk from the orphanage brought me to his house. Titano sent me away with a gold coin and a warning to make myself scarce."

"He rejected his own child? What a terrible thing to do."

"Pedro faced worse."

"Why?"

"He had to live with him."

Anne couldn't imagine such a parent. "How did you meet Pedro?"

"In Mozambique. I was sixteen and hoped if the duke saw me in military glory, he would... Christ, I don't know what I expected. After being sick as a pig on the journey to the other side of the world, I disgraced myself in the first skirmish."

"How did you manage?"

"Pedro saved me on the battlefield."

"He was there." Anne pictured a younger Pedro clashing through the enemy line, fighting to get to his baby brother. The image fit the dashing count so well, it made her sigh.

"For the first time..." Cris took a long, quivering breath. "I wasn't alone."

She pressed his hand affectionately, and he pulled her closer, wrapping her in his arms. Anne hugged him, patting his back. Griffin had never embraced her, and she respected his natural reserve. But tucked against this brother who needed as much warmth as she, she wished to have insisted more.

"See," Anne said. "Everything will be all right."

Chapter 15

Pedro descended the ridge to Barca D'Alva. Each jostle of Erebus's gait on the rocky ground felt like the horse stepped on his wound, pain coursing from his hip to his shoulder. He shook his head, blinking to keep his eyes open. He needed to lie down. At least Anne and Cris would be safe on the yacht. Would she be waiting for his arrival, pacing the yacht's deck?

Elms opened to show the marina. The sun hovered above the Douro's silvery water, and the *Dawn Chaser* floated as if on a mirror, her oblong shape an elegant addition to the sprawling landscape, the majestic hundred-foot vessel lording over the smaller boats.

A few yards more, and he would find his bed, perhaps glimpse her face.

A honeyed voice drifted in the breeze. Her voice. Heart leaping into his chest, Pedro straightened in the saddle, straining to see. Sunlight filtered through the willows, veiling the river. A shaft of champagne in between the branches. Anne. She waited for him.

A few feet more. Just a few.

Erebus picked up speed, breaking through the line of trees.

A couple embraced atop the wooden pier. Anne and his brother. Pedro sucked in a breath through clenched teeth, his vision blurring around the pair. Cris engulfed her, his right hand covering her head, his left at her mid-back, his face buried in the soft place where her neck met her shoulder. Anne's pulse would beat there, the skin warm and fragrant. A river breeze blew strands of their hair together, light and black.

Pedro shut his eyes, pressing the reins until his fingers hurt. Why could his brother enjoy another's touch? How unfair he was so free with his affections, with his body. Cris thought nothing of allowing others too close, making himself vulnerable, while Pedro's skin crawled with the mere threat of being touched by another. He shouldn't feel rage. This was Cris, the only blood relation that mattered to him, and she was a girl that, except for her connection to a man he hated, wasn't his.

How would they receive his return? Did they wish he had perished in the skirmish? With a smile that showed his teeth, Pedro crossed Erebus to the pier. "I'm glad you enjoyed my absence."

She startled and moved away from Cris, a blush covering her cheeks.

"Thank God!" Cris laughed his booming, easy laugh and grabbed Erebus's reins. His brother's eyes were red-rimmed. Worried?

Pedro dismounted. When his boots reached the ground, his hip stung as if the blade had pierced him anew. He leaned over the horse's flank while black dots burned inside his eyelids.

"You are hurt." Anne's gaze trembled from his face to the russet stain on his shirt.

Pedro splayed his palm over the wound. "It's nothing."

Their eyes met, hers so blue it warred with the summer sky, the blue of unfulfilled dreams. Even in borrowed boy's clothes, cheeks smudged with dirt, hair a mess, she dazzled him.

She moved closer, her hand reaching out for him. What would it feel like? Her touch? Right now, with his side bleeding, she could scourge his skin, and he would welcome the pain.

The realization staggered him, and he gulped a breath.

Before she could place her palm on his forearm, her lips a pretty moue of concern, he strode past her in the yacht's direction, his heart pounding in his ears.

Blood washed with the hot spray to pool on the white marble. Pedro allowed the water to pour over his naked body, a balm to scars old and new. Gaslamp light caught on his mother's ring. The band dangling from his chest was a valuable reminder of his goals. Before the year's end, the ring would crown a princess's finger. Cris could have Anne if he so wished.

A wave of nausea swept over him.

Locking his jaw, Pedro applied carbolic soap to the angry flesh between his hip bone and ribs. The two-inch gash burned as if coals were inside. Hissing, Pedro leaned on the tiled wall. With a shuddering breath, he closed the faucet and dried himself. He pressed the terry cloth to the wound, staunching the blood, and shoved his legs into a pair of Cossack trousers. Keeping a steady pressure, Pedro came around the silkscreen to the cabin's bedroom. Cris sprawled on his bed, his boots on the feet rest, hair disheveled as if tangled by a woman's hands.

"I can manage this one by myself."

"May I have a look?" Cris said, his voice grave.

"You've seen worse." Pedro uncovered the cut, glad it had stopped bleeding.

Cris whistled. "Did you wash it?"

"What do you think?" Pedro snarled.

Cris probed the jagged edges. "Dagger? Short sword?"

"Dagger. New." The soldier who stabbed him had been so young, he must have used the standard-issue blade for the first time.

Cris nodded and reached for the medical supplies. "Better sew it. Leave it alone, and it will take too long to close."

"It's just a scratch."

"Don't be a mule, for heaven's sake. You know I'm right."

After a soft knock, the captain's niece entered with a food tray. The yacht's all-men crew had carped about her presence, but Pedro had ignored their superstitions and ordered her uncle to fetch her from the village. The young maid would be a suitable company for Anne on their voyage.

The smell of stew and fresh-baked bread invaded the cabin, and his stomach lurched. Pedro pointed to the table. "Over there." He couldn't stand food, not yet. "Did you find the clothes?"

"The chest is already in her cabin, Your Excellency."

"Has Miss Maxwell eaten?"

Eyes averted to the floor, the girl settled the burden as directed. "She said she wasn't hungry, Your Excellency."

"Take a tray to her cabin, anyway. See that she has everything she needs."

The maid nodded. "She asked about you."

His pulse sped up. "Tell Miss Maxwell I'm in perfect health. That will be all."

"As you wish." She curtsied and moved to the door.

Cris winked at the young maid and followed her trim back as she left. "If you won't allow me to suture you, I'll check if Anne is settled."

Pedro glared at his brother. "Fine. Close the cursed thing."

Cris chuckled but didn't lose time, his hands busy pouring laudanum into a flowery cup.

Pedro eyed the tincture with distaste and dread. "Can't you do it without the foul stuff?"

Cris pursed his lips. "I can't stick a needle into your flesh in cold blood."

"Then you should drink it yourself." If he didn't take the anesthetic, his brother's hands would not cease shaking, so Pedro drank it in a single gulp, grimacing at the bitterness.

Pedro watched Cris strain his eyes to thread a needle, his rough hands ill-fitted for the delicate job. Had Cris developed an attachment for Anne so quickly? If so, what would Pedro do? Endure their blossoming relationship? Warn him away from her, and then what?

So far, Cris's feelings for the opposite sex have been limited to lust. Should Pedro rob him of that?

The boat tossed, and laudanum swam like acid on his empty stomach. "Did you enjoy your afternoon?"

Cris shoved a hand in his hair. "Joy? You worried me to death." He dropped into the chair next to his bedside and exhaled. "How many soldiers today?"

"Does it matter?"

Cris shrugged. "If I'm asking."

Pedro stretched his body atop the velvet counterpane, hissing at the strain on his side. "It was a scouting team. Gabriel must have sent them to inspect the perimeter. I must admit he got better—"

"How many?"

Pedro shut his eyes. "Two."

Cris stopped fumbling with threads and needles, his face scrunched in a frown. "You were distracted."

It wasn't a question. Cris knew him too well. While he had faced the soldiers back at the meadow, rage and concern that they would get her, that they would harm her, had clouded his rational responses. It was guilt, nothing more. He had vowed to protect her.

At least they would cross the river's mouth. Tonight. Offshore. Out of Gabriel's reach.

Cris stared at him, his lips pressed into a firm line, and approached his midriff with the needle. "You taught me a distracted mind during a fight is worse than a dull sword. Fastest way to meet the reaper."

Pedro clenched his teeth when the steel bit into his skin, but the pain was mild. "Would you mourn me, brother? At least you wouldn't lack a shoulder to cry on, judging by the scene I witnessed by the river."

The laudanum spread over his veins, making his heartbeats throb erratically and his vision waver. At the cabin's corner, an oily substance crept up like a black tide. Pedro willed the hallucination away, but it kept coming. He turned his face to the circular hatch spanning most of his bedside. The sickness receded, but the boat's speed made the vineyards outside blur, a metallic green mass flashing as both wind and current propelled them along the Douro.

"Is this why you are being a prick in the arse? I wasn't taking advantage of her or anything. Anne's not for dalliance. We mustn't stray from the plan—find the bodyguard, prove your innocence, and return her to her family." Cris raised his black brows, eyeing him askance. "Exactly as we found her."

Pedro felt him tugging the thread and tying a knot over the first stitch. "You ask the impossible. It is inevitable, her change. The girl lives in a fairy tale, populated by noble people who place others' interests above their own."

"For Christ's sake, she is just a sweet—"

"Don't call her that," Pedro snapped.

"Shit. Don't go there. What happens if you pursue her? Do you think she will enjoy those?" Cris pointed his chin at the commode's drawer.

Pedro didn't flinch and didn't ask how his brother knew about the ropes. Whores talked, and Cris was a gracious listener. "I don't plan to..." The words slurred inside his head. "Forget it."

"Your... er, preferences aren't the only issue. Do you think Anne would welcome your attention if she knew about the past?"

Pedro fisted his hands. If she found out, she would look at him with revulsion. He couldn't allow it. "You won't speak with her about Mozambique, damn it."

Cris's mouth gaped open. "What? Why would I—Sometimes you say things... It's like you don't really know me. I'm talking about your past with her brother. With Julia."

"Maxwell can't protect her from Ulrich. I did what was necessary to keep her safe."

"Whatever you say."

Pedro gripped his brother's arm, stopping his stitches. "I forbid you to reveal it to her."

Cris turned back to his work, his expression sullen. When he finished, he bandaged the wound with more force than necessary and, with an unintelligible grunt, rose and gathered the medical supplies. "I'll go to our guest."

Pedro shook his head, fighting to open his eyes. The shadows' tide swelled, threatening to drown him. Before the drug made him oblivious, he needed to know the truth. "Do you want her?"

The silence dragged out. Pedro focused on his brother's minute reactions.

"She is not my type."

Cris never lied.

Exhaling, Pedro dropped back onto the pillow. "I thought your type was warm and willing."

The shadows reached the bed, and Pedro bunched the sheets in his hands, his breathing coming in short bursts.

His brother's heavy footsteps receded as he left the cabin. "Sleep, brother."

Pedro wished he could.

Chapter 16

Anne could not stay still. At this rate, the plush carpet would be threadbare when she had news. She took deep breaths, but the beeswax scent of her cabin could not calm her. The soft rocking of the boat had long lulled James into sleep, and she envied his oblivion.

Pedro's gray pallor flashed inside her mind, his face contorted in pain. The count would be all right. He had to be. Anne traced the hatch with her fingertips. Drops of water reflected the vineyards outside and painted the cream wood paneling with tiny rainbows. Barca D'Alva had stayed behind, with its shops and riverside restaurants. They floated along a rural countryside like the land around Vesuvio.

How was her family? Griffin would fret. At least he had Julia to comfort him.

She was lucky. She hadn't realized how much until her conversation with Cris. What kind of man would shun his own son? And worse, what had he done to Pedro? Sometimes, in the quiet of her bedroom, she blamed her father for being selfish and abandoning her family. In truth, she would carry his poignant memories her entire life. Even after he left, her brother had been there, growing up before his time to take care of her.

A soft knock on the door brought Beatriz. "May I come in?"

"Have you news?"

"I just left His Excellency's cabin. He was up and about, Miss, so don't you fret." The maid exuded a quiet demeanor, her hands folded on her front, her feet tucked under her gray skirts. Only her mouth, too large for her round face, exuded activity. During the explanation, the maid's lips pouted and grimaced and finally revealed a lovely smile.

"Thank God." Anne exhaled and dropped onto the bed.

Beatriz pointed to James. "Can I hold him?" Anne nodded, and the maid clasped the pug to her chest, cooing. "There is a deck behind the galley where I can take him to relieve himself, Miss. The crew is nice. Mr. Oliveira, the captain, is my uncle. Mario and Dario, the twins, are my cousins. And there's the Italian."

"You don't like Dante?" Anne had seen him speaking with Cris. A stout man in his mid-thirties, he had more drawings on his arms than words on his lips.

Beatriz scooted closer, wringing her apron. "They say he was a war hero, a condottiere in the Revolutionary Army, and fought with Garibaldi. He came to Portugal with the Italian queen, but he had to leave her court because of a duel."

"Do you think he fought for love?"

Her cheeks turned pink. "The twins told me he threatens to club anyone who asks. Anyway, all are curious to meet you. No one knew the count had female relatives."

Anne whirled away. "It is as His Excellency said." She hated to lie but was glad Pedro had come up with an acceptable excuse for her presence.

"Have you seen the clothes, Miss? His Excellency ordered me to go to the village for some. It was rushed, but I did my best. Picked them myself." Beatriz propped James on the bed and crouched near the chest. "All ready-made, but I can adjust them for you if need be."

There were shirts, pelisses, undergarments, dresses, and skirts. Their cloth was more serviceable than Anne was used to, and the designs were simple but fetching. "How thoughtful."

The maid flushed in pleasure. "I can help you with your hair. I haven't seen color such as yours. But I need to go. I promised my uncle to take him his tea." She bobbed a curtsy and left.

Alone in the cabin, Anne drifted to the hatch and was surprised by Oporto's lights twinkling outside. So soon? She hadn't expected to leave her city yet. Her lungs became constricted, as if she traveled under water, dragged like an anchor.

Anne raced to the main deck. Leaning over the railing, she inhaled the scent of cooking fires, lit oil lamps, and the sweet smell of the river. This stretch of the Douro was home. Atop Oporto's high cliffs, the houses stacked one atop the other like toy blocks—their colors reflected in the mirror-like water, blurry yellows, reds, and whites blending with the amber shade of sunset.

How many times had she strolled among those narrow streets? Griffin had grumbled that few were level, and fewer were at right angles with each other. Still, each held a secret to be tasted, touched, treasured forever.

Before she had time to say goodbye, the yacht had crossed the bar to the Atlantic. The boat's sway changed, and she felt it in the pit of her stomach. The smell changed, too, only salt spray on her lips. When the sun abandoned her to dip in the waves, the sky closed into deep indigo. The city lights twinkled far away, and soon they, too, disappeared. Only the ocean now. From south, north, west, and east—vast, mysterious, and immensely lonely.

The infinite blue made her nose burn, and Anne descended the stairs leading to the cabins, the anchor in the place of her heart dragging her steps.

A throaty moan made her pause.

Pedro. He must be in pain.

Brittle legs carried her to his door, and she knocked softly.

Silence.

Anne turned the handle and peeked inside. "Cris?" she whispered.

No one answered. Shouldn't the brother be nursing the count? By the dim light, she could make out an enormous bed, a chaise, and a table.

"Pedro?"

When her sight adjusted to the shadows, Anne stepped over the threshold. A circular window covered most of the wall, and the hazy blue light pulled her closer to the bed. Pillows strewed over the floor, the scenery of a struggle. Moonlight caressed Pedro's bare chest, and a loose trouser hung low on his hips. She shouldn't notice the taut skin stretching over the lean muscles of his torso, but she had nowhere else to look. The bandages tied around his midsection were clean. He wasn't bleeding. A good sign, right? Untied, his golden hair veiled his cheek and shoulder. What would it feel like to sift her fingers through the strands?

A tortured moan escaped his lips, and his face scrunched up as if in deep pain.

Hands trembling, she touched his forehead. His skin was cool. No fever, then. Thank God. "Are you in pain?"

He didn't respond but kept staring at her vacantly.

Anne searched the medical supplies over his tallboy and spooned laudanum into a porcelain cup. She brought the liquid to his mouth. "It will make the pain go away."

He sniffed the contents. Jerking his head, he knocked her hand away. "No more."

The cup fell from her grasp and shattered, staining the carpet. Gasping, she backed away. She shouldn't have disturbed him. His head thrashed, his torso jerking as if he fought invisible ropes. She couldn't leave him like this. He was wounded because of her.

"Please, be at ease. Shhh. Pedro, you'll open your wound."

He seemed beyond hearing. Anne's gaze darted to the exit, and she wrung her hands. What could she do to calm him? He needed a nurse, not her.

There, over his couch, lay a guitar. When Tony had trouble sleeping, music helped.

She kneeled by his bedside. After a deep breath, she sang a lyric *modinha*.

"Rosas Flores, tão bonitas..."

His breathing less strained, he turned to his side, perhaps seeking the melody's source. Anne was admiring his voluminous eyelashes when his eyes opened—precious stones lit from within. Unable to hold his stare, she forgot the chorus, her voice fading into the waves rocking the hull.

"Don't stop," he whispered.

His eyes pleaded, and it tugged her heart. No one should go through pain alone. What comfort she had would be his. Sustaining his gaze, she weaved the song into soothing sounds, a mellow lullaby. The weight pressing against her chest lessened, and her loneliness receded, blinking far away like Oporto's lights.

Pedro's forehead smoothed. When his hand traveled closer to her, she interlaced her fingers with his. The night had a chill, but their shared touch was warm like milk before bed, wool mitts, and Pedro's smile. He sighed. Anne sighed too.

Touching him tasted like the sun filtering through her umbrella pine.

Chapter 17

Pedro fought the shadows, but they tied his arms and pressed against his torso with the weight of dead bodies. He thrashed against it, and his strength seeped away, his limbs powerless to fight its hold.

A voice. Music penetrated the darkness. A lifeline enveloped his hand. The tide receded. He inhaled neroli and rain and knew to open his eyes. Anne. So radiant even the night paled against her. She kneeled by his bedside, her face level with the mattress, her hand holding his.

The touch... the touch grounded him.

Her transparent eyes beckoned, pushing the haziness away. Her outline became clear, faintly illuminated by moonlight—an angel.

His head seemed full of tar, and somewhere it registered that he shouldn't allow anyone near him, not when drugs dulled his reflexes. This wasn't anyone. This was her. She had come for him of her own free will. Not because he paid. Not because he forced her. Not because she had hidden designs.

She sang, her voice the chiming of heaven, lifting and nurturing. Her eyes found him, and she gazed away, the song dying on her lips.

The tide threatened to pull him under again, and he took a ragged breath. "Don't stop."

Notes lilting and liquid, she sang until Pedro's vision cleared, until she dazzled the tide, until her voice faltered, until her chin rested on the bed, until her eyes became heavy-lidded, and her hand turned lax where it touched his.

The angel would have floated to the floor, but Pedro clasped her palm and tugged. With a sleepy murmur, she climbed atop the mattress and lay on her side, facing him with her eyes closed, her mouth half-open, her breathing warm bursts on his chin.

Pedro traced her brows and her bow-shaped lips, learning her contours, wishing to see inside her, divine her secrets. When she stirred, he stopped and settled for holding her hand, feeling the bird-like bones and tendons, the blood pulsing in her wrist.

How strange, seeing her roaming fingers so still. Pedro examined the pads of her fingertips, and when he reached the center of her palm, he found a raised patch of skin. A scar? He couldn't see it in the dim light.

What would her hand feel over his chest? Above his heart? No, he wouldn't risk it. He couldn't spoil this reprieve. For once, touch felt like summer and not blade cold. If the drug had made his skin insensitive, he hoped it lasted through the night.

Too soon, the light changed from soft blue to soft golden, and she blinked, her irises a sliver around raven pupils. "Oh, I'm sorry," she whispered. "I don't remember falling asleep."

"You sang to me." His tone was rough, more question than accusation.

"I... You were in pain. I didn't know what else to do."

"You have a beautiful voice."

"Thank you." A shy smile played at the corner of her lips.

Pedro turned her hand palm up and touched her scar. "What is this?"

She looked away. "Oh, that. You will think it silly."

"Indulge me."

She was silent for too many heartbeats, and then she sighed, and her smile wobbled. "I was six. After my father died, my mother, she... Well, she became distraught and threw a few mementos at the hearth. There was not much left after... letters and a cameo, even her wedding ring. But when she flung my locket into the fire, I rushed after it. Afterward, the doctor said it was not so much that I placed my hand there. You see, the piece had heated, and I held it in my cupped hands like this." She interlaced her fingers and locked her palms. "My mother couldn't pry my hands open. I only let go after my brother reassured me no one would take it from me."

Anne opened her hands like the halves of a shell. Printed on the rosy skin of her palms were twin heart-shaped burns.

Pedro traced the markings with his fingertips more gently than he ever had treated a battle wound, awed by the girl who had leaped into the fire after her father's memory. Another facet of this Anne, who crusaded for her sister-in-law and meant to save the king's life.

"A lot of trouble for a piece of jewelry, right?" she said deprecatingly, all the while caressing the locket with her free hand, the one hand Pedro had not retrieved the moment she had finished her explanation. "My mother forced me to use bandages for three weeks, afraid the skin would scar terribly. I barely remember the pain, but being deprived of touch made a horrible impression on me."

"That is why you always feel the world with your fingers."

"Nobody mentioned... I guess you are right." She exhaled, her eyes lifting abashedly to his. "I'd better go."

He tightened the hold on her hand. "It's early still. No one will notice."

"But it is not decent—"

"Stay for the sunrise."

"Sunrise?" She glanced over his shoulder and gasped.

The circular glass pane occupying most of his cabin's bulkhead offered the best dawn view. Pedro had designed it himself to watch the sun conquer the night after sleepless, shadow-soaked hours.

"Won't you face the window?" Anne propelled her head over a bent elbow, her cheeks reflecting the predawn brilliance.

She spoke of sunrises and sea and summer, but her words blended into a gentle chime, rocked by the boat swaying to and fro. Languidness melted his limbs, and he couldn't muster the will to turn from her. He drank the way her mouth formed sounds and then settled into watching her eyes. While dark still ruled outside, her pupils occupied all, ebony, like night. As the first sun rays reflected on her skin, the blue of her irises unfolded, expanding, breathing out. The dawn she watched avidly spread to his chest—a triumph of light.

"The sun just crested. If I had my watercolors here... look at these blues and the saffron and the waves." She smiled and pressed his hand. "You are missing it."

"I'm not," he breathed, his voice faltering. Aboard the *Dawn Chaser*, he had watched the sunrise from the Port of Malta, where the sky turned crimson above the Mediterranean. He had seen it defeat the darkness from Mozambique's coast, where the aquamarine Indian sea became a mirror for Dhon boats. He had seen it emerge from the English shore, where the horizon caught fire, and the North Sea boiled like a cauldron.

Nothing compared to seeing dawn in her eyes.

She yawned, her skin golden, her hair mussed. "How lovely."

He had to agree, for this morning, the sun had traded places with Icarus and was singed by this fire-leaping angel. If the sun couldn't keep from flying close to her, who was Pedro to resist? He shifted on the mattress, craving her brilliance. The stitches pulled against the bruised skin of his side, forcing him to stop. She had come to succor him. He couldn't repay her by taking advantage of her innocence. Pedro lingered for a moment more on her trusting gaze. Cris was right. She was too pure for him. Reluctantly, he released her hand and crossed his arms above his chest.

"Does your wound hurt?"

"I've had worse."

She frowned. "In battle?"

"And other places."

"Would you tell me?"

"I won't taint you with my shadows."

She lowered her eyes, the gilded tips of her eyelashes brushing her cheeks. "I don't like that you had to live in shadows."

Pedro lived there still.

"You chased them away today, Ana." He tucked a strand of hair behind her ear. "Go. The crew will rise, and the maid will notice your absence."

She sat on the bed's edge. "I forgot to thank you."

Pedro adjusted his pillow and shifted to his back. "The clothes were beneath you in quality and style—"

She whirled and came on her hands and knees to him. Pedro curbed the instinct to push her away, his pulse throbbing inside his veins. She stopped so close she could have pierced his heart with a dagger or slit his throat. In all his adult life, no one had touched him without his express demand, and here he was, frozen while strands of her hair tickled his chest, and her breath fanned his face, stealing his air.

Slowly, she leaned forward and branded his skin with her lips above the corner of his mouth—a kiss. All paused except for the ringing in his ears. Pedro covered the skin she had kissed, the calloused pads of his fingertips a poor substitute for the glow and dew of her lips.

"Thank you for saving my life. The clothes were incredibly thoughtful, but you risked your own safety for me." She flushed from her collarbone to the tips of her ears. "I will never forget."

As the girl with Atlantic eyes and cheeks flaming like port wine scurried from the bed, something moved inside him. A crumbling of sorts, uncomfortable, and then a crack, not unlike a glacier breaking in the sea. He placed both palms above his chest, wanting to prevent it. Still, it continued, opening space with hammer-like delicacy.

"I'll be leaving now, but I'll find Beatriz and ask for your breakfast. You must be hungry because you didn't eat your dinner, and if you are to recover, then eating is necessary. I'm mumbling, aren't I? I'll leave you to your rest. Good night." She curtsied. "I mean, good day."

She stumbled on the rug, and then she was gone.

Chapter 18

Light flooded the yacht's spacious drawing room. To the left, the wall was all glass. To the right, a well-appointed sitting area was situated around a plush emerald carpet. Anne caressed the cushions, noticing no creases as if no one had ever laid down with a book or embroidery. Mahogany paneling with niches for pieces of art covered the inner wall. Pedro's taste was eclectic, ranging from the modern to the classical.

A warrior, an aristocrat, an art collector... What other secrets lay in his past? At least she had uncovered one. She knew why he called the yacht *Dawn Chaser*. He didn't like nights.

But not last night. Last night, she had chased his shadows.

Warmth infused her body, goosebumps rising on her arms. If she closed her eyes, she could still feel his large hand covering hers. Would it be too immodest if she took him a food tray instead of Beatriz? He must be made to eat. Or she could offer to read him from the library. What would he like? Philosophy? Some history...

"Your breakfast is served, Miss Anne."

"Thanks, Beatriz."

The dinner table caught the morning sun from the uncovered veranda. Why did the brothers have their meals inside their cabins instead of here? Anne stretched her arms above her head, her gaze taking in the ocean tinted by the green of the Portuguese coast. The smells of coffee, tea, and baked buns made her stomach rumble, and, hard-pressed to choose, she bit into a *pão de deus*. The sweet roll with marmalade melted in her mouth.

"No seasickness?" Cris's voice came from the deck. "Some people have all the luck."

Startled, Anne perched on her seat. "Are you unwell?"

"My stubborn sea legs take longer to sprout, that's all." Skin sallow and lips tinged with white, he splayed his hands on the linen-clad table.

"Won't you sit? I'll pour you some tea." Anne reached for the samovar. "Beatriz prepared this colossal breakfast. I cannot hope to gobble it alone."

He pulled the chair across from her and dropped his bulky frame onto it. "So, you enjoy the Portuguese *pequeno almoço*? No fry-up for our English guest?"

Anne scrunched her face. "I'm a native Portuguese for food. My brother demanded black pudding, fried eggs, sausages, beans. I didn't like those, but my mother forced me to eat."

He grimaced. "I hate beans. No beans for me to break the fast, or in the midday meal. The brown grubber starred as the staple food at the orphanage."

"Oh, Cris, how terrible." Anne passed him a cup.

He grunted. "When we arrive in Aveiro tomorrow, I will buy *ovos moles* for you. If you have a sweet tooth, you will fancy the city's delicacy."

"You will search for the king's bodyguard?" She shouldn't forget why they were here. "Do you think he can help find the... murderer?"

"I'll see what I can uncover."

"But isn't too soon for Pedro—I mean, His Excellency—to leave his bed?"

"I'll go alone."

"Is it safe?"'

He tilted his head and speared her with an inquisitive gaze. "Safe enough. Some risks we have to take, while others we should avoid."

Anne studied the crumbles on her plate. "I wish to help you... but proper English education is sorely lacking when one is escaping the authorities—"

"I saw you leaving my brother's cabin."

"What?" Her cheeks flared, and she covered them with her hands.

He raised his brows.

"I heard him moaning. I couldn't leave him to suffer alone, could I?"

He pinched the bridge of his nose. "Did he try to... Was he inappropriate? "

"Of course not! He was in pain. Thrashing."

Cris crossed his arms, leaning back in the chair. "You should stay away from him."

His expression and the conversation turned uncomfortable. Throat dry, Anne sipped her tea and forced a smile. "We are in a boat, aren't we? Quite difficult to stay apart in such a confined place."

"Don't you think he is too old?" Cris narrowed his eyes. "You just poked your head out of the schoolroom."

"I'm not a child." She pushed the food away. "Princess Sissi married the Emperor of Austria when she was sixteen. My best friend wed this past winter, and she is a year younger than I."

"He isn't the tame gentlemen your friends take for husbands."

Cris seemed to love Pedro so much. Why would he disparage his brother's character?

Anne lifted her chin. "How long until we reach port?"

"You'll not make this easy, will you? I hoped to..." He shoved a hand through his hair, disheveling the combed strands. "I shouldn't tell you this, but Christ..." He pushed away from the table and turned his back to her, staring at the ocean.

Anne's stomach lurched, and she gripped her skirts with icy fingers. Whatever he meant to say, she didn't want to hear. Out in the sea, two seagulls flew near the deck, their white wings spread far and immobile, their screeches piercing the silence of the morning.

"Pedro cannot bear to be touched."

"I beg your pardon?"

"He can't stand a woman's touch."

Anne fisted her hands. "Why are you saying such things?"

"I wish it was a lie." Cris sighed, and his shoulders deflated. He closed his eyes, and his anguish made her chest ache. "He is broken, Anne."

She grabbed her locket, the edges biting into her palm. "You must be mistaken—"

He laughed, a shrill, mirthless laugh. "My brother is broken, and sometimes he breaks people around him, too."

"Excuse me."

Anne fled to the quarterdeck and gripped the railings. She had wanted to discover more about him, had she not?

Broken. He was broken.

Footsteps sounded behind her, and she hastened through the gunwale. She reached the front deck and descended an unfamiliar ladder, arriving at a cavernous compartment. Hay and horse manure impregnated the place like a heavy cloud, and she blinked, adjusting her eyes to the dim light. Four wooden stalls were tucked against the hull. Hemera poked her head through the door, her long mane braided into neat buns.

Anne sighed, her shoulders sagging, and hugged the mare's neck. Touching was vital, like breathing or eating. Pedro could not go through life without a hug, a caress, a kiss. What of the intimacies shared between husband and wife?

Heat climbed to her cheeks, and she shut her eyes. They had held hands today, had they not? But then... what if he had allowed it because he was drowsy? Nonsense. Had she not touched him in the forest? But then, when she had linked her hands around his neck, he had turned cold, not even looking at her. And he always wore those black gloves...

It was true. Anne stared at her hands, hands that tingled to sift through his golden hair and more. An ache spread to her chest, and she leaned her forehead on Hemera's coat, breathing in her dusty, familiar scent. Look at her, thinking of herself when Pedro suffered. Living a barren life.

A threatening neigh lifted the hairs off her neck. When Anne turned, she caught herself staring into Erebus's glassy eyes. Only a metal bar separated her from the stallion. A cry locked inside her throat, and she left the stall, stumbling on one of the twins. The young deckhand hastily apologized.

"It was my fault." She panted. "Dario?"

"I'm Mario, miss, and the captain always says I should look where I go."

The boys were identical, same olive skin, dark eyes, and curly brown hair. What made it worse, they wore the same sailor's uniform.

"Should Erebus be so close to Hemera?"

"The big brute won't have it any other way, miss. When Dante kept him alone, he carved a hole in the hull."

"But won't he bite Hemera or kick her?"

Mario shrugged. "He seems calm enough to me. I guess he likes to stay close to her. I'll be over there rubbing Mr. Queiroz's horse if you need anything."

Erebus eyed her calmly, behaving like an average horse and not a fire-breathing beast. Tentatively, she ambled closer. Palm up, arm quivering, she offered her hand. Holding her breath, she waited, the silence such that she heard the thumps of her heart.

Neighing, Erebus advanced, his ears glued to his head.

Anne stumbled back a step, cradling her hand.

Anne touched the green baize and flung the ball, enjoying the clacking and the smooth rolling as it reached
the hole. Was this to be how she passed her hours?
Playing billiards by herself? If the day of navigation had
crawled, the night proved to be a snail, so slowly the
hours ticked by. How was Pedro? Had he caught a fever?
He had others to take care of him.

Anne twirled her locket on her fingertips. She hadn't
asked to be here. This... this mad jaunt might damage
her reputation beyond repair, but her future didn't have
to be. Pedro was as different from the suitor of her
dreams as a tiger from a kitten. Broken. Avoided touch.

A faint breeze invaded the billiard room, carrying the
ocean's groans but also a moody twang. Curious, she
slid the glass pane an inch. Waves lapped the coast,
the rhythm predictable, the sea jumping ropes with
the rocks. Beyond the sounds of the sea, silence. She
had splayed her hands over the door to close it when
string notes, guttural, percussive, brushed against her
cheeks, vibrating inside her. Anne slid the door open
and tiptoed along the promenade deck stretched on the
yacht's port side.

Pedro sprawled over a wicker chair, a Portuguese guitar on his lap, his fingers strumming. She couldn't take

her eyes from his hands, the expert way he handled the instrument. How would it feel on her skin? The pressing and pulling and deft tugs?

She must be insane, conjuring the impossible. Anne pressed against the bulkhead, hugging herself. The melody increased the tempo. He fingered the guitar's bridge, coaxing a grave and exotic sound. The cadenza spoke to her of tortured feelings, of pain. How could the hand that wields a sword with viciousness play with such poignancy?

Anne closed her eyes, and the music painted a vivid image in her mind of Salgueiro's dead vineyards, the stalks protruding from the earth like lonely crosses. The desolation made her gasp.

The guitar ceased. "I can see you there."

"I didn't mean to intrude." Anne let go of the bulkhead and sighed. "You play beautifully."

He shrugged. "Art, any art, replaces life's ugliness, even if for a self-deceiving moment."

"But if art mimics life, isn't there beauty in life too?"

His gaze lingered on her face. "I won't contradict you."

Her heart fluttered, and Anne fidgeted with her braid. "How were Salgueiro's vineyards before phylloxera?"

"Green. Terraces upon terraces of emerald hue, if you fancy words. The wine was similar to Vesuvio, the terroir being so close. Well, not all wine." Pedro turned to the ocean and exhaled. "Salgueiro has this isolated hill, much higher than the others. By a miracle of nature, some hundred grapevines bask in the sun's attention for over three hundred days a year."

"How did it taste? The wine from this lucky vineyard?"

"*Vinho Luz* defies description. You would have to try it." He shifted, leaning the guitar on the yacht's railing. "I had despaired of seeing you today."

Anne's cheeks colored. Did he guess she had avoided him? "The music you were playing. A *modinha* about—"

"Illogical desires." He trailed his fingers over the chords slowly, and the melody vibrated in the pit of her stomach.

Anne smiled nervously. "Aren't all desires illogical?"

"Not if the desires are beneficial to us." His eyes had an unsettling intensity.

Could he glimpse her thoughts? How her hands tingled to sift through his hair? Discover its texture? Sometimes she feared he could, so uncanny was his intelligence.

The moon floated above the sea, pouring a veil over the ocean. Silvery waves traveled from the horizon to lap the yacht's hull. Could she bathe in such waters? Feel liquid moonlight caressing her skin? Would it be brisk and slippery like the Atlantic in the morning? Or satiny, the silks of a magic realm just waiting for her to take the leap?

Anne glanced away from her own fancy and recognized the book from his quinta. The tome rested atop a side table. "You brought this?"

"Dom Pedro and Inês's story." He frowned, staring at the leather cover. "The redoubtable Portuguese tragedy enchants poets and wide-eyed women since the Middle Ages. A dashing prince meets a bastard noble and falls in love. The king contests the couple, and the prince refuses to abandon his love. As you may well predict, the ending is not happy. Some believe it the most heart-wrenching tragedy of all time. In truth, it shows that when powerful men allow women to cloud their judgment, the consequences are disastrous."

"How romantic. Why do you carry it, then?"

"It was Braganza's. He asked me to bring it to the Douro. I will never know why."

"How was he? The king's brother?"

Pedro shook his head, and a shadow crossed over his features. "Energetic, idealistic... kind. He would have liked your convictions. Ulrich deprived the country of a great man."

"I'm sorry for your loss." She wanted to massage away the pleats on his forehead or press his hand affectionately, anything to relieve his grief. Since he wouldn't welcome her touch, she felt bereft. Unsure what to do, she opened the book and squinted to read it by the deck's dimmed light.

Queen's Palace - Coimbra, September 1312

Inês's own throat garroted as Dom Pedro, Prince of Portugal, struggled to speak to his father. Why did the king have to humiliate him so? A pox on narrow-minded people who thought a stammer the work of the devil. Before her eyes, the boy, not much older than her sixteen years, went red in the face. As soon as his father left, he crushed his dulcimer against the throne, growling like a feral beast.

The court ladies gasped. Constança Manuel screamed and scurried away, forgetting wives should support their husbands. The prince turned to them, horrified that his outburst had been witnessed. Inês sought his gaze and held it. Instead of showing the pity swamping her chest, she remembered the signs from the silent monks and placed two fingertips below her eyes. I see you.

When a boyish grin played at the corner of his lips, Inês's heart skipped a beat, and she smiled her secret smile.

Anne dropped the book. "He had a wife when... when Inês met him?"

Pedro traced the cover's gilded letters. "Shocked?"

Anne's hand came to her locket, and she took a step back. "No, I mean—"

"Even though his father warned him away from her, he snatched Inês for himself, uncaring of the consequences. And yet, some say he was the best monarch the country ever had and loved Inês desperately, faithful to his dying breath. Do you wish to know love? Real love?" He gave the book a last glance and offered it to her.

An ocean breeze ruffled her neck, making her shiver. Anne lifted her hand but could not command herself to accept it, as if the opposite force of a magnet existed between her fingers and the old tome.

Pedro awaited, tentative but guarded, as if he offered a part of himself.

How could she deny it? Him? When she grasped the worn leather surface, he removed his hand quickly, no doubt to avoid touching her. Cris's words rang inside her head again. Was it distance Pedro needed? To be put away like a rabid animal? Under the moonlight's liquid glow, gazing at Pedro's jewel-like eyes, the words did not seem like a warning to protect herself, but an altogether different plea.

Anne's chest constricted, and she hugged the book. "I promise to take care of it."

Chapter 19

Pedro sat behind his desk in the library. Moored at the Costa Nova Marina, the boat swayed like a child's cradle. Two hours had passed since Cris had left with Dante to find the bodyguard, but he had no reason to doubt their success. The yacht's first mate was a seasoned soldier. In fact, his prudence weighted Cris's recklessness, and unless Gabriel's horse had sprouted wings, the head of the king's guard lagged at least a day behind.

If luck were on their side, the bodyguard would be useful, and this farce would end. The sooner Pedro sent Anne away, the better.

He shoved all thoughts of the girl into the recess of his mind and concentrated on the week-old newspaper. Why did Ulrich want to kill the king? Had the bullfighter foregone his base in Mozambique, or were his interests still linked to slave trading? The pairing of a king's bodyguard with an enslaver did not raise his brows. Political allegiances were as tradable as commodities, if less valuable.

The gray mongrel waddled inside, stubby paws printing the thick rose carpet. Nonchalantly, it crossed the room and lodged close to Pedro's boots.

Her crown of champagne hair appeared first. Pedro reclined in the chair, pulse speeding up as she waltzed into his library, her simple floral dress resembling a spring meadow. Light from the sky dome painted her pale skin in iridescent colors.

She held a tray, her gaze colliding with his. "I've got you tea... but I don't mean to intrude. If you are busy, I can—"

"You keep saying that." A smile crept to his lips.

After pouring tea for them both, she settled on the chair facing his desk, shifting a few times like a kitten preparing a pillow for a nap. Daintily, she sipped, and a pearl of tea nestled on the crest of her bottom lip, only to be swept away by an elusive tongue. She circled the porcelain's rim slowly, unbearably slowly, with the tip of her finger. As if conjured by an enchantress, a vivid image assaulted him. Anne tracing circles over his skin, starting at his neck, teasing his chest, and lowering still.

Pedro pushed the cup away. The few times he'd allowed women to touch him had been the same. Cold, too personal. He cleared his throat and pointed to the mutt, drowsing with its head atop Pedro's toes. "You misplaced the *petit* corporal. Again."

"Corporal?"

"He shirks duty to sleep, and he is always chasing a skirt."

"Do you hear that, James? Your honor is being besmirched." Laughing, she crouched so close her scent invaded his space.

When she picked up the tiny beast, her shoulder brushed against his trousers, and Pedro could not stifle a groan.

She frowned, one arm holding the dog, the other at her waist like a scolding teacup. "The wound still pains you. Shouldn't you be in bed?"

Pedro glowered. If he vented his desires, he would indeed be back in bed, but not alone. The vow to keep his hands from her had slashed him in two. One side chose to protect her innocence. The other wanted to consume it. Unfortunately for her, the ravenous side hadn't seen a ration in a month, and mutiny was rampant.

She brushed the newspaper creases. "Have you found something new? I wish I could help more. Usually, I'm the one doing things."

As long as she stood out of his way, Pedro was content. He grunted and caught his timepiece. Half-past two.

"You are fretting about your brother, are you not?"

"Women fret. Cris is a battle-hardened soldier. I would dishonor him if I didn't trust him to succeed."

She perched back on her chair, the dog snoring on her lap. "Would you like to play a game? To pass away the time while you are not worrying?" Her lips twitched. "I'm a decent chess player."

She reached for the chessboard, eagerly setting the pieces in place.

The game reminded him of his inability to maneuver his own fate. Pedro took the white queen from her hand and dropped it. "I'd rather not."

Her shoulders deflated a notch, but then she perked up again. "Backgammon? Charades?"

Pedro stared deep into her eyes and, keeping her gaze captive, opened the top drawer of his desk. He chose two ivory cubes and rolled them twice in his leather-clad hands. With a practiced toss, he placed them in front of her.

She gulped. "Dice?"

"You said you wanted to play." He extended his hand to take them back.

"Dice, then. But I must warn you. I'm not familiar with the rules."

Of course, she wasn't. No respectable lady played hazard. "The game has two players, the caster and the bank. The caster chooses a number between five and nine."

Her gaze wandered to her lap, and she yawned.

"Are you following me?"

She straightened. "Sorry. I'm listening."

"The number you choose is the main. Then you throw. If you score a two or a three, you lose. If you score an eleven or a twelve, you lose. If you hit your main, you win."

She tilted her head, frowning. "But what if I get the remaining five numbers?"

She was bright, his angel. Pedro's lips tugged up. "Your main number becomes your chance, and you roll again. This time, you win if you hit your chance, but you lose if you hit your main. You keep rolling the dice until you either lose or win."

"Can I cast?"

"As you wish."

She bounced on the chair. "Can I pick seven as my main number?"

He nodded.

Hands cupped, she threw the dice. They clattered twice and settled—a nine. Without a pause, she plucked the cubes and rolled again. Five and four.

"I won!" She grinned as if he had offered her jewels. For three consecutive times, she played and scored. "I'm surprised it's not a child's game. Why do you suppose it is frowned upon?"

"It is not the dice, but the gambling. When gambling, drunk, or in the heat of war, mankind shows its true nature."

"Surely, when under the influence of strong emotions, people can display nasty behaviors, but I can't believe it to be their true nature." She looked at him from under gold-tipped eyelashes.

Pedro made a cage with his fingers. "Enlighten me then. What is man's true nature?"

She raised a pretty shoulder. "I believe people are good before they prove otherwise."

"When they prove otherwise, it's too late."

"When? Not if?" She clicked her tongue. "I must beg to disagree. Our human nature is innately good."

Pedro smirked. "I imagine you have experience to support this belief."

"What would you do if you saw a child drowning in the ocean? Wouldn't you help? I dare say every person would save a child in harm's way." She hoisted her chin in defiance. "Isn't this proof our nature is good?"

"A few would remove the child to hurt it further."

"I cannot believe such evil exists."

With her rosy beliefs and youthful mulishness, she was as well-equipped to live in the real world as a soldier arriving in battle without a bayonet. Maxwell must have been insane to bring her up with such ideas.

"The man behind Salgueiro's attack relishes inflicting pain." Pedro grabbed her wrist. "Promise you won't allow your stupid, reckless optimism to put you in danger."

Her face paled, and she winced.

Pedro realized he had crushed her wrist and released her. Three red marks flashed on her skin. He stared at what his touch had done to her, and bile rose in his throat. "I've hurt you."

"It's nothing." She moved her hand below the table. "My skin is too fair. How do you know this, anyway?" Her voice softened. "Is he part of the shadows?"

Her perception was too near the mark. He should tell her the truth about Ulrich so she could protect herself. But she would not look at him with dawn in her eyes if she found out about Mozambique, would she? He could not bring himself to shatter her trust. Best to keep her close, guarded at all times.

"Since you seem to like thought experiments." Pedro crossed his arms. "Are you familiar with the Gyges ring?"

She raised a brow. "Should I be?"

"I'll tell you his legend, then. Gyges was a shepherd in Ancient Greece. After an earthquake, he found a dead giant wearing a gold ring. Gyges placed it on his finger. To his surprise, it made him invisible. Care to guess what he did with such power?"

She shook her head, and the long rope of her hair came to rest over her shoulder.

"He invaded the king's palace, slept with his wife, plotted with her to kill the monarch, and seized control of the kingdom."

She listened avidly. "And then?"

"There's no then. This is the story. No fairy tale ending. Anyone possessing the means without the risk of being caught will forget moral restrictions."

"Certainly not."

"Are you so sure, Ana?" He kept his tone low. "What would you do if you had the ring?"

She tilted her head sideways, then her face colored, and she quickly glanced away.

"There." Pedro leaned forward. "What have you just imagined?"

She furiously traced the etches of his desk, avoiding his eyes. "Nothing."

"You are a terrible liar. What was it?"

She covered her cheeks with her palms. "I can't tell. Please don't ask me."

What was her sin of choice? Jewelry, silks... voyeurism? What if she wanted another man? Was Gabriel her dream suitor? The one she had mentioned more than once? His gut tightened. He needed to know.

Pedro pushed the dice in her direction. "We could play again. If you lose, you confess your desire. If you win..."

She squirmed in her chair, no doubt preparing to balk. Unless Pedro offered the right incentive.

"I'll take you to see the view from Saint George's castle. It's enough compensation, don't you think? Plus, have you not won four times? You are on a winning streak." Pedro toyed with the dice, rolling them over his fingers.

Her gaze flitted over his face. Pedro kept his expression schooled.

"I'll play." Hands trembling, she picked up the dice. "My main will be seven."

She threw the cubes. A six. Clumsily, she collected and rolled them again. Nine. She stared at the numbers as if pleading for them to do her will. "Why do you think the game is called hazard?" she whispered.

"Portuguese have words for bad and good luck. Do you know them?"

"*Sorte* for good. *Azar* for bad. That's where hazard came from?"

"Some say it is." He pointed at her hands. "Cast the dice again. I want to see who's sitting on your shoulder today, bright *sorte* or murky *azar.*"

She brought the dice to her lips, her eyes closed. After a hopeful brush, she let go.

Pedro tensed. If she managed a nine, he wouldn't know her wishes.

Three dots in the first. The second clattered twice before stopping—a four.

Her shoulders slumped, and she groaned.

"I win." Pedro covered the dice with his black-gloved hands. "Now you tell me."

Face flushed, she left the sleeping dog on the chair and, in a whirl of flowery cotton, hastened away. She stopped in front of the curved bookshelves, arms crossed over her chest.

Pedro moved slowly, so he wouldn't frighten her, and halted behind her. He had played with her innocence. Letting her out of the bet would be the gentlemanly thing to do. He could be a gentleman when he wanted to be. But not today.

"Are you a gracious loser, Ana?" He breathed the words near her neck, and the champagne-colored down covering her skin lifted to meet him.

There was no contact between them. Still, warmth seeped from her spine into his chest, flooding him.

"No, it's just..."

Pedro tucked a stray hair over the perfect shell of her ear. "Your innately good nature recoils from your cravings?"

"I can't." Her cheeks, already flushed, turned into a brighter cherry. "It's too intimate."

"You are whetting my curiosity."

A breeze blustered through the glass panes, and she hugged herself. The need to see into her darker side dimmed. It wasn't worth making her subdued. How fast he had ranked her interests above his own. Wasn't he willing to face enfilading fire just to know her deepest desire? No matter. He had gone too far.

He had opened his mouth to relieve her of the bet when she spun, her chest brushing against him.

"I would use it..." She exhaled and closed her eyes, her brows furrowed. "I would use invisibility to touch you."

Pedro went utterly still. All he could do was stare at her flashing irises.

Heart pounding, he broke eye contact, his muscles contracting. "Cris told you? Of course, he did. And you want it just because you can't have it?" He sucked in a breath, clenching his hands. "A spoiled child denied a sweet?"

"No! Why did you force me to say it only to judge me so?" Her voice broke, and she raced to the door.

Pedro seized her arm, preventing her flight. "Why?" he snarled.

She flinched and lowered her chin to her chest. Clouds raced over their heads, dappling shadows over her slim frame, but the sunlight fought its way to her, illuminating her mouth's dejected slant, the hurt in her eyes.

Pedro rubbed his chest, her pain defeating his own anger. He caressed her cheek, searching her expression.

"Why?" he whispered so softly the words could have been lost in the breeze.

"If you ask for a logical explanation, I have none." Her voice faltered. Her face was serious, if somehow defiant.

He turned her wrist and stared at her palm. He wanted—no, he *craved* her hands on his skin. To allow it would be an unplanned, irrational decision. Those led to failings every time. Yet he needed to know if the bliss of the night before, when she had touched him, had been an effect of the laudanum or if these tiny hands, so breakable, so constantly in motion, could somehow change the wiring of his skin.

Rationality be damned.

Pedro pulled the chain around his neck, removing his mother's ring. The weight was slight, but the absence of it was unbalancing. He opened his palm, the gold carrying his warmth, and displayed it to her. "This will be your Gyges ring."

"But how?" She stared at it, no doubt searching for hidden magic.

"I will close my eyes and won't open them for one minute." He touched her chin and brought her gaze to him. "Only one, understand?"

A nod, and then another. She seemed breathless, and when the pink tip of her tongue came out to lick the seam of her lips, Pedro had to look away lest he devoured her mouth. He turned her hand and traced her heart-shaped scar. "You will be invisible, and you will have your desire. But after your turn, it will be mine."

"But what will you—"

"You will have to wait."

Before she changed her mind, Pedro slid the gold band over her knuckles to the hilt of her finger. The diamond caught the sun's rays from the skylight, shattering it into colorful sparks over her skin. It fit like the well-placed note of a symphony, the rich rhyme of a sonnet, the crowning brush of a masterpiece. "It was my mother's."

"Do you miss her?"

The memories had waned over the years—caring hands, hushed lullabies, shielding arms. Pedro turned from her sympathy. Those emotions had been buried a long time ago.

On stiff legs, he pulled his chair close to the open glass panes and lowered his weight gradually as if his back would meet ice instead of sun-warmed leather. Spine straight, Pedro gripped the sides of the seat and, as agreed, closed his eyes. Darkness greeted him behind his eyelids, and he took measured breaths despite his pounding heart.

Her presence shifted the air behind him, and he locked his jaw to keep still. The brine of the sea gushed against his face. She was silent, and the screeching of gulls and the hull creaking assailed his ears.

Conscious of the vibrations of her breaths, the neroli of her scent, Pedro tapped his foot once, twice, and stopped. His father had beaten him out of the habit long ago. "Your minute is waning."

Muffled words. A tug on the leather string tying his hair. The fluttering of the strands over his neck. Any moment, cold fingertips would brush his nape like burrowers seeking entrance into his skin.

She combed her fingers through his hair. Pedro held his breath. It was too far from his skin for him to feel any contact, mere butterfly wings flirting, shirking from the answer he craved.

"More," he rasped.

"Are you sure? I... yes."

The floor squeaked behind him as she came closer and then closer still. Warm fingers sifted through his hairline, brushing the shell of his ears and then up until they reached the top of his skull. He lowered his shoulders and released all the air inside his lungs.

Points of pressure on his scalp, firm, deep, and then sliding away. Absence, cold. Her fingers returned, breezing touches over his temples. His skin hummed, a current spreading to his arms and legs, flowing from her fingertips right into his core. He lost awareness of where she touched. It was as if... as if she had stripped him bare and wrapped him with a mantle of sensations, unfurling from the soles of his feet to his scalp.

Anne sighed. "So soft."

The words breathed fire into his chest. To be touched by her and to know she enjoyed it? It was acute and allayed an ache within, lulling his muscles yet inflaming his blood.

This girl, his Anne... She soothed him. She seared him.

Gently, he caught her wrist and pulled her to his front. He opened his eyes to an angel standing between his legs, lips parted, eyes glazed with desire. Heat flooded his chest, his limbs. It was her touch, her spark, and now he burned.

"My turn."

Chapter 20

Anne tasted invisibility, exploring Pedro's manly textures, floating in the silk of his hair, skimming the velvet planes of his coat, gliding across the stubble of his beard. Buoyed by the slow rocking of the boat and gentle ocean sounds, she closed her eyelids, suspended as if swimming in warm waters.

He caught her hand, tugging her back to reality. The stubble of his beard whisked her wrist, and then his lips met the skin there, just a brush. Breathless and not a little dizzy, she allowed him to pull her to his front. Had he liked to be touched? Had he liked to be touched by her?

Pedro opened his eyes. No more invisibility. He saw her.

One second he was seated, his head reaching no further than her chest. The other he was standing, engulfing her, her feet between his feet, her shadow inside his. Not an inch separated her nose from the mother-of-pearl buttons of his white shirt, and the scent of clean linen and Pedro drowned her senses. Perhaps she had dived too deep.

"Place your hands behind your back."

Anne gasped, lifting her gaze from his chest to his chin. "Are you sure this is advisable?" Her voice came out high-pitched, and she swallowed. "This... This hardly seems appropriate, and you must agree the bet was so sudden and silly. No gentleman had ever—"

He touched her lips. "You talk too much when you are nervous."

"Do I? No one has told me so before."

He exhaled, his warm breath ruffling her hair. "I didn't judge your desire."

With a heavy sigh, Anne nodded and crossed her wrists behind her, the stone of his mother's ring biting into her clammy palm. He retrieved the discarded hair string and circled her. His breathing teased her neck, and then the flaky leather brushed her skin. Some deft tugs. Anne panted. He had tied her. A twinge of panic shuddered through her, and she twisted her arms.

"I won't hurt you." He covered her hands, and his mouth near her ear made her shiver. "The knots are loose. You can free yourself anytime."

Could she?

He faced her, his presence shading the sun. Anne sought the buttons on his shirt, unable to look up. A simple leather string had her more exposed than if he had stripped her clothes.

"I can release you if you want me to," he said, his hair loose and tousled, his mouth unsmiling, and his eyes—his *eyes*—intense and focused solely on her.

His cloak of restraint had slipped, unleashing wild energy. A proper English lady would run screaming and hide under her berth. But a proper English lady wouldn't have a warrior prince gazing at her as if she was his princess, would she?

Anne raised her chin. "What will you do?"

"You are unbearably sweet." He removed his leather gloves, one finger at a time. "And I've developed a craving for sweetness."

Anne had never seen his hands in broad daylight. How would the calloused palms feel against her skin? Her breath caught, and she blinked several times. "Oh, if this is the case, then—"

"Close your eyes, Ana. It's my turn to be invisible."

She did.

He stroked her brows and ruffled her eyelashes, making her face twitch. Then, gliding lower, first over the bridge of her nose and then the curve of her mouth. His touch was warm and heavy, like the sun at three o'clock. He only wanted to learn her, a sculptor discovering his muse.

Anne smiled and lifted her face, wanting more of his gentle caresses.

Palms cradled her cheeks, and then his breaths came impossibly closer. Anne's heart lurched against her rib cage and then halted. Outside her closed eyelids, the gulls stopped screeching. The waves hushed, and the boat stilled as if airborne.

Warm and firm, his lips joined with hers. A kiss. She breathed in the cedar of his skin, heated by the sun, and it inflated her lungs until she became weightless. If he were not holding her, she would have floated away. Anne held still while his heart thudded close to hers, reveling in the texture of his lips, wishing this moment would last forever.

Something moist traced her lips, and the chaste kiss became more. Pedro embraced her, caressing the ridges of her spine. Anne leaned into him, wanting her hands free so she could sift her fingers through his hair.

He kissed the line of her jaw, and then he touched his tongue to her neck, just below her ear. It was shocking, and she should protest. Instead, she dropped her head back, swaying closer to him. Coherent thoughts sank in the rush of warmth flooding her chest, her limbs.

He trailed his caresses lower, down the curve of her breasts, to press at her waist. Then his palms flattened her dress against her thigh and lifted her knee. The sudden movement robbed her balance, and she leaned on the bulkhead, pressing against her bound hands. She was open to him, and he claimed every inch, moving against her with thrilling intensity. He possessed her mouth, his tongue insistent, invading, seeking. The whirlwind threatened to consume her, making her lightheaded.

If this was ruination, she was beyond caring.

Then it stopped. Where once they touched everywhere, now there was only air.

Would he remove the binding and allow her to touch him? She waited for another heartbeat, but she heard only wood groaning and the ruffling of sails.

"Pedro?"

No answer.

She opened her eyes. The library was empty. She was alone. Invisible.

Chapter 21

Pedro strode out of the library, blood pounding in his temples. He had almost taken Anne against the bulkhead like a common trollop. Fists clenched by his sides, chest about to explode, he halted on the quarter-deck.

Cris and Dante crossed the raised bridge, their easy banter proof of their well-being.

"Finally. What news?" Pedro snapped.

The first mate saluted him, beret clasped in his right hand, and sped to the crew's quarters. Cris approached with narrowed eyes, no doubt taking in Pedro's loose hair and opened coat. For once, his brother's clothes were less disheveled than his. "Something happened in my absence?"

Something had happened, indeed. Pedro had lost control, and his insides still clamored for her. She hummed in his veins, invading his senses. Was it not enough to have her image burned inside his eyelids? He was to have her contours imprinted on his palms? Her taste? By Saint George, she was not sweet. The ridiculous adjective could not describe her layers, spiced, fresh, heated...

Pedro rubbed his neck. "That wasn't my question."

Cris frowned. "We asked around for the bodyguard's address, but the house was deserted. He must have escaped."

"*Merda*." He should have known there would be no simple solution to this.

Gripping the yacht's railings, Pedro stared outside. The moored boats prepared for the night, their cooking fires leaving the air acrid. The rope tying the *Dawn Chaser* to the pier strained and relaxed with the swelling and ebbing of the dark water. Pedro's gut churned, his feet unable to find a place of stability. He needed out of here.

Cris's face split into a mischievous grin. "No need to curse yet. I've asked around. One of the tavern barmaids, a favorite of the bodyguard, visited him at the beach of São Jacinto."

Pedro knew the terrain, ten miles north of here, a stretch of dunes and river marshes delimited by the ocean on the west and the Aveiro's Ria lagoon to the east. Pedro gazed at the setting sun. The place was too treacherous to travel by night.

"We leave at dawn." Pedro exhaled and closed his eyes. "I can't spend another second inside this cursed boat."

"So it seems." Cris raised his brows. "We'll find the wayward bodyguard tomorrow. Tonight, we can hunt for other prey, eh? Aveiro's entertainment is quite agreeable. And judging by your state, you need it."

Pedro remembered Anne's soft, willing moans and hardened again. He couldn't stay near her. A man's vows could only be stretched so far, and his vows were not ductile in the first place. "Fine."

Cris clasped Pedro's shoulder, his laughter booming on the deck. "Come on, then. I've heard it's Gitano night at the local tavern, and I fancy myself a gypsy. Or two." His green eyes flashed. "It will be just like the old times."

Pedro swallowed the *aguardente*. The alcohol burned a path from his throat to his stomach. He cleaned his mouth on his sleeve and slammed the crude cup on the table.

The tavern was the reverse of the colorful Aveiro. Filled with sailors from the bustling port city, it was chaotic, pungent, and crowded. Cris had been right. The guitar playing at the corner wasn't the twelve chord Portuguese instrument but the Spanish one, sounding hollow and harsh. Two flamenco dancers performed near the counter, their red and black skirts flying, chins jutting out and arms raised, their incessant castanets clacking inside Pedro's head. An avid crowd had gathered to catch glimpses of naked skin, their mouths gaping and hands clapping in time.

Cris bounced the two barmaids perched on his thighs, and they giggled. Their Castilian accents were as genuine as fool's gold. The other woman licked her lips, her black hair waving around her shoulders, and stared at

Pedro boldly. Her Gypsy veils were the softest thing of her appearance.

The whore was precisely the kind he needed. Experienced, jaded, unbreakable.

Cris wiggled his brows. "I thought you came here to enjoy yourself, not empty glasses."

Pedro finished his *aguardente* and stood, pushing Anne from his mind and his chair back with enough force to rattle the table behind. A rough-looking sailor, Dutch by the hay-colored hair and blotched skin, rose, a glower on his face. Pedro stared into gray eyes, baring his teeth. After a brittle nod, the man dropped back onto his chair, and the group returned to gambling. A shame they didn't take offense. Pedro craved a fight even more than a fuck.

He turned to the whore. "Lead the way."

Eyes flashing like copper coins, she rose. Cris snickered, but the lurid words faded over string notes, clinking glasses, and drunk guffaws. The scarred planks covering the floor bowed beneath Pedro's feet. She sashayed inside a room, lighting a taper near the window. The squalid furniture flickered in time with the wick, but he didn't need light to navigate the room's shadows. Semen-stained bed sheets, walls too thin to block sex sounds, liquor spilled on the floor. How many hours of his life had he spent in hells like this? It didn't matter. This was a transaction. His body needed sexual release. The whore sold the service.

No attachments and no ocean-gazed girl wishing for a place inside his skin.

Hips swaying, the Gypsy came near, hands outstretched to his waistband.

"You touch me when I say so."

"You are paying, *Fidalgo*." She shrugged, and the movement bared her shoulder. "How is it gonna be?"

He should tie her and be done with it.

"Touch my hair." The words spilled from his mouth before he could contain them. The alcohol must have dulled his wits.

String notes filtered through the thin wall, marked by the castanets. She inclined her head and walked around him, her skirts swishing against his legs. Tobacco and stale green wine intoxicated the air. The whore's breaths brushed his nape, and he ground his teeth. When pointed fingernails grazed his neck like steel needles, nausea punched him in the stomach.

He sucked in a breath. "Cease. Lay on the bed."

The whore nodded, her shoulders coming down a notch as if grateful for a request inside her repertoire, and lay on the mattress. Pedro reached for her left wrist to tie it around the iron bedstead, and she grimaced.

"If you leave bruises, it's going to cost you more."

"This is not about pain." He needed control. Some women found dark pleasure in relinquishing it. Would Anne? What was this obsession for her? Why had she planted this seed inside him? The more he hacked at it, the more it grew.

When he finished with the rope, the whore stretched over the bed, kicking up her legs to expose naked thighs. The tawny skin and ample hips should have fired his blood. Instead, he became detached, observing the scene as if suspended from the ceiling. The woman, the threadbare linen, the cracks on the wall, himself in the shadows, the flycatcher swinging, swish, swish.

A guitar screamed outside. Pedro's heart sent blood crashing into his veins, and he shuddered as images pounded him like claps of the castanets—Ana opening herself to him, Ana moaning, Ana's song, Ana, Ana, Ana.

A chilling realization washed over him with the force of a storm.

Pedro needed release, but the whore wouldn't suffice.

Chapter 22

Anne only abandoned her cabin when the sun had hit it long enough to cook her inside. She ambled to the drawing room where her breakfast awaited, the tea long cold and the bread stale. She dropped into the chair and twisted the linen napkin.

Footsteps on the gunwale made her face flame. How would she address Pedro? The proper behavior would be to pretend indifference, but she was terrible at pretending. If it weren't for the way he flustered her, she would ask him. A simple question. Why had he left after the kiss? Had she displeased him?

By the time the door opened, she had straightened her posture and arranged her face into a serene expression. Beatriz stepped inside, bringing with her a gust of wind. A few brown curls had escaped her cap to frame her pixie face. "Dante is a brute. Can you believe he left a pineapple in my cabin? What am I supposed to do with a thorny monster?"

Anne sighed. "He wishes to please you. It's a delicacy."

The maid blushed furiously, and then she gazed at the untouched food and clucked her tongue. "Seasickness,

Miss Anne? Sometimes it happens after the first few days..."

"I'm fine, really. I got little rest last night."

"You too?" Beatriz lifted her brows, her lips making a pretty moue.

Anne smiled in sympathy, reaching for the tea. "You also had trouble sleeping?"

The maid lowered her voice and leaned closer. "No, not me. His Excellency and Mr. Queiroz. They arrived late. You should see their clothes—"

"Are they hurt?"

"Hurt?" Beatriz giggled, and her cheeks turned red. "That shameless Italian told the twins, who told me they went to"—she cupped her hands around her mouth—"the bawdy house."

The cup fell from Anne's hand, splattering tea. Mechanically, she rose and exited the deck on lead-weighted legs. Shutting her eyes, she dropped to the wicker chair. While her lips still tingled with the memory of his kisses, he had touched another? Allowed another to touch him? Somehow, the latter pained her more. What had she expected? Had she not feared it from the start? She took a shuddering breath and clasped her locket. Pedro had proved to be the kind of man she had hoped to avoid.

On the beach, children played, making castles and collecting shells under the watchful eyes of two nannies. Beyond, so close she could almost touch, was Aveiro's cathedral, its domed belfry glinting in the midday sun.

He was out there, doing only God knew what, and she was to stay cooped inside? She crushed the pillow and shot up from the chair. She was done watching from the fringes while others lived their lives.

Anne marched to the raised bridge, Beatriz on her heels.

"Won't you finish your breakfast, miss?"

"I'm not hungry. In fact, a stroll in the city is just the thing to improve my disposition. Want to join me?"

"Are you sure His Excellency would approve? I saw him leaving today. He was in a terrible mood."

"I don't care about His Excellency's moods."

Without waiting to see if the maid followed, Anne reached the platform. The small bridge connecting the yacht to the pier beckoned, the ocean glittering on both sides.

The captain stepped in her way. "Do you need anything, Miss Maxwell?"

"Yes, Mister Oliveira. I wish to visit Aveiro. Beatriz will accompany me."

"I'm sorry." He cleared his throat, looking terribly uncomfortable. "The count left precise instructions. You are not to disembark."

Anne fisted her hands and forced a charming smile. "What if Mario or Dario escorted me?"

He gave her a pitying gaze. "I'm sorry, Miss Maxwell, but I have my orders."

Tears burned her nose, and she spun away from him. Did they know Pedro had kissed her yesterday and left to see other women? Cheeks flaming, the wind lashing her hair against her chest, she sped over the gunwale, only stopping at the stables. All stalls were empty except for Hemera's.

The mare greeted her with a quiet neigh, and Anne hugged her neck, breathing in the dusty scent of her coat. "They left you behind too, huh?"

Anne tangled her hands through the mare's frizzy mane, tears coming freely. How could he order her around like a child? She took deep breaths, but the burning in her chest would not go away. The boat swayed, and she leaned on the bar for support. Would he smell of another?

She couldn't stay inside, waiting for him to return.

Her eyes latched onto the port door, the one used by the horses. On impulse, she tested the handle, but it wouldn't bulge. She pressed with her shoulders, and the barest give filled her with hope.

Please, please, open.

A clank at the stairs made her stop, her heart colliding with her ribs. When Beatriz's gray skirts appeared at the hatch, she exhaled and turned back to the door.

"*Santa Maria, Pinta e Nina*! What are you doing?" the maid whispered.

Anne blew hair from her face. "Instead of reciting Cabral's fleet, can you help me? Please?"

The maid hastened to Anne's side, her hands folded as if in prayer. "Are you sure this is a good idea?"

Anne closed her eyes, a sigh raking her chest. "I must do this."

Beatriz bit her lip. "I guess a lady's maid remains with her lady when she needs it, right?"

"No." Anne gave her a teary smile and pressed her hand affectionately. "Friends do."

Chapter 23

The treacherous dunes hid holes deep enough to break a horse's leg. Pedro forced the party to walk their mounts. He wouldn't risk Erebus even to rescue the Pope. The wind came from a hot stove, swirling grains of sand and thickening the air. To their right, the Atlantic glinted with a thousand sapphires, calling to its blue depths.

"The fiercest battle was the victory of Garibaldi against the Austrian Forces in Sardinia," Dante bragged.

Cris scoffed. "In your pasta-stuffed dreams. The battle of Aljubarrota topples any Italian skirmish you can name. Nuno Gonçalves bathed the earth with Castilian blood, ridding Portugal of the Spaniards' threat. What do you say, Pedro? Sardinia or Aljubarrota?"

"I'm not in the mood for prattle."

"Do you prefer to talk about last night?" Cris's smile strained his tanned skin.

Pedro would rather forget the fiasco. After he had stormed out of the whore's room, he had fought the sailors. Cris had shoved him from atop the Dutch a second before he had crashed his skull. Pedro glanced at his bloodied knuckles. "Austerlitz. There's never been a more brilliant general than Napoleon."

"Not a chance." Cris shook his head, laughing.

While both men kept a steady stream of battle talk, a crow circling the sky lifted the hairs on Pedro's neck. He watched their flanks, but no one had followed. Still, this could be a trap. Acting without confirmed intelligence was a rotten strategy, but time was scarce. Princess Isabel would return from England in September. With Pedro out of the quest, the king would squander her to an obscure German principality. The fortress he meant to construct, carved on influence, on power, his Torres Vedras, wavered, more unstable than the dunes they traversed.

What if they could not find the king's bodyguard? The Duke of Titano would have sacrificed Anne in the first gambit of his game, using her as his alibi. If he sniffed Pedro's reluctance, the duke would rant about her lack of lineage and incite him to take her as a mistress if he so desired. Pedro recoiled from the words as if his father had whispered them in his ear.

Beyond the marsh, a gray cottage crouched between gaunt olive trees. Pedro pulled the reins. "It's here."

Cris halted Guerreiro by his side. "Deserted?"

They dismounted and approached the entrance. Pedro lifted his hand, halting the others. He pointed at the sets of footprints exiting the shack. "At least five."

"Do you think Gabriel's been here?"

"Not the guards. The regiment uses standard-issued boots. These soles are uneven."

The scarred door hung from its leather hinges, charred at the edges. Pedro entered first. Fire had licked the walls, leaving blackened wood and ashes in the place of furniture. The shack had a single room partitioned with a darkened screen. A cot, fishing implements, and a brick oven completed the squalid decor. Hardly the setting to enjoy a bribe. More likely, the bodyguard had felt the need to hide.

Cris whistled. "A sardine grilling went wrong?"

Pedro strained his eyes to adjust to the lack of light. "The bodyguard could've eliminated evidence."

Dante found an empty bottle and sniffed it. "*Aguardente.*"

Sugar cane alcohol flared quickly, but too fast. "Search every corner. He could have left something behind."

"The sooner we leave this rat hole, the better." Cris affected a shiver and winked. "I bet evil spirits are lurking."

Dante widened his eyes and shuffled closer to the door. For all his bulk, the Italian was superstitious.

"Don't listen to him. The wise fear the living."

Dante lifted the makeshift bed, raising a cloud of fetid smoke. He was lowering it when Pedro spotted a volume below, cloaked in shadows. "What's that?"

Dante crouched and picked it up. "A notebook of sorts."

Pedro took the volume, careful not to damage it further. The fire had burned the edges but left the crest on the first page untouched. Pedro traced the two green dragons and crown of the Braganza coat of arms. The small, organized handwriting belonged to his friend, but the cottage's semi-darkness didn't allow him to read the words.

Pedro went to the window at the back of the house. Meager light and a faint droning seeped through the rattling panes. He pushed the shutters open. Among sage bushes and yellowed oleanders hid the unmistakable shape of a body.

Signaling the others, Pedro strode outside and circled the shack. A man. On his stomach in a crawling position, as if he had died trying to escape. Flies swarmed the corpse, leaving no patch of skin sacred. His spine and legs had been punctured several times, and a bull spear protruded from his shoulder blade. Blood had leaked into the white sand, congealing into crimson rivulets.

"Ulrich," Cris said with disgust. "The man is the worst kind of sick."

Dante crossed himself. "*Dio ti abbia*."

Pedro had heard about Ulrich's games. How he enjoyed staging bullfights with his prey. While he acted as the matador, the victim played the bull part, unarmed. Crouching near the body, Pedro closed the glassy brown eyes. The bodyguard's face would forever be frozen in terror.

Cris looked away, his arms crossed over his chest. "I have this nightmare... Ulrich chases me in an arena, his spear hidden by his red cape, waiting for a chance to strike."

Pedro planted a hand over his brother's shoulder.

Cris shuddered. "Who the hell put him on our paths? If we could find who sold us in Mozambique..."

Pedro's gaze lingered on his brother, and the image came unbidden. The Chikunda's death grip on Cris's neck, the dagger flashing below his brother's chin. With Ulrich's return, it became nearly impossible to shut them out. They clawed to the surface, the memories. Pedro struggled to push them away. He could not go through Mozambique again. Not now. Not ever.

The bullfighter had employed another winning strategy. But if Ulrich was in Aveiro...

Pedro stilled, a wave of acid swamping his stomach. Anne was unprotected on the yacht.

Heart pounding in his ears and throat, Pedro bolted to his feet, brushing sand from his hands as he strode toward the horses. "Bury him."

"Where are you going?" Cris raised his voice.

"I'm returning to the boat. Anne is vulnerable."

Cris frowned, his always cheerful facade somber. "*Se cuida, irmão.*"

Pedro nodded and vaulted atop the saddle. The dunes and bogs of the Ria lagoon stretched endlessly. If Ulrich had reached her, Pedro wouldn't get to them in time. Pushing Erebus to a canter, he trusted the steed to step true over the treacherous terrain. Sand rose in powdery waves to stick in his throat. He avoided looking at the Atlantic. The color of her eyes. If he kept staring at the horizon, he would not lose her.

They clattered over a wooden bridge. The flashes returned, but this time, Anne stood in Cris's place, Ulrich's dagger cutting her skin, tears of pain and horror trailing down her cheeks. The madman quenching the brightness of her spirit.

Pedro shook his head, fisting his hands on the reins. She was safe on the yacht. She was safe on the yacht. She must be safe, damn it. Why couldn't he breathe? If only he could claw his chest open and extricate this madness.

The dunes gave way to a shallow rise, and Pedro leaned over Erebus's neck, urging the horse to a gallop. Atop the crest, the view opened to show both the coast and the road leading to the city. Below, crossing the Ria lagoon pass, a flash of red. Soldiers. Aveiro had become a hornet's nest, no longer a safe harbor for the yacht. As soon as Cris returned, they would have to set sail.

Pressing his heels on Erebus's flanks, he guided the horse down the path. The seaside Marina came into view, and Pedro cantered over the wooden boards to his yacht's bridge. He glimpsed the captain's gray head on the main deck. An aura of normalcy clung to the *Dawn Chaser*. Still, this vise crushing his chest would only recede when he saw her with his own eyes.

He reined in, and Dario took Erebus's reins as Pedro vaulted from the saddle, his breaths coming in short bursts. "Where is Miss Maxwell? I must speak with her this instant." He might lure her into invisibility again to feel the pleasing pain of her hands on his skin.

The deckhand would not meet his eyes. "She left, Your Excellency."

A roar erupted from Pedro's throat. The crew watched, no doubt shocked at his unusual loss of restraint. He was aware the captain had disembarked and was moving closer.

Pedro took great gulps of air but couldn't fill his lungs. "What happened?"

The captain wrang his hands. His ruddy skin was blotched and deep lines marred his forehead. "She wanted to visit the city, Your Excellency, but I told her you had forbidden her to leave the yacht. Miss Maxwell must have left through the stable port. We found it open. They—"

Pedro advanced over the older man. "They?"

The captain gulped. "She took Beatriz with her. I'm sure they are both fine. Why, the city is quite safe, and—"

"Enough." Pedro jabbed his finger at the captain's face. "I ordered you to guard her in my absence."

The sun glared at him, and Pedro shut his eyes, pressing his fists to the sides of his head. What had the little fool expected to gain by ignoring his commands? Putting herself in danger? Bile burned his throat. By Saint George, the devilish angel had torn him in two, taking with her a part of him that was vulnerable, unprotected, leaving behind this battle-hardened hide. She had no right.

He clenched and unclenched his fists. Think. "When?"

"Not forty minutes ago— "

"Dario, take Erebus aboard. I'm going after her. Prepare the boat. Cristiano and Dante will arrive within the hour. As soon as I bring her back, we will set sail."

Pedro swapped coats with the captain and tucked his hair inside a sailor's cap, his only concession as a disguise. If it weren't for Anne, he would relish meeting a soldier intent on arresting him.

He tunneled his vision into the city. When he caught her, she would wish Ulrich had gotten her first.

Chapter 24

After so many days aboard, Anne's balance was off, the stone pavement of Aveiro's square floating under her feet. The channels used in lieu of streets added a smell of salted water to the city, and the absence of carriages and oxcarts made it hushed. Gondolas skimmed their dark waters, bright colors reflecting on the surface.

What a pity. After reading about the charming city in her guidebooks, Portugal's Venice, now that she was here, her mind kept straying to Pedro in another woman's company. Had she been pretty? What had she offered that Anne couldn't?

Beatriz tugged at her elbow. "Miss, shouldn't we head back?"

"So soon? We just arrived."

"I have this feeling someone is watching us."

Anne glanced at both sides. "But no one is giving us the least attention."

Couples and families strolled and visited the shops. Many drank tea at inviting cafés, sitting under the shade of ash trees. All perfectly safe.

She would not allow Pedro's pessimism to taint her. She linked her arm with Beatriz and urged her along. To their right, the Monastery of Jesus rose higher than the other buildings, flanked by junipers, its broken arch pediment windows glinting in the sun. An Avis princess, Saint Joana, had lived there. Typically, Anne would wait in line to visit the museum, but she couldn't muster the enthusiasm.

"If we are staying, let's sit for a bit? I've brought some coins, and you can try Aveiro's famous *ovos moles*."

Anne's stomach lurched at the thought of eating the sweet made of egg yolk and a copious amount of sugar. "I'll have to pass, but we can stop if you fancy one for yourself."

"I don't know..." The maid peeked longingly at the spindly masts beyond the central channel. "If we hurry, we can arrive before His Excellency, and then we wouldn't upset him. You know he is— "

"We should try the *ovos moles*, Beatriz. What an excellent idea." Anne wouldn't consider the Count's sentiments, as he hadn't considered hers. The ungracious thought brought a bitter taste to her mouth, but she was helpless to dispel it. Had he not taught her to put her own wishes above others?

The petite maid sighed and glanced heavenward. "There's a *pastelaria* with nice outside tables. Come, and we'll have a pastry too... Dante told me about the duel yesterday."

"You don't say."

Beatriz looked at her for a short spell, and her eyes darted back to the square. "It wasn't about a woman, but about honor. He had so much to say."

"Dante? Spoke more than expletives?"

Beatriz scrunched the skirt of her dress. "I sent him away. I'm confused. Oh, Miss Anne, he... he frightens me."

Anne sighed, her eyes straying to the marina. "A girl should not settle for less than perfect love. One she feels confident will be comfortable, frictionless, and filled with quiet afternoons by the hearth, drinking tea and discussing literature."

Beatriz frowned. "I'm not so fond of tea..."

A figure approached them. Anne's breath caught, and she gripped Beatriz's arm. An elderly man, face gaunt, clothes wrinkled, and expression somber. When he stepped into the sunlight, he offered a gentle smile.

Anne released her death grip on the maid's arm and pointed to the peculiar instrument the man carried. "What is that?"

Beatriz smiled. "It's a *realejo*, Miss. He wants to see your luck."

The man twirled a hand crank, filling the square with crisp, twinkling notes, and opened a hidden drawer. Thimble-sized papers filled the compartment. A lovebird chirped out of a tiny door.

"What a lovely fellow you are." Anne extended her arm. "May I?"

At the man's consent, Anne cooed to the bird and caressed its green feathery chest.

A gust of wind stole Anne's bonnet, but Beatriz caught the headpiece before it could sail into the channel.

"Thank you, dear." Anne accepted the hat and held it to her chest.

The bird leaped into the drawer, picked a paper with his curved beak, and offered it to her. The music repeated the same notes, spinning and spinning. After a moment of hesitation, Anne presented her palm to receive her luck. Would it be *sorte* or *azar*?

After a deep breath, Anne unfolded the message.

'A flawless heart may find true love, but those who love a flawed heart find the truest love of all.'

Gripping her locket, Anne stared until the lines blurred. A gray cloud covered the sun, and the water breeze seeped into her thin cotton dress. "Beatriz, let's return."

The maid grinned and gave a coin to the *realejo* man. The melancholic sounds of the music box followed them along the street as they retraced the path to the yacht, and Anne urged Beatriz to speed her steps.

A metallic cacophony made them halt. Hooves.

Soldiers entered the square through both exits. Anne covered her mouth and stumbled. Pedro was in danger. They must return posthaste. She needed to alert him before... no, she would not picture him behind bars.

A painful grip on her forearm jarred her balance, and before she could so much as breathe, she was pulled into the shadows.

"Don't say a word."

They hid in the nook between two buildings while soldiers trumpeted their arrival mere feet away. Anne nodded, and the rough palm covering her mouth dropped.

Pedro stepped away from her.

Panting, Anne reached for him. "Thank God. I was worried. The riders arrived—"

"Spare me your concern." Pedro's voice could freeze the channel. He turned to her companion, his expression an icy mask. "For your part in this, you will work in the galley for a week."

Beatriz's shoulders sank, and she nodded, looking at the ground.

Anne hurried forward. "It was my fault. If you are going to punish someone, you can— "

"I know exactly whose blunder this is, Miss Maxwell." He bared his teeth. "Don't despair. I'll reserve your punishment for a private place."

Anne crushed her bonnet against her chest. She barely recognized him, and it had nothing to do with the sailor's clothing. Eyes glinting, mouth pressed into a sharp line, his whole body exuded forbidding energy.

"How many Portuguese women have you seen with hair the color of yours? You are a walking target."

"I didn't mean to. The bonnet flew away. I— "

"Put it back."

She wouldn't let him order her around. Anne raised her chin. "No."

"Now is not the time to try my patience." He yanked the hat from her hands. "Beatriz, help Miss Maxwell conceal her hair."

The maid hastened to Anne's side, face ashen. If Anne provoked the count further, no doubt Beatriz would break down, so she turned, allowing her friend to arrange a bun atop her head and then cover it with the straw bonnet.

Pedro leaned over the wall, staring at the street. When the maid finished, he signaled for them to follow.

Heart thundering in her chest, Anne struggled to keep up with his long strides. Next to the *pastelaria*, two soldiers talked with the *realejo* man. Inquiring about Pedro? God, if they only looked at her, they would know her show of calm to be false.

Pedro guided them to a path veering away from the canal's main branch. Three-storied buildings crammed the street on both sides, blocking the light. A channel appeared a few steps further, forming a natural pier under a rickety bridge, water lapping at the mud-colored sand. A gondola bobbed in the shallow. This was his plan? To take the boat? Anne would ask, but she couldn't muster the words. Pedro had the warmth of a block of ice.

A crash sounded to their left, and he spun, drawing her and Beatriz to a crevice in the wall. He retrieved a pistol and pointed it at the threat—a boy racing after a ball.

She grabbed Pedro's arm. "It's a child."

Pedro's gaze shifted to her, pain flickering in his eyes.

Anne lifted her hand, wanting to retrieve her careless words.

"I've got the naughty child I came for." He concealed the gun under his coat and bade them descend to the pier.

Anne tugged at Beatriz's hand, and they stepped over the damp sand, moisture seeping into her shoes and the hem of her dress. The count helped them into the unstable watercraft, and Anne sat with Beatriz on the bow.

"Are we stealing this boat? Won't the owner miss it?"

"What do you suggest we do? Swim back to the marina? Keep your faces down."

Pedro stood at the stern and rowed them out into the glaring light of the open square. Boats passed them, and people mingled around the stores and cafés. Who could believe Pedro was a rower? He had the posture of a Greek hero, sun rays gifting him with a gilded aura. Any moment, a soldier would sound an alarm.

The channel was narrow, the street just a few feet away. If spotted, they would have no place to run. Cold sweat trickled down Anne's spine, and she tucked her feet under her seat to conceal her shaking knees. Beatriz stared at her lap, her lips moving as if in prayer. Her outing, such a fine idea mere hours ago, now weighed on her conscience. If it weren't for her, they wouldn't be in jeopardy.

Pedro bent to touch Anne's hand, pressing it briefly. "After we cross the bridge, we will be secure."

Anne nodded, forcing herself to stay seated when she wanted to bury her face in his neck. His tender gesture reduced the pressure in her chest. True to Pedro's words, not a hundred feet in their front, the arched bridge became visible. Beyond, the Atlantic bar beckoned, masts and sails poking the edges of the orange sky. After the bridge, the canal would be too broad, the yacht and safety too close for the soldiers to threaten them.

A rider clattered to the bridge, his white trousers spotless, his posture regal.

Gabriel Fontes halted his chestnut horse and called to the soldier guarding the square. Did he lead Pedro's pursuers? What a cruel coincidence. Ages had passed since she'd last seen him, the memories wavering on and off like paper lanterns. How was her family? Did they miss her?

The officer's voice, grave with authority, made her stomach twist. She lifted her eyes to the bridge. If she stood, if she made herself known, this would all end. She could go back to her family.

Anne fisted her hands, her nails digging into her palms. She shouldn't entertain such ideas. Risking Pedro's safety when he had saved her life? How hideously selfish.

The boat's glide turned slower. Pedro had stopped rowing and placed his hand menacingly inside the flap of his coat, as if preparing to use his pistol on Mr. Fontes. Why such hatred?

Slowly, he turned his face to her. His eyes had a suspicious glint. Could he divine her thoughts?

Light flickered out as the current sped them under the bridge.

Chapter 25

Pedro shoved the cabin door, closing it with enough force to rattle the doorknob. Ignoring Anne's gasp, he rested his forehead against the wood, his pulse bursting in his throat. The boat lurched, hastening away from the pier. He should be up with the captain, overseeing their escape from Aveiro. But he needed to know, damn it. Had she been deceiving him? Communicating with Gabriel, luring him into the city to arrest him? He couldn't lodge a viper so close.

The key clicked in the lock. Pedro turned. The dim light haunted the shadows of the cozy space. Stockings, skirts, and scarves populated the back of the chairs, and a book lay forgotten on the rose counterpane. Her delicious scent infused the air.

She stood opposite him, her back to the window, arms crossed at her middle, white skirts splattered by muddy water. Her face was pallid, and her trembling chin pointed up.

Thunder rumbled outside, low and distant. The boat braved the sea, its bow rising and falling. How long had it been going on? Their association? He rubbed at his chest, at this damn thing she had put inside. If only he could remove it. The way he had acted the fool, risking his brother's safety, and Erebus's limbs, to get to her while she worked behind his back?

He should've known better.

He paced around the compartment, hardening his resolve. Fear brought a man to his knees. Never again. In anger, he could be both judge and enforcer.

"Thank God it's over, Pedro. I—"

"Did you enjoy your outing?"

She tilted her head. "I think it's best if we talk later."

Did she think to dismiss him? Pedro gritted his teeth. "Do you understand the risk you put yourself at today? With your childish decision to ignore my orders?"

She lifted her chin, a glint in her eyes. "Perhaps you are not the only one with people to visit in the city."

Pedro sucked in a breath, her words piercing his chest. It was true, then. She had been acting to deliver him to her lover. He averted his gaze, hiding his reaction. "Do you know what happens to disobedient girls? They are disciplined."

The silence strained in the wake of his words. There. He had frightened her. Excellent. Now she would—

"Discipline?" Anne spun so fast that her hair whipped against his chest, and she fisted her hands by her hips. "Don't you mean retribution?"

Silvery blonde hair spilled over her face, eyes defiantly raised to his, sharp breaths pushing her breasts above her corset—she resembled a martyred angel.

What was worse? Her betrayal, or her attachment to his cousin, the ultimate *raguser*? Must he always arrive in second place in a woman's heart? Maybe the order did not matter.

"What's amiss with righting a wrong, seeking retribution? An eye for an eye? I would expect proper, pious girls like you to accept it."

She lifted her palms, taking a step closer. "Something made you afraid, and you mean— "

"Do you love him?" he asked through gritted teeth.

She gazed down. "How did you know I've met him?"

He gripped her chin and forced her to look at him. "Answer me."

"Here." She pulled her face out of his reach. "I think you'd best take your mother's ring back." She fumbled to retrieve the band from her finger. "You forgot it with me before you went away last night."

Pedro caught the ancient ring, the warmth of her skin vanishing after a mere second. "You left today to meet him, didn't you? What did he offer in exchange for arresting me?"

Gasping, she turned her face to him. "No! I would never put you in danger. Don't you know me at all?"

The blue of her irises was fully black, moist, focused on him. He knew about people, about the ways of the world. The innocence swimming in her gaze seemed genuine, but how could he trust her? Trust himself around her?

She lifted her hand as if to touch him. "What would it take for you to believe me?"

Pedro shook his head and turned from her, crossing his arms firmly over his chest.

She placed her hand upon his shoulder. "Pedro, please. I can't. Not like this."

Pedro jerked away from her touch. Staring at the night outside, he counted his breaths. Was she telling the truth? He forced his mind back to their moments together. How could she have alerted Gabriel? Unless she was waiting somehow for him to arrive. It made little sense. An insidious pain found its way inside his brain. Pedro shook his head and crammed his fists against his temples.

"This discipline you mentioned. Will it make you believe me?" she asked, her voice detached as if she spoke from a place he couldn't reach.

What?

Pedro whirled.

With the elegance of a ballerina, she bent over the recamier headrest, arching her spine, a swan reverencing. It would not surprise him if white feathers emerged on her back and she flew away.

Pedro staggered back a step, his eyes widening.

She tucked her hair over her shoulder. "Will you do it already, or will you tie me up first?"

Lightning flared outside, drawing the shadow of his hand on the wall. He had seen that shadow before. Over and over. Holding the back of the chair while his father had administered the rod, the belt, the ruler, sweating to make him mend his ways, to purge his sins, to make him better. His skin crawled with the old wish for an invisible armor to plate his skin against the duke's touch.

"I believe you, damn it!" His doubts came crashing in on him with the force of a steam train. Pedro stumbled forward and circled his arms around her, bringing her close to his chest. "Don't do that. Never do that again."

Chapter 26

Anne panted, unable to move. The distrust in his eyes had wrenched her chest open. The sensation of losing something precious had been too intense. Why his trust mattered so much, she could not fathom. It had bloomed since the moment they'd met in his ballroom, and it pained her to see it gone.

Pedro released her and dropped his weight onto the recamier, shoulders caved, face engulfed by his hands. Without his heat cloaking her, the cabin's dank air brushed against her naked arms, raising prickles on her skin. Dazed, Anne stared at her palms imprinted with the headrest flowers. The boat swayed, the waves crashing against the hull an afterthought of what had passed between them.

Nothing about Pedro Daun was what she needed. When she craved comfort, he was anger. When she wanted company, he was heat. When she expected hate and hurt, he was care. When she dreamed of perfection, he was spiked edges.

Shivering, the floor swaying under her soles, she glanced at the door. That man collapsed on her chaise...

perhaps there would be no mending him. This suffering was worse than his Achilles's wrath.

A lump formed in her throat, her eyes gritty as if sand had entered her eyelids. His misery shouldn't affect her. She pulled in a shaky breath, hugging herself. The door waited five feet away. All she had to do was turn the key. Pedro didn't move, lost inside himself, inside his shadows, oblivious to her presence.

How many times had he been left to his own pain? She dragged herself closer and inhaled to speak, but words eluded her, a cruel game of hiding and seek.

"Do you hate me, Ana?"

Sudden tiredness spread to her shoulders and chest. The weight was unbearable. Anne dropped by his side and stared ahead. Try as she might, she couldn't hate him. Not yet. But the denial wouldn't come out, either. Not yet. "What happened today?"

He shook his head, his lips crushed in a tense line.

She crossed her hands above her chest, restraining her need to curl closer and share his warmth. "Please?"

With a toneless voice, he recounted the discovery of the bodyguard's death. He didn't spare her the horrible details, and her stomach revolted at the cruelty. Then came her absence. For her, he had left his brother; for her, he had risked breaking Erebus; for her, he had chanced capture and a hanging sentence.

For her.

"When I realized you were vulnerable, that Ulrich had— " He shut his eyes and took a grieved breath. "Fear. Horrible. I never want to feel it again."

Anne stared at him, moved by what he hadn't said. He didn't tell her that he'd experienced such fright because he had feelings for her. He didn't tell her these feelings were strong and uncomfortable and new, but she heard it all the same. Like a bucket left in a storm, he had been flooded by emotions, and they had drowned him. Anne might be naïve, as he delighted in pointing out, but she understood her own emotions. "I didn't realize we were at risk."

"Do you see the danger?"

"Never again. I promise."

With a ragged breath, he tensed to stand. Before he escaped to wherever he went to hide his pain, she slid from the sofa and kneeled between his thighs. The things yet unsaid made her bold. She tugged at his wrists and removed his black gloves. Eyes red-rimmed and unfocused, he stared at her but didn't resist her touch. Anne rubbed his icy fingers, tracing the battles etched in the roughed skin of his palms.

"I've met Mr. Fontes only once. He was dashing, and I..." She took a deep breath. "And I admired him. But after we left Vila Nova, I haven't thought of him. Not even once."

He tilted his head to the side, a renewed glint in his eyes.

"Did you kiss another yesterday?" Her chin quivered, and she swallowed the tears. "The way you kissed me?"

"I went to quench the fire you created." Pedro tucked hair behind her ear, the gesture achingly sweet. "Before it burned you."

"Did it work?"

"This fire." He rubbed his chest and gazed away. "Only you can extinguish."

Anne inhaled sharply. They were in the open waters, somewhere off the coast of Portugal, but gazing at him, she was back on the precipice—the wind ruffling her hair and the fall beckoning with inexorable attraction.

"I'm sorry you witnessed Ulrich's horror today." Anne trailed her palm from his brow to his eyelids, his long eyelashes tickling her fingertips. "And I'm sorry it put a new shadow here." She placed her palm on his chest, just above his heart.

He sucked in a breath, his eyes fixed on her. A flush swept through her skin, her pulse so fast she became lightheaded. Before courage deserted her, she kissed the corner of his mouth, his close-cropped whiskers teasing her lips.

"Ana," he croaked, and she loved how boyish he looked, surprised and unsure as if she were his first sweetheart.

Lurching from the chaise, he reached for her and picked her from the floor. She went willingly, eagerly, settling on his lap, intertwining her hands around his neck. Anne breathed in his skin. Then his mouth was on hers, and when his tongue traced her lips, she welcomed him in.

Chapter 27

Pedro pulled away from her kiss. "*Me perdoa?*" Cradling her face, he peeled golden strands from her mouth and eyelashes. "Forgive me?"

Her fingertips rested against his cheek and then his chest, weightless, like feathered wings. He let her. This once, it felt right to have her hands on him. Like they belonged there.

A dainty shrug. "Done."

Pedro sagged against the recamier, bringing her close. Dusk had settled around them. An ivory lace covered the Argand lamp and filtered the light, bathing the cabin in a sleepy haze. Anne's stockings and toiletries contrasted with the golden Sèvres. Sleepers and a boot sprouted from the Gobelin he'd purchased in Paris last season. It was curious how her baubles brought life to his art. Outside, the waves rocked them, the wind too swift to be denied, propelling the yacht forward. Two days and they would cross the Nazaré underwater canyon. And then Lisbon.

"You should reconsider." Pedro closed his eyes. "There are things you—"

Her fingertip on his mouth silenced him. "I shouldn't have left, and you could've"—she frowned—"punished me, but you didn't. It's over."

"But I—"

"Must we remember it?" The wobbly smile returned, and she touched her smile to his lips.

Perched in his lap, she presumed to take command, surer than a green sailor who had never braved a storm. That he let her must be because he needed to feel lifeblood traveling inside the teal veins, pulsing beneath her translucent skin. Reverently, he kissed her eyelids, the tip of her elegant nose, her cheeks. Her tears tasted bittersweet.

He could've lost her. If not to Ulrich, then to his own shadows.

In the dimly lit cabin, against his dark clothes and the furniture's black silhouettes, Anne glowed. She was very much alive, her pliant curves warm and welcoming. Pedro lost his fingers in the silk of her hair and fused their mouths, wanting to nip, lick, devour her. She opened her lips and he explored her slowly, thoroughly, the kiss gaining intensity until his pulse pounded, and lava coursed through his veins. Pedro rained kisses down her chin, her neck, her sighs and puffs of breaths spurring him on.

She moaned, and arousal spiced the air like the sultriest of perfumes. Her first desire. Coaxed by him. His heart drummed a staccato clamor for release, for possession.

He slanted his mouth over hers, pushing his tongue inside. Without warning, she lowered her hands from his neck to his chest, her fingers trailing a path of fire.

"Ana."

"Hmm?"

He bit her lip. "You are not invisible."

Kissing her deeply, Pedro didn't allow her time to argue. If she touched him now, when his skin felt so raw, this would have to end.

While she held still, he massaged her calves, delighting in the skin prickled by goosebumps, the suppleness beneath. Drinking her sighs like the richest of wines, Pedro skimmed his hand up over her thighs, over the curves of her derriere, up inside the slit of her pantalets. The sheer cotton unveiled her core, moist for him. Her puffed breaths stilled. Undeterred, Pedro tempted her with fleeting caresses, then gentle thrusts, until her hips sought him.

She clamped her eyes shut.

He needed her to see him. "Look at me."

Anne opened her eyes, hazy like a misty morning. Her lips were parted, her skin glowing a deep rose. Pedro had never beheld a more erotic sight. He kept touching her until her stomach quivered. She gasped and hid her face in his chest.

If an army charged her cabin, it would not wrestle her from him. His soul could be damned, and he would not care as long as he gave her pleasure. "Let go for me, angel."

A sob, and she arched her back, her breasts pushing against her corset. Her tight passage clenched his finger, her release placing him at once in heaven and hell. Hissing, he pulled his hand away. While she lay languidly in his arms, a fallen angel, his breathing sounded harsh and out of control.

He stood from the recamier, bearing her slight weight, and strode to the bed. When Pedro lowered her atop the counterpane, her hair clung to him, whispering over his clothes, inviting him in. As if he needed an invitation. He would follow her to Hades.

Anne opened her arms, offering her embrace. Hope and a new light curved the bow of her lips, pressing the dimple on her cheeks, sparkling her eyes.

Panting, fists poised at the waistband of his trousers, Pedro froze. She invited him to a meadow filled with flowers and sunshine all year, no fortifications in sight, open to attack. A general's nightmare. Had he not envisioned what her absence meant to him this afternoon? She was the exposed flank of his corps, the unguarded wall of a fortress. A vulnerability he couldn't allow.

With shaky fingers, he pulled the merino wool quilt until it left only her face uncovered. Then he turned away, his gut churning. "Good night."

"Won't you stay?"

Pedro halted, staring at the cabin's door. "Would that be wise?"

"I don't want to be wise." Her words fizzled around his skin, the girlish rebellion sugary and tart.

He told himself he did her a favor. She would want a piece of his soul, she would want in, she would *want*. What could he give? Love was what she expected, and he knew nothing about love. "This was desire. Your first glimpse." Pedro shut his eyes. "It will fade."

"No, I'm sure—"

Pedro spun, facing her. "It must be a husband's privilege, not mine."

She propped herself on the bedrest, the merino pooling on her lap. "You saved me from a battle. You guided me over an abyss. You taught me how to gamble. You made me invisible. And my first kiss... all you." She gifted him her wobbling smile. "Why not this?"

Pedro closed his eyes. Every tendon, every muscle, every patch of skin demanded him to accept her invitation. "Do not offer a man more than you are willing to give."

"But I thought... I mean, between us—"

"What would you say to your perfect suitor if you went to your marriage bed deflowered?"

Playfulness gone, she wilted before his eyes. "I understand."

Chest hollow, he extended his hand, needing to hunt back the words, but she flinched as if he had attempted to strike her.

"You have made your point clearly enough." Her voice trembled like the lamplight. "Good night."

Chapter 28

S aint Anthony's Church had more flies than believers on this hot Wednesday afternoon. Below the Nossa Senhora image, the choir boys practiced the *Requiem das Lágrimas*. A falsetto voice rose above the others, mournful notes climbing the granite walls.

As a good Christian, Gabriel shouldn't stay near. A purple cloth hung from the door, and the side curtain was closed. All signs Santiago was inside, entertaining, so to speak. But what could take so long? He had already prayed to the Saint's effigy and counted the mosaic of the crosier's floor. Still, no one came out. This one must have a heavy conscience.

Gabriel tugged at the intricate knots of his neckcloth. At least one advantage of being an officer—the uniform was more practical than these bothersome civilian clothes.

The velvet curtains rustled, and a slender woman emerged. Face hidden under a black veil, she bustled past him. Before the drapery settled, he pushed inside, kneeling on the miniature pew. Stuffy and dark, the cramped space had incense and mold embedded in the scrolled oak. Why force the sinners to sit in such a depressing box? If it depended on him, he would redesign the whole concept. An open ceiling and better seating accommodations would do wonders for a man's soul.

The latticed partition wouldn't allow for visual contact, but a shuffling on the other side alerted Gabriel of his presence.

"Forgive me, Father, for I have sinned."

A heavy sigh. "When will you heed my advice, Gabriel, and just tell your father?"

Gabriel fisted his hands. "Were you not supposed to listen first, Santiago?"

"Not when your confessor already knows your sins."

"Well, not this time," Gabriel said, his voice rough.

"What changed?"

"Have you ever questioned your choice? After Mozambique? You were the regiment's best scout..."

"It was a blessing to relinquish this earth's grievances, to rise above lies and sins."

Gabriel hadn't wanted to be a soldier until he had to become one. "You are happy, then? In the church?"

"I am content. But I assume you didn't come here to speak of my vocation."

Gabriel pinched the bridge of his nose. "There were new developments in the king's attempt investigations." The recitation sounded distant and brassy. "Pedro is not guilty."

After realizing Pedro had slipped from the siege back in the north, Gabriel had gone straight to the crime scene and uncovered a trail of bribes. The witness's written confession awaited in his saddlebags to clear Pedro's name. Before he could impart the news to the king, the doomed message had arrived. Gabriel touched the crude paper and contained the impulse to rip it off.

Silence on the other side. A dry cough. "It doesn't surprise me."

"You too? I thought only my father could not believe Pedro, the great promise of our time, of any wrong-doing." Gabriel spat the words and cursed under his breath.

"When will you surmount this old hate?" Santiago chanted, the disembodied voice sounding like a warning from the heavens.

How could one forget growing up under Pedro's shadow? He'd been the best sword fighter, the best horseman, the best student... How could Gabriel compete? Pedro was better than a son—he was a godson. "I try. For the past ten years, this lie has occupied my every hour. Ten years living in fear of Father discovering, ten years pondering the effect I had on Pedro's life, ten years wishing I hadn't spoken those words."

"Then tell your father the truth."

"I can't."

Santiago exhaled loudly. "You mistake me. I always knew Pedro had a dark side, but I've read the newspaper. The shooter missed the target. Pedro wouldn't have failed."

Gabriel shifted his weight, his knees protesting the hardwood. "Do you remember how he became impossible after receiving the command of our battalion? Decided to order us like a grand marshal."

"That is Pedro Daun... But you didn't come here to chat about the past."

Gabriel shoved a hand in his hair. "Christ— "

"Don't say the lord's name in vain."

Gabriel glowered. "I am being blackmailed. If I don't confirm Pedro's accusations, my lies will be revealed. To my father."

"This is a godsend. Your father is an honorable man, and you were a boy. We all were. He will understand."

"It's not that simple."

"God is simple, and so is justice."

"If Father finds out, it would be too powerful a blow for him. I can't— "

"You blamed Pedro for a crime he didn't commit in Mozambique. Are you willing to do it again? Send an innocent man to the gallows?"

Gabriel's gut churned. "That's why I'm here."

Silence stretched. Santiago's breathing mingled with Gabriel's feet rasping the slate floor. A tired sight. "What do you want?"

"I cannot do this alone. I need your help."

"Impossible. I'm not the lieutenant of his Majesty's Hunters anymore. I wear the cloth—"

"Ulrich is in Portugal."

Santiago stopped speaking. A charged silence filled the confined space.

Gabriel's heart sped, and he leaned forward. "Listen to me. Pedro says Ulrich shot the king. I need to find the slave trader before Pedro is arrested."

The organ blared metallic notes. Rising again, the falsetto chimed a lifting Agnus Dei. When he'd been a choirboy, he had chafed at having to show up on Wednesdays and Sundays. If only he'd known how his obligations would change...

Gabriel gripped the back of the pew. "Do you think I would come here if I had any alternatives? Lives are in danger. Not only Pedro's, but he has a girl with him, an innocent girl he claims as his alibi. My blackmailer sent me a note. He wants to meet me in the new club, the Siren."

On the other side, a loud creak, and then steps clattering. A second later, the curtain was jerked open. Light invaded the confessionary. Gabriel blinked. Seeing his friend in the black cassock, even after ten years, was still a shock.

Santiago crossed his arms, glowering. No wonder the ladies chose him as their confessor. His straight posture and classic features differed from the saggy priests available elsewhere. "If I help you, it will not be to save your lies."

Gabriel rose, his thighs cramping. "I promise, after this is settled, I will—"

Santiago raised his palm. "We should have helped Pedro after we returned, but..." He sighed and glanced at his pointed black shoes. "The bishop gave me absolution, but my conscience is less forgiving."

"Pedro decided to keep away from us, to return to his father's fold."

"Still, we should have stood with him. He was an arrogant ass, but he was one of us."

"Will you help me find Ulrich?"

Santiago pointed his chin to the exit. "Not here. If you will force me to visit a brothel, at least buy me a glass of port."

Chapter 29

Anne missed the brilliant dawn. This morning, it had been just darkness turning to gray, the dismayed light oozing through the circular hatch and invading her cabin without her consent.

Inês's book rested above the tallboy, and Anne reluctantly reached for it.

Coimbra, Quinta das Lágrimas - November 1335

"Dona Inês, listen to your mother. Return to Albuquerque. It's been two months since the prince came here last. He left you alone, isolated in this godforsaken cottage. You are vulnerable. Think of the enemies you made at court."

Inês picked a hyacinth, her heart clenching around the emptiness of her lover's absence. He had a reason to be away from her. She only wished the king had not humiliated him again. Her feet crunched fall's dry leaves. Soon, winter would come. "Do you know what the hummingbird said to the hyacinth?"

"Madam, think of yourself. Think of the danger."

Inês touched the lilac petal to her lips. "The hummingbird kissed her and told her she was the loveliest flower in the garden, and winter would pass."

"I don't know why—"

"He showed her love and warmed her from within. For the first time in her life, she knew joy."

The maid harrumphed and returned to the house.

Inês looked beyond the sky cut by umbrella pines. "Return to me, love."

Anne shut the book firmly. Inês should have left the prince. Why pour her love over a man like this? If Dom Pedro loved her, he would not have left her, would he?

Anne jumped away from the bed and rummaged through her clothing, pulling skirts and bustles from the armoire. Printed cotton and striped satins piled atop the vanity, but no color matched her disposition.

Since Pedro had saved her life, he had captured the reins of this... this relationship like Saint George holding the spear. Implacable, in control, aloof. Pedro alone decided when she could come close, when she had to stay away, when she should be delighted by his presence, when she rued his nearness. When and if she could touch him. Without a by-your-leave, he became protector. He became tormentor. The man was altogether too much and... and not nearly enough.

As a child, she'd played with magnets. Trailing two gray pieces on the sides of a vellum fold, watching as they held each other. She had driven her mother insane, running around with the stones, marveling at the magic gluing them together even when something thick stood between them. When she'd flipped the sides, a perverse force had pushed the magnets apart. How could a mere change of position turn attraction into repulsion?

Anne stared at the scar on her palm. When Pedro had traced the ugly mark, she had felt his gentleness in her heart. Hadn't she glimpsed a soft side to Pedro's ruthlessness? For a perfect moment, they had bonded. But how easily he had flipped their bond.

James whined and stared at the door, pink tongue lolling.

"I'm sorry, dear. I shouldn't bemoan my fate while you need to go."

She covered her nakedness with a chemise and petticoat and settled for an ivory shirt and a chestnut skirt. What did she expect? An aristocrat with bloodlines linked to royalty wouldn't marry a foreigner, a girl with a dubious past.

She rubbed her chest, willing the pain away, and held her locket. There was only one solution—guard her heart, at least the part he hadn't yet touched.

Pedro would uncover the truth about the attempt on the king's life. She didn't doubt his cunning and persistence. How hard could it be to stay away from him during these days?

Anne braided her hair and coiled it on top of her head, the pins pricking her scalp. Straightening the velvet of her skirts, she stooped down to James and hugged her pug close. With a heavy sigh, she opened the door.

Pedro lorded over the corridor, leaning on the bulkhead, a leg bent at the knee. He had chosen a dashing black frock coat. His hair was tied, but a few envied strands were allowed to touch his face.

By the light of day, her behavior seemed incredibly wanton. A telling flush rose on her cheeks, and her legs turned weak. Anne tilted her head in a polite greeting, but before she could rush toward the ladder leading to the rear deck, Pedro stepped to the side, blocking the passage.

His eyes bore into her. "Are you well? I came to—"

"Perfectly fine, thank you." She bent her knee, the curtsy restrained by the narrow passage. "If you'll excuse me, James needs his morning constitutional."

Her tone, icy and polite, would make her former governess proud.

He startled, and she seized the opportunity to move past him. Strides constricted by her skirts, she kept going until she arrived at the narrow deck aft of the ship, where a square flowerbed had been arranged for James's toilette. A breeze poured from the sea, humid and hot. Grayish clouds hung above her head, as if threatening to fall on her any minute. The waves lashed out angrily, the ocean punishing the coast.

Pedro emerged behind her, his coat hanging from his shoulder, and rolled the sleeves of his linen shirt. He paused at the railing, his gaze lost at sea. "We'll arrive in Lisbon tomorrow."

Silence stretched uncomfortably, both staring at James as the pug left the flowerbed to sniff the mincemeat on his plate.

He cleared his throat. "After this ends, you can visit the sights—"

"That would be fantastic, thank you."

She ignored his hurt look. Why did he haunt her? The distance was for the best. According to Pedro, there was no future for them. Anne must remember the list. She grabbed her locket, but the gold brought no comfort. The qualities of her perfect suitor blurred, overly simple, and childish in the face of a man like Pedro Daun. It felt this way because of this impossible situation. When she returned home, her list would make sense again. She would be safe if she remembered Pedro's words from last night and protected her heart.

James finished his meal and padded straight to the statue-like man leaning on the railing. When she took a tentative step closer to pick James and leave the servants' deck, Pedro crouched. Her eyes widened as he petted James behind his ears, the place she knew the traitor loved, and spoke to the dog in hushed Portuguese.

Before her resolve melted, she hurried away.

"He admonished me for disobeying his orders." Anne poured tea, her lips compressed in a thin line. "Sugar?"

"Yes, please."

Cris had foregone the cravat today, another piece of gentlemen's clothing he had ignored during their travel. She was sure he would soon adopt a pirate's attire, corsair pants and some rags for a shirt. If he wore an eye patch, his flashing green eyes wouldn't probe her so.

Anne averted her glance to the windows. White foam bubbled in the yacht's wake. Near the horizon, charcoal clouds clotted together like a band of outcasts.

Cris wolfed down a pastry. "When I arrived, he had locked himself with you in the cabin. I find it hard to believe—"

"If you were so concerned, then why did I hear no one knocking on the door?"

Cris flushed and averted his gaze. It had been rude of her, but still... he shouldn't judge her if he could not stand up to his older brother. Cris and Pedro's speech was often charged with innuendos and veiled criticisms. At first, she'd thought love and loyalty bonded them, but their relationship was more complicated. The hurt she sensed simmering below the surface tied them together and ripped them apart.

"Good morning." The smoky voice made her heart jump.

Anne glared at Cris. He shrugged but mercifully dropped the questions as Pedro strolled inside, his eyes sweeping the room she had commandeered since boarding the yacht. Her things disturbed his decoration, the easel with watercolors near his prized landscape, novels scattered over the escritoire, her shawl draped over the brocade chaise. She straightened in the chair, hoping he would reprove her and ask her to remove them. But he didn't register displeasure, just frowned, perhaps surprised to find them seated at the breakfast table. He never joined her for meals, instead eating alone in his cabin.

She watched his expression from beneath her eyelashes. He had cloaked himself in a mantle of aloofness, like a lake covered with a layer of ice. How could he be so self-possessed when she lacked balance, her body alternating between shivers and cold sweats? An urge gripped her to break his composure, to throw a stone and shatter his ice, and she cringed at the ungracious thought.

Pedro raised his chin, greeting Cris. "I was looking for you."

He was after his brother, then. She should be relieved.

Circling behind her, Pedro pulled the chair at the table's head. "I've been trying to make sense of the notes we found at the bodyguard's cottage." Not sparing her a single glance, he threw a book atop the table and sprawled like a king. "The pages are innocuous, but this caught my attention."

"A telegraph?" Cris lowered his cup.

"Yes, signed by Fernando and addressed to me."

Cris squinted his eyes, intent on the strip of paper. "Blasted codes. Did you try to break it?"

Pedro raised his brows. "What do you think?"

Cris sneered and rose. "I have code keys in my cabin. I'll be right back."

Anne wanted to ask the safe brother to stay, but Cris had already crossed to the doorway. Pedro's gaze caught hers. His attention felt like a burner too close to her skin. Anne averted her eyes and picked up a pomegranate. She pressed a knife against the waxy skin, but her hand quivered, and the obstinate fruit slipped from her grasp.

Even the food conspired against her.

Clenching her hands below the table, she closed her eyes, trying to forestall humiliating tears.

Pedro seized the pomegranate. "Allow me."

"Do you think me a child? Unable to cut my food?"

He placed it in front of him, his long fingers engulfing the coral sphere. His expression belonged to a perfect statue. Had yesterday meant nothing to him?

"There is a trick." With an elegant turn of his wrist, he sliced the fruit, exposing a core filled with bright pips.

"Do you know Hades fed the seeds to Persephone when she was in the underworld? To force her to return to him every year?"

He extended his arm, offering her the pomegranate. Anne stared at his hands, the same ones that had caressed her so tenderly only to push her away. Her stomach hardened, and she crossed her arms. "He must have loved her exceedingly, wanting to keep her close."

His eyes flashed, and he lowered the plate. "Do you think the sacrifice of her freedom an act of love?"

Wasn't love supposed to be all-consuming? She glanced away, her voice faltering. "I know little about mythology."

He leaned back in the chair, a crooked smile on his lips. "I thought the British took better care of their ladies' education."

No doubt he believed her beneath him in station and breeding, a commoner and worse, a foreign hussy. Heat climbed on her cheeks, and she pushed the plate away. "We learn all that matters, Your Excellency." She drawled the honorific and cringed at her voice's bitterness.

"Ana, about last night—"

Why did he have to voice her name like that? She rose, her legs quivering like a foal's. "I've lost my appetite. Please excuse me."

"No." He stood, his height shadowing the table. "I didn't intend to ruin your meal. Have a good day."

Bowing stiffly, he turned to leave. It was better this way. He had made it clear that a future between them was impossible. Still, her chest ached at seeing him go, his neck strained, shoulders hunched.

"Wait."

Slowly, he faced her, eyes alert.

"I'm sorry. If we can't... if we can't be..." She hugged herself, the tips of her ears flaming. "We could be friends."

"Define what you mean by friends."

How like Pedro to have relationships agreed upon. Did he honestly believe she meant him harm? Anne sighed. "Friends converse and share confidences. Sometimes they pursue common interests. But above all, I think, friends care for each other in times of need."

"Talk, interests, care." He considered the matter, looking at his knee-length boots. "It is acceptable."

She forced a smile. "We are friends, then."

Pedro nodded twice and returned to the table.

Anne sank into her chair. Friendship with the Count of Almoster? The Portuguese sun had finally cooked her brains.

Cris rushed inside, his chest heaving. "I have it." He straddled a chair, comparing some brownish cards with Braganza's message.

Anne reached for the forgotten notebook. Sending a prayer for the poor man's soul, she scanned Braganza's handwriting. Sonnets, odes, and free verses occupied the lines. A few were copied from Luis Gama, a former Brazilian slave. Others were signed by the deceased man himself. Those had a recurring theme—freedom and the absence of it.

Cris shoved his papers away and grimaced. "The code is unbreakable. With the bodyguard killed, how will we ever prove your innocence? We are back at the beginning, aren't we? I expected answers. Jesus, Pedro, I... I can't stay locked up here."

Anne's shoulders sagged, and she closed her eyes. She, too, would not survive Pedro's presence forever.

"*Fique calmo.*" Pedro clasped his brother's shoulder. "We'll sail to Lisbon. Since our lead proved fruitless, we will find others in the capital. I will access my contacts there."

Pedro sounded confident, but a crease marred his forehead, and a tick pulsed on his jaw. She couldn't help but wonder if his reassurance was warranted or meant to calm Cris.

"Braganza was your only true friend. Your political pawns can't be trusted. They will sell you to the highest bidder." Cris pushed his cup away, splashing tea over the table, and gripped his own hair.

Cris's desperation sank into her chest. Lives were at risk—hers, Pedro's, and the royal family's. The frail paper with the scrabble of letters was their only hope. She had never seen a coded message, but she was skilled in games and riddles. "May I have a look?"

Cris raised his palms. "Dear, you'll burden your-self—"

"Yes," Pedro cut in, passing her the telegraph.

Anne leaned back in the chair, staring at the rectangular strip of paper. Instead of words, there were duos of numbers. At the bottom, the title Braganza. A tiny marking at the top caught her attention, not in the black typo of the telegraph but in pencil.

"What does this mean?" she asked.

Pedro pulled his chair near, his breathing ruffling her hair. "Where?"

"Here. Could it be IdC?"

He came closer, his cedar scent challenging her concentration. "It's faint. I missed it."

A smile transformed his face. Heat infused her at his admiration, and she shook her head, focusing on the lines. The first numbers of the pair ranged from forty to one hundred and ninety, while the second didn't surpass thirty-eight. She left the telegraph and flicked through the notebook's pages. "The Duke of Braganza was an abolitionist."

A pained look crossed Pedro's face. "Fernando fought for curbing illegal slave trading in the African colonies."

His unresolved grief pained her, but she controlled the impulse to place her hand above his, knowing he would not welcome her comfort. "Enough to die for it?"

"Do you think Braganza may have died for the cause?" Pedro rose from the table and paced to the hatch. He stared at the glass as if trying to find answers overboard. His chest expanded and contracted forcefully. Which shadow haunted him? Without warning, he whirled. "You are right. Braganza's killing was no accident. Fernando battled slavery by investigating illegal shipments from the colonies and pushing for harsher laws. This is the link we missed between the attack and Ulrich's involvement. The slave trader *wanted* to kill Fernando."

Cris frowned. "Why shoot the king, then? Why not simply eliminate his brother?"

"If Ulrich went directly to Fernando, it would shed light on his activities. Think, brother. He eliminated the single voice against slave trading and masked it with the gravest crime in a kingdom. The *coup de man* would be brilliant if he did not use me as the scapegoat."

While they discussed, Anne forced her mind from the hateful subject, turning to the message.

"IdC," she said, gliding her finger over the curved letters. She cast her mind to what she had learned of

Fernando, and her eyes widened. "The book! You told me your friend asked you to bring Inês's story to the Douro. IdC must stand for Inês de Castro."

Chapter 30

Pedro paced the yacht's library, forcing himself to keep away from his table where Anne wrestled with the code. He should leave her alone instead of hovering around her under this friendship disguise. If he had an ounce of character, he would be on the command bridge, overseeing the underwater canyon's cross, allowing her to forget her temporary attachment to him. But how could he keep away? Concentrating, Anne looked like Calliope, the muse of poetry. The afternoon sun reflected on the desk's travertine top and glinted off her skin, forgetting the rest of the library.

Through the glass panes, the sea rippled with shallow waves. The wind was behind them, and soon they would sail the underwater canyon. The captain was seasoned. He could manage without him.

Pedro yawned and leaned on the curved shelves. The code had not kept him awake all night, but Anne. Each time the clock had struck the hour, he had stared at her closed door, wanting to accept her invitation. Only his iron self-control had kept him outside.

Anne tapped the pen on a sheet of paper. "I think the first number of each pair stands for the page and the second for the line. It will take a while, but I believe I can translate Braganza's message."

Could she? After Pedro and Cris had failed? He had his doubts. But he would support her. The last thing he wanted was to discourage her. "Have you finished reading his book? Inês's story?"

A pleat appeared on her forehead, and she caressed the page. "I've read until Dom Pedro left Inês alone in a cottage in the middle of nowhere. After he seduced her, he abandoned her there so her presence in court wouldn't offend his wife and father."

"He had his reasons for—"

"No reason justifies sacrificing her happiness."

Her vehemence struck him in the chest, the hurt of the night before shining in her eyes. He wanted to soothe her pain, to give her what she desired. But Dom Pedro's inability to stay away from Inês had doomed her. If he had resisted their attraction, Inês would have lived. Everything in Anne was delicate, hands made for caresses, not swords, her body made for nurturing, not fighting. Eyes that couldn't see evil, even when evil lay within her finger's reach. Her life was too fleeting. How had Dom Pedro survived after his Inês had been brutally stolen from him?

"Inês was not the only one who suffered from their impossible love. After his father sentenced her to death, the prince waged war against the old king. For months, he trod the line between lucidity and madness. Died alone. He had the worst side of the bargain."

"I find it hard to believe."

Pedro stared at her defiance, and the verses came tumbling out of his mouth.

"Cloud the air,

Stop guitar,
Die, heart,
Inês is dead,
Wretched spouse,
Cease the sorrow,
For your tomorrow,
Is no longer yours."

Their eyes locked. He could swear she saw right through him. As if the Gyges ring had given her the power to see invisible things. The lies, the fortress he had built around himself, the truth of why he had rejected her last night. He stopped breathing, waiting for her to call his bluff. He wouldn't be able to resist her a second time.

But she glanced away, a sad smile on her beautiful lips. "A great musician and a poet. You surprise me with your talents."

Pedro released a pent-up breath. "The verses are not mine. They are Bocage's. The best Portuguese poet after Camões."

"Have you read Camões?" Her long, slender fingers wrapped around his fountain pen. Yesterday, those hands had clung to his neck. How would her explorations feel on his skin? Not agony. Not with Anne.

"Who didn't? When I was eight, I wanted to be his Vasco da Gama. Embark on the Odysseus-like adventure to find a route to the Indies. I knew several stanzas by heart. And when I was fifteen..." Pedro closed his eyes, remembering the old tutor, a bohemian poet with a fuzzy white mustache and ruddy nose, reciting the rousing lines, teaching him their hidden meaning.

"When you were fifteen?"

Pedro shrugged. "The Lusiad's patriotism inspired me. I foolishly believed I could help the country regain its past glories."

"I don't think patriots are foolish."

"You wouldn't." Too many years had passed since he had dreamed those glory-filled dreams. How different from the plans he had pursued. His political games, as Cris called them. Pedro cleared his throat. "I thought proper ladies were taught Camões in the schoolroom."

"Not English ones. Griffin banished Portuguese authors. You know how he was, at least before Julia."

Pedro could not say he did, and turned from her lest she saw the lie on his face. For the first time, her brother's name didn't make his gut clench in hate. What would she do if she discovered the truth of his past with Maxwell?

"What's wrong? You can tell me. We are friends, remember?"

He wondered if friends lied to each other. "More friendship rules? This wasn't on your list."

She gave him a mock scowl that wouldn't scare a toddler. "Rules? I meant those as general guidelines. You don't seriously believe there are rules to being friends."

"English love their rules."

She raised her brows, a mischievous grin on her lips. "You are awfully talkative today. If you want me to decipher this, you better hush."

Pedro looked heavenward, feigning exasperation. Waves pummeled the hull, spraying the glass. He breathed in the brine, the chill helping to keep sleep at bay. A trio of cormorants flew east, to shore. Pedro searched the sky. Cirrus clouds raced across his line of vision, white strips up high, their feathery tails flickering. As if to confirm the changing weather, the bow dipped in the lull after a four-foot wave, and the hull groaned.

Anne ignored the lurch and concentrated on her task. She scribbled with the pen. She tapped the edge of the table with the pen. She frowned in great concentration at the pen, but when she bit the pen with her dewy lips, Pedro wanted to break the pen in two.

"How much longer will you take?" Pedro asked, his voice gruff.

"Not long."

Grunting, he stretched on the couch. The knife wound protested the position, and he shifted. Anne hummed the *Rosas Flores* melody. Her voice made his eyelids close. The clock ticked away the minutes, then the hour.

"Pedro?"

He blinked awake, rising with a start.

She stood beside the chaise, a sheet of paper in her hand. "Oh, you were resting. I'm sorry. Here it is, but I confess, the content—"

"What?" He took the piece from her, unable to register the words' meaning. "You succeeded?"

He had spent several hours last night staring at the telegraph, comparing it to each code key he had, as Cris had this morning. Both had failed, while Anne had done the impossible.

"Why, yes. You thought—?"

Pedro didn't allow her to finish. Heart speeding, he grabbed her waist and lifted her high.

She laughed, the sound slightly out of breath. "Don't you want to hear the message?"

He lowered her slowly, her body brushing against his, and she blinked several times, her eyelashes fluttering.

He grinned. "Your wit astounds me."

"Oh, it was nothing." Cheeks glowing red, she bit her bottom lip.

"It was much more than nothing." He dropped his arm, the page forgotten. "Why won't you accept my praise?"

She pulled away from the cage of his arms. "Pride is one of the deadly sins. I—"

Pedro scoffed. "Just because an old priest deemed it a dangerous emotion?" If Anne wasn't proud of her accomplishment, he was enough for both of them. "Religion is fickle about what is supposed to be a sin. The Greeks were right to call pride a virtue."

The warmth of her skin seeped into his shirt. He wanted more.

"But... isn't it unbecoming for a young lady to display something other than humility?"

He would like her to display much more than humility. "The opposite of pride is not humility, but shame. Pride has its virtues. It is deserved. It is decadent. It is your due. Don't shy from it. I forbid you to feel ought but prideful."

"Why, if you have the power to dictate one's feelings..." She curtsied and then dazzled him with a smile full of dimples and white teeth. "It was pretty marvelous, wasn't it?"

Pedro thought so, too, more than he cared to admit. "That it was, Ana. That it was."

They found Cris lounging at the parlor, a Figaro magazine forgotten on his knees.

"Anne solved the code."

"Really?" Cris's glance shifted from him to Anne, his voice slurring. "And what does it say?"

Pedro narrowed his eyes at his brother. Cris usually held his liquor. But he read Anne's flourishing calligraphy for all to hear. "All my findings are close to my hero's grave. Third pew." He lowered the paper. "Fernando must be speaking of Dom Pedro's tomb. Both the King and Inês were buried in Alcobaça. The monastery is only a few miles from Lisbon."

Cris flung the magazine. It landed on the coffee table, upsetting a half-empty bottle of brandy. "Another stupid clue? We are chasing our tails."

A wave jostled the boat, and Anne stumbled. Pedro steadied her with an arm around her shoulders and escorted her to the divan opposite his brother. When he sat beside her, she searched his eyes, her face pale.

Pedro pressed her hand in reassurance. "Just a rough sea."

Cris stared at their joined hands. "Since you are in such a great mood, why don't you go to your godfather? Ask for his help?"

Pedro crossed his arms. "What if Fontes is involved?"

Cris scoffed. "You cannot be serious."

"Everyone is capable of evil, given the right incentive."

"But your godfather?" Cris raised his palms. "When will you put Mozambique behind us? It hazes your judgment."

Pedro gritted his teeth, his gaze straying to see Anne's reaction to Cris's careless words. "Careful, brother. You are allowing the brandy to speak for you."

"Mozambique?" Anne placed a hand on his shoulder, and the touch burned him to the bone.

Pedro glared at his brother. "Cris will return to his cabin."

Cris rose unsteadily. "I won't be shut up this time. Fontes wasn't responsible. Why not ask for his assistance?"

Since when had asking for help served him? After Mozambique, at the most excruciating time of his life, Fontes had shut the door in Pedro's face.

"Anne, you are so high in his regard. Try to sweeten him. Our Pedro here must be made to understand. But don't raise your hopes. The position as Pedro's advisor is short-lived." Shoulders hunched, Cris retrieved his brandy tumbler.

Anne stood, raising her hands placatingly. "Cris, please, I don't wish to intrude."

Why had Anne become the target of Cris's barbs? His derision clearly made her uncomfortable. And drunk, he might blurt out things better left buried in the past. "He doesn't mean it. Right, Cristiano?"

The parlor shook as the yacht lurched. The hatch swung inward, and a gush of wind swept inside. Anne gasped, and Pedro brought her close to his side. With a clash, the bottle fell, spilling alcohol over the table and dripping onto the polished floor.

Cris lost his footing and held the wall for balance. "Jesus!"

Pedro strode to the hatch. Water spattered the glass panes. Outside, a light blinked two seconds on, one second off. He went cold. The lighthouse atop São Miguel Arcanjo's Fort. What the hell was the captain doing? They were nearing the shore, too close to Nazare's giant waves.

Pedro glanced at Anne, but she seemed too affected by Cris's diatribe to register the altered sea. At least she wouldn't grasp what the flickering light meant.

Cris sobered, his eyes alert. "What do you want me to do?"

"Escort Anne to her cabin and meet me on the bridge."

The ocean churned, waves swaying the *Dawn Chaser*, threatening to expose her keel. Swells of fifteen feet rose from the indigo surface, their foam-covered heads exploding against the hull and quarterdeck. Gunmetal clouds swallowed the sun, soaking the command room in shadows. Dante rushed to light two gas lamps, his bare arms carrying more markings than the charts spread on the table.

Pedro swept his eyes over the travel log, zeroing in on the mistake. He slammed the compass on the scarred desk. "Your dead reckoning is biased, Oliveira. You missed by a league."

And that explained why, instead of sailing a safe distance from the shore, they risked being awash by Nazare's waves. The captain's face blanched. Stepping away from the steering wheel, he covered his mouth as a dry cough shook his torso. Pulling in a breath, Oliveira justified himself, but Pedro ignored his feeble excuses.

"You can retire. I'll assume command."

Captain Oliveira raised his bushy brows. "But, Your Excellency, I may be of assistance."

Assist them in meeting the bottom of the sea? Pedro shut his eyes and exhaled forcefully. The old man was not entirely to blame. If Pedro had been on the bridge instead of spending the afternoon enjoying Anne's pr esence...

Even now, the impulse to run to her cabin and assure himself of her safety twisted his chest. But to pull them out of this, he needed total focus.

"Indeed, you can help." Pedro narrowed his eyes. "Make sure those not on watch stay inside, especially Miss Maxwell. Under no circumstance is she to leave her quarters. Better yet, ask Beatriz to sit with her. This time, Oliveira, I'll not admit failings."

Pedro didn't wait to see the man stumble out of the threshold. Gripping the helm with both hands, he raised his voice above the waves' low-pitched roar. "Dante, tell the boatswain to rig the storm sail and reef the rest. We'll heave to. Keep the crew on a two-hour rotation. I don't want them exhausted and failing their tasks."

"Yes, sir." The Italian saluted and left.

Pedro turned to the twin deckhands. "Hook the horses to the hammocks. Cinch the cloth close to their elbows." If the beasts thrashed around without support, they could break their legs. "Stay there. If I catch sight of either of you on the quarterdeck, you'll wish the ocean washed you away."

Glancing down, their pimpled-ridden cheeks bright red, they bobbed their heads and rushed out.

Cris crossed his arms. "They are good boys."

"Yes. And I want them living boys."

His brother grunted. "Must we face the weather? Wouldn't it be better to lie ahull?"

"Not for this. If we reef all sails and drift, the swell will capsize the *Dawn Chaser*. Our only chance is to keep the bow ahead, perpendicular to the waves."

Pedro steered leeward, gazing beyond the iron-reinforced glass panes. Lightning flared, followed by the rumble of thunder. Sea and rain merged in a gray vortex of air and water. Not long ago, Pedro would have relished nature's gauntlet, keen to prove his might against the ocean's power. If he survived, he would emerge as the victor and prove himself better. If he lost... well, there were worse ways to heed heaven's recall.

But not anymore. She had changed everything. Pedro couldn't fathom a place where Anne wouldn't also be. He now understood Maxwell's plight. The same fear that had twisted Maxwell's face back in the Douro swam ice cold in Pedro's stomach.

Pedro, too, had something to lose.

A wave hit the yacht's broadside, and he braced himself to avoid losing his grasp on the wheel.

Cris paced around the cramped cabin, gait wobbled by the heaving deck, and crossed himself. "What have we done to anger the ocean? Not natural. More like the work of demons."

"Nothing mystic about this." Pedro removed his coat and rolled up his shirt sleeves. "Below, there's a chasm. Some say over three miles deep. It magnifies the size and speed of the waves as they approach the coast, creating these behemoths."

They were already too close to shore, the lighthouse blinking at them ominously.

"What do you want me to do?"

"Watch the wings. Call my attention if you see a breaker."

Cris nodded, sweat glistening on his forehead, and positioned himself to the left, his broad shoulders spanning the iron hatch. So far, they had faced large but not breaking waves. Dante screamed orders on the quarterdeck, his voice rising above the maniacal wind. The crew reefed the mainsails, and the jib soared. Canvas sheets and cordage writhed and twitched like kites. The *Dawn Chaser's* speed decreased by a knot, but the steering was lighter.

A massive wave rose, the blue hill coming straight at them.

"Brace yourself, brother. Here comes the first."

This one topped twenty feet. The bridge swung, a giant seesaw, bow plunging deep and ricocheting up toward the sky. Cris had a point. They rode the heaving breaths of Poseidon.

Pedro sought the smooth water. They passed the summit and gained a few degrees away from shore, from the canyon. He exhaled and cracked his knuckles, sore from the tight clasp on the handles.

Cris cleared his throat, his eyes sparkling like a child's. "After we clear your name, we should go away for a spell. It's aways hot in Ilhéus. Do you remember the Bataclan? Best bawdy house in the world, not the prudish sort we have here."

The thought of a Brazilian city with more humidity than morals had the same appeal as letting the shadows consume him. For once, Pedro wanted to stay in one place, do other than war, other than destroy. "You should go."

Frowning, Cris stared at the ocean. "Do you have a better plan?"

A lull allowed him some respite, and he released the helm, rubbing his fingers. Numbness spread from the first knuckle to his wrist, but his arms hurt like a bitch. "My plan is to survive this night."

Through it all, Pedro steered. Cris brought coffee, and he gulped it down between waves. At some point, Dante offered to take his place, but he refused. The weight of Anne's life and everyone else's rested on his shoulders.

Cris gasped. "Are you seeing this?"

"Barely." His eyes were gritty as if salt had found a way inside.

An overblown wave billowed ahead—a massive glass wall streaked by white veins.

Leaning closer to the hatch, Pedro sucked in a breath. "Brother, if we can't reach the other side of this one, I want you to take Ana to the lifeboat."

"It is Ana now? What a sweet Portuguese endearment. What's next? You will forget who her brother is? You should see yourself. Drooling all over the floor she walks. Can't you see where this is going? Soon you will become obsessive, like when you wasted ten years to marry Julia."

"It is different with Anne."

"Different how?"

For Julia, Pedro had felt a platonic, pure emotion. For Anne, he felt a whole maelstrom of them. But that was not all. Unlike Julia, Anne wanted him in return. "She is our guest, and you will treat her with common courtesy."

"You won't listen, will you? It will be left to me to clean up your mess when this farce explodes in your face."

"You have my orders."

"You own my loyalty." Cris pointed his finger at Pedro's chest. "Not her."

Christ, didn't he realize this was not about loyalty? What was loyalty but an empty word compared to the generous angel aboard this ship? "If by loyalty you mean the debt from Mozambique, you owe me nothing."

"You won't forget I left my post, will you?"

Pedro stared straight ahead, unable to face Cris. His brother was right. Pedro could not swallow it. Why had he not stayed at his bivouac that night? Straggling down the wharf, drunk, Cris had been easy prey.

"You should have let Ulrich cut my throat."

"I don't have time for your drama."

"And they say I am the bastard." Cris laughed bitterly and barreled out of the cabin.

Grinding his jaw, Pedro gazed ahead. The melted mountain neared, the summit rising endlessly. It grew, it swelled, it bulged. At the crest, so high as to overshadow the *Dawn Chaser*, foam burst like powdered chalk.

The swell couldn't sustain such heights. This one would break, and them with it.

The roar was deafening. As the ocean rose, the current pulled them inexorably to the wave's hollow. Pedro steered leeward, searching for a smooth entry away from the breaking point. Wind swelled the rig and propelled them upward on the wave's wall. The gray giant was endless, the yacht but a speck. His legs tingled, and a knell clanged in his ears, obliterating other sounds.

Aft, too close, the wave erupted —a volcano. Spray speckled the windshield. The deck inclined precariously. They were almost at the summit. Either they crossed, or they plummeted, a heap of wood and steel straight to the ocean's depths. Pedro felt the engine's strength faltering in his gut. They needed more steam. He grasped the engine telegraph, but the boat heaved violently. Pedro crashed to the floor, grunting as pain exploded on his side.

He called Cris, but there was no answer. He was alone.

Unattended, the steering wheel spun on its axis, out of control. The yacht's bow swung aft, straight toward the wave's breaking point.

Cursing, he crawled to the telegraph and hefted the marker from HALF AHEAD to FULL. The engine's screw responded, increasing the yacht's steam power. Struggling to his feet, Pedro wrestled the spinning helm to a stop, the muscles of his shoulders burning. With a grunt, he adjusted the steering angle. They resumed the climb.

Only a few yards more.

Time stopped, the wind hushed, a suspended moment of stasis where they were weightless, balancing, poised over a landscape of gray-blue hills and swirling white.

And then it was over. With a last surge, the yacht ascended to the crest.

Pedro descended the ladder to the companionway, splaying his hands on the hull to keep upright, the wound at his side throbbing with each step. The corridor gas lamps spread phantom fingers over the bulkhead. Beyond overturned furniture, the storm had caused no structural damage, but there would be time for repairs tomorrow. He needed a bed. Eyes closing against his will, he ambled to the main cabin.

A whine, high and mournful, pierced the silence.

Pedro rubbed his eyes and straightened. Anne's dog.

The whining sounded again, followed by scratching.

Gut clenching, Pedro sped to her cabin and knocked. Nothing.

He tested the knob. Locked.

Holding the latch to avoid hitting the dog, Pedro slammed his shoulder into the door. Once, twice, it gave way on the third try.

Inside, there was darkness. Her neroli fragrance wasn't there, just the sour scent of vomit.

The dog shuffled close, pawing Pedro's leg, its bark feeble. Pedro stepped on the carpet, boots crunching broken ceramic. The bed was empty, the recamier overturned. Where was she?

Unable to fill his lungs, he raced to the opposite wall. Her slight frame crouched near the hatch, knees bent, face hidden in her palms.

Pedro dropped to his knees beside her. "Anne?"

Desperate to rouse her, he tapped her cheeks. She didn't move, her skin clammy, her hair grimy and plastered around her shoulders and face. Pedro peeled away the matted strands. Her eyes, glazed, didn't acknowledge him. After a battle, a few soldiers became paralyzed, fear and shock sinking them into oblivion.

Wanting to pull her up, to shake her, he grabbed her hand, but she flinched. Her fingers bled.

"What happened?" He lifted her chin. "Talk to me."

Again, no response. Pedro sagged against the wall. The weight of a cannon bore down on his shoulders, and he closed his eyes, dropping his head at the bulkhead.

James rested his head over his thigh, his bright eyes pleading.

Pedro petted the mutt's ears. "You are a faithful guardian, are you not? All ten inches of you. You are no longer a corporal. I promote you to brigadier." Rubbing his eyes, Pedro shook himself. "I'll take care of her."

Panting, he lifted Anne, one arm around her torso, the other under her knees. His back and shoulders burned under the strain, her familiar weight too heavy tonight. He exited to the companionway, James following close.

Kicking his cabin door open, he carried her inside. They needed a bath. Then sleep.

His hands shook when he opened the faucet. Hot water poured from the shower, soaking his arm and misting the air. Thank God the pipes had not been damaged. Pedro unhooked the buttons of her shirt, but she batted his fingers aside. Her large pupils didn't seem to register his presence.

"Shh. Let me take care of you."

Hands falling limply to her sides, she leaned on the wall, mouth pressed into a thin line. With efficient gestures, Pedro peeled away the clothes but decided against removing her shift. Her skin was freezing. Breathing heavily, he wrestled away his shirt and tugged her into the shower. Under the warm spray, her skin regained color, but still, she wouldn't look at him, her gaze fixed on the tiles lining the wall. Ever since they'd met, she had never failed to respond to him, and her insensibility raked at his chest.

"What horrors have you traversed, angel?" Pedro's voice echoed in the bathroom.

No reply came.

She would get better. She had to. No room for despair.

He needed to make her comfortable. Pedro enveloped her in a towel and brushed her limbs. Averting his eyes to her nakedness, he removed the wet chemise and dressed her in one of his shirts. It fell below her knees, engulfing her in white cotton. Her locket shone, a heart-shaped lamp carrying her secrets. His hand tingled to open it, but he restrained himself. He had no right.

After shoving his legs in Cossack's trousers, he guided her to the bed. While he treated the cut on her forefinger, she stared at the merino covers, her shoulders wilted like a wounded doe.

With a heavy breath, he brought her a glass of brandy. "You will feel better."

He touched the chalice to her bleached lips, and she sipped. A cough racked her chest. He tried again, but she pushed the glass away.

"No more." Her voice rasped as if she had screamed her throat raw.

"Please."

She drank, holding the cup with two hands, and when he took the glass from her, she closed her eyes. She was too quiet. He hated seeing her fingers poised above her knees, immobile and hurt. The dim light cast shadows below her eyelashes, and even pale, her skin glimmered with an ethereal glow. Before his eyes, she wavered, incorporeal as a vision. What if his angel faded?

Unable to breathe, Pedro cradled her face and touched his lips to her forehead. "*Meu amor, volta.* Come back to me."

She opened her eyes as if released from a nightmare and took a ragged breath. A single tear left the corner of her eye, a silvery trail flickering in the cabin's tired light.

"Pedro?"

Embracing her as if he held the substance of light, he brushed the tear away. "I'm here."

"Locked." She sobbed. "Inside. The waves... I thought you dead."

Chin trembling, she stared at her hands, at the scraped skin and broken nails.

She had gone through the waves alone? Buried in her cabin? A roar rumbled in his throat. Pedro should have asked Cris to bring her to the bridge. With a shaking breath, he embraced her. He hadn't much comfort in him, but whatever he had, he vowed to give her.

After a heavy exhale, she sagged against him, but the sobbing ceased. "He locked the door. Why would he do that?"

Pedro shifted on the bed to face her, his gut tightening. "The captain?"

Her gaze dropped. With a finger below her chin, he brought it back to him. She nodded.

Pedro gripped the bedpost with enough force to rip the wood. "I asked Oliveira to see that you stayed inside. The *pulha* locked you in. I'll have him flogged."

She gasped and covered her throat. "No. Please, no. Don't leave me."

Pedro stared at the wreckage of his cabin and then at the girl wrecked on his bed. He shut his eyes, counting his rasping breaths. Rage would have to wait. He pulled the bed coverings. "I won't. Try to sleep."

She crawled over the white sheets. Her breaths were silent, tranquil, her cheeks regaining color. Her hair fanned over the bed coverings. Pedro deposited James at the bed's foot. The dog chased his tail once and dropped to sleep. He had done well this night and deserved his rest.

A heavy sigh escaped Pedro's lungs, and he circled to the bed's side and lifted the counterpane.

Anne gazed at him, a frown lining her forehead. "Friends don't share a bed, Pedro."

He yawned. "Can we resume friendship in the morning? We'll just sleep."

She closed her eyes. "I... I can't understand what is between us anymore."

"There's nothing to understand." Pedro lifted his arms wide and dropped them at his sides. "You need me. I am here."

After what she had gone through, his company would be better than staying alone.

"I cannot come back and forth like this." She hugged the pillow. "It's too painful."

She was wary of him. Could he blame her? After he had told her they had no future? A better man would bunk elsewhere. Still, they had been one wave short of being buried in the ocean. She had been one wave short of being buried alone in her cabin.

He shoved a hand through his hair. "Christ, Anne, I need you too."

Her eyes widened, and she stared at him.

He waited, counting the rises and falls of her chest. The boat rocked to and fro, the sea settling after the storm.

She scooted to the left, opening a space for him. It was twenty inches of linen and down. It was the best gift he had ever received.

Groaning, he stretched on the bed, muscles melting over the mattress. Anne hid her face on the pillow, the tip of her ear cherry-red. At least a hand separated them. Pulse racing, he scooped her close, pillowing her head on his chest. She startled, a weightless butterfly fluttering on his side.

"Sleep, nothing more." His voice was husky.

After a moment's hesitation, she acquiesced, her cheek settling on his chest, her weight covering him like a blanket. Pedro moved his shoulder and adjusted her head away from the old wound at his collarbone. Sharing a bed made his sword arm useless. Her chin poked his ribcage, and her hair was all over him, tickling his neck. He buried his nose in the fragrant strands, inhaling her essence, now merged with his. It was new, but good. They fit. Her shivering stopped and her heart slowed, soon matching his rhythm.

"I didn't know you were alone." He sifted his fingers through her hair, the strands still damp. "If I had known—"

"The cabin was dark. I couldn't find the lamps. I rattled the door, but water hit the hatch. Over and over. As if I was inside the clipper again."

Pedro stilled. "When were you inside a clipper?"

"A long time. But the memories... they haunt me still."

"Tell me."

She exhaled. "When we left London, I was six. Our cabin was way below. There were no windows. One night, I woke up to screaming, wood groaning, thunder. I called my mother, my brother, but no one came. I tried to open the door, but I couldn't. Later, Mother said I locked myself inside. I screamed and got sick all over the floor. Afterward, I couldn't sleep alone until we arrived in Oporto."

Had her family traveled in steerage? When Pedro had uncovered Maxwell's past, he had found only his success in turning a small trading firm into one of the largest in Oporto. He had assumed they had been born in wealth.

"Why did you come to Portugal on such a ship?"

She stiffened. "It's too painful. I—"

"Shh. Say no more." Pedro rubbed her shoulder, and she relaxed again.

"Thank you." She lifted her hand to his cheek.

The movement was too sudden, and he jerked, unable to restrain the instinctive reaction.

She yanked her hand back as if he had burned her. "I'm sorry."

She shifted to the side. It was only an inch, but he felt it on his chest, on his legs, her absence, the skin now cold. She didn't ask for an explanation, and her silence was somehow worse. She didn't feel he owed her anything. Not even words.

"I never could bear it." He exhaled. "Others touching my skin."

"Not even someone close? A caregiver?"

"My father forbade it. He thought touch would make me weak." All his adult life, he had blamed his aversion to a physical condition, but the truth had always hovered within his grasp. "Only for punishment."

"I wish... I wish you didn't despise my touch."

Didn't she realize her voice caressed him?

"Anne." Her name tasted like a quiet prayer. He should warn her away from him, not encourage her. "Your touch. It singed my skin, but not with pain."

He kissed her hand and placed it over his heart. Pedro waited for his skin to crawl, but the aversion never came. Not with her. There was nothing erotic in her touch. No pain, no desire, no greed. Just warmth.

Water dripped on the hatch, punctuated by the hissing gas lamps.

"Do you know how the church says when a person," she swallowed, "ends her own life, she won't go to heaven? Do you believe it?"

"I must believe all are bound to the same place, angel."

"My father... he killed himself." Her pained breath spread over his chest. "I should have helped. Prevented it. But I wasn't attentive enough. I wasn't listening."

He searched her face. Where did she hide such grief? She didn't possess a trace of hardness or bitterness. As gently as he could, he traced her heart-shaped scar, wondering if it still pained her. "You were but a child."

Chin trembling, she shook her head. "Griffin believed Father thought only of himself when he left us behind, but he was wrong. That morning, Mother asked me to cheer him up, but I didn't go. If I had not left him alone, he would be here. You were right. I'm not truly noble. Deep down, I'm selfish."

Eyes moist and red-rimmed, she sighed. Pedro stared at the bulkhead, exhaling through his mouth. He knew guilt's faces intimately, knew how it consumed a person's joy. Unlike him, she had no reason to carry such a burden.

"Your father's problems must have loomed higher than the giant waves we crossed today. Otherwise, he wouldn't have left you."

She lifted shimmering eyes to him. "You think?"

If he had one certainty in this world, it was this. Anne's nobility shone brighter than any star. Pedro tucked hair under her ear. "I know."

She smiled that wobbly smile that was hers alone, and then she sighed, a deep sigh that emerged from her soul. She gazed at him as if... as if he was the man he was meant to be.

Pedro's breath caught, and he dove into her eyes. The Atlantic depths accepted him. The restlessness, the vise roping his lungs, ruptured. One thread snapped, then the other. Pedro inhaled, letting her acceptance fill him, willing it to last.

God, it felt good to be that man.

He placed her palm over his chest, where his heart beat, and brought her flush against him, trapping her hands between them.

Outside, the waves quieted. Anne's breathing turned even, soft bursts of air over his skin. Pedro joined her in Orpheus's realm, confident sleep would bring no nightmares.

Chapter 31

Their small party rode over the chalky path, the clatter of hooves buffed by acacias lining the road. A soft breeze rustled through the fernlike leaves and cottony blooms, exhaling a sweet, jasmine-like scent. Hemera fought with the bridle, wanting to stretch her legs after so many days confined. Anne didn't care, the jarring impact of the trot infinitely better than the languid rocking of the *Dawn Chaser*. The azure sky had pushed yesterday's storm into the past. All had survived, and the memories of the waves would fade.

Hemera tugged the reins from her hands. The jerk made the leather rasp on Anne's injuries, and she flinched. The salve had done wonders, but it still hurt. Her days with Pedro, and especially the nights, had brought to light a surprise. A warrior who could also heal?

Pedro had mended more than her fingers with whispered words in the dark of his cabin.

He rode by her side, his posture straight, carrying aloofness like a mantle. By now, she was familiar with his moods. He was preoccupied. She couldn't blame him. So much rested on his shoulders. The need to search for Braganza's evidence and the situation with his brother.

"It's my fault, isn't it? Cris's departure?"

A heavy exhale. "You are not the reason for our dis-agreement."

The usually cheerful, boastful brother had left after they'd disembarked this morning, cantering away with-out a goodbye.

Anne fidgeted with Hemera's mane. "Does it have to do with Mozambique?"

Pedro glanced away from her, ostensibly to inspect the horizon. A sudden rustling in the bushes made Ere-bus prick his ears and dance to the side. Whispering in Portuguese, Pedro quieted the stallion. "How are your hands?"

Anne raised her brows. "Just fine, thank you."

She let the matter drop. For now. Were they not friends? How could a friend watch another suffer from a sore in the past and not try to relieve it? What could have happened between the brothers so far away, so long ago, and still carry such weight in their lives? With any luck, she could ease his burden after they arrived at his villa.

Anne peeked at him from below her eyelashes. "You owe me a lesson on Lusitanos."

"What do you wish to know?"

"The English thoroughbreds are bred for racing. What are the gifts of the Lusitano?"

"War and bullfights. The Lusitano has innate courage and obedience. Both traits needed to face a raging bull or charge a plain stormed by heavy artillery."

"I thought they didn't use horses in bullfighting," Anne said, pronouncing the detested sport with distaste.

"The original *corrida de touros* is performed by horse-men. But in Spain, the Bourbons forbade the aristoc-racy from it. It became a sport for the masses, done on foot. But Portuguese nobility kept on as before, and the *matador* still rides a horse."

"Do they train horses for such brutality?"

"No. The Lusitano knows instinctively how to corner the bull."

They were knee to knee, and her mare bumped his stallion's flank. Their names fit them. With her lily-white coat and long, frizzy mane, Hemera was the perfect Goddess of Light. Erebus, the God of Dark-ness, was raven-black and exuded magnetic energy.

Anne patted the mare's neck. "Do you have her off-spring with Erebus back at the coudelaria?"

Pedro eyed her as if she had spoken blasphemy. "No."

"That's a pity. I would love to see a colt with Hemera's gentleness and Erebus's fire."

"Erebus is a warhorse. He would hurt Hemera. She is too valuable, bought from the king, directly from the Alter Real Stud—"

"When she is near, he's calm and happy. Plus, you gave her to me, remember? Shouldn't I have a say in this?"

"You refused her as a gift." He raised his brows. "So, no."

Anne rolled her eyes. She was ecstatic they were only friends. She really was. Pedro Daun was a tyrant, if a dashing one, and she pitied the woman who would have to accept his dictates. "Since this is such a touchy subject, tell me about our destination. This villa."

"It's safe, secluded on a private beach. My grandfather built it for his French bride. My grandmother grew up in Dieppe and wished to continue her medicinal sea bathing after the marriage."

Anne sighed, searching his eyes. "Were they in love?"

"I doubt it." He gazed ahead, breaking the contact. "He was a count who owned half of the Minho region. She was the only daughter of a wealthy *emigreé*. It was a political arrangement."

"Oh, of course."

How silly of her to even ask. An aristocratic family like his would settle only for advantageous marriages. As would Pedro. Her shoulders slumped, and a sharp ache pierced her chest. Weren't they supposed to be friends? Then why did the thought of him marrying an heiress hurt so much?

"It's here."

Pedro guided Erebus through an iron gate, and Anne followed, Dante trailing behind with Beatriz bundled atop his horse. The poor dear was still queasy after the storm, and the Italian had refused to let her ride with Anne.

A courtyard opened in front of them. Palm trees flirted with the breeze, their stalks festooned with lilac and yellow orchids. A charming two-story house sat poised on the bluff, magenta bougainvillea climbing its whitewashed walls. Portuguese *sombreros* and cypresses offered tantalizing glimpses of the sea.

Pedro vaulted from the saddle and secured Erebus on a hitching post. Dante and Beatriz alighted from their mount and were busy removing the saddlebags. Holding her breath, Anne waited for Pedro to help her dismount. His leather-clad hands lingered on her waist for only three heartbeats, and too soon, her feet touched the ground. Their eyes met. Then he stepped back so Dante could take Hemera's reins.

Beatriz handed her James's basket. Her cheeks were bright pink.

"The ride did wonders to your pallor." Anne winked.

"Miss Anne was right. Pineapple is quite agreeable. Once we remove the thorns, that is," Beatriz whispered, her gaze darting to Dante.

Perhaps Anne had been too harsh in warning the maid away from Dante. "I'm glad you found sweetness in him. I mean…it." Anne giggled and linked her arms with Beatriz.

While the men conversed, they strolled to a patch of grass, and Anne crouched to release her dog. The pug sniffed a carnation bush and sneezed, upsetting an orange butterfly.

Beatriz chuckled and brushed her hands on her skirt. "I'll be inside if you need me, Miss, arranging your clothes."

"Thank you, dear."

Pedro strode to her side. The sun loved his hair, highlighting the golden and flaxen tones. Her wayward fingertips tingled to touch the silky strands, and she clasped them around her middle.

Anne straightened and shielded her eyes. "Would you show me inside?"

"The housekeeper will provide you with anything you want. Dante will stay, and I trust him implicitly. It is safe for you to roam the gardens and the beach. You can visit Hemera at the stables, but I ask you not to ride."

She tilted her head to the side. "What about you?"

"I'll be absent for a couple of days."

Her breath caught. "So soon? I hoped—"

He frowned. "I must go to Alcobaça to retrieve whatever Braganza wanted me to see. This is not a vacation, Anne."

Just like that, he flipped the magnets again, pushing her away. She covered her cheeks with her palms, wishing to hide her obvious reaction. "I know. Of course. Must you go alone?"

"I act better alone." He bowed stiffly, already turning to leave.

Anne's gaze shifted from him to his warhorse. A knot clogged her throat, and the air became scarce. "Wait."

He halted, his features set in granite. Why could he hide his feelings so masterfully? Anne was sure her face hid nothing of what she felt.

Uncaring, she went on her tiptoes and kissed his cheek. "Godspeed."

His fingers covered the place where her lips had been, and he stared at her with an intensity that left her legs completely useless. She needed to be away from him. Friends said goodbyes with simple handshakes, *adieus*, or *tchaus*, not with a waterfall of tears.

Anne turned on her heels, intent on racing to the house.

A hand on her shoulder stopped her. When the familiar leather of his gloves encircled her wrist, she stifled a cry.

"You will be here when I return." He tugged, forcing her to face him, his voice hoarse. "No leaving the property. No impromptu travels to the city."

Anne tried to swallow past the lump in her throat. "Must you decide everything?"

With a heavy sigh, he pulled her to his chest, and his solidness and warmth seeped into her. She gazed into topaz-colored eyes, into the swirling brown lines. Why couldn't she see inside them? Just a glimpse? Her heart, so close to his, fluttered against her ribcage.

Thoughts babbled through her mind—friends didn't look at each other this way; how she missed being this tight to him; if only he would never let go—and then his lips touched hers, and her mind hushed. She closed her eyes, her insides melting, but not with tears.

Pedro deepened the kiss, his tongue tangling with hers, and his taste made her head spin. Circling her spine, his arms pressed her closer, intimately.

"Ana." He broke away, panting. "I haven't heard your promise."

"Friends don't kiss like that," she mumbled, refusing to open her eyes. Instead, she glided her hands around his neck, willing his lips back.

He touched his forehead to hers, breaths ruffling her hair. "This friendship arrangement was your choice."

"But it was you—"

"When I return, you will be here. And it will be my turn to choose." He rubbed her lips with his thumb, and the heat in his gaze made her weak.

Then he stepped away. Cold and thin air replaced his presence. The sun filtered through the palm leaves, pooling on the grass and glinting off his horse's ebony coat. Anne watched, still reeling, as he mounted Erebus. Dressed all in black, Pedro looked like the God of Shadows, and when he left, cantering through the iron gate, he stole all the courtyard's light.

Pedro's parting words followed Anne around the house. Unable to face Beatriz or the cheerful house-keeper, Anne found the bedroom with her suitcase and shut the door. Alone, she leaned her back on the wall and closed her eyes. At some point, she would have to stop reading meaning where there wasn't any. Parting words or not, Pedro had done it again. Left her behind.

What of her resolutions? What of her future?

Her hand came up to her locket of its own will. Would she sacrifice the promise of perfect love for a man so different from her ideal? With a cry, she released the necklace. She couldn't think about it.

The book was there, Inês's story, atop the escritoire, along with her toiletries. The last time she had read it, Inês awaited Dom Pedro. Heir to the throne of Portugal, mortal enemy of her family, possessor of mercurial moods, a married man.

Anne settled on the bay window seat and opened the tome.

Coimbra, Quinta das Lágrimas—June 1336

Chirps filled the trees' foliage. Still, Inês's garden hadn't survived the drought. Her hyacinth had brown leaves, lifeless. She couldn't remain in Portugal, not without the hyacinth, not without happiness.

Hooves sounded outside her cottage. The baggage train had left for Albuquerque, but her escort was expected only tomorrow. Who could it be? Heart leaping, Inês dropped the baby cap she had been knitting and tiptoed to the front door.

Dom Pedro cantered inside the courtyard and halted, lifting plumes of dust in the bright morning. He vaulted from his steed and raced to her as if he had left for a hunt, not two seasons.

Inês lifted her fingers below her chin in the silent language for him to stop. Pain washed out the joy on his princely face, and Inês trembled.

For several months a widower, he could've made her his wife. His queen. Perhaps he never would. It was not in him to defy his father.

But he loved her, and her heart could not beat without him.
Inês opened her arms.

Anne closed the book and sprang to her feet. Dazedly, she left her bedchamber and climbed the stairs to the second floor. A sliver of light wavered from the master's bedroom, calling her in. The window invited inside a fragrant breeze, the gauzy curtain flowing like a bride's veil. Beyond, the ocean, blue and vast.

Anne swept her gaze over his possessions, the Almoster coat of arms carved on the four-poster bed, his guitar poised by the bedstand, the two sabers crisscrossed as if locked in perpetual battle. She picked up a linen towel, tracing the embroidered P and D, and raised the cloth to her face, but his cedar scent eluded her.

Pedro was everywhere in this airy chamber, but he was nowhere at all.

She closed her eyes, trying to picture the faceless gentleman that had accompanied her since her heart had begun dreaming of fairytale love. But she could only see Pedro's sharp edges—a warrior, a cynic, a fugitive. A future with him would not be the comfortable, gentle family life she had envisioned with her perfect gentleman. Pedro would be a dictator to his wife, but only when it concerned her safety. He would also demand a woman's constant guidance to understand his emotions and respect hers. A future with him would not be frictionless.

Still, he would be a fierce father, and nothing would bring her more joy than him falling in love with their first child. Fridays would be for riding, Saturdays for sea bathing. He could teach the boy how to fence and ride, eyes shining with the same pride he'd shown her when she had solved the code. She could teach their daughter to play the piano, and Pedro would follow with the guitar.

Tears slipped from her eyes, and she cleaned them with the cloth.

Inês had stayed for her Dom Pedro, and the obstacles to their love had not been the childish whims she carried around her neck or the shadows of Pedro's past. Inês had dared to fight for her love, risking her pride and her own life.

Anne's fingers shook as she opened the clasp and removed the chain. The gold locket's weight was slight compared to all the hopes she had placed inside it. She kissed the pendant and, smiling through her tears, closed the chain around Pedro's bedpost.

Beatriz burst inside the bedchamber, her pallor gray. "Thank God, I found you."

Anne dried her cheeks. "What happened?"

The maid leaned on the threshold, panting. "There are strangers. Outside."

Anne grabbed her skirt and rushed downstairs. She addressed the housekeeper, her voice cracking. "Have you discovered what they want?"

Dona Hilaria rubbed her thick arms, her face twisted in anguish. "They say they work for the king and are searching for the Count of Almoster."

"Did you tell them there are only women here?" Anne closed the French doors to shield the house, but its delicate portals and oversized windows would grant them no protection.

"Yes, Miss. But they are rude men. Quite insistent, one of them is. They say they won't go away until they see my employer."

Dante, a mean-looking rifle on his shoulder, stopped pacing and turned to the window. He tugged the curtain and stood there, trying to glimpse these strangers. Anne glared at the Italian's back. He had yet to speak since they had congregated in the parlor. Granted, he was a man of few words, half of them Italian imprecations, but this went too far. Would he be of no help? If Pedro were here, he would know what to do.

Beatriz touched her arm. Her face had lost all color. "Can't we let them in? Won't they leave us alone if they don't find His Excellency?"

Anne shook her head. "If they set foot inside the count's bedroom, they will realize the house belongs to him."

Pedro's warnings flashed in her mind. What if the men outside worked for Ulrich? Would they hurt them or take them hostage or worse?

A sharp knock on the door made her jump so high she almost bumped the chandelier. Anne calmed her breaths. Acting like a frightened hen wouldn't help.

Beatriz cried, covering her head with a pillow.

Dante pushed away from the window, his face impassive. "Miss Maxwell, go upstairs."

Anne stood but paused halfway to the landing. His grim expression chilled her spine."What will you do?"

He lifted his shoulders and dropped them in a resigned gesture. "*Il finirò.*"

What if the strangers didn't mean them harm? They could have families. She wouldn't have their deaths on her conscience. "No."

"I have my orders, *signorina.*" He waved to the stairs dismissively, as if she weren't better than a child. "Beatriz, accompany Miss Maxwell."

Anne had enough males ordering her for two lifetimes and didn't need another. "What if there are others?" Planting her feet on the carpet, she crossed her arms. "Won't they notice if these men disappear? What if they send replacements to investigate? Will you kill them all?"

The rugged Italian shifted his weight from side to side, rubbing his forehead. He seemed nervous. Beatriz looked about to be sick.

Sick...

Sick!

"I have a plan," Anne said, her mind already listing all the things they would need. It was daring but better than murder.

The Italian stared her down, but his chestnut eyes wavered.

Anne didn't budge.

Dante glided his forefinger below his chin. "The count will have my neck."

"If my plan fails and they discover the house belongs to Pedro, you can shoot them."

This had to work.

Wringing her hands, Anne addressed her motley crew. "We'll need dirt, a large camisole, and all the chamber pots."

Anne perched on the settee, her back not touching the upholstery, fingers crossed on her lap, heart pumping madly. She adjusted Hilaria's mantilla around her head and shoulders, so no single strand appeared. She would not make the same mistake twice and expose her hair.

The housekeeper entered the parlor, leading the strangers. Anne swallowed and forced her eyes to meet them. They both wore identical clothes, a frock coat reaching mid-thigh. The color must have been forest green, but the stiff linen had degraded to some mossy tone. It resembled a soldier's uniform. Though they dressed alike, the stocky one with the triangular beard was older and looked meaner. His pointed face reminded her of a ferret.

"Hilaria, please bring refreshments," Anne said, hiding her nervousness under a polite facade.

Without invitation, the leader sprawled on the armchair. Crossing his leg, he caressed the tip of his beard and eyed her from slippers to mantilla. The not-so-subtle leer made her skin crawl.

The other kept a soldiering stance behind the bearded one, looking straight ahead. His face was clean-shaven, and the skin above his collar had an angry slash. Younger, perhaps her age, he seemed to take his job quite seriously, whatever that job was.

Perspiration trickled down her spine. The air was stiff, with all windows closed and the gas lamps burning.

Anne touched her lips with a kerchief. "May I help you?"

"We are looking for a criminal, Pedro Daun. Have you heard of him?"

She perked up. "I know no criminals, sir."

"The man is highly dangerous." He trailed shining eyes through the Rubens and the silverware, no doubt accessing their value. "I'll have to search the house. For your safety, of course."

"But sir, two men wandering a widow's home? I may be foreign, but I'm certain this isn't proper. Even here in the Peninsula."

"We are under His Majesty's orders. The count's ship was spotted in the bay. We have the king's authorization to inspect the houses from the right margin of the Tagus to Carcavelos beach." He hardened his face. "So, if you—"

A cough came from upstairs, a tremendous, dog-like cough.

Anne grimaced. "Do forgive my poor mother. We came for the medicinal baths, but instead of sunshine, I'm afraid the dear soul contracted a terrible sickness."

A moan started then, followed by some straining, long and suffered.

The leader shifted in the chair. "What's wrong with her?"

"The doctor just left." Anne pouted. "He said it's cholera. Are you familiar with it? Chol-leer-raa?" She stretched out each syllable like a simpleton, and they echoed in the wake of another terrible moan.

Anne watched the effect of their ruse. Both men's eyes widened, and the younger turned a sickly shade of green.

"I didn't know it progressed so fast." She leaned forward as if imparting a secret. "*Maman* was fine yesterday, but today... so much blood." Pressing her nose with the kerchief, she sniffed. "And worse."

On cue, the housekeeper brought a tray with two glasses. The dirt mixed inside made the water brown. Hilaria placed it on the coffee table and cleaned her hands on her apron. "If you will excuse me, madam, I'll take your mother's soup upstairs."

"Of course, dear. Thank you for such kindness." Anne held the housekeeper's gaze and then turned to her audience. "Please, have a drink. The landlord told us the cistern's water has curative properties. If only my poor mother would keep any in her stomach."

It had the desired effect, as it was common knowledge foul water caused cholera. The men eyed the glasses as if they contained eels. The younger one stepped back, hands lifted.

A groan and a pungent scent invaded the parlor. Their unwanted visitors squirmed and shared an alarmed look.

"I'm not thirsty, thank you. We'll search the house, and you can return to your mother." The leader stood, his face resolute.

Anne nodded resignedly. "I'll take you upstairs, then."

She twisted the kerchief in her hands, not daring to breathe, as she led them through the hallways. They needed to convince them the house didn't belong to Pedro. She fervently hoped she was doing the right thing.

Anne showed him to her room first. As she feared, they took their job too seriously, opening the chests and cabinets, inspecting the bathing area, and even looking under the bed. Her heart beat so loudly that they probably heard it downstairs.

After checking every room, they came to the last, the master's chamber. Anne paused, willing away the tremor in her hand. Exhaling deeply, she twisted the doorknob and flung the door inwards.

A miasma of sickness invaded her nostrils. The closed shutters concealed the room in shadows. Paralyzed, a sheen of sweat covering his brow, the leader gaped at the room's tableau. On the four-poster bed, a heavy matron lay, face hidden by the bed curtains. Hilaria's sturdy frame bent over the patient, a steaming bowl of broth in her hands.

Anne covered her nose with the kerchief. "Is Mother better?"

The housekeeper turned to the door, eyes wild and cap askew. "I wouldn't come near, madam. The poor lady spilled out her entrails, a fetid flux of blood and pus." Placing the soup on the tallboy, she grabbed the chamber pot. "Cholera is eating her alive."

The prone woman groaned.

Hilaria discarded the chamber pot and hastened to the bed. "Want soup?" she yelled as if the patient was deaf. "Here, have more."

From inside the bed curtains came a scream of pain and anguish so loud it lifted all the hairs on Anne's nape.

The youth whirled on his feet, chest heaving, and raced downstairs.

"I'm sorry to bother you, *madame*. Have a good day." The leader nodded curtly and followed his companion.

Anne had to hoist her skirts to follow their longer strides. They flew to the exit, and the youth flung the door open. Anne stopped at the stairs landing, covering her mouth. Through the window, she saw their visitors racing to see who reached his horse first. She never thought it possible to mount so fast.

Beatriz hurried to lock the door as Hilaria descended the stairs. Anne motioned for them to be silent and listened. Only when the clatter of hooves vanished could Anne fill her lungs.

Dante, still wearing the camisole, limped closer to their group. He had pulled the cap covering his hair, but the fake breasts remained. Grinning, Beatriz sidled up to him, and the Italian hugged her, lifting her from the ground.

Anne smiled, admiring the disgruntled couple.

Hilaria slapped his shoulder. "I hope you didn't soil my underwear, Italian! God forgive me. You are as ugly as a cow."

The swarthy Italian puffed his chest, the false bosom framing his square chin. "*Bella or brutta*, I fooled the sod, didn't I?"

Anne laughed, cleaning some tears of relief. "Where did you learn how to act? Those screams were horrifying."

"*Caspita*, I didn't act." He wiggled his finger at a brownish stain on his midriff and then pointed it accusingly at Hilaria. "She dropped scalding soup on me. The madwoman burned my bollocks!"

Chapter 32

Pedro dismounted and led Erebus through the narrow alleys of the medieval village. Peasants leaned out of their windows, but the horse attracted more attention than Pedro did. He emerged from the cramped shadows to a brightly lit courtyard. The Alcobaça Monastery presided over the square, the facade's marble yellowed by the centuries. A tower reached high in the sky, and from their perch over the belfries, the apostles judged newcomers. Pedro would go in, find whatever Fernando had hidden in the temple, and leave.

Pedro opened the arched portal, expecting a moldy, dark interior, but heavenly light bathed the nave, pouring from a rosette-shaped window over eight meters high. The acute silence weighed on his ears. A profusion of chrysanthemums laded the air with a mournful perfume.

Count on medieval architecture to turn a man of his stature the size of an ant.

Unwilling to stay longer than necessary, Pedro strode to the third line of pews. He cupped his hand and tapped the wood until he found a hollow spot. With a folding knife, he removed the lid, uncovering a leather satchel. A quick perusal revealed documents, maps, and photographs.

Pedro had folded it under his arm and turned to leave when the light changed, illuminating the end of the cross-shaped cathedral. Pedro recognized it at once. The final resting place Dom Pedro had built for himself and the love of his life.

Pedro tensed. He should go away. Had he not endured enough sentimentality in the past few days to last him a lifetime? Still, his legs took him to them.

On opposite sides of the altar, Dom Pedro and Inês rested under a shaft of milky light. The air was brisk, with a trace of rosemary, and strangely rarefied. Her image rested above the grave's lid, serene, surrounded by angels, a crown atop her head. The effigy had a haunting quality, art that had stood the test of centuries, a Gothic beauty that made the most stoic of souls glimpse the power of love found and lost.

Pedro turned to the king. Like Inês, his image lay atop the marble coffin. But unlike her, he had his eyes open, gazing at the heavens. His expression was melancholy, anguished even.

Pedro sighed heavily. "Was it worth your eternal peace, this love?"

Standing behind Dom Pedro's tomb, Pedro could see Inês's grave. Dom Pedro had demanded it this way, so on judgment's day, the first thing they would look at would be each other.

And Pedro had his answer.

"She saw you, didn't she? The only one who did? Your precious Castilian girl, your haven among a court that didn't understand you."

Circling the grave, he trailed his hand over the carved symbols, images, and inscriptions. A rosette stood below Dom Pedro's feet—the wheel of life. Pedro traced the inscription above it.

Until the end of time.

Eighteen scenes decorated the spaces. Their fateful meeting, their chess games, and the birthing of their sons. When he arrived at the last one, his chest constricted painfully. Her death sentence. Anger burned in his stomach and traveled to his chest, so acute it fisted his hands, and a roar thundered out of his throat.

"Why didn't you fight for your Inês? Why didn't you marry her and make her your queen when you had the chance? Instead, you worried about politics, intrigues, locked in the shadow of a father who didn't love you."

The statue didn't answer.

"Why wait until her death to make her your queen? *Agora não adianta, Inês é morta.* It doesn't matter now. Inês is dead."

Beneath the heavenly light, Pedro felt bare. All he had constructed in his life was this—a monument to regret.

The villa seemed deserted. No bells of her voice or the dog's bark to greet him.

Had Anne left again?

Pedro pushed the thought away. She had promised to stay, and Anne was loyal. Still, the twenty hours without seeing her had dragged like a century.

Midway to the kitchen, Pedro found the housekeeper. "Where is she?"

The woman twisted her apron. "The poor dear moped about the house, pallid. I've shoved her outside to enjoy the sun and the water, Your Excellency."

Pedro strode through the French doors. His pulse jugged erratically as he navigated a path through bougainvillea and sage bushes. The ocean glittered in his line of sight. His heart thrashed against his ribs as if wanting to get out, to be the first to see her.

Pedro took off his boots and stepped into the sand, forcing himself to walk when his legs wanted to run. The beach extended a mile in both directions, protected by a cliff.

Dante and Beatriz clasped hands by a checkered cloth spread on the sand. Were they together? He would have to speak with the condottiere later.

Following their gazes, Pedro found her.

Anne faced the horizon, the ocean reaching her thighs. The sun caressed her skin, glowing over her glorious hair. A breath he was unconscious of holding went out from his chest.

Dante cleared his throat. "All is well, sir. We had some—"

"Leave us."

Grinning, Dante nodded and tugged Beatriz toward the house.

Pedro walked into the ocean, ignoring the water soaking his trousers. The sea and sky blurred into a bluish mass. "Ana."

She whirled, and a smile illuminated her face, sparkling her eyes. "You are back. Thank God!"

Pedro rubbed his chest. Who was ever so happy upon his return? He had been so intent on finding her that he had not noticed her clothes. Her short dress exposed her legs, arms, and curves. How was he to keep his restraint? The fairness of her skin in daylight threatened to dazzle him. He wanted her dewy lips rubbing against his, her wet skin gliding over his, her silky hair teasing his chest. "What are you wearing?"

She trailed her hands over the navy-blue fabric. "It's a bathing suit. The latest fashion from Paris. Do you like it?"

Pedro closed his gaping mouth. "Who bought you this?"

Her lips tugged up in a mischievous smile. "Why, Your Excellency, it was you. When you sent Beatriz to Barca D'Alva to provide me with a wardrobe, of course. She thought I would enjoy—"

Pedro jerked his chin in the house's direction. "You will cover yourself."

She sighed and pouted, her eyes twinkling. "But the water is so nice."

Pedro circled his hand around her forearm. Her moist skin slipped from his grasp, and she dove. Pedro held his breath, watching for her shape, but the foam made it impossible to see below the surface.

"Anne?" he yelled, his voice unsteady.

He tensed to dive after her when she emerged behind him. Laughing, she sprayed water on his shirt. He caught her, tightening his arms around her waist, but before he could taste her lips, she splayed her hands over his chest and pushed. Caught off balance, he splashed backward.

Holding his lapels, she came with him and kissed the corner of his mouth. "I've got you."

Surprised, he grappled for purchase, whipping his arms to keep afloat. Like a water sprite, Anne fled, long legs bared to the elements, and skipped back to shore.

Pedro stood, and coldness seeped into his skin as he watched her leave.

"Too old to catch me?" Her laughter reached him as she raced along the shore.

Panting, he gave chase. The sand sang beneath his heavy strides, the breeze ruffling his soaked clothes. He felt none of it. Not the salt in his eyes or the coat's drag, just this weightlessness, a sense of floating, of being able to follow her across the Nile, the Danube, the Rubicon.

She ran, pumping her elegant arms, hair flowing in rivulets down her back, her slim legs carrying her more up than forward. Pedro had never seen a person run more inefficiently or more beautifully.

She turned her head to see if he still chased, and their eyes met. It happened so suddenly that if he had not been so close, if the sun had not left the cover of clouds at that precise moment, if his soul had not been looking for it every second of every day for as long as he could remember, he would have missed it.

She gave him that look. Sultry and playful, woman and girl, Ana and Angel.

It was better than the statue, for it was real, and it was for him.

Pedro vaulted the distance between them. It would've not mattered if it had been an abyss. He caught her in his arms and pressed her to his chest. She laughed, the sound a little strained, and intertwined her fingers over his neck. After trailing his tongue over the seams of her lips, he plunged inside, exploring her warmth.

She was different, her eyes flashing, her hands lingering over his chest, setting him on edge and at ease, promising delicious things that would pierce his defenses but make him deliriously content.

He pulled away, breathing hard. With Anne, he had no control, his body demanding total possession. "The sun is setting. We will head back."

"I love the golden hour. When the sun rests behind the mountains, the colors turn brighter. A parting gift from nature to last us until dawn."

"I don't like sunsets." In the sun's absence, sins had a way of crawling from hell to haunt him.

She placed a warm palm on his cheek. "Let's saddle Hemera and Erebus. We can gallop east. The sun won't set for us."

"Do you think we can run from shadows?"

"If you allowed me inside."

Her earnest plea wrenched open the hole she had made in his armor. What did she hope to find? If she but glimpsed his past, she wouldn't look at him as if he were the suitor of her dreams. The one she carried by her heart. Already she was a part of him he treasured unreasonably. A sensation of grasping thin air flooded him, and he kissed her desperately, drinking her moans like a parched man.

Pedro broke the kiss and leaned his forehead over hers. "My life is at risk. I'm a fugitive."

"Why are we wasting precious moments with words?"

"There are things you don't know about me. About the past."

"What you did before cannot change how I feel. For once, let's live in the now."

"Ana," he warned.

"Don't leave me. Not again. Not when I'm offering my love to you." Her voice rang true and steady, but her Atlantic gaze shimmered like the water's surface, held together by an ephemeral force so delicate anything could rupture it.

By God, he did not want to hurt her.

She kissed the corner of his mouth and then nibbled his bottom lip. He could have resisted, but he allowed himself to be reeled in, ever so close to her, to the source of this madness. Light poured from her eyes, her smile, her touch. He had spent years deprived of it, and now she plunged him into this open meadow, filled with the light of a thousand suns.

Chapter 33

The Marialva Palace, former residence of the Dukes of Abrantes, had undergone expensive... butchering. The facade had been crammed with gaudy plasterwork, including some erotic depictions of Gods frolicking, all fitting decoration to the Siren, the newest addition to the city's demimonde. A private club, bordello, and casino.

Gabriel removed the enigmatic invitation from his pocket, inspecting the crass handwriting for further clues of the owner's identity.

The Duke of Madeira invites Mr. Gabriel Fontes to a meeting at the Siren.

His heraldic consultations had brought no such titles, either old or recently given by the king. Nonetheless, Gabriel knew who it belonged to. His blackmailer. Who else would summon the head of the king's guard so authoritatively but the blackguard who held him by the collar?

Gabriel rolled his neck, waiting by the front porch. A boat marred the Tagus's surface, breathing plumes of smoke in the sky. To his left, neighboring the property's fence, the Mosteiro dos Jerônimos sprawled over Empire Square. The Manueline building, with its symbolic decorations, was the best Portugal offered in terms of architecture. Their own Gothic style. A crew gathered around scaffolds, preparing to resume the restoration.

Enough stalling. Facing the heavy oak portal, Gabriel knocked two times. A pompous majordomo opened the door, and Gabriel delivered his calling card. "His Excellency awaits me."

The butler ushered him inside a private study. A rosewood escritoire crouched at the center of the room, surrounded by leather-backed chairs.

"Gabriel Fontes. Time has favored you." The voice, shrill and sure, came from the doorway.

Below the threshold stood the ghost of their past—João Ulrich.

Blinking repeatedly, Gabriel stumbled back a step. By God, it was him. Same greased black hair and leathery skin, all razor-edged angles. "What are you doing here?"

"Why, I'm a Portuguese subject, just like yourself." Ulrich pushed a square monocle into his left eye. An extravagant ermine pelisse covered his pointed shoulders, but the veneer fit him poorly.

Gabriel advanced a step, his heart speeding. "I arrest you for the illegal—"

"For what?" Ulrich sneered and strutted inside as if presenting himself at court. "You have no proof against me."

Whose fault was that? If it weren't for Gabriel's lie, his father would have continued the investigations. The only reason he had ceased the inquiries was to protect his beloved godson.

"I was there, in the Zambezi. You attacked our camp. You captured the families under our protection."

Gabriel grabbed the hilt of his saber, tensing to unsheathe the blade.

"Careful what you do." Ulrich jutted his jaw at the sword. Raising his voice, he peeled the ermine pelisse and, with it, any trace of civility. "I arranged this as a friendly meeting. Our little encounter happened in the colony. You are no imbecile. There's no jurisdiction to arrest me here in Lisbon."

Ulrich petted the fur with slow movements of his bejeweled fingers. "It's easy to flaunt these English liberal mottos and blame me, the low-born subject from Madeira Island. Don't force me to tell you who supplied the ships, gave us fake notes, and insured our cargo. Oh, and let's not forget, bought the merchandise produced by the slaves."

"I don't think this is relevant—"

"All the glittering court. The entire society."

"You threatened the king. If you think I will condone—"

He clicked his tongue. "I thought you would have figured it out. Braganza was the target. He poked his nose where he shouldn't. I have no business with the king. I'm diversifying my talents, you know? Using my expertise for entertaining. And that is where I can use your... favors."

"What do you want?"

Ulrich sprawled on the chaise. "No need to sweat. A few birds told me you are quite the *chique* here, that Lisbon's gentry loves you. I need a fine bloke to introduce me to high society."

Did Ulrich mean to parade in respectable company? The dandified, naïve Lisbon court wouldn't survive the strike.

Gabriel gritted his teeth. "And if I refuse?"

"We all have secrets, have we not? I assume Papa Fontes would be displeased to learn yours."

Gabriel could imagine his father's shock if Ulrich appeared at their doorstep, spilling his accusations. Several scenarios had crossed his mind when the summons had arrived this morning, but not this. How could his situation have turned for the worst so quickly?

Hands clenched, Gabriel struggled to fill his lungs. He could deny Ulrich. He certainly should.

He pictured his father's dismay at realizing his own son had lied for the past ten years and, in doing so, had unleashed this viper.

He gazed away from the oily bastard, heart thumping in his ears. Through the window, the Mosteiro dos Jerônimos restorations were underway. The architects and stonemasons no doubt argued if an eroded sculpture was a gargoyle or an ouroboros. What would he give to be among them and far from this?

Gabriel tugged at the collar of his coat. "I expect you'll want to attend the races, an invitation to the Grêmio, and the Havanesa House, of course."

Ulrich shrugged. "If I must. It will bore me to death. Mingling with those gents, pretending to enjoy horse racing and fancy balls... don't you think it goes against our Portuguese blood? We were made for Fado taverns, *bordoadas*, and bullfighting. Not this foreign shit."

"For when do you plan your grand entrance?"

"Soon. First, I have this thread to knot, and you, a truant count to catch." Grinning, he flung the pelisse over his back.

Gabriel covered his mouth, nodding several times. With a last look, he turned to the exit. Halfway to the door, he halted. "Why Pedro?"

"There is much you don't know about my past with Almoster. But I can tell you this. I remember the five of you swaggering out of the frigate that ripped you from your mamas and took you to Mozambique ten years ago. Fresh from your military academies, shoulders crowned by diamond studded epaulets, and no stitch of beard in your cheeks. I liked how the reality of that godforsaken place dimmed the brightness of your eyes... but not Pedro Daun. The Count of Almoster. Up on the hill, he thought himself a new Caesar." Ulrich shrugged and smiled apologetically. "I wanted to shove him from up there. Can you blame me?"

Gabriel stared at Ulrich, throat so thick he could not swallow his own saliva, his chest so tight he feared his heart would not have room to keep beating.

Had Gabriel not wished the same?

Chapter 34

Pedro carried Anne to the villa, heart pounding faster than a drum boy during his first march. He took the steps to the house two at a time and arrived at his bedroom with his prize atop his arms, only stopping when his knees touched the bed.

Anne smiled, clinging to his neck. "I've never thought it possible to arrive here so fast."

"If you have second thoughts—"

She placed her fingertip on his lips. "I'm told this happens atop the bed. Not hovering above it."

She did not know the myriad places he had imagined doing this to her, but instead of sharing this detail, he lowered her to the mattress. She bounced to a seated position, her cheeks turning the port color he loved.

He must remember her innocence.

Pedro kneeled in front of her. She gazed at him expectantly, vulnerable and enchantress, girl and goddess. She was more than he expected, more than he deserved, but she was his. With a trembling hand, he skimmed the mobile eyebrows that questioned his beliefs, the eyelids that unveiled her gaze, and vowed to earn more of her adoring looks.

She caressed his cheek. "All that matters is the now."

Pedro nodded. He could live in the now. Now his hands brushed pinpricks on her arms, now he breathed the same air as hers, now he slanted his mouth over hers. He stretched the now into a fabric of desire until they were both panting. He tugged the bands of the bathing suit free, revealing the curves of her breasts. Another pull and nothing was concealed from him. Pedro sucked in a breath, awed. He couldn't say Anne was naked. With her skin revealed to the sunset, creaminess made golden by the caressing light, she didn't seem bare. Bare meant lacking, and nude, Anne was complete.

She lowered her eyes for a moment, and Pedro thought she would cover herself, but then she dazzled him with a luminous smile. It was not the conceit of women who knew themselves to be perfect but the absence of malice, of shame. It enchanted him.

She peeked at him from under golden eyelashes. "I want to see you, too."

Pedro took off his shirt and forced himself to stand still. While she was Aphrodite, his body was the product of war, hard-wired muscles covered by scarred skin. Pedro held his breath as she traced the bayonet wound above his shoulder, and the dagger slashes frozen into a spiderweb above his first rib. He knew her intention. She wished to heal him. And then she arrived at those scars. They were faint, as his father had controlled himself before ruining the skin of his heir, but they ran deep.

She lingered over the markings, and a tear wet his shoulder. "I hate him for hurting you."

"I barely felt the pain." Pedro had learned to shield his body, and by the end, his father had looked worse after one of their lessons than Pedro had. It was not about the pain. The damage the duke had done to him was inside. But he didn't tell her that. His father's shadow had no place between them.

Reverently, Pedro glided his palms over her shoulder blades and brought her to his chest. Lush and silky and smooth, how delicate she was, how precious. If only he could fit her inside him. "I keep thinking you will open your angel's wings and take to the sky." His voice came out gravelly, and he exhaled.

Anne sifted her fingers through his hair and brushed her lips against his neck. "If I had wings, they would only serve to bring me back to you."

Pedro kissed her, exploring her mouth, sucking her tongue. The thrill of her lustrous skin against his was incendiary, and Pedro guided her to lie on the bed. He followed her there. He would follow her anywhere.

When he rose above her, a sizzle shot down his spine. They fit, her legs opening to receive his hips, his hardness meeting her softness, cradling him like the most perfect nest.

Pedro feasted on her pliant curves, stroking and massaging, tugging her impossibly closer. Her sighs of pleasure demolished his will to go slow, and he pushed inside her. Her mouth opened in a silent moan, and Pedro stopped.

"Tell me if I'm hurting. I don't—I don't want to hurt you." The instinct to invade the last barrier and make her his clouded his vision, but he forced himself to pull away.

Before he could withdraw, she locked her legs around his waist and lifted her hips. Her maidenhead gave way in his downward thrust, and he covered her whimper with a kiss. He shuddered and buried his face in her neck. He had denied this attraction, but now, entrenched in her, he didn't know if he could ever leave.

She flitted her palms over his back, feeling for the ridges of his spine. If he felt an ounce of annoyance at her touch, he could not bear her so close, but everywhere she touched, his skin ignited. She strained, moving restlessly beneath him, and he knew to thrust. He kept pace with her movements. Though he had had sex countless forgettable times, in this, in lovemaking, he was the novice.

When she trembled, erupting in a wordless gasp, Pedro lost control, thrusting mindlessly, breaching her with the pound of his hips, consuming her innocence with all his desire, all his lust.

With a groan, he poured himself into her and then collapsed atop her. They lay chest to chest, skin to skin, his breaths stirring her light hair. Pedro's limbs trembled. Everything in him hushed, his thoughts blanked, strain left his muscles, and he simply *was*. Connected with her. His chest expanded to engulf her, her scent mingling with his, her soft breaths mixing with the ocean waves. Her skin, moist and heated, melded with his.

She lay still, her eyelashes resting against her flushed cheeks. Had she felt the same? Undone and complete, overwhelmed and starved, scorched and blissfully free? He had taken her like a savage. She would be afraid of him, of the entire experience. His gut twisted, and Pedro tensed to pull away.

She closed her heels over his legs and enveloped him with her arms. "Don't leave."

"You will be sore," Pedro whispered, his heart soaring, and kissed her forehead.

She yawned. "I don't care."

Pedro adjusted his position, propelling his weight to the side so he would not smother her. She rested her head on his chest, and her breaths evened out until they turned soft and rhythmic. He kept his hand splayed over her spine, wishing to absorb her through his fingertips.

When night fell and the clock chimed eight hours, she stirred. Her eyes sparkled in the moonlight, and a shy smile played at the corner of her lips. "Have you been watching me for long?"

"Since I saw you in my ballroom."

"That long? I—"

"Do you regret it?"

"Only that you took forever to—"

"Ruin you?"

"To make love to me."

"Can you tell love from ruin?"

"Let me see." She kissed him, lips luring his, daring to trace the tip of her tongue over his bottom lip. Fluttering her eyelashes, she tapped her chin. "I am positive it is love. I tasted a ruined apple once, and I dare say it wasn't so sweet." She giggled, mussed and smug, her hair fanned against his pillow.

Pedro gave her more of his weight and tucked her hair under her ear. He gazed into her eyes, and the intimacy they shared while the fires of desire were still banked, joined at a primal level, moved him deeply.

He kissed her tempting lips, and when she entangled her tongue with his, ripples of desire traveled through him, and he lengthened inside her. Her eyes widened, and her mouth opened in a breathless *oh*. He pressed against her pliable curves without thrusting, allowing her to get used to him.

"Pedro, this is... I think—"

He kissed her jaw and brushed his lips over her neck, lingering where her pulse beat. Sighing, she relaxed on the pillow, eyes closed, a sleepy smile on her lips. He kneaded her breasts, and when Anne arched her back, he accepted her offer, sucking her peaks with long pulls. She moaned, lifting her hips against him. But this time, he would not be rushed. He gave her deep, slow thrusts. Her breathing turned shallow, and when the *petite mort* gripped her, Pedro followed her to oblivion.

Chapter 35

Anne awoke and stretched languidly. A breeze bowed the bed curtains, brushing against her naked skin. Only a sliver of moonlight illuminated the bedchamber. For a second, she believed herself in her own room, but the waves brushing against the sand sparked her memories. Her skin heated, and a fluttering started in her stomach.

They had made love, not in her dreams, but in his bed. Anne felt inside herself for changes, like one who glides a finger on the rim of a precious vase after dropping it, searching for chinks in the porcelain. She found none. Instead, a profusion of new colors and textures startled her. She had known love—not the perfect, frictionless love of her fantasies, but edged, bristled, even sweaty love. Real love. She had been touched by it, warmed from the inside out, a glow not unlike the hummingbird had shown the hyacinth in Inês's story.

And she wanted more.

She reached for his side of the bed. Her palm touched the coolness of empty cotton. He had left. Anne's heart ached, and she hid her face in his pillow. He had pushed her away yet again.

A melody whispered against her cheeks, floating just out of her reach. Guitar strings, poignant, exotic. Pedro's notes caught her senses and tugged. He had stayed. Anne wrapped her nakedness with the sheet and padded barefoot to the veranda.

He sat with his foot propped on the balustrade, the guitar blurring under his fingertips. The moon caressed his profile and loose hair, and thousands of stars twinkled, casting their light closer to him. Even the tide swelled, wishing for a better view of Anne's lover. Light-headed, she inhaled the salty air and leaned over the threshold, mesmerized by the music he coaxed out of string and wood. His notes carried feelings for her he had not yet spoken, sensuous, joyful, and vibrant. Then they changed, turning melancholy, singing of his shadows, and her heart wept.

The music ended, and he splayed his hand over the rosette, stopping the chords.

Would he send her away? Sorry for having seduced her, claiming to put her interests first? Anne took a tentative step closer, but hesitated. If he rejected her after the night they had spent together, she wouldn't recover.

Pedro lowered the guitar and caught her gaze.

Anne sustained it, surprising herself with her steadiness. "I woke up and didn't find you... I will go back to my room—"

He grabbed her wrist and pulled her onto his lap. "Your room is here."

Her heart registered his words, pounding madly against her ribcage. Could it be true? "Will we...? I mean—"

Pedro nibbled her lower lip, silencing her. Then he pulled away, and his eyes sparkled. "I want to show you something."

After carrying her to the bedroom, he lit a candelabra and placed the light atop the table, revealing a tray. "You asked about Salgueiro's wine."

Anne gasped. "Is this *Vinho Luz*?"

"I found a casket in the cellar." Pedro poured the pale liquid into two glasses. "Some say the Arinto grapes have a distinct passionfruit scent."

Anne swirled the golden wine in her glass. The candle gave the liquid a mystic glow. Wine was alive and, in a sense, a special vault, capable of capturing a moment in time. Be it a season, a community's effort, a person's dedication, or a unique blend.

What moment of Pedro's life did Vinho Luz preserve?

Anne peered into the crystal, wanting to catch a whiff of his past. A woodsy, fresh scent teased her nose, reserved but playful. Closing her eyes, she sipped. The nectar coated her tongue, unctuous and rich, taking her to the top of a hill, among buttercups and daisies, kissed by sunlight.

He circled her waist and gazed at her intently. "Do you like it?"

The doubt in his eyes wrenched her chest, and she cradled his cheek. "How could I not? I've tasted summer, I've tasted the ocean breeze, I've tasted light. Your light."

A part of him untouched by shadows.

Pedro's breath caught, and then he frowned. "You see too much."

Anne went on her tiptoes and nipped his lip. "I want to see all. If only you would show me."

"Now, remember? The past has no place here."

Anne sighed and hugged him. She was patient, and one day she would convince him to abandon his shadows.

"Are you hungry?" Pedro tugged her to the table.

With infinite care, he fed her cheese and olive-filled pastries and tiny pancakes with caviar. The candle cast a secluded aura over their private banquet, a bubble of intimacy just for them. Anne drank his wine and accepted morsels from his fingertips, but it was the man gazing at her with jewel-colored eyes that left her intoxicated.

"What are these?" Anne picked a cluster of little ruby grapes, marveling at the lush color and translucent skin.

"Red currants. They are typical of the region."

Anne placed a currant on her lip. "Should I pop them in my mouth, or do they have seeds?"

His stare heated, and he took the fruit from her. "That's not how we will eat them."

Pedro burst the tiny grape between his long, aristocratic fingers. A thrill of giddy anticipation coursed through her as he smeared her lips with the tart juice, and then licked her bottom lip clean.

Anne's chest fluttered, and she tipped her head back, wanting more. But Pedro had other plans, and linking their hands, he guided her to the bed. Her heart bolted inside her chest, and a flush rose on her skin. They had made love already, and the intimacy was wonderful, but still new. Gently, he unwrapped the sheet from under her arms. Anne stretched on the mattress, the breeze lapping her skin.

Pedro bolstered her back with a cushion, arching her spine. Warmth drenched her, and she stifled the impulse to cover herself. He drew on her collarbone with currant juice, his fingers searing her skin, then bent his head and licked his designs. When he arrived at her breasts, Anne was breathless, her nerve endings tingling. He stared at his drawings, his face so close his breaths rolled deliciously over her cooling skin.

He lay by her side and caressed her heated flesh, soothing her with Portuguese murmurs and moist kisses.

"I've dreamed of this." He painted her nipples with the syrupy juice and then covered them with his mouth.

Anne lost any semblance of decorum and moaned, holding his neck, sifting her fingers through his hair. She had enough currants for a lifetime and caressed his flanks, willing him closer. Instead of entering her, he rolled the pillow under her buttocks. The position forced her legs apart, opening her to his gaze. Anne should protest. But propriety was the least of her cares, desire making her bold. He placed currants above her mound and stopped.

"Pedro, please."

He licked and laved and nipped. Stars exploded behind her eyelids, and shudders of pleasure traveled up and down her limbs. Her pulse throbbed, and she tipped her head back, a sigh emerging from her soul. When she could not bear more of his unrelenting exploration, he removed the pillow and climbed up her body, melding their chests.

His weight atop her fulfilled her, and she opened her legs to accommodate him. He had currant juice above his lip, and Anne stole it with her tongue. Groaning, he held her head and fused their mouths, his heart beating desperately against her chest.

Panting, he pulled away. "I need inside you."

His eyes still had shadows, and she would soon want to take part in those, but not tonight.

"Always," she vowed, welcoming him with all her being.

He entered her, stretching her inch by inch. When he was lodged in her core, he stilled. His pulse beat inside her, and her passage clenched around him. She pressed against him, and only when desire made her plead did he deign to give her what her body craved, moving deliciously. Each lunge instilled his essence into her. Anne entangled herself in his hair and splayed her hands over his shoulder blades, loving the ropy muscles of his back straining and relaxing under her palms, the sweaty glide of skin against skin. An exquisite tingle overcame her senses. Anne arched her back as spasm after frenzied spasm radiated from her core, and pure white light flooded her.

Shuddering, Anne sought Pedro's mouth. He drank her moans and crashed into paradise with her. Afterward, he kissed the top of her head and held her close. The questions he wouldn't answer and the words he wouldn't say quieted themselves, leaving only the peaceful silence of his breathing.

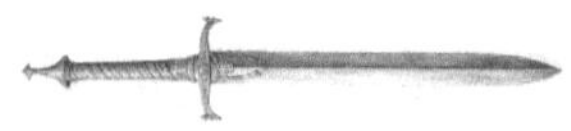

After breakfast, Pedro left the dining room and came back with a package. Anne admired how the velvet coat emphasized his broad shoulders and narrow waist, but she much preferred him sans the gentleman's attire. The naughty thought startled her, and warmth rose on her cheeks.

Pedro placed the leather satchel atop the table and seated himself. "This is Braganza's evidence."

Anne touched it reverently. Would they finally be able to prove Pedro's innocence? "Was it really there?"

"Exactly where you discovered it would be." A note of pride colored his voice.

Anne flushed with pleasure at his praise. They had shared so much yesterday. How was she supposed to behave outside the bedroom? Pedro usually preferred to be alone...

Anne eyed his furrowed brows and businesslike attitude, already missing their passionate interlude. Did reality have to intrude so soon? "Do you want me to go away, so you can—?"

"Stay. Your help proved invaluable, and I—"

Anne leaped into his lap and rained kisses down his face.

"I will take that as a yes." He chuckled and kissed her back with abandon. Then he pulled away, his eyes heated. "You best control your enthusiasm, or the documents will have to wait another day."

"I'll behave," she said but refused to relinquish her spot on his lap.

When he opened the leather envelope, foreboding curdled her stomach. He hadn't spoken of their future. What if they returned to their normal lives after they proved his innocence? Their flowering relationship forgotten? Was it too selfish of her to want to preserve this moment? Anne would gladly exchange an uncertain future for a prolonged stay in this villa, listening to his guitar, drinking *Vinho Luz*, and making love.

The scent of paper and ink brought her back to reality. Pedro scattered notes, documents, letters, lists, and maps. Some were old, yellowed at the edges, and some were clearly new.

Pedro stared at the papers, his gaze distant.

"Are you all right?"

"Fernando collected enough evidence to bring down the entire illegal slave trading operation. No wonder Ulrich wanted him dead. With this, he won't be able to evade justice."

"There are so many. How can I help?"

"We will organize the evidence by type and chronological order."

Anne covered his hand with hers. "After you bring this to light, no one will remember the baseless accusations. You will be a hero."

He stilled, and she felt the tension on his thighs and the arm circling her waist. Anne kissed his frown until it became acceptance, her own misgivings forgotten.

Whatever happened to them, of one thing she was certain: Pedro deserved redemption.

Anne picked a sheet with estimates for the number of slaves leaving Africa and reaching Brazil and Cuba. The middle passage took three months from Mozambique to Rio de Janeiro on the Brazilian Coast. Each ship carried four hundred passengers, with a fifteen percent mortality rate. Seventy percent were males, and twenty-five percent children.

Anne gasped. "One-quarter of the transported Africans are children? This is awful. Why didn't the numbers decrease after 1832, when the king made trafficking illegal?"

Pedro caught the paper from her. "It's a brutal enterprise, but a profitable one. After the British made slave trading a capital crime, the operation simply changed hands. While ownership of slave trading ships turned to Portuguese and Brazilians, North America builds most of the slaving ships, and investment comes from British banks."

"And the whole of Europe buys slave-produced goods," Anne said, her voice dripping with disgust. Her efforts at avoiding Brazilian products were paltry when faced with the scale of the problem.

She filed the list and reached for a discolored photo taken on the coast of Zanzibar by John Armstrong, lieutenant of the Royal Navy, in June 1870. With unsteady hands, Anne uncovered the parchment protecting the image. Several children huddled on the deck, dressed in rags, their bones poking out from their skin, their heads disproportionately big compared to their frail bodies. They had been rescued, and yet their eyes seemed dead.

Anne exchanged Pedro's lap for a chair facing him. They'd been working for at least an hour when a letter caught her attention. A dispatch addressing the colonial army's general, headquartered in Mozambique. It was dated January 1862. A quick perusal revealed Pedro's title. Hiding her gasp under a cough, she peeked at her lover, but he was still engrossed in organizing the evidence. This must relate to his past.

A past he had chosen not to share with her.

Anne's pulse sped, cold perspiration trickling down her spine. If he kept the hurt inside him, how would he heal?

Before she could change her mind, she scanned the contents. It was a list of slave trading suspects. And Pedro's name figured among them.

Anne dropped her head to the back of the chair, the blood draining from her face. This must be a mistake.

Pedro stopped reading. "Is something wrong?" When she didn't respond, he stood. "What is it?"

Anne watched him, unable to ask the questions locked in her throat. She couldn't ask him why his name was included among slave trader conspirators. She could not ask why Mozambique haunted him. She couldn't voice her doubts.

He grabbed the paper from her hand. The concern for her washed out from his face, replaced by gelid composure.

Chapter 36

Pedro sent his bedroom door crashing against the wall. He shrugged out of his coat and cravat, unable to breathe. She had seen his name mixed with the horrors of slave trading.

Anne's ashen face, her horrified expression...

Sunshine burst through the gauzy curtains, illuminating a heart-shaped piece of jewelry hanging from his bedpost. Anne's locket. With unsteady hands, Pedro opened it and removed a little paper. It wasn't a name or a photograph, as he had feared, but a list. She had underlined one of the flowery adjectives penned to describe her dream suitor.

Noble.

It ripped through his chest like a knife blade.

Footsteps sounded outside. Pedro closed his hand around the necklace.

"Pedro? Are you all right?"

He turned slowly as she took a step in his direction.

Pedro opened his hand, revealing his finding. "You removed this. Why?"

"Does it really matter? Pedro, I..." She inhaled sharply, her voice cracking. "I need to know if—"

"You took it off because you gave up your dreams for me."

"No! You've got it all wrong." She placed an icy hand on his arm, her eyes moving rapidly, trying to catch his. "I removed it because I found my dream suitor."

Pedro extricated himself from her touch. "Did you? Then why do you tremble? Ask me what you need to know about Mozambique, Anne."

She closed her eyes.

The absence of her gaze unmanned him.

"Is it true?"

Pedro pressed his fisted hands over his temples. "You wanted a noble prince and chose the villain."

"I know you. You are sometimes ruthless, sometimes cold, sometimes too sharp, but you are not evil."

"No? If you ask the one hundred and forty families I sentenced to a life of slavery, I'm sure they would disagree. But then, most would not be alive to share their opinions."

"I don't believe you," she whispered.

"They were not like the ones from the photo. Malnutrition did not assail my villagers. The tribe was healthy. At least compared to others in the interior."

Anne stood still, and a single tear sprang from the corner of her eye. He couldn't help but admire her courage. Others would have raced away, clasping their ears.

Pedro shut his eyes and dropped his weight on the bed. "If they could speak to you, they would tell you it was ten in the night when the shooting began. My troop had bivouacked at the arrowhead of the Zambezi, halfway between the village and the port. I formed the soldiers in two columns. The darkness was complete, and I marched toward the torches and occasional flashes of gunpowder. If the wind had not blown so heavily, we might have found the location sooner, but when we arrived, it was too late."

As if he had been transported to that moonless night, Pedro saw it again.

Orange light flickered over the hull and outlined the spiked masts. A slave ship, a human trap, bobbed on the Zambezi River. To the east, Chikunda warriors poked and bullied villagers, forming a thick line. Fires licked the tents, spreading cinders and illuminating their terror.

Hardening his heart against the screams, Pedro rallied his company to stop the captives from boarding. He could hear the rapid breaths of the young soldiers under his command.

Gabriel deployed by his side, his rifle pointed to the ground. "What is happening?"

"Slave traders."

"What will you do?"

"Fight."

No matter what happened on this side of the riverbank, he wouldn't allow the families to be taken from under his protection. His mission was to take them to a safe location, and he would see it to completion.

A white man disembarked from the ship. He strutted as if on a stage. The leader. An eerie silence descended on the riverbank as ashes floated on the wind like black snowflakes. Ignoring the soldiers, he inspected the lined Africans, brutally parting the old and the sick from their families.

The rage his father strove to make Pedro curb surfaced, heating his face and blurring his vision as the leader continued his stroll as if he owned them all. Pedro's soldiers stood their ground, pointing their guns at the Chikunda, waiting for his orders.

Pedro raised his voice above the wailing. "These families are under the Portuguese Army's protection."

The leader sneered. "Count of Almoster, right? Who do you think sold me this cargo?"

He opened his arms wide but kept coming closer. The man was too sure, too cynical.

Understanding spread over Pedro's chest like black oil. These people had been traded, and he had been the delivery boy.

He would persecute whoever had given the slave trader the information about their mission.

Pedro eyed his soldiers, reading the determination on their faces, and he knew what he had to do. "Slave trading is illegal. The king—"

The leader scoffed. "Go back to the coast, to the girls you soldiers enjoy so much. This is not a matter for boys. Visit the *danguro*. Tell them João Ulrich sent you. They'll give you the house special."

Pedro brought the rifle to his shoulder and aimed at Ulrich's head.

The man's eyes widened.

Pedro took a step forward, enjoying the shift in the power balance. Soldiers around him did the same, rifles clicking and pointing at the foe. If Pedro felled the leader, the Chikunda would retreat. Some soldiers would lose their lives, but they would save the families from a fate worse than death.

But Ulrich recovered too quickly, a sneer replacing his fear. "I have a cure for your lofty values."

Ulrich snapped his fingers, and a Chikunda warrior brought Cris forward. His brother had his arms tied behind him, and a dagger flashed at his neck.

Cris didn't struggle. He was calm. They locked eyes, the black ash smearing his skin, his white trousers, his red coat. The air solidified, tunneling around them, and Pedro could not focus on anything else. Not on the ship, like a gaping mouth wanting to be fed, not on the Chikunda, the white of their eyes dead as they wrestled with their own kind, not on the Portuguese soldiers, far from their homes, their bodies humming with tension, not on João Ulrich's cruel sneer.

Pedro gripped the rifle, his forefinger battling with the trigger. He had to do it. These people couldn't be carted away under his orders, not because of personal interests. Not because of his brother. The brother he had just found, who had been denied him when he was growing up and who would be taken away from him again.

The weapon hovered over his shoulder for a minute or an hour, but he didn't pull the trigger.

When Pedro lowered the standard-issue rifle to the side of his body, he was no longer the same. Somewhere, his father was laughing.

Pedro had turned into the Duke of Titano.

Anne's hands on his face pulled him away from the ravaged village. Pedro shut his eyes, unable to face her. For ten years, he had avoided the painful memories. Was reliving that night supposed to make him feel better? Then why did it feel like his chest had been ripped open?

But now Anne knew the truth about him. When he looked at her eyes, he would see only disgust. Shame for having gifted her innocence to a morally corrupt man—one who had exchanged the safety of dozens of families for his own benefit.

Even after all these years, he could not regret his decision on that godforsaken plain. If given a chance, he would choose his brother again, his bastard relation, dearer to him than if he had royal blood.

Pedro clenched her locket in his palm. He wasn't worthy of such honor. A better man would place it back on her neck and tell her to keep looking. But how could he let her go? After what they shared? She was the only part of him that mattered.

When Pedro opened his eyes, it wasn't revulsion saddening her lovely face. She cried. Her hands were cold when she circled her arms around him, placing her cheek above his heart. "Please, you must abandon the past."

"How can I? When it has solidified inside me? Turned into stones?"

"But they hurt you. They drag you down. Tell me how to mend this, Pedro. Tell me, and I will do it. Whatever it takes."

He didn't deserve her comfort and held her at arm's length. "Mend? Now you know the sort of man you spent the night with."

"Don't do this. Don't push me away."

Pedro relinquished his grip on her arms and paced to the window. The cloudless sky touched the ocean, giving the illusion that the horizon waited within reach. "You should do the pushing this time. Aren't you disgusted by my true nature? My selfishness?"

"Do you think I'm surprised? You love your brother. You are not to blame for this. If I'm crying, it is because of the terrible situation. No one should be put in that position. Ulrich is evil."

"Only him?"

"Of course. You taught me men could be evil. But not you. Never you."

"I always knew mankind's true nature. I lived with the best teacher. Before that night, I thought I was different. I prided myself on placing others' interests above my own. Of being noble. Mozambique showed how wrong I was. About myself."

She pursued him around the bedchamber, her eyes flashing with determination. "I removed my necklace because I found who I want to be with. Your tragic tale has not changed how I feel."

Pedro shook his head, hiding his truth from her trust.

She placed her palms on his cheeks, crying freely. "I love you."

Pedro stilled, his heart crashing against his ribs.

"Look at me. See if I'm telling the truth," she said, her voice clear. "Please."

He stared at her long and hard. It was all there, swimming in her ocean gaze. But she offered her love without knowing Pedro's relationship with her brother. Pedro had not asked to meet her, and he certainly was not proud of what he had done to keep her close. He could end the string of lies, but what if she demanded to return to her family? Or worse, escaped from him? Either would place her in danger.

But he was done forcing his will on her. After he proved his innocence and Ulrich was no longer a threat to her, Pedro would allow her to choose. She deserved his honesty.

He pulled her close and brushed away her tears. "I will take Fernando's evidence to Lisbon and do what is right."

"I know you will." Anne gifted him with her wobbly smile.

James padded into the room, and Pedro bent to pet his little head. "If you take care of her until I return, brigadier, I will bring you a medal."

"I thought he was a corporal."

"He was long due a promotion." Pedro straightened and pulled Anne closer for a kiss, tasting her trust, her love, her light. Opening his palm, he revealed her locket once more. "You once leaped into the fire to save this."

"Pedro—"

He placed a fingertip above her lips. "Would you keep it longer?" When he secured the chain around her neck, the heart-shaped locket caught the light from the morning sun, but it didn't rival Anne's luminous skin. "After I return, I will take you to your family. If you still believe I deserve this honor by then, you can remove it for good."

Chapter 37

Wandering through the orchard, Anne couldn't stop thinking about Pedro's revelation. She wished bringing Braganza's evidence to light would help diminish Pedro's guilt over Mozambique. Would it work? Or were his scars too deep? Too entrenched in Pedro's belief of himself to ever heal?

Pedro was a man of deep feeling but a harsh judge of his own actions. Witnessing his pain without being able to help had wrenched her heart.

Heavy clouds gathered atop the villa, and an unnatural stillness had turned the scenery into a painting. A storm brewed, and unwilling to get drenched, Anne took the trail back to the house.

When she entered the garden, a coach awaiting at the courtyard made her stumble. Her brother's brougham! Grinning, she collected her skirts and raced to the front door.

Griffin held James in his left arm and brandished his finger in Hilaria's face. "You will tell where my sister is this instant, or I will demolish this house."

The housekeeper glowered, her face a furious red. "Sir, you are stepping over his lordship's begonias—"

"I will step over much more if you don't give me an answer."

Anne laughed, breathless. "Griffin?"

Her brother stilled and then turned slowly. His clothes, always so impeccable, were wrinkled, and several days of beard shadowed his jaw. "Anne? Thank God."

Anne leaped into his arms. Griffin pulled her into a genuine embrace, not the customary taps she used to receive from him.

Pressed between them, James groaned.

Griffin passed her the dog and pushed her in the coach's direction. "Wait for me inside."

Anne planted her feet into the grass. "No, I—"

"Anne, not now." He dismissed her and turned to Hilaria. "I demand to speak with Almoster."

"Do you know this brute, Miss Anne? Will you tell him the master isn't here?"

"Pedro Daun will not leave this situation unscathed. This time he will pay for his crimes," her brother said, looking positively murderous.

There must be a mistake. Certainly, Griffin was right to feel out of sorts, even emotional, but why such hatred? A lot had happened since last they'd last seen each other, but she wasn't the child who had left Vesuvio, and Griffin would have to understand she would no longer take his orders. "Hilaria, can you please give us a minute?"

The housekeeper seemed about to club Griffin with her wooden spoon, but Anne smiled reassuringly. "This is my brother, and he usually has more manners than this." As soon as the housekeeper entered the kitchen, Anne turned to her brother. "I don't believe—"

"Is he watching? Is that why you act like a gracious guest and not a kidnapper's victim? I've traveled through this entire country after you, stopping at all his properties. In every bloody one, I expected to find you cowering, locked against your will in a dank room. Imagine my surprise to find you tanned and glowing as if—" His eyes widened. He pointed at her, and then he groaned. "By God, he seduced you, did he not?"

Her cheeks flamed, and she crossed her arms over her midriff. He had the right to be displeased that she had lost her virtue. Still, he would reconsider when he realized her feelings for Pedro. "Griffin, please, it is not what you think—"

"This is all my fault. When I learned Almoster was back in the Douro, I should have warned you away from him. I should have predicted the corrupt count would use you."

Anne's heart clenched, beating out of rhythm, and she placed a hand above her breastbone. "You are not making any sense. I thought you were old friends. Why would he use me?"

Griffin combed a hand over his windswept hair and stared at her, eyes flashing blue fire. "He didn't tell you about last summer? Of course, he didn't. If he had, how would he get his twisted revenge?"

Anne entered the hotel's foyer behind her brother, her arm numb from being pulled along the Chiado neighborhood. Her grand adventure had ended in Lisbon, after all. Still, the city of her dreams loomed overcrowded and gray. Pedro's lies had dulled the colors and hills as if her eyes had a lens turning beauty into ugliness.

Griffin paused in front of his suite at the Central Hotel. "You don't need to fret," he said gruffly, fumbling with the door key. "Whatever he did to you, I will... I will make it all right."

Anne averted her eyes. Griffin was confident he could salvage her. To him, a girl's reputation was a cracked vase. One glued it back together and turned the repaired patch to the wall so guests would not see it. Anne wondered if a girl's heart could be mended the same way.

Griffin pushed the door open, and Julia shot to her feet. Even with her advanced pregnancy, she was beautiful, and mature, and intelligent, and very much Portuguese. It made perfect sense Pedro had loved her so desperately. Did he love her still?

Standing in a strange room, Anne chased the buttons on her glove, searching for clues on how a wayward relative should return to her family's fold after falling from grace.

Griffin cleared his throat and whispered in his wife's ear. Julia's eyes widened.

Shame coloring her cheeks, Anne inspected the sun-burned carpet, envying the part in shadows, protected from the light by the dinner table.

Griffin kissed Julia's brows and her mouth. Suddenly cold, Anne brushed her arms and looked away, unable to witness their intimacy.

"I will leave you ladies to your, er... subjects," Griffin said and exited the room.

Anne had taken Julia from her beloved Vesuvio, and her sister-in-law had the right to be angry. Anne was prepared to receive a lecture, even an outright tongue-lashing. But when Julia exhaled and opened her arms, a watery smile on her lips, Anne cried out and rushed to her. Instead of reproach, Julia's hug was all understanding. Coaxed by her steady heartbeats, Anne cried freely.

Julia bade her sit on the couch.

Anne obeyed dutifully and told her everything with a detached voice. By the time she had finished, her throat was hoarse, and she shut her eyes. "So, you see? I've been trying to help this man I thought was the hero, but it turned out he was the villain..."

Julia grabbed her hand. "When we are young, we believe people are absolutely good or absolutely bad. But the greatest vintage is not perfect, and the simplest wine can have redeeming qualities."

"But I trusted him." How could he have manipulated her so? "He took me with him only to avenge himself on Griffin."

"Can I tell you a story?" Julia asked, holding tight to Anne's hands.

Her sister-in-law had a gift for storytelling, but Anne didn't care for one of Julia's tales now. She had heard enough horrible things about Pedro this morning to last her a lifetime.

Julia ignored her reticence and took a deep breath. "Once there was this golden boy, quiet and mature above his years. While all the children his age spent their time fishing and riding, he had more tutors than toys. His father hurt him terribly. One day, a girl found him by the river, his lip bruised. Back then, the girl believed herself quite a heroine." Julia's lips quirked up, her onyx eyes twinkling with unshed tears. "She treated his wound. The boy was starved for kindness, and he vowed he would marry her. But fate had other designs. The girl was betrothed to another, and the boy was sent away."

Anne couldn't help the ache squeezing her chest any more than she could halt Julia's words. Julia had known the noble Pedro who left for Mozambique, the boy who believed he could save the world.

Julia closed her eyes. "Ten years passed, and he returned. Changed. Hardened. But the man still carried the boy inside, and the boy still needed the girl's comfort. He fought, and he connived to make the girl his, because his father taught him—"

"Please don't justify Pedro's actions. Griffin told me how he tampered with your carriage and lied about you being his bride—"

"When I was sick and vulnerable, Pedro could've forced me to marry him, but he didn't. Last summer, I didn't think he wanted love. Not the love I share with your brother. He wanted salvation. In the end, he realized I couldn't give him what he desired." Julia, her gaze shining with determination, caught Anne's hand. "You are the one who will unlock his heart, who will show him what love is—"

"Please, stop." Anne had fervently wished for the perfect love of fairy tales, only to discover sharp-edged, broken, real-life love. Now she wanted neither. "It's over. I will accept whatever future Griffin will offer me."

Chapter 38

Lisbon's crammed buildings, their balconies wrestling above his head, engulfed Pedro in stark reality. Fernando's dossier against slave trading wasn't direct evidence of Pedro's innocence. He needed to speak with the king to explain his findings, but if he as much as put his feet inside Ajuda Palace to ask an audience with Dom Luis, he would find himself in iron chains.

But who could he trust? His brother's desertion brought to mind a practical and painful realization. Pedro had no one else.

A pair of officers on patrol crossed Pedro's path. Striding west, Pedro left the alley to Santo Amaro Avenue. He grabbed the railing of the Americano tram and propelled himself inside. Keeping his gaze down, he dropped to the backbench. The vehicle chugged along, the mule's hooves beating a staccato rhythm on the cobblestones. Pedro felt several pairs of eyes on him and lowered his hat. When the tram turned onto São George Street, Pedro jumped out.

The trees and green iron fence of the Estrela Garden poked his line of vision. Inside the park, he found the same old bench below the dragon tree. With a heavy exhale, he settled on the unforgiving seat, stretching his legs and crossing his arms.

Eight o'clock, and the sun began its descent beyond the Tagus. The view hit him in the chest. Lisbon's favorite summer pastime: an evening in the park. Children fed swans, their pinafores and short trousers mirrored on the lake's surface. Brazilian rosewoods, rubber trees, and the majestic Lebanese cedar shaded the walkways. A waltz spilled from the bandstand, and laughter flowed in the breeze. Couples strolled, their hands clasped. And in the center, the grand carousel spun, colors whirling in a rainbow of cheers.

He had often sat under the shadows of this dragon tree, staring at others' lives, not being part of it and not really wanting to. Today, as the ride turned, that angry indifference, the feeling of being denied something he despised in the first place, never came. It used to repel him, this warmth of mellow smiles, of snug afternoons, of a lover's embrace. Now he might as well be sitting on a glacier, so desolate was the bite of its absence.

Anne would love it here. She would bring her children, a girl with the same champagne hair, a toddler hanging on her skirts, waiting for a turn on the carousel.

Pedro rubbed his chest right above where his heart was supposed to be. He wanted inside that carousel, too.

If he and Anne were to have a future, he must focus on what had to be done. There weren't many options. He could proceed alone, hunt Ulrich by himself, force his confession. But he was tired of war. He needed his name cleared to start a new phase in his life, not destroying but building.

Pedro crossed the garden, heeding the call of another familiar place. With brittle legs, he stopped in front of São Bernardo Street, number 33. He stared at Fontes's solar, and the house glowered back at him, cross-eyed and gray-faced. Built after the earthquake that leveled the city in 1755, it was a prime example of the Marquis of Pombal architecture, only three floors, a revolutionary anti-seismic system, and absolutely no decorations protruding from the walls. The result lacked beauty, but the efficient style perfectly matched his godfather's puritanical beliefs.

Night had fallen with all its shadows. While he stood in the darkness, the glass surrounding Fontes's door sparkled. Girding his resolve, Pedro climbed the steps to the front porch and knocked.

The door swung open, his hand still mid-air. A mop of brown hair and vivid gray eyes peeked at him from the other side. He would recognize that freckled nose and coltish disposition anywhere. Gabriel's baby sister. Only she was no baby. She must be the same age as Anne, a girl of eighteen.

"Are you opening doors, Manuela?" Pedro drawled.

"Tista is feeling poorly." She eyed him from his boots to the saber hanging from his belt. Placing gloved hands on her waist, she cocked her hip to the side. "Have you come to kill Father?"

"No."

She raised her brows. "Gabriel?"

Pedro's lips twitched. "Only if he provokes me."

"Pity." She shrugged, opening the door wide. "He never does, nowadays."

"Is your father home?"

She nodded.

Pedro stepped inside and was swept to the past by the scent of pastry and beeswax, the brass Argand lamps, the Norman tapestries, and the toile du jour wallpaper. He used to come here daily for his afternoon lessons, notebook under one arm, bumping Santiago's shoulder and tweaking Manu's ponytails.

"Are you coming? I'll let him know you are here."

Exhaling, he followed Manuela's petite frame. A painting in the corridor made him pause. His mother. She sat with her hands folded on her lap, an indulgent smile on her lips, gazing at an infant. The boy played with wooden soldiers at her feet.

He had forgotten the love in her caramel eyes.

"I missed you here, cousin." Manu smiled and pointed to the open library. "Take it easy on *Papa*."

"What do you want?" The voice, stern and rough, came from the doorway. Fontes circled his customary chair by the hearth but didn't sit. Instead, he crossed his arms, his face a mask of contempt.

Pedro emerged from the shadows into the light of the chandelier. "Assistance. I discovered evidence that can extinguish slave trading and prove my innocence."

Fontes frowned. New lines radiated from his eyes, a hardness to his mouth Pedro hadn't seen before, not even when he had shut the door on Pedro's face after Mozambique. "It's too late."

Coming here had been a mistake. Pedro unclenched his hands and touched Braganza's dossier. "Too late for the truth?"

"For a long time, I wanted to believe in your truths. Your mother, *Que Deus a tenha*, would understand I strove to turn you into a noble subject."

"What a grand job you did." Pedro paced to the window. Outside, the carousel spun in the park dizzyingly.

"She was my sister, and I loved her above all else."

Then why abandon him after his return from Mozambique? Pedro had needed him, damn it. His guidance, support, understanding... Instead, the only welcome he had received had been his father's. Pedro shut his eyes. "Stop talking about her."

"You were a prince among men, the noblest heart, the keenest mind, the strongest physique. You could have changed the world. But what did you do with your greatness? You squandered it on petty acts of revenge. Fighting for profit, for power, for yourself." Fontes took a sharp breath, his eyes shining feverishly. "You are not like her. You are the spitting image of your father, vain and selfish. I made a deathbed promise to your mother that I would take care of her beloved son. I covered your villainy once, but never again."

Pedro turned and faced his godfather, eyebrows raised. "Covered for me? When have you ever—"

"Pretending ignorance doesn't become you. But perhaps it does, only I was too blind to see. To this day, I can't believe how you fooled me so completely." A catch in Fonte's voice betrayed emotion, a reminder of the uncle Pedro had grown up with, had looked up to.

Fontes fisted his hand over his heart. "I loved you better than my own son."

All these years, Pedro had waited to hear those words. Throat constricted, he reached for Fontes. For a second, he glimpsed his uncle inside the granite facade, but Fontes raised his palms to shield his chest. Pedro stepped back, arms hanging by his sides.

Silence stretched. Music from the park wandered through the window like children lost from their mother, too light and pure to belong here.

"I should have denounced you after the Zambezi mission, but I reasoned that recklessness and some stupid dare had made you sell those Africans under your guard. I wronged you." Fontes inhaled and stood up, erasing all traces of emotion from his countenance. "Because I didn't punish you, your crimes escalated. You are beyond redemption."

The floor swayed beneath him, and Pedro held the back of the couch. All this time, Fontes had believed he'd delivered the village to slavery? How? He opened his mouth, but words wouldn't form. His throat had crippled into silence.

A clatter of feet and raised voices came from the corridor. Before Pedro could process what was happening, a trio of red-coated officers entered the library, pistols pointing to his chest.

Outside, the carousel spun without him.

The tower's naked stone walls dripped with humidity. A single gas lamp hissed, casting unreliable shadows over the caskets and blackened bottles. As a courtesy to his rank, Pedro had been locked alone in the old wing of Saint George's Castle instead of the common pits. The ancient cellar became a perfect prison—steel reinforced door, iron bars crisscrossed over the single window, and no chance of escape.

Seated on a bench, Pedro dropped his head to his palms. While the granite froze his spine, he scored the numbers of his downfall—two wars, three years in Napoleon III's court, seventeen living under the Duke of Titano's roof, and never had he been ambushed like this.

Yet here he was. Locked. His godfather must have sent for the officers when Manuela had alerted him of Pedro's arrival, choosing to disregard whatever he had to say beforehand. So wretched was Fontes's opinion of him that he concluded Braganza's dossier to be evidence of Pedro's crimes.

For ten years, Fontes had considered him capable of convicting two hundred and fifty-five adults and eighty-one children into slavery. No wonder he supposed Pedro guilty of shooting his best friend. When a wolf with blood on his jaws claimed he didn't kill the sheep, was it to be believed?

Fontes judged Pedro to be the image of his father. Growing up, Pedro had rebelled against his father's enlightened self-interest, a philosophical excuse to expropriate personal gain from political advantages. To his father's delight, Pedro had come back from Africa reformed. After Mozambique, Pedro had thought the world was out to get him, and he had sought to get the world first. Expecting the worst of others, he had shown others the worst of himself.

The reality of his situation sank in slowly. As he wouldn't confess to a crime he didn't commit, the best he could hope for was a rotten stay here, like the wine inside these barrels, aging without light, echoes of previous seasons, vulnerable to the whims of others.

Why this? Damn it, he wanted to leave the shadows of his past.

Pedro inhaled the cool air, the scent of aged wood and alcohol dulling his senses. Outside, no park, no bandstand, no carousel, just sentry torches moving in the darkness, pools of light wandering the mosaic paths.

He closed his eyes, picturing what could have been. A life with Anne in a sunny place, like Crete or Nice or Algarve, where he could've watched her skin turn bright honey, the sun freckling the bridge of her nose. She would've gifted him with her gazes, and he would've started each day tangled in her hair.

The image brought a painful jolt to his chest, and his eyelids shot open. He stared at the flickering flame until his pupils burned.

What if Ulrich persecuted Anne to eliminate a potential witness? A vise closed around his rib cage. He must speak with Gabriel. His cousin was honorable and could take her to the Douro. Once there, Maxwell would protect her.

The door creaked open. Pedro reached instinctively for his scabbard, but his hand came out empty, the saber removed before they had imprisoned him.

A guard shoved Cris inside and locked the door again.

Cris, hands tied, glared at the door, then faced Pedro. "So, this was your great idea?"

Of all the times his brother could show up, he had chosen now?

"What in the blazes are you doing here?"

"I've read the newspapers." Cris presented his arms for untying. "I would appreciate a thank you. At least some brotherly affection."

"Did you bring reinforcements?" Pedro loosened the knots on Cris's hands. At his brother's sheepish smile, he sagged on the bench. "Where have you been?"

"Here and there. I visited Quinta das Lágrimas. The place where Inês de Castro was killed."

Pedro eyed his brother wearily. "You became a tourist?"

"The gardens are beautiful. When the wind blows, it whispers over the willows, and one can swear it is Inês, calling for her lost lover."

Throat dry, Pedro studied a spider climbing the wall. "Why are you telling me this?"

Cris exhaled and lifted his palms. "I was scared. I've said it. I feared losing you, and instead of welcoming Anne as a little sister, I tried to keep you apart. What a fool, eh? I should have seen the obvious. You love her."

Love? Was that the word for what he felt? This need to pursue, to possess, to protect? Men loved their prize horses, their weekend hunting, their games.

Pedro placed his palm above his chest. His heart pulsed stronger than ever but was no longer his. The keeper, infinitely more vulnerable and precious than him, was Anne.

His connection to her was more like a state of being—a place. A meadow he'd glimpsed when she had appeared in Salgueiro. One he had denied, barricaded himself outside, scoffed at its poor defenses, and now would wage a war to see its sunlit grass one more time. A place of drowning in dry land and breathing underwater, where the skin hummed with energy, where pain became pleasure, and shadows became light.

Cris waited for an answer, eyes humid.

Pedro glanced away, reluctant to say it out loud. It wouldn't matter. The tower's stones harbored no lovers, no meadow. "Now I have a heart?"

Cris touched Pedro's shoulder. "I think you have the biggest heart this side of the Tagus. You're just damn good at hiding it."

Pedro grasped his brother's broad frame. God, he had missed the rascal. He should have embraced him more. Who would take care of him now?

"Perhaps a tad rusty, too." Cris chuckled, slapping Pedro's back. "But you'll manage. After we break free."

Pedro held Cris at arm's length. With his brother here, his accusers had more leverage against him. The last time someone had attempted to kill a king in Portugal was in 1758, and his fate had been exemplary. Dom Jose had killed not only the Duke of Aveiro but wiped out all his household, including his servants.

Cris leaned his hip on a port pipe. "So, what is our plan?"

"I will propose a deal." Pedro's stay at the tower would be brief, after all. Those convicted of killing royalty had short life expectancies.

"Always with a card up your sleeve, eh?" Cris smiled. "What will it be?"

Chapter 39

Anne woke up with a terrible migraine. She opened her eyes to a strange, opaque hotel room. After living in a perfect dream, reality had plucked her back. She pressed her fists to her head, trying to return to the dream. But it was useless. Every time she opened her eyes, it was to dull mahogany walls and Pedro's absence.

Restless, she turned to lie on her stomach. The locket pierced the skin of her chest, and she yanked it away. She stared at it, regret making it hard to breathe. She could not keep the memories from coming, from Pedro's protective rages to his unbridled lovemaking. Their last moment together had been the most bittersweet. Pedro had lovingly traced the burns on her palms and promised to accept her heart if she thought he was still worth it.

Anne clasped the locket. Perhaps he regretted his lies.

What if Julia was right? Could Pedro have changed because of her? He would return to the villa eager to see her, to celebrate his success, only to discover her absence. She would join the ranks of people in his life who had abandoned him. She could not bear to think of his pain.

Voices floated from the connecting chamber. Anne sat up, pulling her legs to the side of the bed. Julia and Griffin. She covered her camisole with a wrapper and crept silently to the half-opened door, peeking in at the adjoining room.

"But Griffin, don't you see? She is in love with him." Julia caressed her tummy, worrying her lip between her teeth.

Griffin snorted, his brows cocked arrogantly. "Love? My sister is an incurable romantic. According to Anne, love is the cure for all maladies. Have recurrent sadness? Put the fellow to love. A bad tooth? Put him to love. A sore back? Put him to love. Tender digestion? Put him to love. A habit of telling lies? Love! But even you must admit, love is no cure for Pedro Daun."

Her brother was wrong. Had love not cured his own prejudices? Before he'd met Julia, he had lived a barren life, obsessed with work. Why couldn't love cure Pedro's anguish?

Julia glared at her brute of her husband. "But— "

"Don't give me that face, Julia. I know exactly what you are thinking. But you won't maneuver me out of this. I'm sending her to England. She can stay with my mother's relations and have a Season. The scandal would not have reached there and with a proper dowry..."

Blood climbed Anne's head until the tips of her ears burned. She fisted her hands so hard her nails bit into her palms. "No."

Griffin stopped his ranting and turned, his mouth hanging open. "What did you say?"

"You don't know Pedro as I do. He made mistakes in the past, but he deserves a second chance."

"I will tell you who Pedro Daun is. Pedro Daun is a scoundrel, a blackguard, a ravisher of young women."

Anne took a fortifying breath. "Griffin, I'm a grown woman. I love Pedro, and he needs me."

Julia let out a squeal but hushed when Griffin turned to her.

Griffin recovered from his shock and crossed his arms above his chest. "He is beyond your help."

"What do you mean?"

Griffin picked a newspaper and passed it to her. Anne gazed at Pedro's picture and lifted her eyes to her brother, searching for answers on his face. "He was... he was arrested? Griffin, Pedro is innocent. I told you! I saw everything. Please, you must help him."

"It is time that blackguard paid for his crimes." Her brother stood and adjusted his coat.

Anne grabbed his arm, tugging it desperately. "Please, he has no one else."

"You won't change my mind."

"Then I must go myself."

Her brother ignored her. "You will board the *HMS Victoria* for Liverpool tomorrow. Until then, you will take your meals inside your bedroom."

Anne raced to her room and shut the door. Her legs collapsed beneath her, and she bit the side of her hand to contain her scream. She couldn't allow it. They could not hang an innocent man.

She brushed away her tears and forced herself to stand. She had no time for despair. She must speak with the king. Many said he was a just monarch. Anne chose a sober day dress and arranged her hair into a severe bun at her nape. Surreptitiously, she checked the room by her side. Julia hummed softly, folding her clothes into a valise.

She could speak with her sister-in-law and ask for help. Though Julia could be counted on to understand, Anne didn't want to cause her problems with Griffin.

James padded close to her and nibbled her leg.

Anne crouched and kissed his furrowed brow. "I'm sorry, James. You cannot go this time. But Julia will take care of you, I promise."

Anne emerged from the dark foyer into the bright Rossio Square, the sunshine leaving black spots in her vision. From her Lisbon brochures, she knew the king resided atop a hill by the city's east side. She placed her hand atop her forehead to shield the light and located the neoclassical facade. The windows glinted like tiny stars, leagues away from her.

All her logical reasoning dissolved like frost in the harsh morning sun. Would the king even receive her? Ignoring her doubts, she sprang into motion.

Clerks and storekeepers hastened with their over-coats strained over their chests. Patrons shouldered her out of the way. Carriages passed, their harness jingling, the hooves pounding inside her head. The Americano tram sped through the avenue, sounding the bell. If she could catch it, she would reach the palace in a fraction of the time.

When Anne crossed the street, a dog cart screeched to a halt an inch from her chest. Heart speeding, she apologized for her clumsiness and weaved through the traffic.

The streetcar reached the crossing.

Her legs protested as she increased her speed, confined by the narrow skirt of her dress.

Four feet from the tram, a figure trapped her attention. The man who had come to the beach house after Pedro. She remembered his ferret face. His gaze caught hers, and a flare of recognition sparkled in his leery eyes.

Her mouth went dry, her hand coming up to touch the top of her head. In her haste, she had forgotten a bonnet, and though her hair was pulled up in a tight chignon, the coloring stood out like a beacon.

Anne gave up the tram and moved in the opposite direction, tripping over the hem of her dress, her breaths coming in short bursts, the constricting corset fighting her breaths. She left the main street and entered a side alley, hoping it could give her a better cover, and glanced over her shoulder.

No one had followed.

Gasping, she leaned her back on the scratchy facade of a building, closing her eyes in relief.

A cloth clamped over her mouth. She didn't have time to scream before alcohol invaded her nostrils. And then she couldn't think anymore.

The ropes chafed Anne's wrists and ankles. Gray light poured from slits in the heavy drapery. On her stomach, hands tied behind her back, she lifted her chin to inspect her surroundings, but the movement made the room spin. She rested her forehead on the satin sheets, wheezing her breaths.

"Can you untie my hands, please?"

"So polite." A rough hand circled her neck and pulled, lifting her head. "How is your poor, poor mother? You are an excellent actress. It's a pity Ulrich has his eyes set on you. But after he is done..."

The ferret man tapped her cheek, and his fetid breath made her recoil.

She fought the dizziness and stared at her assailant's face. Black, opaque eyes oozed malice. A wave of nausea washed over Anne, and she controlled the impulse to retch. His hatred slapped her in the face. She had never been the recipient of such animosity in her life.

Anne considered her options. She needed out of here, but trussed up, her chances of escape were dismal. "Do you think your master will approve if my skin is brutally chafed?"

The man brooded, and Anne counted his rasping breaths. Somewhere in the house, a door opened, followed by a woman's guttural moan. Just when Anne began to despair, he untied her wrists and ankles. Thousands of prickles coursed through her as blood returned to her limbs, and Anne had to clamp her mouth shut to avoid crying.

He grabbed her hand cruelly and, pulling her upward, shoved her face against the window. "Ulrich chose this bedroom for a reason. Do you see the square? You will have a prime seat to watch when they hang your lover."

"No—"

"Ulrich has a man working in the jail, you know? If the trial takes too long, the famous Count of Almoster will be gutted like a common thug."

Laughing, he strutted out of the bedroom.

When the door clicked shut, and she heard the ominous turn of a key, Anne slid to the floor. Ice crept up her spine, and Anne fought its gripping tendrils.

Pedro needed her.

She launched herself onto the drapery and pulled it away. Outside, night still reigned. The window latch would not budge. It had been sealed shut. She pushed all her weight against it, to no avail.

Tears of frustration gathered in her eyes, but she kept tugging. If she had a sharp object to peel off the plaster...

Anne searched the room, opening drawers, and wrenching an armoire open. Finding only gaudy dresses and flimsy lingerie, Anne shoved the cabinet's door shut, a scream locked in her throat.

Panting, she gazed from the door to the window. After Ulrich came for her, there would be no saving Pedro. A vase rested atop the commode. It would have to do. She enveloped it in a pillowcase to avoid unnecessary noise and smashed it, then chose a pointed shard from the remains.

Anne stumbled to the window and worked furiously over the plaster. When the first chinks of paint fell over the floor, she felt a glimmer of hope.

Chapter 40

Dawn had colored the sky when Gabriel found the will to leave his club and return to the solar. He climbed the carpeted steps to his room, secluded at the back of the house. By God, how had he become trapped in this? Implicated in Ulrich's conspiracy, a participant in his schemes. Exhaling, he pinched the bridge of his nose and dropped on the tall-backed chair. Bile rose in his throat, and he took a swig of *aguardente* to push it down.

Fumbling with his jacket, he felt around the inner pocket for the note. The paper was of the lowest quality, and his vision blurred as he stared at the crooked handwriting. Ulrich champed at the bit for his society's entrance. He asked—better yet, demanded—that Gabriel arrange it for next Friday. How could Gabriel uncover proof of his involvement in Braganza's murder and slave trading in only eight days? All his hopes rested on Santiago scouting Ulrich's address. Would his friend be able to enter the Siren and find clues about Ulrich's den? What if Ulrich caught him? Gabriel shouldn't have involved him in this sordid mess.

Gabriel gulped another mouthful of the volatile drink. He pushed the bottle away and grabbed a pencil. Rolling his shoulders, he brought the graffiti to where light pooled on the paper and freed his hand to draw. A curve of a cheek, the down-sweep of long hair, an impish nose, arched brows. A silhouette took form. Anne Maxwell evading her eyes, just like she had back under the umbrella pine. Why possess the ability to conjure her image so well when she was beyond his reach? He crumpled the drawing in his fist and sagged against the chair.

His bedroom door crashed into the wall. Manu bounded inside, hair flowing around her face, freckled cheeks bright red.

"When will you learn to knock, imp?" Gabriel exhaled and rubbed his forehead. "I don't have time for your antics."

She tugged his arm. "Come quickly."

Gabriel pulled away and stored the drawing in his pocket. This wasn't the right day to try his patience. He had caught her wrist to guide her out when he saw her eyes. Disturbed, they couldn't seem to focus anywhere.

He cradled her face. "What is it, dear?"

"Pedro Daun came last night. He spoke with Father. I don't know what happened, but Father is distraught."

Gabriel sucked in a breath. Had Fontes somehow discovered the truth? "Where is he?"

"Good morning, sir." Gabriel entered his father's bed-chamber, glad his voice rang even.

Father buttoned his military coat, watching his reflection in the mirror. The jacket sagged on his frame, evidence of the weight loss since Pedro had been accused of murdering Braganza. He seemed older, his carriage hunched, the skin around his face sallower. "Why didn't you attend dinner last night? I'm on my way to Saint George's Castle."

"What happened?"

"You should accompany me." He lifted his eyes from his reflection, and their gazes met in the mirror. "I've done *your* duty and arrested the Count of Almoster."

Gabriel's breath caught. "Arrested Pedro? How?"

"It is not important." Father's voice wavered, and he lowered his gaze.

Gabriel loosened his cravat and exhaled through his mouth. "Did he say something?"

"I am done with his lies." Father tried to pin the Order of The Christ above his chest, but his hand shook, and with a soft click, he dropped the medal back into the onyx box.

Gabriel ambled to the bed, his gait unsteady. If Fontes had arrested Pedro, the population would clamor for a swift resolution, and the other ministers would push for a public execution. The republicans had gathered strength in congress, and the king couldn't afford to show weakness. Good-hearted Dom Luis would have no alternative but to concede.

Gabriel knew what he had to do. The truth about Pedro's innocence, about his own participation, swelled in his chest, wanting out. "Father."

"Yes?"

Gabriel opened his mouth, gathering the strength to say it.

Father came closer, halting a mere breath away. "I'm sorry for my curtness." He placed his hand over Gabriel's shoulder. "I'm proud of you, son."

Gabriel stilled, stunned by the unusual praise. The hand was cold and bony, but the warmth touched his chest.

Nodding once, twice, Father strode out of the room.

The menage tower of Saint George's Castle loomed on Gabriel's front, the sun igniting the stones. Atop the city's highest hill, the majestic pile of rocks had housed Roman garrisons, defended the Moors inside its impregnable walls, nursed the cream of Portuguese aristocracy, belched cannon fire to repel Napoleon's advances, and now imprisoned their criminals.

Gabriel gave a last look at the city, sprawled beneath the fortress moat. Where was Santiago? If the priest appeared with a clue to Ulrich's location, Gabriel would donate all his billets to the church. But as he followed his father's resolute steps into the ward's office, the Roman portal remained empty.

The news of Pedro's arrest had spread like typhus. If he could convince Father—no, there would be no changing his mind. Fontes was an oak, set in his ways. In comparison, it made mortals look like willows.

The stocky ward greeted them with a clumsy bow. "The prisoner requires a word with His Excellency, the defense minister."

Father grunted. "Very well."

Gabriel touched his father's shoulder. "Are you sure this is advisable? I can go in your place."

"You will wait here."

Gabriel nodded and lowered his weight onto the ward's couch. The *aguardente* churned in his empty stomach, nausea sweeping him in waves. He would give anything, anything, to go back to that day. God, he'd been so relieved. To return with the regiment after an entire year, only to plunge himself into a deeper hell than the dusty bloodshed of the Zambezi.

The clock struck the half-hour, and Gabriel stood. What could Pedro have to say that took so long? Cleaning perspiration from his brow, Gabriel descended the stairs to the cellar, feet tactless in the dark, the air brisk as a crypt's.

Movement downstairs. Officers. He recognized who they were escorting. Cris. Pedro's brother dragged his feet over the steps, his hands tied. He looked like a beast being herded to the slaughterhouse.

The officer saluted Gabriel.

"Where are you taking him?"

"To the ward's office. The count wished to speak with the minister alone."

Cris lifted his eyes, straining against the bindings. "Gabriel, you mustn't let him do it.

"What?"

Cris groaned and shook his head. "He wants to confess, but he is innocent. It's my fault. He sacrificed his honor for me in Mozambique. I can't take his life too."

"Sacrifice? I'll... I'll see what I can do." Gabriel pressed his spine to the wall so the group could proceed upstairs. Coldness seeped into his lungs as the guards' crimson coats vanished above, swallowed by the corridor's light. Would Pedro admit to a crime he hadn't committed to save his brother? Be forever branded as a murderer and a traitor?

Gabriel laughed bitterly. Of course, he would. How utterly like him, to take command of the situation, set his own terms, and lead. Even cornered, the perfect Pedro Daun had honor to spare.

Gabriel descended to the landing, his legs negotiating the steps slowly. Voices spilled from the open door, not the ramblings of prisoners pleading for their lives, but the serious timbre of statesmen discussing the fate of nations.

Kept outside, not being invited to their conversation, Gabriel was... what? A sulking child? Father should have asked for his presence. He was the head of the king's guard, and arresting Pedro was his duty. Cursing under his breath, he pushed the door open.

Fontes's expression made him halt. White brackets surrounded his mouth, and his lips were purple as if he had drunk red wine. Pedro leaned against the wall. He didn't resemble a prisoner but a Greek hero sculpted from precious ivory.

Fontes wouldn't meet Gabriel's eyes. "I'll wait upstairs."

His father left, closing the door behind him.

Gabriel sprang forth. "What is going on? I don't understand."

"Fontes agreed to release Cris in exchange for a written confession."

Gabriel gasped. "Your brother isn't willing to—"

"It's done." Pedro stepped closer. "I have a final issue to discuss with you."

Pedro watched him with clear, focused eyes. How could he be so composed?

A trickle of sweat descended on his spine, and Gabriel swallowed. "This is so sudden. What happened to your innocence claims? I can't believe you won't—"

"That's not why I asked to speak with you alone."

"Then what?" Gabriel's voice cracked.

"I have a request." Pedro rubbed his chest, and for the first time, his expression revealed high emotion. "I suppose you remember Miss Maxwell?"

Gabriel pushed his hand inside his pocket, feeling for the girl's portrait. Indeed, he remembered her. Much more than he should. "What about her?"

Pedro took a shaking breath. "I need you to escort Anne—Miss Maxwell—to her brother."

Somewhere from the Douro to Lisbon, Pedro must have become attached to Anne Maxwell. Gabriel pressed the sketch into a tight ball, his legs unsteady.

Would events turn this way, then? Pedro, imprisoned and possibly killed, the girl returned. Worried about her reputation, Griffin Maxwell would welcome an offer of marriage from him, son of the defense minister, head of his majesty's guard. This should bring him joy, right?

Why, then, did it feel like a drawing lacking the notion of perspective, flat and hollow? Why hadn't Gabriel called on her the day after he'd met her? He could be married, free from this whole sordid mess.

Gabriel gazed away from Pedro's fathomless eyes. He walked the few steps to the bench and sat, staring at the rough granite covering the floor.

"Gabriel, this is vital." Pedro raised his voice. "Will you go to my villa and return Miss Maxwell to her family? You must advise Maxwell to protect her."

"Do you think he will go after her?" Gabriel blurted and instantly cringed. "You spoke of Ulrich the last time we met."

Pedro stilled, his eyes assessing. "I believe Ulrich will."

Gabriel pushed away from the bench and paced to the farthest corner of the cellar. "After I left the coudelaria, I couldn't find evidence of others' involvement. To prove your innocence."

"I understand. Your father is waiting." Pedro took a long breath and strode to the door. The flickering lamplight touched his silhouette, erasing the passage of time. No longer the Count of Almoster, a ruthless politician, Gabriel saw his eighteen-year-old cousin. The cousin who had shared his meager paper supply and shot his candle at night so Gabriel wouldn't shame himself during morning drills.

"Pedro?"

His cousin turned.

Gabriel shut his eyes. "I'm sorry."

They gathered in the ward's office. Gabriel held the back of a chair, his knuckles white. Cris slumped on the couch, eyes red-rimmed. Under the shadow of the entailed cross, face resolute, Pedro wrote the confession.

While Father stared at the unlit hearth, conflict raged inside his rigid facade, invisible but as salient as the naked walls of the castle—his heart pleading to let his precious godson go while his unflinching honor demanded justice be served at all costs.

Gabriel shifted his weight, his legs tingling, begging for movement. He could leave the castle and take the Geira road to Spain, keep going until he reached Santiago the Compostela.

Would the path wear out his sins?

They had agreed Pedro would sign a confession. Cris would be set free and stay under the Fontes's protection. Gabriel would return the girl to her family and assure Maxwell and society that she had been a hostage but treated with decency.

Pedro stood. "It is done."

A breathless silence pervaded the room. Gabriel wanted to apologize for the insensitivity of the brass clock pounding the hours, the gas lamps hissing insistently, and his own rasping breaths.

Cris rose first, hair disheveled, clothing rumpled. He ambled in Pedro's direction, rubbing his forehead, then latched himself to his brother, sobs racking his torso.

Throat constricted, Gabriel had to look away. Father leaned on the mantelpiece. His hands trembled, cadaveric in the dim room. It would not happen in front of them, but Father's structure wouldn't survive this earthquake. He would crumble.

The weight of a thousand concrete tons pressed against Gabriel's chest, constricting his lungs. "He is innocent."

His words echoed in the ceiling's beams as if spoken by another man. He had the audience's full attention, but he ignored everyone except his father.

Fontes frowned, deep pleats appearing between his brows. "What are you saying, son?

Gabriel took a shuddering breath, fisting his hands. "He wasn't even close to the king's procession. Pedro was locked in his quinta, drunk. One of my soldiers confessed to having planted the evidence."

Cris gaped at him. "How long have you known this?"

"A few weeks."

Pedro's brother lurched into action. Before Gabriel could raise his arm to protect himself, Cris's fist connected with his jaw. The blow jerked his face with such force that his balance faltered. He took a step back, pain exploding behind his eyelid, and touched his cheekbone. His fingers came away sticky. Ears ringing, he knew he had to defend himself, but his arms wouldn't respond.

Cris grabbed his lapels, and Gabriel stared into his feral green eyes, willing Cris to knock him cold.

Pedro clasped his brother's shoulder. "Let him speak."

Fontes stepped closer, frowning. "Why have you kept this, son?"

Gabriel cleaned the blood with his shirt sleeve. No more lies. "I'm being blackmailed by João Ulrich, the true assassin."

His father flinched and retraced several steps, muttering to himself. A second passed, then two. Gabriel knew what must be poisoning his father's thoughts and braced himself for the question that would no doubt follow.

Fontes's expression hardened, and he squared his shoulders, the statue of authority so familiar to Gabriel. "What leverage does the scum have on you? Why did you choose to convict an innocent man instead of acting honorably?"

Gabriel flinched at the hardness in his father's eyes, but he couldn't escape. He opened his mouth, and the lie that had shaped his life broke free. He told them how he had disembarked in Lisbon after an entire year in east Africa, waiting to see his family, his country. How Father, using his best uniform, had come in person to greet the returning army. But Pedro hadn't been aboard the frigate. God, Father's disappointment at seeing him instead of the golden godson...

Gabriel held his father's gaze. "It hurt, and I wanted to hurt you. I've lied to you. Pedro did not sell the African families into slavery. He risked his life to save them."

He stared at his father's stony expression, the rest of the room blurring. The silence was too thick. A compulsion to scream flitted through his mind, and he clamped his mouth shut.

"You shame me." Father's voice shook.

"Believe me, I'm quite familiar with your shame."

Santiago had told him the truth would make him feel better. The priest had lied.

A cough wracked Father's torso, and his face lost color. Wheezing, hand clawing his coat, he collapsed to the floor.

"Father?" Pulse racing, Gabriel stumbled in his direction.

Fontes raised his palms. "Don't call me that."

Chapter 41

Pedro's first impulse was to leave the castle. His godfather and Gabriel had done enough and could deal with their woes. Gritting his teeth, he tried to harden his resolve. It didn't work. With two strides, he reached Fontes and held his hand. The older man's face was rigid, mouth opening and closing, eyes shining with a voiceless plea.

"Summon the doctor," Pedro ordered a shocked Gabriel. "Cris, help me carry him to the couch."

It took a lot of effort to move his godfather's solid frame. Fontes reclined on the cushions, his color ashen, but the strain had left his expression.

Cris passed him a crumpled paper. "It must have fallen after I punched the *pulha*."

Opening the sheet, Pedro recognized both artist and muse. His cousin's talents had not evolved, his traces still beautiful but lacking confidence. Anne's gaze, though, he had captured brilliantly. While once jealousy would taint Pedro's judgment, now pity swept him. How had Gabriel suffered, being in love and knowing Pedro had Anne all these days? If the situation had been reversed, Pedro would have scourged hell to bring her back.

"You must call him out," Cris whispered, his nostrils flaring. "The damn straight arrow stomped on your honor."

Pedro stared at his brother's eyes, the green fire a strange substitute for his usual optimism. Wrath had been Pedro's close companion for a long time, and before, a duel would have been the right choice—the only choice. But he was stunned by the tremendous shift Gabriel's confession had produced in his life, to consider a moment beyond the next second, the next heartbeat.

The doctor arrived. While the man examined his godfather, Pedro paced to the window. Outside the tower, Lisbon awakened. The Tagus River caught fire, and sunshine sparkled over the whitewashed residences. Anne was right. Dawn from Saint George's Castle was a feast of light.

Gabriel's revelation swirled in his mind like the tide filling the recesses of a cave. Pedro waited for anger to arise, the need for vengeance. It never came. Instead, tiredness weighted his bones, a numbness to the whole drama playing out around him. He also felt regret for the years lost. With his clear conscience, Cris wouldn't understand, but Pedro was grateful Gabriel had dared to speak. Pedro had spread more than his share of lies, and God knew they were hard to admit. Because Gabriel had faced his shadows, Pedro had a place to come back to—Anne.

"Your Excellency?" Adjusting his spectacles, the doctor fixed him with a professional glance. "I believe the defense minister will recover. He only needs rest."

The doctor left, and through the open door, Pedro watched Gabriel receiving the same news and then slumping to the floor, his face hidden between bent knees.

Pedro had failed to see before, but now it glared at him—the truth. What had it been like to grow up feeling inferior? He had suffered Titano's lessons, but in his twisted mentality, the duke had given him full attention. And Pedro had grown up with Fontes.

The afternoons spent studying with his uncle, the hunting, the dressage, played in his head, but this time depressingly, as Pedro saw it through his cousin's eyes. It must have been unbearable to never feel good enough.

"My own son." Fonte's voice sounded like a requiem. Pedro approached the bed. His uncle's eyes moistened, and he grabbed Pedro's hand. "I'll never forgive him."

Uncle locked himself in a tower of stones. The same rocks Pedro carried inside his chest.

"A bright person told me the past drags us down, making us sink. I ignored the advice then, but now I can see its wisdom. Letting the past occupy the present is easy, but it makes us bitter. True courage, though, is to forget. To forgive."

Fontes sighed. "He had no right. God, when I think of the suffering... I believed I knew him."

"No one knows him." Pedro pressed his uncle's hand. "Not even himself. He tried to be somebody else, for your sake."

"No." Fontes looked away, but deep lines marred his forehead.

"Gabriel acted wrongly, but it took him a lot of courage to admit the truth."

"You have the right to process him for libel. I won't object."

"The past no longer concerns me."

"What will you do?"

The question resonated with the promise of a thousand beginnings. Pedro had several plans, and all involved a girl with Atlantic eyes.

"I'll speak with Gabriel, and together, we will bring to justice the real criminal."

Pedro rode to the Ajuda Palace with Cris and Gabriel. While they waited for the king in the dispatch room, Santiago limped through the door. Pedro had trouble recognizing his former comrade in a dandified frock coat and cheap cologne. He slumped into an armchair and promptly fell asleep. According to Gabriel, he had passed the night reconnoitering the Siren.

Pedro ignored Santiago's snores and the strife between Cris and Gabriel and paced the threadbare carpet.

Where was Dom Luis?

The king's dispatch room was exactly like Pedro remembered. The dark wood paneling was stifling like a frigate's interior, trapping dust and tobacco like old political enemies. Pedro and Fernando had often hidden behind the blue partition to smoke cigarettes and drink *aguardente.*

Cris glared at Gabriel. "I can't believe you lied all this time. You should be warming the cell in Pedro's place."

Gabriel slumped back in the chair, beaten. "Don't you think I regret it? Life has not been an endless party for me, I assure you."

"What are you implying, you traitorous —"

"Stop," Pedro commanded, staring down at both men. "The past has no room here. Brother, if I forgot it, so will you. Gabriel, I need you focused. We can reverse all the harm done by Ulrich if we deliver him to justice."

Gabriel nodded, sobering.

Pedro drummed his fingertips on the rosewood cabinet. The sooner they planned their actions, the faster he could return to Anne. If he left now, when he arrived at the villa, she would be asleep. His lips tugged up, and warmth flooded his chest as he imagined all the delicious ways he could wake her. "What is taking Dom Luis so long?"

Santiago yawned and inspected his timepiece. "It's too early for him to be at the tavern, so my guess would be his mistress's house." At Gabriel's confusion, Santiago shrugged apologetically. "I'm the queen's confessor."

Cris chuckled at the king's peccadilloes, but Pedro could not muster the same flippancy. This sort of marriage awaited him if he married the princess. A cold, cynical affair punctuated by infidelities and political intrigue. He could thank Ulrich for delivering him from such fate. He would do so after he shoved the slave trader's carcass into prison.

The door opened, and everyone stood. Instead of the king, Henrique poked his head inside. Viscount

Penafiel, the wine connoisseur, celebrated scientist, and womanizer, strolled to meet them with the same elan he used to lead a cavalry charge.

Pedro shook hands with his comrade. "Where is the king?"

Henrique cleared his throat. "Well... His Majesty expressed his uttermost satisfaction that you are innocent, but he is otherwise detained."

"I thought he would want to avenge his brother's death. Does he not grieve Fernando's—"

"The king grieves for his brother." Henrique raised his voice defensively and then sighed. "It's only he needs a female shoulder to cry on. But he nominated me as his plenipotentiary to deal with these fresh developments, etcetera."

Gabriel raised his brows. "Let me guess. You were at hand when the messenger arrived at his club, and Dom Luis sent you in his place?"

Henrique blushed and dropped to a chair. "We were at Madam Grassine's house, and yes."

Pedro pointed at the remaining chairs circling the oval-shaped table. "We should get this over with." He seated himself, pushing away the assortment of maps, letters, and music sheets cluttering the surface.

The others followed his example.

Henrique smiled. "All the officers from Mozambique gathered. I must say, the last ten years were not gentle to you. You look like shit."

Cris bumped Henrique's shoulder and laughed. "I don't hear the ladies complaining."

"Is that what you call them nowadays? I thought you only bedded—"

"A little decorum is in order," Santiago said, and his priestly voice battled with his debauched appearance.

Henrique lifted his palms. "All right, all right. It will be like our old war councils. When Pedro starts issuing orders, Santiago will nap, and I will exchange messages with Cris setting up the night's entertainment. Gabriel will pretend to be taking notes while drawing furiously, and the only one paying attention will be Fernando." Henrique's smile died, and his eyes sought Pedro's. "But Fernando is not here, is he?"

"Each of us returned from Africa a different man. We carved our paths to erase that place from our lives. But not Fernando." Pedro's voice faltered as grief clotted his throat. "Fernando was not changed by Mozambique. He toiled to change it instead. He is no longer with us, but we have the chance to finish his life's work."

Henrique nodded, his expression serious. The others quieted, assuming their places at the table.

Pedro settled into the leading role as if he had donned his military uniform. "We will telegraph the royal navy and our outposts in the colony. With Fernando's evidence, we can shut down Ulrich's operation. What have you discovered at the brothel, Santiago?"

Santiago rubbed his red-rimmed eyes. "Ulrich is the owner of the Siren. He brings the girls from exotic places and keeps them against their will."

The blackguard planned to keep exploiting people right under their noses. Pedro's stomach churned as a wave of apprehension burst through him, and he forced his breaths to calm down. Anne was safe at the beach house with Dante. "How long have you stayed inside? Did you discover anything else?"

The priest flushed. "I spent the night, but Ulrich did not appear."

Pedro nodded. "We must place a lookout and storm the Siren as soon as Ulrich arrives. Gabriel, can you draw the club?"

Gabriel sketched the premises. According to Santiago, at least twenty guards guarded the former residence of the Duke of Abrantes.

Pedro needed to consider the innocents inside the club. "How many women does he have?"

"I don't know the precise number, but there are several rooms upstairs, and I believe he also keeps them in the basement. I stumbled upon one of his men when I scouted the service stairs. The fellow carried an unconscious girl."

Pedro's chest caved in. No, it could not be.

He gripped Santiago's arm. "What did she look like?"

Santiago frowned. "I couldn't see much in the dark. But I saw her hair. A blonde so pure, it was nearly white."

The room spun. Pedro's heart lurched, pounding in a painful rhythm. He shot to his feet and took several steps backward. Ice coursed through his veins instead of blood, and time stopped.

Ulrich had Anne.

The door flung inward, and Maxwell burst inside, brushing away the king's secretary. His face was gray as ash. "What have you done with her this time?"

Pedro sucked in a breath as rage hardened his chest, his heart. His vision tunneled at the Englishman. He grabbed Maxwell's shoulder. "Where. Is. She?"

"Don't pretend ignorance—" Maxwell's gaze searched his, and he must have seen something that forced him to pause. "My sister is gone."

Chapter 42

Gabriel watched Pedro and Maxwell circle each other. The aura of menace and hate emanating from them raged too wild to be contained. Miss Anne Maxwell's disappearance sank into Gabriel's chest. He had wrecked Pedro's life, and an innocent girl had suffered for his lie.

Gabriel shook away the stupor and pushed away from the table. He would carry on Pedro's orders and summon the guards.

Halfway to the door, the thud of a fist hitting flesh made Gabriel wince. Pedro punched Maxwell's gut, and the Englishman retaliated by shoving Pedro from him and crushing his fist against Pedro's face.

Gabriel could not watch them kill each other, but before he could separate the pair, Cris blocked his way. "Let them blow some steam. It will help clear the air a bit."

Henrique followed the struggle, his expression a mixture of excitement and concern. "I bet two caskets of port on Pedro." At Gabriel's perplexed look, Henrique shrugged. "What? Inflation, of course. I only accept wine these days. But If Pedro sends the Englishman back to his maker, I'll volunteer to care for his lovely widow. Second time is a charm, eh?"

Santiago held Gabriel's arm and whispered, "Who is the Englishman with the death wish? Should I retrieve my cassock? I cannot perform last rites smelling of lavender."

"Let's hope it will not come to that," Gabriel said with more conviction than he felt.

Pedro held Maxwell by his lapel. His eyes had a ferocity that would put a lesser man into a drop-your-musket-and-run-for-your-life kind of retreat. "You took her from under my roof and let her wander unprotected? Didn't you know she was at risk? If Ulrich got her—"

"Better this fellow than you. At least he is not after some petty revenge," Maxwell spoke through clenched teeth.

Pedro stabbed his finger at Maxwell's chest. "I never transferred my hate from you to her. Anne appeared on my doorstep by herself. She... She brought light into my life, and she is with him. Ulrich is a sadist, and now he has the power to push me back into the darkness. And you with me."

Maxwell backed away, shaking his head. "I loathe the day you stumbled into our lives. Anne is a sweet—"

The hiss of metal sliding against a scabbard chilled the dispatch room.

"Don't call her sweet." Pedro held the tip of his saber to Maxwell's Adam's apple.

Cris shot to his feet, no doubt rethinking his strategy of letting them resolve their issues.

Maxwell didn't cower. The strained set of his jaw was the only visible sign he had poked a lion with a short straw.

Gabriel had seen his cousin in battle, radiating reckless energy and deadly intent. But not like this. Pedro sustained the sword, his body charged with animal aggression. "She is the strongest, brightest, most selfless person I have ever met. Never call her sweet."

No one breathed. Gabriel feared his cousin would kill Griffin, and by their companion's faces, they shared his dire opinion.

With a slash of his arm, Pedro flung away the sword. The saber clanked twice, and a pregnant silence ensued.

Pedro's frame shook as if he was receiving invisible blows to his chest.

Gabriel shifted his gaze from Pedro to Maxwell. What would he do? If the stoic Englishman proved immune to Pedro's pain, Gabriel would kill Maxwell himself.

The Englishman stared at Pedro for several heartbeats, his fists cocked by his side, his breathing harsh and loud. But as Pedro's dry sobs gained intensity, the fight drained from the Englishman's expression. He took a tentative step forward and placed his hand over Pedro's shoulder. "I... I did not know. You love her."

Pedro lifted his eyes to the taller man and grabbed the Englishman's arm. For a second, Gabriel feared Maxwell had gone too far.

Then Pedro clasped the Englishman, hitting his back with closed fists. Maxwell held firm. Pedro's punches stopped, and he splayed his hands on Maxwell's coat. A collective breath sounded in the dispatch room as the bitter enemies held each other in a strained embrace.

Gabriel nodded at Cris, who took it all in with apparent relief.

Henrique flung his arm around Gabriel's shoulder. "Good God, are they going to kiss?"

"Are you crying?" Gabriel asked, sure he hadn't witnessed so much emotion on their group's staunchest rake.

Henrique brushed his eyes with the sleeve of his impeccable coat. "Bite your tongue. My eyes... They are sensitive today, that's all." Henrique exhaled. "What the hell... I always loved our Pedro, and it turns out I'm partial to the Englishman too. He might be a grumbler and a wife thief, but he has a good heart."

Chapter 43

The day had long lit the sky when Anne had scraped enough of the plaster to allow the window a shuddering slide. The bedroom was on the second floor, but a sturdy cork oak, its branches stretching to brush against the windowsill, would deliver her safely to the ground. And then to Pedro.

Footsteps sounded outside the bedroom. Anne clutched the porcelain shard in her hand and closed the drapery. Slowly, she backed away from the window, her heart beating so painfully fast she feared it might burst.

The door opened. She caught a flash of a green uniform and then the youthful, serious countenance of the boy who trampled Pedro's begonias. She clamped her mouth shut so as not to laugh like a raving lunatic.

"Good morning, Miss Maxwell." He bowed as if she wasn't a prisoner and he wasn't an accomplice in the crime.

Still, his politeness brought a sheen of normalcy to her predicament, and Anne inclined her head.

"My lord Ulrich sends this with his compliments." He produced an ivory gown made of sheer lace. "He desires you to wear it for your breakfast with him."

Anne smoothed her own dress, eyeing the boy askance. "I thought you worked for the king."

He flushed and glanced away. "We all lie when the need is upon us."

Her eyes flicked to the window, and she wrung her hands. A few more minutes alone, and she could open it. "Very well. I will require privacy to change clothes."

"You will dress with the help of Angelina."

He clapped his hands, and a scrawny maid entered the bedchamber. She curtsied clumsily. Her black hair covered the right side of her face. Anne cringed at the sight of the ugly star-shaped gash on the other woman's cheek. No man could be so evil. Still, her body mocked her feeble attempts to rationalize her fears.

"Please, Ega. Your name is Ega, no? I'm sure you are better than this." Anne glanced at the other woman. "Help us escape."

"You best forget any foolishness. There is no escaping Ulrich." The boy's gaze was sad, and she couldn't avoid a glimmer of sympathy.

"Please hear me." Anne linked her hands in front of her chest. "You don't need to do anything. All I ask is that you leave for five minutes. I will—"

"If you... If you please Ulrich, he will not hurt you." His face flushed a terrible shade of red, making the scar on his neck stand out in high contrast.

Anne lifted her chin. "Pleasure and hurt shouldn't be uttered in the same sentence."

He grabbed her hand, and panic settled into his features. "Please, Miss Maxwell, don't act foolishly. He will make you regret it. I promise he will."

Anne sat in front of Ulrich. Only the dining table separated her from his lascivious looks. He wore a golden *robe de chambre*, and his dishabille heightened her sense of discomfort. She knew she should converse with him—if anything, to extend this meal and avoid whatever he had planned for after—but her mouth would not cooperate.

Anne's eyes went to the table knife, and quickly gazed away, praying Ulrich had not gleaned her intentions. Why had he placed a sharp knife so close? A coincidence? Or did he toy with her?

Ulrich passed his hand over his slick hair as he gnawed a hunk of beef. "The Portuguese bullfight is a superior sport. A man who believes otherwise is a wimp. Spanish *Torada* is a mockery to our *Corrida de Touros*."

Light from the gaudy candelabra gleamed over her knife's blade. The clock struck the hour. A trickle of perspiration descended between her breasts, and Anne pressed her napkin to her lips. "Is there a difference?"

Ulrich hacked at his meat, and the blade slid through it like butter. "Imagine the scene in your lovely head. You are sitting at the *sombra*—"

"*Sombra?*"

He snapped his fingers. "The shade, of course. Do you think I would buy cheap tickets for my new pet? The *matador* enters the arena, riding his steed. The bull's rage is at a fever pitch. Bull blades pierce its back, and blood leaves red streaks over his black coat. The crowd goes wild. The beast attacks. The *matador* gallops to deliver the killing blow..."

Anne flinched.

"What, no stomach for the sport?" He shoved a raw piece of meat in his mouth and chewed.

"I fail to see the pleasure in hurting animals."

"You have so much to learn."

Anne made a decision. Game or no game, she would conceal her knife in her dress.

"Do you toy with people like the matador taunts the bull?" Anne's heart picked up speed. She treaded dangerous terrain with this subject, but she needed to know. "Was that what you did to Pedro in Mozambique by forcing him to make an impossible choice?"

Ulrich's eyes glittered, and he turned his head to the side. "I did not know you would be more than a pretty pet." He clicked his tongue and inspected her with renewed interest. "I always loved the sport, but the choices... Those came later. I used to scrape for four months to find stragglers and misfits to fill my ship. Then I received this visit. An all-important duke, straight from the king's court. We struck a deal."

Anne leaned forward and placed her napkin over the knife. "Deal?"

"The duke said he would help me catch an entire tribe. In exchange, I had to teach this young general a lesson."

Anne gasped. Pedro's wound had been a deliberate blow?

Ulrich shushed her. "The duke told me the general would kick his morals to high heaven if I spilled his brother's blood. It worked. You see, the right choice is a mirror. It reveals who a person really is. And I learned the lesson. After dealing with the duke, I went straight to the tribe leaders. Sometimes it took a blonde wench like yourself. In others, I had to torture a wife or a child, but it never failed. While other traders sweated four months to fill a slave ship, I did it in one. You do the math."

Who had betrayed Pedro so? Changing him from a noble youth to a cynical man? Anger swept through her at such calculated cruelty. Still, she forced herself to hear his ramblings, hoping her expression didn't show her disgust. "Except you didn't give Pedro a choice when you implicated him in the king's brother's assassination."

"Is that so?" Ulrich smiled, and his head leaned to the side. "Are you so eager to be a part of my tests?"

The corset squeezed her rib cage, making it hard to breathe. Anne tugged the napkin, and the knife fell onto her lap. A wave of heat climbed to her cheeks, and she kept her gaze on her plate.

He tapped his finger over his chin. "I'm not very creative today, and lust is impatient. You can lie with me willingly and become my pampered pet, or you can fight me, and after I finish with you, you will join the ranks of the Siren. An English lady will be a success in my new collection."

Anne held her breath, her hand going to her lap. Her muscles became so tense she feared they would snap, and she gripped the knife until the handle bit into her palm. How could she do this? Hurt another? Still, she couldn't live with herself if she allowed him to touch her.

He stood and swaggered near, a secretive smile pulling up the corners of his thin lips. A drop of blood had congealed on his mustache, and Anne could not look away from that single drop.

"What will it be?"

Chapter 44

Pedro spun the cylinder of his gasser revolver while waiting for the others at the Siren's front entrance. Cris and Gabriel flanked him. A detachment of the king's guard screened the street, and the rest deployed to block the exit.

Pedro, who had never prayed in his life, did it feverishly, praying for Anne to be strong, to protect herself by whatever means necessary. He prayed for Ulrich to find a spark of decency, to spare her of hurt. Had Anne not told him human nature was good? He had scoffed at her naivete then, but now he hoped she was right.

The dead bodyguard lying on the sand flashed through his mind, dissolving any doubt about the truth of Ulrich's nature.

He signaled the men to be silent, unwilling to rouse Ulrich's guards. An unnatural quietness pervaded the mansion. A kick in the brass lock, and the door crashed open. Pedro stepped inside the foyer, his boots crunching glass. Light shied away from the black and red drapery. Cigars littered the floor, and the carpet had liquor stains.

All was hushed until a wave of footsteps resounded from above. Women stampeded down the stairs, some wearing flimsy nightgowns, others dressed in rags. Heart accelerating, Pedro searched for Anne's face among the group. She was not one of them. Pedro left Gabriel to deal with the distraught women and dashed to the second floor.

A door lay ajar at the end of the corridor, spilling bright color on the Persian rug. Dust motes flew with the shaft of light, their sparkle reminding him of his last morning with Anne. Dread swam in his stomach like venom. What would he find inside that room? The image of Anne's body, lifeless and bloody, threatened to push him to his knees.

The bed was empty. Anne's fragrance floated inside, a fresh mist over the gaudy bedchamber. A breeze ruffled the curtains, and they billowed like old sails in a storm, emphasizing the utter stillness of the room. Empty. Atop the bed, a golden chain caught the light. It was her locket. Below the jewelry, a vellum card.

Meet me at the Bullfighting Arena. Alone.

Pedro rode Erebus to the hill on the outskirts of Lisbon, his breaths straining his chest. When he arrived at the crest, he thanked the terrain's layout. From his position, he had an unobstructed view of the circular bullring, from the uncovered arena where the *tourada* took place to the surrounding stands. Ulrich's guards swarmed both entrances of the coliseum-like structure, but no sign of Anne or Ulrich.

Pedro lay on the schist soil, oblivious to pebbles poking his torso, and placed the Chassepot rifle over his shoulder. The midday sun punished his back, and an army of bruise-colored clouds gathered above the city.

Pedro cleared stray thoughts from his mind, preparing for his life's most important shot. While Gabriel's soldiers distracted Ulrich's men, Pedro would shoot Ulrich as soon as he settled over the bleachers. And then he would remove Anne from this hell.

Cris and Santiago formed behind him, while the others, including Maxwell, had followed Gabriel. One had to admire the Englishman's courage. He had insisted on accompanying them, even being a civilian without military training.

Down the hill, red flashed among the grove of cork oaks. Santiago settled by Pedro's side and signaled with a mirror. "The royal guard is in place."

Perspiration trickled down Pedro's spine as he inspected the roads leading to the bullring. "Why is Ulrich taking so long?"

A bull bellowed mournfully. Another replied, and then silence. The wind ruffled the olive leaves and lifted clouds of sand from the empty arena. Minutes crawled into hours. Pedro checked the sun's position. At least three o'clock.

Dust lifted beyond the hill, and then the clap of hooves neared. A team of harassed horses came into view. They pulled a crestless barouche, windows covered by black curtains. The coach winded down the road and halted at the building's main entrance.

Pedro held his breath, his finger hovering over the trigger.

The coachman jumped from his perch and limped to the door. Pedro stopped breathing. When Anne alighted, Pedro shuddered, his eyes closing briefly, and he released a painful breath. Thank God she was alive.

Ulrich exited the carriage next.

Pedro tensed to pull the trigger, but the slave trader flung his arm over Anne's shoulder, the black of his clothes engulfing Anne's slight frame.

Red hot rage clouded his vision, and Pedro cursed under his breath, lowering the rifle.

"Easy, brother. You will have another shot."

Ulrich led Anne through the entrails of the bullring, and Pedro followed their progress through the rifle's scope. The couple oscillated from Pedro's sight as they navigated the wooden maze below the tiered stands. Pedro's heart drummed against his chest, and he took measured breaths.

The slave trader emerged at the highest bleacher. Pedro kept aim as Ulrich circled the ring through the glaring light until his vision plunged into darkness. Panting, Pedro lowered the scope and realized his error. An error that could cost their lives. Ulrich had timed his arrival with precision. Unlike the noon's brightness, the three o'clock sun illuminated only three-quarters of the bullring. Ulrich had chosen the one quart plunged in shadows. The *sombra*.

Pedro strained his vision but could make out only vague silhouettes.

Dread gnawing his stomach, he lowered his Chassepot and stood. "Signal the guard to wait. I will enter the arena."

Cris grabbed his arm. "This is utter madness. Ulrich will butcher you."

Pedro had no intention of dying today. But he could no longer let Anne remain at Ulrich's mercy than he could stop breathing. Pedro stared at his brother's red-rimmed eyes, the desperation in his familiar face tugging at his heart.

Pedro clasped his brother's neck, kissed his forehead, and yanked him in for a hug. His voice, when it came, was rough. "You were right. I never forgot Mozambique, and I didn't allow you to forget. I'm sorry."

"Why are you telling me this drivel?" Cris demanded, his eyes humid.

"Because I love you."

Cris nodded, his chin trembling like a child's. "You better bounce back alive, or I will chase you to hell."

Pedro held his brother's gaze, then ruffled his hair and handed him his rifle. "I will try to lure him to the light. When you get a clear aim, shoot the blackguard."

Chapter 45

Ulrich forced Anne to sit at the bullring's top. The sand glimmered white, the pureness marred by russet spots. Whose blood was it? The bull or the *toureiro*? The relief of being spared Ulrich's proposition had worn out, replaced by dread. What kind of brutal act had Ulrich planned? She peeked at him, trying to glean his intentions, but since Ega had interrupted their meal, he had become a sphinx. Anne eyed the exit with longing. With Ulrich slouching by her side and the two guards flanking the bleacher, she had no chance of escaping.

A flock of doves flapped their wings desperately and took to the sky. At the opposite side of the ring, a wooden gate flung inward.

Ulrich stirred, and a demonic smile lit his face. "*Querida*, won't you look? The spectacle begins."

Pedro strode through the arena, his black clothes contrasting with the sand. Anne's heart sped as she drank in his beloved face, and without conscious thought, she rose to reach him.

Ulrich grabbed her wrist, grazing his nails over her skin, and forced her to sit. "Pets move when they are told so."

Anne cradled her bruised wrist and touched the knife resting in the folds of her dress. Hate for their tormentor poisoned her veins, and a vivid thought of her plunging the blade into Ulrich's flesh made her wince. Could she do it? Kill another?

Pedro halted at the arena's center, his posture regal, his chin lifted, his hair gleaming golden in the harsh sun. Didn't he see the trap? A scream locked in her throat, and she gripped the wooden plank to stay still. By God, wasn't he so clever? A strategist? She scanned the wings of bleachers behind him, looking for Dante, for Cris, anyone to help him fight the madman seated by her side. But he was utterly alone.

"Our major attraction has arrived." Ulrich placed his hand above hers and raised his voice. "I will have your weapons, Almoster."

The ferret guard dragged his feet in Pedro's direction. She couldn't see his expression, but she could bet he sneered. Still, he didn't step close until her Pedro was disarmed, and then he hastened out as soon as he took the guns.

Pedro's gaze touched hers. Concern and desperation warred in his lovely eyes, and Anne managed a feeble smile, trying to reassure him.

Pedro turned to Ulrich and opened his arms wide. "I'm here, as requested. Release Anne." His voice rang with unbreakable authority.

"So soon? And keep my lovely plaything from her entertainment? Don't you think the foreign dove should learn of our pleasures?" Ulrich caressed a strand of her hair, and when she flinched from his touch, he twisted the strands in his grasp.

Pain coursed through her scalp, but she clamped her mouth shut to keep her cry inside. Pedro needed his wits to defend himself, and her distress would distract him.

Ulrich clapped his hands, the strident call resounding in the arena. The wooden gate swung. Hooves chafed the sand, followed by a terrible bawl that lifted the hairs on her nape.

A bull trotted inside, black coat gleaming under the unforgivable sun. Anne couldn't look away from the yard-long horns. Ulrich had bragged bulls were selected for uncommon strength and ferocity. Still, nothing had prepared her for the gargantuan beast, his heavy breathing lifting plumes of sand into the air.

For a breathless moment, her prince and the creature faced each other.

Ulrich squealed and bounced on his seat, his black eyes oozing excitement. "Look at them. The bull is planning his best attack. Your former lover will have the honor of being killed by the best *touro* in Portugal."

The bull lowered its head, and Anne cried out. "Stop this madness, please."

"Smile, *querida*. Otherwise, I will think you are not enjoying the spectacle."

No, no, no. Her eyes darted from the bull to Ulrich, her mouth so dry she could not swallow her own saliva. Her legs and arms shaking, her chest so tight she feared it might crush her heart, Anne pleaded, "Let him go, and I will do whatever you want."

"You love him." He grabbed her chin painfully, examining her eyes. "A loving heart can fit a vain count, but not pride. Interesting. But for what I have in mind, your obedience is not required. I'm charmed at this turn of events, though. An English maiden offering her company, a proud aristocrat providing the recreation. Not bad for an emigrant from Madeira Island. Not bad at all."

Anne recoiled from his scrutiny, realizing she had just given him more ammunition to use in his cruel games. A low-pitched report, like thunder rumbling, sounded from the back of the arena. Ulrich signaled impatiently for his guards to check the noise.

The bull pawed the ground once, twice, and lowered its rectangular head, displaying ivory horns. Pedro flexed his knees, his hands stretched like claws in front of his chest.

With an ear-splitting bellow, the bull charged, speeding like a black locomotive, tons of muscle barraging forward, spear-like horns aimed at the man she loved.

Ulrich shot to his feet, gripped by an unnatural excitement, and held to the railing, a sick smile contorting his lips.

Pedro veered gracefully to the left as the bull careened to the other side of the arena.

The guards had yet to return, and Ulrich was so engrossed by the bull he would not notice if...

Anne felt for her knife in the folds of her dress and shot to her feet. She could end this. She must. Anne hardened her stomach and forced herself to grab the knife. Glancing around nervously, she plodded in his direction. Her chest shook violently, and her arm fell limply to her side. Anne shut her eyes and rebuked herself. She couldn't kill him.

A neigh, shrill and desperate, lifted all the hairs in her body. Erebus.

She knew how to help Pedro.

She raced away from Ulrich, making her way among the chairs lining the bleachers, her steps clumsy, her hands trembling. Through the dusty wood planks, she saw Pedro remove his coat and wave it like a flag as the bull charged again.

How long could he keep the bull from tearing him up? Lungs burning, she gained speed and reached the exit of the second-floor platform when Ulrich's shouted displeasure froze the blood in her veins. Anne forced her feet forward.

Hoping her instincts were right, she followed the rhythmic pounding of Erebus's hooves. She arrived at a paddock hidden under the bleachers. The stallion pummeled the ground, head lifted, ears pricked.

When she dragged herself into the paddock, he fixed her with his fathomless black eyes. She lifted her palms in submission. The last time she had come near the war horse, he had tried to trample her. Cooing softly, her voice brittle with her need to cry, she shifted closer. All the while, he observed her, his gaze bright with uncanny intelligence.

Murmuring praises, she unlatched the reins from the wooden post. Erebus stood stock still, as if restraining himself not to frighten her. She tugged the reins, and he followed her to the arena's entrance. Not for a second did she fear his hooves or his teeth. Going on her toes to reach between his ears, Anne removed Erebus's bridle.

Then she crashed her shoulder into the arena's gate, swinging it open.

Erebus charged, his long mane flying like a black halo, powerful legs pumping the sand, coat gleaming ebony light, the pure expression of a Greek God of Darkness.

Oblivious to the new threat, the bull charged Pedro again. Anne screamed as the beast's horns grazed his torso.

Erebus reared, front legs ramming the air. It was over ten feet of horse, reaching more than double the bull's height. The beast halted.

Anne leaned her weight on the gate, catching her breath, relief making her dizzy.

Before her eyes, the bull turned his flank and fled to the arena's corner. Erebus gave chase and corralled the beast.

Anne spotted blood on Pedro's white shirt and moved to run to him when her arm was yanked behind her.

Ulrich slapped her hard.

Anne's head jerked, and she collapsed onto the sand. Fighting the starbursts behind her eyelids, she hugged herself. A coppery taste invaded her mouth, and she lifted her chin, eying Ulrich with dread and defiance.

"Treacherous bitch."

Chapter 46

Pedro splayed his hands over his knees to catch his breath. Erebus kept the bull blocked, neutralizing the threat. Pedro lifted his gaze to the bleacher—empty. The sound of palm hitting flesh pierced Pedro's chest harder than the bull's horns. The gate swung inward, and he glimpsed Anne's hair flailing as Ulrich felled her.

Hatred as fathomless as Dom Pedro must have felt for Inês's executioners coursed through his veins, and Pedro reached the gate in two strides. When it swung open again, he blocked its path.

Ulrich startled. Fear flashed in his black eyes.

Pedro caught him by the lapel and fisted his hand. He punched Ulrich's face with all the pent-up rage from the hours he had spent wondering what Ulrich had done to Anne. The crack of the bastard's bones under his knuckles was not enough, and he pummeled him again.

"Is this any way to thank me? Before our affair at the Zambezi, you believed yourself noble, didn't you? A hero," Ulrich sneered, twisting the words. "I freed you from morality. You can lie to yourself, but you are just like me."

"You are wrong." Pedro crushed his fist against Ulrich's cheekbone.

Ulrich tumbled onto the sand and crawled backward like a spider. The fence separating the paddock from the arena contained his retreat. His face had turned ashen, and he lifted his palms. "Go ahead. Smash my skull with your bare fists. Show the girl your evil side."

The hairs on his nape lifting, Pedro stilled, his gaze darting from Ulrich's bloodied teeth to Anne. She hunched in a ball, hugging her knees, terror clear in her gaze.

"That tribe..." Ulrich clicked his tongue. "They were troublesome, you know. The children whined too much, and the women cried pitifully when I had to dump the loudest ones topside." Ulrich's singsong voice penetrated Pedro's skull. "All your fault."

Pedro covered his ears.

"No, Pedro, don't listen to him." Anne's plead became distorted, as if underwater.

Images from Mozambique bombarded him—scattered wooden toys over the trail, bloody garments, scorched tents, the flight of carrion, screeching and screeching. Pulse hammering against his ears, Pedro staggered back a step as vertigo robbed his balance, and he took short gulps of breath.

Ulrich cannon balled at Pedro's chest. With a flick of his wrist, he flung sand at Pedro's face and, whirling out of reach, unsheathed a pistol. Before Pedro could react, he grabbed Anne's hair and forced her to stand.

Pedro didn't feel the grain abrading his eyeballs, and his legs became useless as Ulrich pointed the pistol at Anne's head. She trembled. Her lips were bleeding, leaving a crimson trail on her opalescent skin.

Ulrich's face distorted into an expression of malice Pedro had not encountered in all his years serving in blood-soaked battles. Ulrich lifted the barrel from her temple and, still holding her hair in his grasp, pointed the gun at Pedro's chest.

An explosion brought a breath of hope to their impossible situation, but it was futile. The royal guard couldn't change the balance of power. Ulrich held the cards. Their position would not allow Cris a clear shot either, as the hill stood behind the bleacher's platform.

Ulrich traced Anne's slim brows with the obscene barrel of his gun. "Since you ruined my bullfight, I thought of a little game to brighten our afternoon. None of you will leave this arena alive, but I'm not without mercy. The Count of Almoster will pick his lover's fate."

Ulrich stared into Pedro's eyes. "You can watch Miss Maxwell die or choose to go first. Think about it carefully. Watching a loved one's death is not easy, but if I end you first, you won't know what I will do to her after I put a bullet into your heart."

Blood congealed in Pedro's veins, his arms going slack by his side. Thunder rumbled, rash and ominous. Lightning flashed white over the sand, and the sky turned black. Pedro's mind rebelled against Ulrich's game. He would not see her die, and he would not leave her in Ulrich's cruel hands. His heart exploded out of control. He was a youth again, facing an impossible choice. And Anne... she was his very life. His light.

Rain lashed the arena, drops indenting the sand, coursing through their clothes, plastering Anne's hair, washing away the blood on her lips.

Pedro held Anne's gaze. Too much had been left unsaid. He had never told her that he loved her. And now...

He should never have allowed evil to touch her meadow of light.

She shook her head as if she knew the direction of his thoughts and then gifted him with her wobbly smile. While a volcano raged inside his chest, she was ethereal, translucent, untouched by evil. She closed her eyes, and a tear shimmered down her cheek.

When she opened her eyelids, her chest expanded, and a new strength radiated from her gaze. She wrenched herself from Ulrich's grasp and produced a blade from the folds of her dress, touching it to her own neck. Lightning flashed, illuminating the sharp steel. A knife. Her skin there, so delicate, would require only a nudge, and then her light would be forever extinguished.

Pedro's heart slammed against his ribs, and he lifted his hands. "Anne, no!"

Ulrich's eyes widened. "There now, pet. Drop the knife."

She lifted her chin, her eyes gleaming with unfathomable strength. "If I kill myself, you won't be able to play your twisted game, will you?" She pressed the blade against her neck and turned to Pedro. "Your father sold you to Ulrich ten years ago. He arranged the attack with a single purpose. To destroy your values."

Pedro's gut twisted, and he fisted his hands, his nails drawing blood from his palms. His father had given Ulrich their location in Mozambique? Had forced him to choose between his brother and the people he'd been sworn to protect? His mind shot back to his return from Mozambique. Father had awaited him with open arms, eager to receive him back into the fold. Pedro had played into his hand, his lesson well learned.

Eying Anne as if she had become a ghost, Ulrich stepped back, leaving the cover of the bleachers. He cocked the gun and aimed at Pedro's chest. "I'm sorry to do this, Almoster. Your father was a mentor to me. It's with regret that I make him childless."

A shot exploded, startling the doves into a frightened flight. The pistol whizzed from Ulrich's grip. The slave trader fell backward, cradling his hand. Pedro's eyes flicked to the hill, and his brother waved. Thank God for Cris's marksmanship.

Pedro grabbed Ulrich's pistol and hit the slave trader's head with the butt of the gun. Ulrich dropped to the sand, evil eyes closed, unconscious.

Pedro rushed to Anne. Gently, he pulled the knife from her neck and tossed it away. He'd thought he had the impregnable armor, but it turned out she carried all the strength. An angel covered in steel.

She lifted her eyes to him and placed a cold palm over his cheek. Tears ran quietly from her eyes. "Do you understand? Your father revealed a monster in Mozambique, but it was not you."

Chapter 47

Her legs gave way, and she tumbled to the sand. Pedro kneeled at her front and cradled her cheeks. Their gazes met. Rain poured on them, washing away the blood, the sand, the grit. The kaleidoscope in Pedro's eyes turned, revealing new shades, lighter, brighter shades. No words left their mouths. No words could express the horror, the trial, the relief, the love.

The rain stopped. The sun slashed the black clouds, and sunlight descended over the arena, glinting off the pools on the sand.

Anne brushed diamond drops from Pedro's cheek. "Is he gone?"

Pedro glanced at the man slumped not ten feet from them. "Ulrich will live to face justice—"

Anne brought his gaze back to her. "I'm not talking about Ulrich."

He frowned, his chin dipping down. Then his eyes lit from within. "My father is gone for good."

Anne clung to Pedro's neck. Relief washed over her like one of Nazare's waves, leaving her trembling as if reborn. Pedro's heart beat close to hers, the blood flowing with his vitality, his breath ruffling her temples.

He fused their lips. A breathless, possessive kiss. Anne drank him in with desperation, so thirsty for him that she forgot to breathe. Pedro held nothing back, and her heart sang as if a thousand angels had found their way inside her chest.

Pedro broke the kiss and pulled her behind him, his stance turning protective. Guards poured into the arena, their red and white uniforms contrasting with the bloodstained sand.

"You should have saved some of the battle for us." Gabriel clasped Pedro's back and smiled at Anne.

A middle-aged gentleman dressed in severe civilian clothes padded near, his striking blue eyes taking in the felled Ulrich. He then turned to Pedro and grinned.

His Majesty.

Anne gasped and dropped into a hasty curtsy.

Other officers surrounded them, their rapid-fire questions making her dizzy. Anne recognized her brother among the strangers. He weaved through the crowd to get to her, and Anne flung herself into her brother's arms.

He kissed her forehead and then embraced her. "I hope Julia births a boy. I won't survive this kind of excitement a second time."

"Yes, you will, Mr. Maxwell." Anne laughed, tasting the salt of her tears.

The king slapped Pedro's back with such vigor he would have felled a lesser man. But not her Pedro. Hair disheveled, clothes dusty and bloodied, he exuded self-confidence. Anne linked her arm with Griffin's, watching their interaction with love and fierce pride. Pedro deserved every inch of redemption the king would grant him.

The king stared into Pedro's eyes. "I told these fools you were innocent. I never doubted your honor." He turned to the others, his voice grave and loud. "It is our most fervent wish that Pedro Daun, Count of Almoster, resumes his rightful place in Portugal's court. We nominate him as Minister of Foreign Affairs."

The audience cheered. What brightened their smiles, Anne had been the first to discover. Behind Pedro's aloof armor lived a man, fiercely loyal, protective, and noble, who loved with the same intensity he fought. She wasn't jealous to share this side of Pedro with the world. While everyone could be dazzled by him, only Anne could touch all his nuances, drench her palate with his reserved playfulness, and immerse herself in his scorching lovemaking. Only she could taste his light.

The king raised his palms, asking for silence. The claps dwindled and then stopped altogether.

"I will no longer speak as the monarch. Pedro, you avenged my brother. Fernando will rest knowing you have finished his life's work. You have my gratitude. I could not ask for a more worthy addition to my family." He clasped Pedro's shoulders. "I want you as my brother-in-law. Princess Isabel's husband."

Chapter 48

The mid-morning sun pushed inside her bedroom. Vesuvio's peacock engaged in a fight with the D'Angola hens outside her window, and Anne covered her ears with a pillow. Lying on the bed, Anne gazed at her possessions. The rose wallpaper, the flowery candelabra, her row of books, her music box. If only she could fit inside her old clothes, but they had shrunk. Either that or she had swelled out of proportion, unfit for her previous life.

James whimpered and touched his humid nose to her cheek.

"I won't cry, James. I know you hate when I cry, so I won't." Anne burrowed into his warmth. As long as James remained with her, she would resist the tears. The pug had partnered her in Pedro's adventure, and they would survive its aftermath together.

"May I come in?" Julia peeked through the slitted door. Her time must be near. She was much larger than when Anne... had left.

Tony sauntered inside after his mother, his hands shoved inside his pockets.

Julia placed a breakfast table beside her. "Tony misses his teacher."

Tony shrugged, rubbing the carpet with the balls of his feet. "The new tutor stinks of ear wax."

Julia covered her chuckle with a cough. "Tony, you shouldn't say that. It's not polite."

James whined and turned on his back, displaying his stomach.

Anne caressed his ears and tried to make him comfortable, but he wouldn't stay still. "I don't know what is wrong with him. He seems restless."

Tony petted James's head. "I think he needs to go outside. Can I take him to the garden? I promise the peacock won't come near him."

Julia laughed and brushed Tony's hair. "I'm sure peacock Zezé won't die if James barks at him. He is quite sturdy."

Tony snorted. "It is James that is scared to death of the old boy."

Anne consented, and Tony carted James outside. Alone with her sister-in-law, Anne wondered how long it would take for the subject to arise.

Julia straightened the counterpane and then perched on the edge of the bed. "It's been a week since the arena. I didn't prod on the train trip here, but... has Ulrich raped you?"

Anne shot to her feet. So that was why they walked around her as if stepping on eggshells. "No, of course not."

"You hardly touch your food. You don't speak. Tony misses his playmate, and Griffin worries constantly."

"How would you feel if Griffin were to marry somebody else?" Anne said the words as one might handle a thin crystal. A torrent of feeling sprang to the surface, raw and uncomfortable. Anne halted the whirl by locking her teeth and closing her hands into fists, her nails digging into her palms.

"Dear, if you love Pedro this much, why leave? You haven't given him a chance to—"

"When I was growing up, Griffin made fun of me because I wanted to meet the perfect prince." Anne took a shuddering breath. "I just didn't expect I would not be his princess."

"Go back to Lisbon. I will start your bags."

"And ruin his redemption? Pedro deserves this so much." He needed this. He had taught her that love wasn't selfish.

"Do you think it is fair to take the choice from him?"

"What choice?" He would be the third in line for the throne, the king's closest advisor, and marry a princess. How could she compare? "If I stayed, he would have married me out of obligation."

Julia sought Anne's gaze, her expression nurturing and kind. "You don't know the treasure you are, do you?"

"Please, Julia. I'm trying so hard." Love was selfless. Love must be selfless. "Why is it so hard?"

Julia opened her arms. Anne accepted her embrace, trying desperately to swallow all the tears. An entire ocean of them waited to pull her under, and if she succumbed, she would never return to the surface.

Julia sighed and held her at arm's length. "It helps to cry."

Anne put distance between herself and Julia's comforting arms. She shook her head, rubbing her nose. The back of her throat burned, but she wouldn't weep.

Tony raced inside the room, and Anne welcomed his interruption. Julia would leave, and with her, the constant reminder of what Anne had lost.

But when Anne's gaze landed on Tony, the boy's condition struck her. The always cheerful, unflappable explorer-to-be was distraught, his eyes glassy and unblinking.

Anne held his shoulders. "What is it?"

"I promise it wasn't my fault. I took James outside, and then... he lay down, so still—"

"Take me to him," Anne croaked, her words coming out as if from another's chest.

Tony clasped her hand, and she held it like a lifeline. They exited the house into the shadowy garden. A breeze from the river rustled the flower bed, waving the greens stalks and raining white petals over James. Anne stumbled to her knees.

His chest did not move.

Carefully, she hugged his furry body, rocking back and forth.

Pedro had lied. He had asked James to take care of her, and James had left. She was alone. Pain spread through her heart and radiated to her lungs, limbs, and soul, pulling her into its vortex. A torrent of tears flooded her, and she was helpless to avoid them.

Julia was wrong. This wasn't a broken heart. It was grief, the grief of abandoning a future. Their future. Her plans were swallowed by the swirl, never to return. She wouldn't see Pedro's children, wouldn't witness the gruff shows of love he would shower them with, and she wouldn't grow old with him. Her vision hazed, and then shadows engulfed it. There was only now, and the yesterdays they had shared. She couldn't bear a tomorrow.

Without Pedro, her tomorrows were dead.

Chapter 49

The yacht bobbed in the marina's calm waters. Gabriel grabbed the railings, staring at the quarterdeck. The crew hastened to hoist sails, their boisterous voices ringing above the gulls' screeches. He would not look back. The Mosteiro dos Jerônimos, Saint George's Castle, the closed Siren club, the places that had played a part in his lies would stay behind. He stared at his hands. The smooth kid of his gloves gave him a new sensibility. Adapting to civilian clothes would take time.

Cris sauntered close, inhaling the brine. "A fine day to sail."

"Are you sure you want to do this?" Gabriel's place in Fontes's house had vanished. While Pedro forgave him and even Cris had decided to abandon Portuguese shores in his company, his father had loftier ideals. Wherever this journey took him, Gabriel hoped there would be no standards to achieve, impossible rules to follow, or fathers to please.

"Better leave before this epidemic catches us, don't you think?"

"Epidemic?"

Cris grimaced. "Love."

Gabriel chuckled. "I mean it. Now that you are officially a duke's son..."

Cris slipped away from his devil-may-care attitude. "I've never had a father. And I didn't ask Pedro to force the duke to recognize me. He did it on his own."

One would think the removal of the bastard stigma would leave Cris satisfied. But Gabriel wouldn't judge. Some subjects were best left buried. If Pedro's brother was willing to accompany him into this escape wrapped in a grand tour, he wouldn't complain.

"I thought Pedro would want to confront Titano. I still cannot believe the duke betrayed us in Mozambique."

Cris sighed. "Take his revenge on what? A bedridden, babbling old man? The duke has been senile for a few weeks. Pedro got the news from his solicitor."

Gabriel whistled. "I'm sorry. I—"

"Pedro did what he had to. He conquered the duke's voice inside his head, where it hurt him the most."

"I'm glad. You have a generous brother." Gabriel touched Pedro's expensive gift. The loaned yacht could take them to every corner of the world.

"Pedro has his reasons to be happy," Cris said under his breath, his voice pensive. "And your sister?"

Gabriel filled his cheeks with air and blew, racing his hands through his hair. "Honestly?"

Cris raised his palms, flashing his amiable smile. "If we are doing this, there'd best be no more lies."

Gabriel chuckled. "None. I guess she will miss me. I will miss her. But she is different. She—"

"Doesn't give a damn?"

"I wouldn't put it in so many words." When he had met her to say goodbye, Manuela had embraced him and cried. She had also told him Father had spoken to her. He had apologized for his indifference and asked for a chance to be a better father. Gabriel knew Fontes wouldn't forgive him, but if his lie meant Manu would have a loving parent, then good had come from his sins. "The girl will land on her feet."

"That's what happened to Pedro, too. There were times I despaired of ever seeing him recovered..."

The captain approached, his cap beneath his armpit, and offered a wooden salute. "All is ready."

He bowed and left.

"Where to?"

The question hung between them. Gabriel had made few decisions in his life, and most of them had pertained to his lie. The ability to make any choice he desired, even the most outlandish, filled him with breathtaking freedom and a yawning emptiness. The sensation of skipping obligations. Guilt, his oldest friend, lifted an accusing finger at him, but Gabriel ignored it. He had resigned his post, and his father had shunned him. He had no duties left.

Gabriel took a long, brine-soaked breath. "Where does one go to find himself?"

Cris laughed, his green eyes crinkling at the corners, and pointed to the glittering horizon. "I know fig about finding oneself. If you ask me of a place to lose oneself... I can think of none better than Ilhéus."

Gabriel nodded. "Ilhéus it is."

Chapter 50

Anne placed a flower atop James's resting place. He had loved the shade of her umbrella pine. A good-bye waited inside her chest, but she could not force herself to say the words. How could she sail without him? Several days in a cabin without his quiet company?

The first fall gales had started, shaking the trees lining the riverbank. The wind warbled the willows; the wind pestered their branches; the wind hassled the tiny leaves—they shook vibrantly, they shook vigorously, shook valiantly, until the wind shook them free.

"I'm late." Pedro's husky voice sounded behind her.

Anne stilled, every single part of her awakening. She shut her eyes and splayed her hands on the ground, hoping the roots could moor her, that her mind would stop playing tricks on her.

Pedro crouched by her side and placed an object atop James's grave. "I promised him a medal for taking care of you, but I didn't arrive in time."

Anne picked up the enameled piece and held it in her hand, tracing the dragon inside. A single tear left the corner of her eye.

"Would you look at me?"

Anne rose and brushed dirt from her hands. "No. It was... James was tired. The weather in London is cold this time of year, and he much preferred Portugal's sun."

"I won't allow you to go."

For a second, she imagined herself back under his roof, chafing and thrilled at his highhandedness, but she didn't obey him anymore. Anne inhaled the brisk air and, hardening her resolve, faced him.

A shaft of sun found its way to him, and he soaked up all the light. Pedro was handsome in black or gray, but he looked dazzling in military uniform. A blue sash emphasized his lean waist, and a ceremonial sword rode low over his hip. Several medals decorated the chest she had explored with her fingertips, golden epaulets crowned the shoulders that had supported her, and his face...

For once, she dared to say his face was transparent.

Surprise and adoration played in his changeable eyes as they swept over her. Then his jaw locked, hurt and anger replacing the joy.

Why had he come? Did he want her to be his mistress? She prayed not. Her resolve couldn't stand such a direct hit. Only oceans and miles could keep her from him. If she was to be the brave, strong woman she hoped to be, she could not ruin his redemption.

Anne glanced at the sunlight pooling in the grass between them. "It's not your choice to make."

He crossed his arms above his chest. "You left me."

Anne lifted her palms. "Pedro, I think—"

"Is this about Julia? I shouldn't have omitted my past with your family. My feelings for her were platonic, and I—"

"No. She told me everything, and I felt betrayed at first, but I don't think it is fair to judge. You were a victim of the situation, just as I was."

"Then what? You don't love me anymore? Is that it? Do you hate me?"

"No!" Anne regretted her outburst and exhaled, trying to compose herself. "No," she whispered. "I was confused. My feelings changed. I only feel… I only feel indifference."

The lie tasted like ashes on her tongue, and she closed her eyes, hoping she had not hurt him too much. But how could she make him understand?

"Indifference?" He frowned, then his gaze traveled from her shoes to her brows.

Anne pleaded with her body not to betray her.

He advanced a step, then another, and breathed the same air as her. The wind fluttered strands of his hair close to her cheeks, and she willed them closer still so she could feel their texture one last time. His scent enveloped her in a warm blanket. She held her hands in front of her chest to avoid the temptation to revel in the heat he shed.

He caught her hand in his and caressed the heart-shaped mark on her palm, once, twice, painfully slow, until Anne's breath hitched. Warmth flooded her, every tiny part of her body celebrating his touch, wanting more of him.

"You lie." He released her, his lips compressed in an unforgiving line. "When you floated inside my ballroom, I assumed you were a feeble angel. But then you showed me a girl capable of leaping into the fire to save her memories. Who solved codes and defied the cruelest man in his own twisted game. I thought you the strongest person I ever met."

He pointed at her, his nostrils flaring. "I was wrong. You are afraid, a weak girl who—"

"Don't call me weak," Anne shouted, her heart twisting at his insult. "If you knew the effort I'm making to stay apart when every fiber of my being clamors for you!"

He grabbed her shoulders. His gaze was insistent and left her no shadows in which to hide. "Then why?"

Anne shook her head, tears pooling at the corners of her lips. "Don't ask me to be your Inês, Pedro. I might accept it, and then we will both be miserable. If Inês had dared to leave Dom Pedro, she could have spared so much pain."

Pedro hid his acute feelings under an aloof mask. "Do you believe Dom Pedro would have accepted her choice?"

Anne nodded and reached for his hand. "He would because he loved her, and love isn't selfish. He wouldn't want her to suffer."

Pedro flinched at her touch. "You think Inês alone suffered? I saw their graves. The monastery drips with his pain, with his regret for not fighting for her. After they took Inês from him, Dom Pedro went mad. This is what you want for me?"

"No! I want you to be happy." So much she couldn't breathe.

He stepped closer, shielding her body from the wind and the sun.

Anne hardened her shoulders, her fingertips, her heart.

Please, don't touch me. I will crumble.

She gazed up at his chin and swayed, her body searching for solace only he could offer.

He caressed her cheek with the back of his finger. "You are not my Inês de Castro, Anne." His hair had fallen loose from the string, two golden curtains shading the side of his face.

"Pedro," she breathed, and her heart broke again.

"Unlike Dom Pedro, I will allow nothing between us. Not the king, and not your family, not shadows from the past, or this nonsense you created in your head to leave me. Not in this life and if there are others, not in any of them."

She shut her eyes. "The princess is your redemption. You have earned it. It is not my right to take it from you."

"*You* are my redemption."

She shook her head. It couldn't be true. She couldn't let herself believe in his words, only to have her hopes shattered again. "But I doubt—"

"If it's doubt you want, then doubt my character. Doubt everything I ever told you, for I have lied, I have deceived, and I have manipulated to be with you. But never doubt my love."

Anne opened her eyes and was dazzled by the emotion in his eyes. Pedro kissed her palm and drew her to him. The distance between them took forever to cross, but when their chests met, Anne took a shuddering breath and dissolved into him. A sob racked her, and she buried her face in his neck. Her knees gave way, and she clung to him for support.

Pedro dried her tears. "I shall love you when you are beautiful as you are now, and I shall love you when you are gray, and I shall love you when you are innocent, and I shall love you when you are not. I shall love you forever, Anne. I'm not asking you to be my Inês."

Pedro reached into his collar and pulled the chain with his mother's ring. He slid the band over her finger, and the diamond scattered the sunlight into tiny rainbows over her skin. "I'm asking you to be my angel, my wife. Ana for me, and Lady Daun, Countess of Almoster, for everybody else."

Chapter 51

Three months later...

"Go to sleep, countess. After weeks of toiling to restore Salgueiro's ballroom, you don't want to sport shadows under your eyes at your grand reception tomorrow." Pedro shifted to his back on their four-poster bed and tucked Anne into his side.

He was right, of course. They would open Quinta do Salgueiro's doors to friends and family. Anne had prepared a lavish ball, the first since Pedro's mother had died. Anne closed her eyes, picturing Pedro leading her in a waltz under the light of thousands of candles, and she cuddled closer to his chest. His warmth was better than any fantasy she could conjure. Her skin came alive, and sleep waved as elusive as the soft sights of the cicadas singing outside.

Pedro was still, and his breathing was even, but she knew he was awake. He always waited for her to sleep first, no matter how tired he was. Smiling, Anne traced circles on the golden skin of his chest. His breath caught, scarcely loud enough to be heard. Encouraged, Anne drew arabesques down his torso, aiming for the trail of golden hair below his navel.

He grabbed her hand, placed a chaste kiss on her palm, and held it. She tugged, but his grip had the give of shackles.

She chanced a peek at his face. His eyes were closed, his long eyelashes casting playful shadows over his cheeks. Anne kissed his puckered nipple.

His chest rumbled. "Sleep."

Anne smiled against his skin. "I would rather do other things."

"Just close your eyes," he said gruffly.

Anne wiggled her toes over his calves, but the insufferable man blocked that too by placing his knees atop both of her thighs. Anne huffed and shimmied her legs, but his limbs seemed made of iron. Winded, she laid back on the pillow and blew hair from her forehead.

His chest shook suspiciously. He chuckled!

Measuring her breaths, she relaxed, pretending defeat. One heartbeat, two, and then ten. When his hold slackened, she pulled free and climbed atop him.

"Ha!" Laughing, she placed her hands on both sides of his face, her hair cascading down his torso.

Their breath mingled. Atop Pedro's chest, she could fight any battle, discover new countries, or, better yet, conquer a recalcitrant count. While gloating, she missed how the light changed in his eyes. Before she could catch her breath, Pedro splayed his hands over her thighs and, holding her tight, switched their positions, rolling on top of her.

He kept his weight on his arms, caging her with his male bulk. She tried to wiggle free, but he was as movable as a Grecian column.

But even naked, she still had a card up her sleeve. Grinning, she brought her hands up as if asking for mercy, but at the last moment, she tickled his armpits.

One second, she was lying beneath him on her back. The next, she was flipped to her stomach, an unwieldy male pressed against her.

Anne huffed, trying to buck his weight from her back. After succeeding only in getting herself breathless, she gave up. "Have you no soft spot on your body? No vulnerabilities?"

He pushed closer, his furry chest tickling her nude spine, and breathed the words near her neck, raising goosebumps over her arms. "I have."

"And what, pray tell, is it?"

"You."

Anne shuddered, and with a sigh, she turned her face to the side to receive his open-mouthed kiss.

Too soon, he released her tongue and fluttered kisses down her shoulder blades, following the arch of her back. His lips were warm on her overheated skin, and everywhere he touched her, he branded her.

She held her breath when he arrived at the base of her spine. With the ease of one who knew his welcome, he hooked her leg up, opening her to him. When his fingers found her entrance, a shiver of pleasure raced through her body, making her toes curl. He chuckled at her desire, no doubt ecstatic with male pride. But instead of shyness, she felt only the truth of their bonding.

When he placed his tongue where his hands had just been, she widened her eyes, but he was too skillful a lover to be denied, and she gave in to his blissful kiss.

He pulled his mouth away. Incoherent thoughts flew to her mind, and Anne blubbered a protest at his absence, but it did not last. He soared above her and, chest pressed to her spine, plunged inside her. Slowly, deeply, devotedly, his thrusts stoked her desire to a fevered pitch. She thought she couldn't take anymore when he burrowed his hands beneath her, caressing her breasts. Anne released her weight on the mattress as Pedro took them to new pleasure heights.

Chapter 52

From the shadows of the grand staircase, Pedro tracked the guests' progress. Like a tide, they floated from the open doorway, dressed in their finery, their eyes admiring Quinta do Salgueiro's ballroom. More than the Gobelins, Sèvres, and priceless works of art, Pedro had the impression their gazes lingered over the subtle pieces of evidence that his house had a countess. Roses in every vase, music spilling from the gallery, a scent of beeswax floating with the breeze. Windows opened to catch the sunset.

Not a single space left for shadows.

Pedro stifled his irritation at having guests after only three months of their wedding. He had to share her with the world. At least a few hours of her time. Braganza's cause justified it. Anne had arranged everything, down to the miniature pastries she served with port.

The only detail missing was his countess.

Minutes ticked by, and Pedro turned to the stairs.

Julia and Maxwell mingled with the other guests. His new sister and brother had arrived that morning. Julia had delivered a healthy baby girl, as her fuller figure could well attest. Pedro's regard hadn't changed since he'd first met her by the river. Seeing her happy, her face glowing with health, brought him pleasure. What had guided his entire life for ten years was love, but not the same love he felt for Anne. His feelings were brotherly tenderness.

Fitting that they had become siblings in the eyes of God.

For Maxwell, the only emotions left were a mild annoyance and a grudging admiration. Anne loved him, and Pedro would tolerate him on her behalf. On preset dates, not exceeding four times a year.

Cris would laugh at the turnabout of his feelings. Where was he? Probably some shady place, doing Saint George knew what. As long as he didn't get himself killed.

Laughter tinkled four paces from him. No doubt Henrique had made a joke, entertaining the small group. Pedro looked as pleasure softened their features. Their postures were open. They felt safe here, in his residence. Pedro could be a part of it.

With a pang of surprise, he realized he wanted to.

Pedro approached them with a genuine smile lifting the corners of his mouth. His new in-laws noticed his presence at once, Julia with pleasure shining in her black eyes, Maxwell with a tick in his jaw.

Julia kissed his cheek. "The decoration is lovely, but I must say, I'm thrilled you rebuilt the vineyards."

"You must congratulate my countess. Hers is all the credit." Pedro glanced at the stairs again.

"Where is my sister, by the way?" Maxwell shook Pedro's hand with jerky movements.

"My wife will be here shortly. I hope you had a chance to ride Sarpedon?"

Maxwell flushed behind his beard and grumbled, "You didn't have to give me a horse, Almoster."

Julia cleared her throat and linked her arm to Maxwell's. "My dear husband means to say he appreciates the gift and accepts it gracefully."

Pedro shrugged. "Since you have embraced Portugal as your home, you might as well ride a Lusitano and not that British horse of yours."

"My thoroughbred is the finest specimen—"

Henrique cut Maxwell's diatribe and kissed Julia's hand, smiling seductively. "Darling, you should wear red more often."

Maxwell forgot the horse, and Pedro enjoyed seeing him flustered. Was Pedro as ridiculous when he was jealous of Anne?

Henrique ignored Maxwell's murderous stare and turned to Pedro. "Congratulations on your ministry appointment. With the extra ships patrolling the colonies, slave trading will soon reach its doom."

Pedro inclined his head. "It should've been done a long time ago."

"You are right. But you are the first Foreign Minister with the guts to defy the criminals."

The clock tolled the tenth hour. Pedro's eyes magnetized to the gallery. Anne floated down the grand stair, her gloved hand skimming the balustrade. Her gown swirled like a cloud, the transparency revealing her collarbone and rounded shoulders. A princess-like skirt flowed to the floor, and the silver thread sparkled with the chandelier light.

Conversations halted, and a murmur of admiration swept through the guests.

Pedro strode in her direction. People called to him, smiling in greeting, but he had eyes only for Anne. He met her at the stairs landing and bowed. "You took too long."

Her eyes widened like they always did when faced with the intensity of his desire. "I'm sorry to have—"

"You are stunning." He bent his head and gave her a chaste kiss below the crevice of her cheek. "I will enjoy peeling away every stitch later."

A delicious blush rose on her cheeks, and she glanced around to see if they'd been overheard. "Dear, we have a mission tonight."

"Your success is a given. Portugal is eager to enter your charity fund. Soon you will have enough to finance the Braganza Foundation."

"*Our* success."

She had been right. The best way to repent for his guilt was to help the Africans sent to Brazil. While she raised funds to support local charities, Pedro used his influence as foreign minister to foster abolitionism and police the sea for illegal trading. It would take time, but their efforts would bring relief to many families.

The orchestra struck the first notes of a waltz. Pedro swept Anne into the steps, leading her to the dance floor. Guests opened space for them, the gentlemen following Anne with open admiration while the women sighed at the incredibly handsome couple.

Anne floated in his arms. "We need to decide where we will winter this year. Griffin wants us to go to Vesuvio, but I think it is too soon."

Pedro caressed the ridges of her spine. "Paris, Milan, the Alps... You can decide wherever you want to be. I've made my decision."

"Humm?"

Pedro turned her in a wide circle. When she returned to him, he immersed himself in her Atlantic eyes. "I will winter in you."

Anne smiled, weightless. "I cannot wait."

Pedro touched her wedding ring. "What would you do if you were invisible now?"

Anne went on her tiptoes to speak in his ear. "If I were invisible, I would..."

The ballroom faded until they were alone, dancing in a meadow of light.

The End

"Step through the castle gates and journey into the opulent world of Portuguese royalty. The secrets, the scandals, and the splendor await! She's the prudish princess. He's the rake with a devil-may-care grin. Together, they're the last pair anyone expected. Can these opposites overcome their clash of wits for the sake of a nation?"

Isabel started in the ballroom's direction. She knew Dolly meant well. If she had too many hearts in her eyes and nothing in her head, it wasn't her fault. Poor

Dolly. Her father had abandoned the family to live with a courtesan, and the mother had died of a broken heart.

The music got louder, string notes interspersed with laughter and clinking glasses. A volume littering the carpet caught Isabel's attention. When she bent to retrieve it, a gasp escaped her lips. A collection of Sappho's poems. The Greek poetess' work had resurfaced a few years before and caused a furor. Several countries had forbidden it.

Looking at both sides to assure herself she was alone, she opened it, half expecting exotic dancers to tumble out, wiggling their hips and shaking their cymbals.

"With sweet myrrh oil worthy of a queen, you anointed your limbs..."

Cheeks flaming, she ripped her eyes from the lines and searched the front matter. A scrawled dedication read, "My lovely porcelain Doll, meet me tonight."

She turned the book around and located a name—Charles Whitaker. She had never forgotten a rake, and that one she had seen several times in London. The Englishman, not much older than she, belonged to the Prince of Wales' set, partaking in his debauchery. What did he want with Dolly? As if Isabel didn't know. He would either rob her fortune or her virtue.

The book alone could ruin a girl's reputation. Isabel concealed it inside her skirt pocket and hastened through the dimly lit corridors. More than ever, she needed to find Dolly. Heart speeding, Isabel lifted the hem of her gown and maneuvered between the furniture.

A shadow shifted five paces ahead. The door to her mother's garden lay open, a soft breeze blowing through the curtains.

Foreboding rippled through her stomach, lifting the hairs on her arms. Isabel had avoided the garden since she let go of her childhood. What nonsense, she told herself. Her body is only aware of brute urges. Her conscience ruled her. Gingerly, she opened the glass panel.

Cool night air touched her cheeks with invisible hands. Moonlight washed the tiled floor, casting shadows over the pathways. A single cicada sang. Water flowed in a soothing cadence.

It took a few moments for her eyes to adjust to the darkness, but when they did, her steps faltered. The silvery leaves of an olive tree concealed the dark shape of a man. The stranger lounged on the fountain's rim, his frame so still he could be one of the statues. Isabel tiptoed closer and crouched behind the begonia bush. Could it be Mr. Whitaker? Waiting for an amorous tryst?

Wings flapped, the sound coming from the pond's direction. Isabel inspected the surface, unable to glimpse any feathered creatures. When she gazed back at the fountain, the stranger had disappeared. She bent over the rim, inspecting the rose bushes and the oriental pagoda—all empty.

"Where is he?" she muttered.

A smoky voice sounded behind her. "Who are we looking for?"

Isabel jumped, the top of her head colliding with an object as hard as marble. She lost her balance and flailed her arms, dreading the encounter with the chill water.

Something caught her waist, pulling her backward. With a swoosh, she landed on her posterior, her crinoline taking the brunt of the impact. Isabel blinked at the starry night, her breath stuttering. The petticoat moved underneath her. Gasping, Isabel rolled to the side.

A silhouette materialized on the floor.

It groaned.

Isabel's cheeks burned with mortification. She had felled a stranger. How... how undiplomatic of her. Well, he shouldn't have startled her in the first place. He unfolded himself to a considerable height. A garden torch cast flickering shadows over his full dress attire. He sported the black and white finery with the ease of one who wore it every night, unlike others who only succeeded in looking like overgrown penguins. When her perusal arrived at his face, jewel-blue eyes returned her gaze, the color made riveting by his tanned skin. His hair fell in waves over his ears and collar as if windswept, the style too messy. She preferred the neatness of the pompadour, but at least the dark color ruled out Charles Whitaker.

"Pardon me. It's not my custom to startle fountain sprites." His voice belonged in the opera, not singing the heroic tenor, but graver and more velvety, like the seductive baritone who always tried to steal the heroine.

The stranger bowed and offered his arm. He seemed contrite, and it had been an accident, so Isabel used expression number five, meaning she was mildly aggravated but willing to forgive, and allowed him to help her stand. A little shaken by the stranger's regard, she smoothed her skirts. They were considerably less weighty.

The book! It must have slipped during the fall. Biting her lip, she scanned the tiles.

Lo and behold, the volume lay sprawled near the begonias, less than two feet from her. Her determination flared, and she reached down, her fingers poised to grasp it. Swift as a meddling hawk, the gentleman swooped in. His gloved hand met hers in a burst of electric energy. He came out with the prize, and Isabel clenched empty fists.

While she mentally berated him for his sharp reflexes, he took his time bringing the proof of Dolly's indiscretion to the front of his nose.

Isabel swallowed a groan.

A devilish grin transformed him into an overly handsome satyr.

Who had dimples like that? A hazard, they were. One could get lost inside them. She bet many did. The humane thing to do would be to send an expedition. Women must be trapped there, dazzled. They were lured within and vanished without a trace.

Lowering the book, he aimed his gaze at her, raking her from the hem of her gown to the braids crowning her head. His demeanor changed from solicitous to speculative. It didn't take telepathy to see the wheels turning in his head. He found a lady alone carrying erotic tales. What would he do next? Assume she was fair game?

He gave her no alternative but to use her expression number seven, the one she'd been grooming to repel rakes. Lifting her chin as high as it would go, which was a lot given her flexible neck muscles, she looked down at him. Well, she pretended to look down at him, his lofty height making it deuced uncomfortable.

He tilted his head to the side, unaffected by her efforts. "Have I died? Are you here to take me to my heavenly abode? If so, lead the way, lady knight."

Isabel's chin dropped to her chest, and she stifled a groan. Why in Athena's name had she not removed the breastplate? "I played charades. The armor was part of my costume."

"I see... What were you? Penthesilea, the Amazon queen?"

"Joan of Arc," she said, hoping the martyr would cloak her in respectability.

"Saintly Joan carrying Sappho's poems... Interesting." He shrugged and leaned back over the garden wall. "Should we play a charade for your real name?"

He had not recognized her, even though her life-sized portrait crowned the gallery not a hundred paces from here. But the light was dim, and she wasn't wearing her tiara. Perfect. She would just retrieve the book and leave.

Isabel sucked in a breath, but before she could speak, he placed his finger atop her lips. "Don't tell me. Are you one of the princess' Vestal Virgins?"

Beneath his touch, her face flushed. Did they call her court The Princess' Vestal Virgins? "How dare—"

"Did you leave Olympus on a night of revelry? I can't say I blame you. And if you ask nicely, I might be of help. Gardenia's performance was quite entertaining, but I'll make an exception for a lady in need."

This was getting out of hand. She gritted her teeth. "Your Excellency—"

"Call me Henrique. I don't stand on formalities." He shrugged his broad shoulders, flaunting protocol with the same ease he flaunted his... his taunting male grins, and expertly cut male clothes, his male squinting eyes, and his gravelly, absurdly low male voice.

"Pity. I do." Isabel presented her hand, palm poised up. "I require the book. Now."

He seemed taken aback by her curt reply but then gazed at the cover. "Is it everything the critics claim?" Frowning, he flicked through the pages until one caught his interest. A devilish smile lit his face. "Come to me and loosen me from blunt agony. Labor and fill my heart with fire."

The words brushed against her, the breastplate no protection against such intimacy.

He closed the book. "I can see the appeal."

"It's not mine," Isabel blurted and cringed. Why explain herself to this man?

He studied her. "It isn't yours, but you want it back?"

Isabel raised her brows. "At least your observation skills are better than your literary taste."

He chuckled, and the sound lifted pinpricks on her skin. "Thank you. I'm proud of my senses. Especially touch."

Isabel crossed her arms above her chest. "Careful. Words enlighten the spirit, while the senses can lead you astray."

He came closer. "I've been allowing the senses to lead me astray for a long time now, but I would gladly give you the reins."

Was this the sort of banter that enthralled other ladies? "You should return to the opera singer, Your Excellency. Your company is quite tedious."

"Ouch." A rakish grin lit up his swarthy face. "The princess is doing us a favor by keeping you locked away. Your tongue can crumple a male's pride."

Isabel ground her teeth so hard her jaw hurt. She didn't imprison her ladies. She protected them from males like him! "If your pride can crumble so easily, then it was not much to begin with, was it?"

His chin dipped low, and he lifted his dashing eyebrows. "Do you blame the moonlight? Or is my presence enough to ignite such passion?"

"I don't allow passion to rule me."

"I know passion when I see it. Right now, it is staring at me with flaming green eyes."

Controlling her breaths, Isabel pretended to clean a speck from her bodice. "Flaming? Sir, your senses are running ahead of you again. Where you see fire, there is only ice. Nothing you do or say affects me."

"No?" His gem-like eyes sparkled, and he bent forward.

His cheek brushed against her, the bristles of his stubble tickling her skin. Locking a gulp of air in her lungs, she mentally slapped her hand. Why provoke a reposing rake? Warmth wafted from him in waves, and her nostrils flared at the citric spice of his cologne. His gaze drilled into hers, consuming her space. Unnerved but unwilling to lose the advantage, she stared right back. A mistake. Up close, the curves drawn into his irises had a hypnotic symmetry—a maze seen from above. One more inch, and they would trap her.

Pulse speeding, she arched her back. "Release me."

Her glance shifted from his bottom lip to his heavy-lidded eyes. Quite suddenly, he dipped his nose to her collarbone and sniffed her—neck to earlobe—waking up the down covering her skin.

"Are you sure, Joan?"

She was sure her heart had become a treacherous belly dancer, as it literally danced in her belly. "Yes?"

"I'm not holding you." He stepped back.

The heat engulfing her vanished, replaced by the drafty air.

Disoriented, Isabel blinked once, twice. Indeed, he wasn't. Then how? She had felt trapped by him as clearly as if he had woven a web of crystal threads around them. Was it all in her head, an illusion? Or did he possess a hidden power of seduction?

He eyed her expectantly, smirking, and she realized he had proved his point. How easily he affected her.

"Keep the book." Clutching her skirts in her clammy palms, she brushed past him.

He grabbed her arm, his black-gloved hand shockingly hot. Isabel sucked in a breath.

His eyes twinkled mischievously, and he placed the book into her hand. "You should read a few verses, little Joan. Perhaps it can thaw ice maidens."

Her wrist tingled where he touched her, and she jerked free from his hold. Panting, at a loss for a proper set down, she watched as he swaggered away.

Read The Truth about Myths! https://amzn.to/3UXe b8Y

Author's note

Dear reader,

If you read my first novel, *The True Purpose of Vines*, Pedro Daun was no stranger to you. Many wished to see a book that featured his story, while others were skeptical of his redemption after he wreaked such havoc in Julia and Griffin's lives.

While writing the True Purpose of Vines, I never intended Pedro to become more than an antagonist. Mid-book, I took a course on writing villains, and the teacher challenged me to write a scene from his point of view. The moment I freed him on the page, he escaped my control, emerging as a complex character, his strong personality carved out of hate and abuse. That scene compelled me to keep writing about him, and I knew he would have his chance at redemption. I owed it to him.

The plot of *The Taste of Light* was the most challenging brain exercise I've ever accomplished. Not because the story is complicated but because it needed to be enough to redeem Pedro. His transformation would not have been credible and fulfilling any other way.

Anne was a complete surprise. I envisioned her as a pure, innocent character, a rebirth of the girl Pedro had met by the riverside when he was a boy. Still, she didn't stay put in the mold I built for her, surprising me at every difficult choice with a core of strength and kindness. In her, I visualize a model of women's toughness that does not require bloodshed.

My novel does not mean to analyze slave trading in detail or depth, but it intrigued me to uncover the other side of this hateful commerce. Most of us only see it from the final destination of the Africans' perspective, and I wanted to show that it was disruptive at its origins too.

The attempt at regicide was inspired by the wave of political assassinations in the nineteenth century. Every European ruler was under threat, including Emperor Franz Joseph of Austria, the Kaisers Wilhelm I, Friedrich III and Wilhelm II of Germany, the Tsars Alexander II, Alexander III and Nicholas II of Russia, the kings Victor Emmanuel II, Umberto I and Victor Emmanuel III of Italy, and Napoleon III. Queen Victoria endured seven attempts on her life while her husband, Prince Albert, and the future kings of England, Edward VII, and George V, were targeted. The son of Dom Luis I, King Manuel, was murdered during a carriage procession, an event that catalyzed the end of the monarchy in Portugal.

Bullfighting is a distasteful sport to me, so I chose it to characterize my villain, João Ulrich. To this day, if you want to watch a *Corrida de Touros* in Portugal or Spain, you can choose between sitting in the sun or at the sombra.

Pedro and Anne are fond of modinhas, a music style characteristic of the salons of both Portugal and Brazil in the nineteenth century. The romantic, sentimentalist melodies were always accompanied by the guitar or the piano and enlivened the court receptions and bourgeois gatherings of the age.

Dom Pedro and Inês de Castro's tragic love story is heartbreakingly true. I have a vast biography about the couple, and their story never ended for me. Dom Pedro still calls for his Inês. I included their love in The Taste of Light firstly because I wished to divulge it to the rest of the world and secondly, to give it resolution inside my head.

When you plan your next visit to Portugal, don't forget to include the Mosteiro de Alcobaça in your tour. Only a few miles from Lisbon, the visit will immerse you in Dom Pedro's infinite love. Google provides a great virtual tour, too.

Thank you so much for embarking on this great adventure with me. I hope Pedro's story has touched your heart as it did mine. I can't wait to share Henrique's novel with you!

Also by Giovanna Siniscalchi

Meet The Winemakers – Passionate and head-strong, the Portuguese will capture your heart in these sun-drenched novels.

The True Purpose of Vines

A Portuguese winemaker meets her match in an arrogant Englishman who threatens her beloved lands. When the wine plague strikes her vineyards, they put differences aside to find a cure, blind tasting their way into an intoxicating passion. "True Purpose of vines - An intoxicating blend of romance, Portuguese history, and winemaking lore." ***Kirkus reviews*** Available on Kindle Unlimited

The Wedding Surprise

An overly rational Englishman attends his superior's wedding. When a meddling godfather risks the ceremony, he must ally with a passionate Portuguese to save the day. Can he put logic aside to embrace love? "When you stop following love, it follows you back... and it will meet you in the most unexpected manner. Witness the heartfelt and beautiful love story of Edmond and Elise from "The Wedding Surprise," a brilliant work of Giovanna Siniscalchi. A perfect bedtime read!!!" ***TheBigReads*** Join my book club and download this delightful novella for free! https://BookHip.com/QNJCNVJ

The Truth about Myths

Princess Isabel de Orleans would do anything for Portugal. When her brother, the king, asks for her help, she agrees to travel to Spain to defuse a diplomatic crisis. Until she discovers who will be her nanny on the trip... Henrique Penafiel is a womanizer and delights in showing how her morals are outdated. The sister of Henrique's best friend should be off-limits. Still, he glimpses the princess' passionate side and cannot understand why she keeps it frozen. When an exiled king threatens Portuguese independence, he has to take drastic measures to save his country and their new-found love. Available on Kindle Unlimited

About me

My name is Giovanna Siniscalchi, and I have two passions: History and Romance. My goal as a writer is to transport readers to Portugal, where they can watch the sunset through majestic umbrella pines, taste bold wines, and sway to the sound of a Fado.

I research every detail of my novels, hoping to make you treasure my grandparents' country as I do. I grew up reading sweeping romances like Gone With The Wind and Count of Monte Cristo. What I love most about reading a novel is the sensation of having experienced something special. My goal is to recreate this feeling. You won't find instant love in my books. My characters need to grow and overcome their flaws before they can experience true romance. I have a loving husband, who still is my hero and two amazing kids.

Let's keep in touch

Don't miss out on exclusive character photos, contests, updates, and more! Follow me on social media for all the latest news, behind-the-scenes glimpses, and a chance to connect with fellow readers. Let's embark on this exciting journey together!

Giovanna Siniscalchi's
LinkTree

Dear reader, please share your thoughts on this enchanting tale. Reviews are like beacons in the literary world, guiding readers to stories that resonate with their hearts. In "The Taste of Light," Pedro and Anne's journey through love, redemption, and a web of conspiracies unfolds, offering a glimpse into their complex souls. Your reviews hold immense power, not only in supporting authors like me but also in helping fellow readers discover a narrative that might touch their souls. Thank you for being a part of this literary voyage, and for sharing your impressions of "The Taste of Light."